'TIS THE SEASON TO BE KISSED

"Rebecca."

She gazed up at him. His face lowered toward hers, his hand slid to the back of her neck. He brushed against her mouth with his own very gently, a soft, wisp of lips touching lips. It felt warm and firm. It felt wonderful.

She felt his hand go around her waist, gripping her flesh with a force that should have caused her discomfort but felt secure instead. He kissed her again, angling his head and pressing strongly.

All question of right and wrong fled from Rebecca's conscience as she parted her lips and allowed his tongue to caress the softness of her mouth. She stayed quietly in his embrace, feeling a delicate warm glow.

Their tongues twined, playfully, erotically. It felt so achingly good. She spread her hand over his chest and let herself go, let herself enjoy the moment, savor the sensation. How long had it been since she had felt wanted? Desired? A long time. A very long time . . .

Books by Adrienne Basso

HIS WICKED EMBRACE

HIS NOBLE PROMISE

TO WED A VISCOUNT

TO PROTECT AN HEIRESS

TO TEMPT A ROGUE

THE WEDDING DECEPTION

THE CHRISTMAS HEIRESS

HIGHLAND VAMPIRE

HOW TO ENJOY A SCANDAL

NATURE OF THE BEAST

THE CHRISTMAS COUNTESS

Published by Zebra Books

CHRISTMAS COUNTESS
THE

Adrienne Basso

ZEBRA BOOKS
Kensington Publishing Corp.
http://www.kensingtonbooks.com

ZEBRA BOOKS are published by

Kensington Publishing Corp.
850 Third Avenue
New York, NY 10022

All Kensington titles, imprints and distributed lines are
available at special quantity discounts for bulk purchases for
sales promotion, premiums, fund-raising, educational or
institutional use.

Special book excerpts or customized printings can also be
created to fit specific needs. For details, write or phone the
office of the Kensington Special Sales Manager: Attn. Special
Sales Department, Kensington Publishing Corp., 850 Third
Avenue, New York, NY 10022. Phone: 1-800-221-2647.

Zebra and the Z logo Reg. U.S. Pat. & TM Off.

ISBN-13: 978-1-4201-0432-5
ISBN-10: 1-4201-0432-2

First Printing: October 2008
10 9 8 7 6 5 4 3 2 1

Printed in the United States of America

Chapter 1

Taunton, England
November 1845

Somewhere in the distance Rebecca could hear the sound
of a baby crying. Soft, muffled. The pitiful, lonely whimpers
tore through her heart. She got to her feet and forced her limbs
to move forward, seeking the source that conveyed such anguish. But it was dark and difficult to see and she had no
candle to light the way.

The whimpers ceased suddenly, then began anew, this time
as an indignant howl. The infant's cries grew steadily
louder, stronger. Disoriented, Rebecca quickened her pace,
rushing toward the noise, frantically trying to reach the babe.

She found herself turning down a long, winding corridor
and her confusion mounted. The sounds of the infant's distress engulfed her but there were so many chambers. Where
was the child? Panicking, she randomly threw open the nearest door. All was instantly silent.

Had she found the infant in time?

The chamber was bathed in shadows; all Rebecca could
distinguish was a table in the center of the room, upon which
rested a basket covered with a thick blanket. Cautiously, she

approached. As she drew near, the night clouds parted and a shaft of moonlight fell on the basket. With trembling fingers she reached down, gently pulled back the soft wool and peered inside.

Nestled beneath the covers was a tiny, newborn baby. With a cry of pure joy, Rebecca stared down at the perfect little face, so sweet, so innocent. There was a thatch of downy dark curls upon its head, a blush of rose coloring on its cheeks, the hint of a dimple in its chin.

"Oh, my."

At the sound of Rebecca's voice the infant stiffened, then slowly lifted its spiky wet lashes. Solemn dark eyes regarded her quietly and a delicate curled fist flailed toward her.

"Precious, love. No need for tears. I'm here now. I'll keep you safe."

Eagerly, Rebecca reached inside to pick up the priceless bundle. Yet when her hands drew near, the baby arched its back and let out a lusty wail. Startled, Rebecca pulled away. But the crying continued and Rebecca knew holding the child was the only way to bring it comfort.

She reached out a second time, yet her arms were suddenly too short, the basket too deep. Stretching on her toes, Rebecca leaned forward yet still could not touch the infant. The cries grew louder, more frantic, more distressed.

Rebecca doubled her efforts, but it was impossible. She could not grab hold of the child, could not pick it up and cradle it in her arms, could not soothe and protect it.

Tears of distress and frustration ran down Rebecca's cheeks. If only she could—

"These letters just arrived with the afternoon post, Miss Rebecca. Among the bills I am certain there are one or two expressions of condolence. Your father, the Good Lord rest his soul, was respected and well liked by one and all. Do you want to sort through the mail now or would you prefer to wait until afternoon tea?"

Rebecca Tremaine opened her eyes with a start. Disoriented, she blinked rapidly, then sat upright.

Gradually, the familiar furnishings of her father's private study came into focus. There were papers arranged in neat piles on the floor, half-full boxes were clustered along the wall beneath the window, stacks of books sorted and waiting to be packed in the appropriate containers.

"Miss Rebecca?"

Rebecca turned her head. Directly in front of her, the short, round form of a middle-aged woman hovered close.

"Mrs. Maxwell?"

The family housekeeper patted her shoulder. "Aye, 'tis me. You must have fallen asleep. Poor lamb. No surprise, with all that's been going on these past few months. Naturally you are exhausted. Oh, dear, were you dreaming about your father?"

The housekeeper fumbled in her pocket, pulled out a clean white handkerchief, then pressed it into Rebecca's hand. Absently, Rebecca lifted it to her face, hastily wiping away the tears she had not realized were on her cheeks.

"Thank you," she said, putting her usual calm expression back on her face. She had no intention of correcting the housekeeper's misconception that the disturbing dream had been about her father. "You are always so kind."

"I wish I could do more," Mrs. Maxwell replied sincerely. "I know how hard it has been for you, first burying your father and now having to give up your home. Trying times, indeed."

"There are many who carry burdens far greater than

my own," Rebecca answered. "Besides, I shall be fine now that Daniel has arrived." Rebecca wiped her nose, then stuffed the handkerchief into the pocket of her black mourning gown. "I will miss you dreadfully, of course, and am sad to say farewell to so many of the kind and generous members of our parish. Still, I know how lucky I am to have a brother willing to take care of me. You need not worry so, Mrs. Maxwell."

The older woman clucked her tongue and Rebecca could tell she wasn't convinced. The housekeeper had been employed by the family for the past four years and during that time Rebecca's older brother, Daniel, had been out of the country. His letters had been infrequent, conversation about his activities and the life he had built for himself away from the family home limited.

Suspicious by nature of most men, especially those who traveled to foreign lands to make their fortune, Mrs. Maxwell clearly did not know what to make of Daniel Tremaine, whom she had met when he arrived from the American Colonies to help settle Vicar Tremaine's very modest estate.

"I only hope the new vicar they have assigned here will be half the gentleman your father was to this parish," Mrs. Maxwell said with a worried frown. "Have you heard anything about him, perchance?"

"Not a word," Rebecca admitted, mentally echoing the housekeeper's concerns. Yet she refrained from voicing any doubts; the housekeeper was already worried about keeping her position once the new family arrived. "I'm sure he will be a great asset to the community."

"We'll just have to see, now won't we?" the house-keeper mumbled.

"Yes." Rebecca gave the older woman what she hoped

was an encouraging smile, telling herself she would stay in touch and make certain Mrs. Maxwell was favorably situated. If not, she would do all that she could to ensure a suitable position was found for her.

"I'd best continue packing Father's personal books and papers," Rebecca added. "I know you will want to give this room a thorough cleaning before the new residents arrive next week."

"I do, but it can wait until tomorrow. You must not work too hard or else you'll catch a chill. Your brother can take care of some of these things."

Rebecca shook her head. "Daniel is handling other business. And truly, I don't mind."

The housekeeper looked at her dubiously. "Well now, I suppose you know best. But don't overdo."

With that final admonishment, Mrs. Maxwell left. Rebecca heaved a weary sigh and sank back against the cushions of the settee. For a moment she was tempted to close her eyes and let the exhaustion of her emotions drift away. But fear held her back. If she fell asleep again, she might start dreaming.

Years ago, right after it happened, the dreams were a nightly occurrence that haunted her relentlessly. Gradually, blessedly, over time they had become less regular. Yet they still occurred, always more vivid in the month of August, the anniversary of the event.

But it was not August, it was late November. Perhaps the trauma of her father's death had brought on the dream? Though it had been three months since his passing, she still grieved her loss. *All* her losses.

Rebecca's breath hitched as another sob threatened. For six years the essence of the dream had remained constant, yet this time, for the first time, she had clearly seen the baby. So small, so delicate, so innocent, so very much alive.

Rebecca took a long, shuddering breath. While the dream might have changed, the emotions it evoked remained precisely the same; pain, regret and an almost unbearable sadness.

Rebecca felt those emotions start to crowd in and she abruptly stood. Activity was the best way to clear her mind. Bustling with purpose she practically sprinted across the room, attacking the pile of books with a vengeance. Once they were sorted, she focused her attention on the desk.

There was a pile of church documents, along with a diary of notes her father had made over the years discussing the needs of various families in the parish. Those would be left for the new vicar. The rest were copies of his favorite sermons, personal papers and a small prayer book that he had always carried with him.

Feeling too tired and edgy to give the papers a thorough look, Rebecca placed them in a crate. She and Daniel could review them at a later time and determine if there was anything they wished to save.

She made a final inspection of the desk drawers and to her surprise found, wedged in the very back of the bottom drawer, a packet of letters neatly tied with a white satin ribbon. Curious, Rebecca removed the top one, opened it and began to read.

My dearest Jacob. A poignant smile formed on her lips as she recognized her mother's distinct handwriting. She turned the letter over, checking the date in the corner. *May 6, 1811.* Her smile broadened. The note had been written before her parents had married, most likely while they had been courting. She had found their love letters.

The pile was thick. 'Twas a testament indeed to the strong bond of love and devotion her parents had shared throughout their marriage that her father had kept these special missives all this time.

Feeling like a voyeur, Rebecca slipped the letter back inside the ribbon and placed the bundle to the side of the desk. They were too private to read, yet she could not leave them behind. She would ask Daniel's opinion on what to do with them. She turned to place the prayer book inside the nearest crate, shifted too quickly and knocked her hip against the desk.

The letters tumbled to the floor and the ribbon came loose, releasing the notes and scattering them all about the carpet.

"Oh, bother," she muttered.

Rubbing the sore spot on her hip, Rebecca knelt. Her arms stretched wide, she gathered the letters together. Yet as she started stacking them in a neat pile, she noted the handwriting on one was distinctly different and clearly not her mother's hand.

Her brow raised. Gracious. Had there been someone special in her father's life before he met and married her mother? It seemed ridiculous, yet life had taught her that only a very foolish or naive individual believed that all was always as it appeared. Rebecca opened the note and began reading.

I received your latest letter and read it with a feeling best described as relief, pleased to discover that you and Meredith are finally being sensible about this grave matter. Giving Rebecca's child to the Earl and Countess of Hampton to raise as their own is the only possible recourse, the only road to salvation for our family. 'Tis the only way we will be saved from certain disgrace and ruin, the only way to save your reputation and our family's honor. A parish will forgive a beloved vicar much, but the bastard grandchild of a man of God is

*not something that would ever be tolerated or accepted.
Nor should it be.*

Rebecca's child? Bastard grandchild? Given to the
Earl and Countess of Hampton to raise? Rebecca
gasped for air. Her lungs felt tight, her chest heavy. She
couldn't breathe, couldn't think. The child had been
given to another? How could this be? Surely there must
be some mistake? The babe she had carried within her
body for nine long months had been stillborn, robbed
of life before it even began.

They had told her. The midwife first, then her
great-aunt. They had told her it was a merciful act of
God and that she should feel grateful that the infant
had not survived.

But Rebecca had not felt grateful. She had felt
hollow and distraught and sad. She had cried for
months, had mourned for years, had dreamt fre-
quently, *still* dreamt, of the infant girl, the baby that
had been created from love and passion. The baby
she had never seen, had never held.

The child that was alive! It had survived! Pain, shock
and confusion rolled around in Rebecca's head. She
felt herself pitching forward. Shaking, she clutched
the edge of the wooden crate so hard her knuckles
turned white. "Is this another dream?" she whispered.

At that moment the study door opened. Rebecca
panicked, thinking Mrs. Maxwell had returned, but to
her great relief it was her brother, Daniel, who walked
into the room.

"My God, Rebecca, what's wrong?"

Her heart and head pounding, Rebecca pushed
herself to stand upright. Daniel moved close to grasp
her elbow and steady her and she was grateful for the
support. Her knees felt so weak.

"Rebecca?"

She shook her head. So many thoughts pounded through her mind that she could not seize upon any one, could not make sense of anything.

"The letter . . . I found a letter . . . here among Father's papers. I don't . . . please, just read it."

Daniel took the letter from her trembling hand and began to read. Rebecca drew in a tight breath, her eyes fixed on her brother's face. It seemed to take forever, but suddenly his expression changed dramatically and she knew he had reached the section about the baby. Her baby! With a sob, Rebecca closed her eyes, trying to slow her breathing, struggling to calm the accelerated beat of her heart.

"Bloody hell, Becca, this is a shock."

Rebecca cleared her throat, searching his face for a glimmer of hope. "Then you believe it is the truth? The infant was given away?"

"Oh, sweetheart."

The kindness and sympathy in Daniel's voice was her undoing. The tears began to trickle down her cheeks and then the sobs overtook them.

Wordlessly, Daniel gathered her close. Rebecca leaned into his strength, pressing her face against his linen shirt. He smelled faintly of tobacco and starch and expensive, spicy cologne, an oddly comforting combination.

"If only I could spare you this additional pain," he whispered.

"'Tis agony to learn of this betrayal . . . and yet . . ." Rebecca's sobs lessened as the full impact of this discovery began to register in her mind. "I cannot comprehend why Mother and Father did this to me and frankly my head is spinning too fast to even consider forgiving them for their part in this cruel duplicity. Yet miraculously the initial hurt and bitterness I feel has not succeeded in overshadowing the joy in this news."

"Joy?"

Rebecca smiled as the final tear ran down her cheek. "She is alive! My sweet little girl, the best part of me and Philip is alive!"

"And apparently the daughter of an earl," Daniel interjected dryly.

It did not matter. Rebecca pushed that reality swiftly to the back of her mind. "I must find her. Oh, my darling baby. Well, not a baby really. She is six years old. Daniel, please, will you help me?"

He did not say anything at first. She had always suspected that her brother suffered pangs of guilt because he had not been here to support her during this tumultuous time in her life. They had been close as children, but the passing of time and the physical distance between them had taken its toll on their relationship.

Beyond a surface knowledge of his business and financial success, Rebecca realized she knew very little about the man her brother had become, knew almost nothing of his attitudes and opinions. As adults they were in essence strangers. Did he believe her parents had acted in her best interests? In the best interest of the child?

Would he refuse her request for help or even worse, order her to drop the matter entirely? The silence went on for so long that Rebecca began to fear hearing his answer.

"We have never spoken of your child, Rebecca." Daniel's voice was rough with contained emotion. "Father wrote to me, first to tell me about the child and later to say it had not survived. Both letters contained very little details. Will you tell me what happened?"

The request startled Rebecca, bringing forth a rush of emotions. The memories of her past were difficult to endure, wracked with pain, regret and sorrow. Yet if she wanted Daniel's help, he deserved to hear the truth.

Fearing her legs would not hold her, she moved back, seating herself in her father's desk chair. Daniel remained on his feet.

"We were very much in love, Philip and I. He was a wonderful man. Kind, intelligent, ambitious. Handsome. How I wish you could have known him. You would have liked him, Daniel, I am certain of it."

Her brother smiled, but made no comment. Rebecca continued.

"I was over the moon when Philip asked me to be his wife and beyond delighted when Father gave us his blessing. Philip was just beginning his career as a barrister and his future success seemed assured. We became engaged and then rather reluctantly agreed with Father's strong opinion that it would be best to wait until Philip became more established, more financially secure before he took on the burden of a wife.

"It was difficult waiting to be married. As much for me as for Philip, I believe. We missed each other dreadfully when we were apart and schemed constantly to have time alone together. We were clever, Philip and I, and succeeded more often than not. Yet beyond the love we shared, there was deep longing and passion between us and then one night, when we so boldly managed to be alone, things got . . . carried away."

"Did he pressure you? Force you?"

Rebecca flinched. "Oh, no. It was nothing like that at all. We were mad for each other, equal in our delight of the . . . the physical expression of our love and commitment. I thought it was wondrous and blissful and beautiful."

Her cheeks heated with embarrassment, but Rebecca did not regret her words. She wanted her brother to know the depth of love and devotion she and Philip had felt for each other.

"Unfortunately your bliss had consequences," Daniel interjected.

"Yes." Rebecca's throat tightened as she remembered her disbelief when she realized she had fallen pregnant. Remembered too, the embarrassment she felt standing before her parents, feeling like a condemned prisoner confessing her crimes, telling them she was expecting a child.

"Philip had been offered a very promising position with a law firm in Salisbury and we all agreed he should take it. He left Taunton before I realized my predicament, so I was forced to explain to Mother and Father that our agreement to wait for the marriage needed to be altered. Our wedding had to take place far sooner than we had planned."

"But there was no wedding," Daniel said softly.

"No. There was an accident. The roof of the building that housed Philip's offices collapsed in the middle of the afternoon. Most of the others were out that day, but Philip was working at his desk. They told me he was killed instantly." She muffled a cry. "I was inconsolable, numb with grief. Losing Philip was a horror I could not comprehend and then there was the unborn child to consider."

"Who decided you should go to Great-Aunt Mildred?" Daniel asked, arms crossed as he leaned against the desk.

"Mother, I think? Or perhaps it was Father? I honestly don't remember who first broached the suggestion to me. As the weeks passed, 'twas obvious I could not remain here in Taunton in my condition. At the time, retreating to Cornwall and having Aunt Mildred care for me seemed a godsend."

"It was the only sensible choice," Daniel agreed.

"Was it? I trusted them; our parents and Aunt Mildred. Believed they would help me." Rebecca blinked as the tears welled in her eyes. "Yet in the end they betrayed me."

Daniel sighed. "It was cruel to tell you the child had perished. Still, were there any other choices? Forgive me, Becca, for asking, but what had you planned to do with this baby? Did you really believe you would be able to keep it, to raise it as your own?"

Rebecca shrugged helplessly. "I was in deep despair, Daniel, living day to day. I was incapable of thinking beyond the moment. We never openly discussed what would happen once the child arrived. I assumed the decision would be made soon after the baby was born. I also assumed I would be a part of that decision." Her voice grew soft. "I broke the rules and knew I would pay dearly for my mistake. But I never expected to be betrayed by those I loved and trusted. Heavens, I was a fool."

"We have all been foolish at one time or another."

Rebecca bowed her head, appreciating her brother's efforts to make her feel better. "The past is gone. It does me no good to dwell on my heartache. However, I have been given a second chance, an opportunity to see and hold and love this child. I must find her. I must meet her. Please, will you help me?"

A wary expression, quickly suppressed, flickered across Daniel's face. "I have lived outside of England for eight years, yet even I know of the Earl of Hampton. He is a powerful, wealthy man, with influential friends. It won't be easy."

"I don't expect it to be," she answered, a sad, bitter

smile forming on her lips. "All I know is that it shall be worth it."

Cameron Sinclair, Earl of Hampton, was enjoying a quiet afternoon at his gentleman's club, reading a fresh copy of *The Times* and drinking a glass of exceptionally fine port. Since his household was comprised and dominated by females—his mother, his sister and his daughter—he had found over the years that in order to maintain his sanity it was necessary to on occasion seek the exclusive company of men.

"For you, my lord."

Puzzled, Cameron lowered his newspaper and lifted the note off the silver salver the servant extended toward him. Social invitations as well as letters of a business nature were sent to his London home. This was the first time he had received such a formal document at his club.

Curious, he broke the seal, which he did not recognize, and read the note. *Mr. Daniel Tremaine requests a private meeting with you on a matter most urgent and personal.*

The name was also unfamiliar to the earl. "Is the gentleman who gave you the note here?"

"Yes, my lord." The servant bowed low and discreetly pointed to a young man, conservatively and expensively dressed. He was tall, lean, with short dark hair and handsome angular features. Cameron judged him to be two or three years his junior. He did not recognize him, further deepening the mystery.

"Is he a member of White's?" the earl asked.

"No, my lord. He was admitted today as a guest of the Duke of Aylesford."

Cameron's brow rose with interest as he contemplated the information. The duke was a shrewd man, known for his successful business investments as well as his high social standards. There were not many who could count upon him for such a personal favor.

"Tell Mr. Tremaine I will meet with him." Cameron folded his newspaper and placed it on the nearby table. "Is there a room available where we can have some privacy?"

"The corner study is currently unoccupied. I will escort the gentleman there and make sure you are not disturbed."

"Excellent."

The earl strolled casually through the club, finding the snug corner study empty as the servant had promised. He waited but a moment for the other gentleman to join him.

"I am Daniel Tremaine," the man said, coming forward to offer his hand. "Thank you for seeing me, Lord Hampton."

Putting a pleasant expression on his face, Cameron shook hands. "Your note said it was urgent and private, yet you have the advantage, Mr. Tremaine. I do not recall making your acquaintance."

"Actually, we are related, though rather distantly. Fourth or fifth cousins, I believe."

"Ah," Cameron replied in a noncommittal tone. Perhaps Tremaine wished to presume upon that exceedingly weak family connection for a favor, something the earl decided he would consider, if the request was reasonable. "I understand you are a guest of Aylesford's."

"Yes. The duke and I have joined together in a few business ventures that have proven lucrative for all parties." The comment was not made in a boastful manner, but rather stated simply as a matter of fact.

"I am most intrigued by successful business ventures," Cameron responded with a congenial smile, appreciating a soft sell when it came to investments. "However, all proposals are first reviewed by my man of business. I can give you his name and address if you wish to send along a report that you would like me to consider."

A frown insinuated itself between Tremaine's brows. "I am not here to discuss business. The matter is personal, and truth be told, rather delicate. It concerns your daughter, Lily."

A tap came at the door, and a servant entered, bearing a tray with a wine decanter and two goblets. Tremaine declined a glass; Cameron did the same. The earl exchanged a glance with the servant, narrowing his eyes with impatience. Understanding the silent command, the servant nodded and quickly exited the room.

"My daughter is six years old, Mr. Tremaine. You cannot possibly wish to make an offer for her."

"I know her age," Tremaine responded in a brittle tone. "I also know that she is not your natural child."

Cameron stared at Tremaine, his gaze steady and sure. Tremaine stared back.

"Nonsense," Cameron stated firmly, because he did not know what else to say.

"Hardly nonsense. 'Tis the truth, and we both know it."

The silence was charged and heavy as the earl contemplated Tremaine with an unfriendly gaze. "Blackmail, sir? I thought you said your business ventures were lucrative. Is this the means by which you have built your fortune?"

Tremaine did not even blink. "Strange, my lord, that you do not deny it."

Cameron did his best not to react. "To do so would only give further credence to your outrageous lie."

His expression inscrutable, Daniel Tremaine leaned closer. "Six years ago, in Cornwall, on the 26th of August, Mildred Blackwell gave a newly born infant girl into your care. She told you the babe's mother was unmarried, of genteel birth, and in need of assistance. For whatever reasons, you and your wife decided to help. However, when you brought the child to London the following spring, you declared the little girl, whom you had named Lily, was your daughter, born of your wife."

Cameron's chest tightened. It took every ounce of his hard-earned self-control to remain seated. *Good God, did he know everything?* "Why should any of this matter to you, Tremaine?"

"Lily's natural mother is my sister."

For the first time, there was a crack of emotion on Tremaine's face. As he leaned back in his chair, he looked vulnerable for just an instant. Then all too soon the intent, determined expression returned in full force. Cameron was not surprised Tremaine was so successful in business. 'Twas a useful talent to be able to contain and mask one's emotions at will.

The earl cleared his throat. "What do you want?"

"My sister, Rebecca, would like to meet her daughter."

The earl's angry, disbelieving reaction was swift, instinctive, protective. "You need to get one thing perfectly clear, Tremaine. Lily is *my* daughter. *Not,* your sister's daughter."

"Understood."

Drawing his frayed temper back under control, Cameron pulled down the cuffs of his tailored linen shirtsleeves, stalling for time. "Enlighten me. What does your sister expect to accomplish?"

A light of doubt entered Tremaine's eyes. "She wants only to meet the child."

"Lily is six years old. 'Tis a bit late for a burst of maternal instinct."

Tremaine's face clouded with anger. "I shall allow that insensitive remark to pass, my lord, but caution you to make no more. Rebecca was told the infant did not survive. She only recently discovered her child's fate."

"How?" Cameron asked in disbelief.

"Mildred Blackwell was our great-aunt. She wrote a letter to my parents outlining the plan to give the baby to you. It was found among my father's personal papers."

The earl rose from his chair. "While not entirely unsympathetic to your sister's plight, you must consider my position. I lost my wife three years ago. Christina adored our daughter and Lily was very close to her mother.

"Though young, Christina's death was a frightening, painful time for her. She has adjusted, as children do, and now finds female guidance and love from her grandmother and my sister, Charlotte, who is unmarried and lives with us. I absolutely refuse to expose Lily to anything that might cause her confusion or distress. Above all else, I will protect my daughter."

Tremaine also stood. "Rebecca means her no harm."

Cameron frowned skeptically. "That is of little assurance to me."

"'Tis the best I can offer." Tremaine inclined his head. "That and my promise that Rebecca will not reveal her identity to your daughter."

Cameron's chest tightened with an unpleasant sensation. His initial instinct was to have Tremaine forcefully removed from the club, but the earl knew he must temper his emotions. While not of the nobility, Tremaine was clearly a formidable opponent. One who had money and resources, not to mention influential friends like the Duke of Aylesford.

"I need time to consider your request," Cameron snapped, annoyed that he had to compromise, yet knowing in the end he might have no other choice. "I shall let you know of my decision in a fortnight."

"No. I need an answer by the end of the week," Tremaine countered. "I have made inquiries, my lord, and have heard you are a decent, honorable man. I pray that you will find compassion and sympathy in your heart for my sister's pain and suffering and grant her this simple wish."

Cameron sighed, deciding it probably would be better to have the matter settled sooner, rather than later. "I will contact you by Friday with my decision."

"Thank you." Tremaine bowed respectfully and headed toward the door, but before he left he faced the earl one final time, his eyes glittering with purpose. "I appreciate that you have been rather suddenly thrust into a difficult position. One that no other man would envy. But as you ponder your decision, I would ask you also to remember one crucial fact, Lord Hampton. Mildred Blackwell's letter naming you as the man who was given this child is in my possession."

Chapter 2

Cameron left White's in a foul humor. He practically stormed from the club, barely acknowledging the greetings of friends and acquaintances as he stood on the front steps and waited for his horse to be brought around. Once mounted, the earl began the ride home at as fast a pace as he dared, wishing all the while he was at one of his country estates, so he could race home and exercise away some of his edgy frustration.

His marriage had been an arranged affair, a blending of families and wealth, but he had been very lucky. Within a few months of taking his vows, the earl had fallen deeply in love with his charming bride. And she with him. From that point on, their marriage had been passionate and loving and full of happiness. The only blight on their otherwise perfect life was Christina's inability to bear a child.

Sadly, she had no difficulty becoming pregnant; the problem was that she could not bring the babe to term. On the occasion of her fourth pregnancy, they had journeyed to one of his smaller estates in Devon. The countess's physician had advised that the country air, quiet daily routine and wholesome environment could prove to be the difference.

Alas, he was wrong. Christina had miscarried the child late in her pregnancy and subsequently sank into a deep depression. Isolated and grieving, the couple had kept the news from their families. Receiving the letter from Mildred Blackwell, a distant relation, requesting that they consider aiding her in finding a home for an illegitimate baby had seemed providential.

The change in Christina had been instantaneous. The sadness lifted and she eagerly embraced the notion of taking the infant girl into their care. Cameron was elated with anything that made his wife happy, and thus they became parents.

Ironically, they had not set out to deliberately deceive anyone that the baby girl was not their natural child. There were few servants at the Devon estate, fewer still who knew the countess had miscarried her child. The initial sad news had not been shared with the family and by the time they brought Lily to London in the spring they no longer thought of how she had become their daughter.

Everyone commented on the baby's striking resemblance to Christina and it quickly became a notion that neither the earl nor countess saw fit to correct. Even with their closest family members.

Perhaps that might have changed over time, but Christina became ill and the focus shifted away from the joy and excitement of the new baby. The illness lingered, worsened. As Christina's health steadily declined, it was the presence of Lily that kept them all sane, that brought the only joy and laughter in the household. And when Christina died—Cameron closed his eyes, as if shutting them could miraculously release him from the persistent pain of those three-year-old memories.

If not for Lily, he very well might have gone mad with grief. His little girl was the sole reason he had forced himself to move forward each day. To rise from his bed, to dress, to shave, to make the effort to resume a normal routine.

His love for the child was all encompassing and unconditional. She was his daughter, in all things that mattered, and as he told Tremaine, he would protect her at all costs.

A chilling gust of early December wind hit as Cameron slowed his mount and expertly negotiated the heavily clogged streets. He turned into Grosvenor Square and trotted through the gates of his London residence. Sliding out of the saddle, the earl flipped the reins to a waiting groom.

The front door opened before he reached it.

"Where is Lady Lily?" Cameron asked as he handed over his riding crop, hat, gloves and capped greatcoat to the waiting butler.

The servant opened his mouth to answer, but his reply was drowned out by a squeal of delight echoing from the top step of the winding staircase.

"Papa! You are home at long last!"

The earl smiled at the greeting, silently acknowledging it was a bit dramatic, since he had seen Lily earlier in the morning when they had eaten breakfast together. Nevertheless, he enjoyed the child's obvious enthusiasm as she bounded down the stairs.

"Lily!" The voice of his sister, Charlotte, standing on the upper landing, invaded the space. "Be careful. The staircase can be slippery."

Ignoring her aunt's reprimand, Lily jumped from the final step to the patterned marble floor of the foyer.

Recovering her balance, the little girl straightened, curtsied to him, then skipped over for a kiss.

"Oh, Papa, your beard is scratchy," she complained, but she snuggled closer for a second kiss.

Cameron tightened his hug. "Hey, Puss. How was your day?"

She pulled back and gave him a puzzled frown. "You sound funny, Papa. Is your throat feeling sore?"

Cameron swallowed and shook his head. His voice had become hoarse with emotion as he held her tight. The overwhelming impulse to bar the front doors and have his pistols brought at once nearly destroyed his common sense, so great was the need he felt to protect her.

"It must be the cold that makes me sound so odd," he replied lightly. "The wind is blowing fiercely."

She accepted his explanation trustingly, her blond curls bobbing. "You must wear a scarf around your neck when it is so cold. That's what Aunt Charlotte tells me."

"Aunt Charlotte is wise in such important matters."

His eyes traveled to the staircase where his sister Charlotte was slowly descending, limping awkwardly down each step. She had been born with a malformed hip socket making one leg slightly shorter than the other and her gait always seemed more pronounced on cold or damp days.

"Mrs. James is suffering from a migraine," Charlotte informed him when she finally arrived at the bottom of the staircase. "I volunteered to look after Lily this afternoon."

"We had a tea party in the nursery, with lemonade and my favorite cream cakes," Lily announced. "But it was dull without any male companions."

"Male companions?" the earl repeated, with a raised brow. "Where on earth did you hear such a term?"

"From my best friend, Jane Grolier. She is nearly eight years old and knows so many important things. Her governess is Mrs. James's sister. We play in the park together."

"She is the daughter of Viscount Harding," Charlotte supplied.

"She sounds like a very bold little girl."

"Oh, she is bold!" Lily replied happily. "Jane has three sisters and two brothers. I want you to meet her. She told me if she is presented to an earl her eldest sister must come along. And once her sister sees you then she will want to marry you. Did you know you are a brilliant catch, Papa? That's what Jane says."

Good God. Cameron sent an annoyed glance at his sister. Charlotte shrugged her shoulders helplessly. "Jane is the youngest of the children," Charlotte said, as if that explained everything.

"I am not certain that she is fit company for Lily," the earl whispered back.

"Jane is a tad precocious, but still a polite and well-mannered child. We shall be leaving for Windmere manor next week to begin our Christmas holiday celebrations, so the girls will be apart for at least a month or more. I suppose we can put a stop to the meetings before that, if you wish," Charlotte said skeptically. "But I do believe it will greatly upset Lily."

The earl glanced down at his daughter. She was out of earshot, playing a game in the foyer, hopping on her left foot from one black marble square to the next. "We might as well wait. Though I expect you to keep a close eye on this budding friendship for me, Charlotte."

"Of course, Cameron. You know I want only the best for Lily."

"I know." The earl leaned forward and gave his sister a gentle kiss on the forehead. He had overreacted, thanks to his unsettling meeting at White's and it was hardly fair to take out his bad humor on Charlotte.

His sister was a timid woman, protected and cosseted since birth. Her bodily imperfection had curtailed not only her physical activity, but her social interaction and she usually had difficulty speaking her mind. Even with him.

"Do you have to work now, Papa?"

"For a few hours, but I shall join you for dinner."

"Will you dress?"

"If you'd like." The earl grinned. Lily had recently become very interested in fashion and adored the idea of dressing formally for dinner.

"Oh, yes, please. I have a brand-new yellow gown with three ruffles of lace on the bottom that I shall wear."

"I am sure you will look very fetching."

"I do hope so." Her mind preoccupied with her dinner outfit, Lily skipped from the room.

The earl expected his sister would follow her, but as she turned to leave he caught a slight frown on Charlotte's face.

"Is something wrong?" he asked.

Charlotte hesitated. "Well, 'tis a bit indulgent for a child of Lily's age to dress for dinner."

"Harmless fun," he countered. "Besides, it makes her happy."

"Perhaps." Charlotte lowered her gaze, which annoyed him, because with her expressive eyes hidden, Cameron had no way of telling what she was really thinking.

"Hurry, Aunt Charlotte. I need you."

Lily's voice, filled with childish excitement, carried

down from above stairs. Cameron watched his sister open her mouth, then suddenly shut it.

"I suppose it would not be an effective lesson to lecture Lily about the inappropriate and unladylike behavior of shouting by yelling back at her to stop screaming," Charlotte remarked with a self-deprecating grin. "I believe I shall simply tell her that is something Jane Grolier would never do."

"Brilliant."

Charlotte looked over her shoulder at him and grinned, then slowly, carefully climbed the stairs. When she disappeared from view, the earl stepped across the hallway to his private study, pleased to find his secretary, Robert Baines, still hard at work. The older man put down his pen and started to stand when the earl entered the room, but Cameron waved him back into his seat.

"I have reviewed the reports and the earning statements for the textile mill in Lancashire, my lord," the secretary said. "My notes are in the margin, if you wish to read and discuss it now."

"It can wait."

Feeling too agitated to sit, Cameron paced behind his desk. "I have a far more urgent and delicate matter I wish you to attend to at once."

Baines lifted his pen and shifted the clutter on his desk, searching for a fresh sheet of paper.

"I need background information on two people, a brother and sister. Daniel Tremaine and Rebecca Tremaine, respectively."

The secretary peered down at the parchment and carefully wrote a few notations. "Do you wish me to hire a Bow Street man?"

"No," Cameron said quietly, torn between his need to find the information quickly and the equally important need to keep this matter very quiet. At this point there were only three living people who knew the truth about Lily—himself, Daniel and Rebecca.

The last thing he wanted was a Bow Street man sniffing around this situation. Secrets were far easier to keep with fewer individuals knowing them. "I want you to handle this personally, Baines."

"What precisely do you wish to know about this pair?" the secretary asked.

"Tremaine is a businessman—a successful one, from what I gather. I want to know where his fortune came from, where and how he made it, and what precisely he has been doing for the past six years." Cameron leaned against the edge of his desk. "As for the sister, I want as many details as you can find about her family history, where she grew up, where she lives currently, who she has associated with, that sort of thing. Also, if there are any scandals about either of them, widely known or otherwise."

The secretary jotted down a few more notes, then glanced up. "If I may ask, are you considering hiring Miss Tremaine for a household position?"

"Not exactly." Cameron furrowed his brow. "I need the information as soon as possible, but discretion is key in this matter, Baines. I do not want you to arouse any suspicions when making these inquiries and above all, I want no one to know of my interest. Do you understand?"

"You may count on me, my lord." The secretary gathered up his papers and turned for the door. "If you will excuse me, I will start working immediately on this matter."

Cameron nodded. Baines had been in his employ for nearly ten years and had always done his job with professional discretion. His loyal service was yet another indicator that hiring skilled, competent people and paying them a generous salary was the best way to conduct business. Short of doing it himself, Cameron knew Baines was the right person to handle this most delicate matter.

Once alone, the earl tried to settle down and read the mill report that Baines had left, but it was a useless endeavor. His eyes saw and read the words, but his brain did not comprehend the sentences.

Instead, he replayed his meeting with Tremaine over and over in his mind, trying to decide the best way to move forward. For a few moments, Cameron toyed with the idea of buying the pair off, but if Tremaine were as successful as the earl suspected, money would hold no appeal.

Disgusted, he resumed pacing, then realized he was clenching his hands so hard that his fingers were growing numb. This was ridiculous. He needed a plan. The information Baines would uncover would be useful, but the earl knew from the conversation at the club today that no matter what was discovered, the Tremaines would not easily go away.

He had agreed to give them an answer by Friday, but Cameron was hardly ready to allow this woman to meet Lily. No, she must first meet him and somehow convince him to allow a brief introduction to his daughter. *His* daughter. Perhaps it was possible to intimidate Miss Tremaine sufficiently so she would drop the notion of meeting the little girl altogether? Or maybe he could find another means to dissuade her interest?

A smile lit his face as an idea formed in his mind. There were few society events of note at this time of year, since many of the members of the *haut ton* had left London for their country estates. Those who stayed behind would be planning Christmas celebrations, but any holiday events would not take place for several weeks.

Yet he was sure with careful planning he could scare up a sizeable crowd for a society dinner party. His mother would enjoy the opportunity to entertain. Perhaps even Charlotte might be persuaded to join them.

But more importantly, a social evening would mask the true intent of meeting Miss Rebecca Tremaine and, if he were very lucky, intimidate her with his wealth, power and position at the same time. Scaring her off would quickly end this problem to his satisfaction. Feeling far more in control now that he had a reasonable course of action to follow, Cameron stormed from the room to search for his mother, eager to set his plan into motion.

Her new satin evening slippers were silent on the stone steps as Rebecca climbed to the front door of the Earl of Hampton's town home. With each step she took, she clung tightly to her brother's arm, her fingers flexing with nerves. Daniel lifted the brass knocker, but before he could bang it, the door swung open.

"Sir, Madame."

"Good evening. Mr. Daniel Tremaine and his sister, Miss Rebecca Tremaine. We are expected."

The expressionless butler bowed, then stood aside to allow them entrance to the vast foyer. Servants rushed forward to take their outer garments; a footman wearing a powdered white wig, dressed in black and gold livery, stood at the ready, waiting to escort them upstairs.

"I thought you said this was to be a casual dinner party," Rebecca whispered to her brother.

"That was how the invitation was worded." Daniel snorted. "I suspect part of this might be meant to impress or more likely intimidate us. Then again, the nobility never need much of an excuse to showcase their wealth and waste their money."

"Daniel, please."

Rebecca placed her hand on her brother's forearm. She knew well her brother's opinion of the majority of men in society. Vain, foolish wastrels who neither understood nor appreciated the value of honest work, who lived purely for their own pleasures. A blight on the British landscape of industrial success, he often remarked, and a disgrace to the ingenuity and hard work of so many others around the world.

"Sorry." Daniel lowered his head contritely. "I shall try to be on my best behavior this evening."

"You will succeed at being utterly charming, well bred and congenial to one and all," she admonished, feeling a small measure of relief when Daniel nodded in agreement.

Taking her brother's arm, they followed the liveried servant. As they ascended the winding staircase to the second story, Rebecca's eyes darted anxiously to the third floor, her head turning quickly in all directions.

"I doubt you will catch a glimpse of the little girl tonight, Becca. Try to relax."

Rebecca let out a frustrated sigh. Of course her brother was right. The girl, who had been named Lily, would be safely ensconced in the nursery at this time of night, most likely already asleep.

Rebecca let out a deep sigh, hoping to steady her nerves. It had been an agonizing few weeks since discovering the truth about her baby girl and her need to see the child had grown with each passing day. Daniel continued urging her to have patience, but it was becoming harder and harder.

As soon as Daniel was able to ascertain that the Earl of Hampton was in residence at his London home, they had journeyed to the city. Foolishly, Rebecca thought she would be able to see Lily the moment they arrived. Fortunately, Daniel had anticipated that it would hardly be easy to make contact with the child and had formulated a more realistic approach to the problem.

Knowing they would be staying in the city for several weeks, he had leased a lovely mansion in the fashionable Mayfair district. It was far more pleasant than residing at a hotel, but the beautiful surroundings and interesting sights of the neighborhood had been lost on Rebecca. All she cared about was her daughter, all she thought about was finally meeting, and holding, the little girl.

Rebecca had been exceedingly distressed when Daniel recounted the details of his initial meeting with the earl, but hope had blossomed when a few days later the invitation to dinner had arrived. She felt certain if she made a favorable impression the earl's objections would evaporate. Then she would at long last achieve her greatest desire and set eyes on her child for the first time.

They entered the drawing room and Rebecca was very glad of the support of her brother's strong arm. The room was filled with a glittering array of people, all beautifully and expensively dressed. They were gathered in small groups, drinks in hand. Conversation was animated, laughter frequent.

For one dizzying moment Rebecca felt as if she had just set foot on the moon. Nothing in her simple life had prepared her for this sort of event. Social gatherings where she had been raised in Taunton were far more simple, casual and understated. In that instant, her lack of society experience and sophistication hit her hard. *How would she ever handle this evening without making a fool of herself?*

"They are just people, Rebecca. No better than we," Daniel muttered calmly, as if sensing her sudden insecurity.

For all his vocal disdain of this glittering world, her brother seemed remarkably calm and secure when set among it. Taking her cue from him, Rebecca attempted to place the perfect expression of nonchalant friendliness upon her face.

"Mr. Tremaine. Good evening."

"Lord Hampton."

Rebecca battled a surge of panic and lowered her gaze. She had been so preoccupied with bolstering her courage that she had missed the approach of the earl.

"This must be your sister."

Rebecca lifted her eyes and the pleasant, generic greeting faltered on her lips when she looked at the earl.

Openly looked at him. As if she were struck mute, as if she had never before met a gentleman until that moment.

His eyes held her. Dark brows arched over hazel eyes, accentuated by thick dark lashes. His nose was straight, the nostrils slightly flared above a most sensuous mouth. His firm jaw and strong cheekbones completed the picture of pure masculine beauty.

His long, leanly muscled body was clad in formal black evening clothes, stark white shirt, intricately tied cravat and a black, silk waistcoat.

A tremor ran down her spine. Though she had vowed she would not be, Rebecca felt intimidated by him. She had met only minor nobility before, but there was an aura about the earl that proclaimed him stronger, more powerful, more dangerous than other men, those who held titles and those who did not. He carried himself with masculine arrogance and nearly unnerving personal command.

She knew she must cease staring at him. It was abominably rude, bordering on crass. But then, he was staring at her. After all, turnabout was fair play.

"May I present my sister, Miss Rebecca Tremaine."

"I am pleased to welcome you into my home, Miss Tremaine."

His low voice sent a peculiar wash of heat through her veins, making it difficult to execute a smooth curtsy. "Thank you, my lord. I am delighted to be here."

An older woman, wearing an enormous diamond choker, bustled between them, giving them a friendly, appraising glance.

"My mother, the dowager countess," the earl said. "This is Mr. Daniel Tremaine and his sister, Miss Rebecca."

"A pleasure to meet you both." The older woman smiled pleasantly and Rebecca was impressed by the tone of sincerity in her voice, especially given the thick, ripe tension that filled the air.

She wondered if the dowager countess knew the truth about her connection to Lily and decided it was unlikely. Her manner was too open, too friendly. A marked contrast to her son, who seemed to pause and measure each word before it was uttered.

Further introductions were made to those guests closest around them. Rebecca was grateful that Daniel received the majority of attention and interest. Several of the men were familiar with his business achievements and many of the women were impressed by his handsome countenance.

They next moved slowly about the room, so they could be introduced to the rest of the crowd. Rebecca could not help but note how most of the guests seemed anxious to have a moment to engage the earl in private conversation. A select few were overt with their fawning efforts to garner his attention, most notably the younger women. Or their mothers.

'Twas either his ignorance or arrogance that made the earl seem oblivious to that fact, though secretly Rebecca suspected it was his arrogance.

There were so many people to meet it was difficult for Rebecca to remember which names went with which faces, but one woman dressed in a striking gown of blue watered silk with a round neckline that emphasized her graceful neck made a lasting impression. She was introduced as Lady Marion Rowley, Viscountess Cranborne.

"Hampton is my first cousin," the pretty young viscountess confided to Rebecca as they stood alone together. "Our mothers were sisters. Yet I fear he claims the relationship only when hard-pressed. I have a terrible habit of allowing impulse to rule my behavior. Truth be told, I'm a bit of a family scandal."

"The earl strikes me as a man filled with pride," Rebecca mused, feeling sympathy for anyone who dared to annoy him.

"My yes, it is excessive. Have you known Hampton long?"

"Goodness, no. I just met him this evening."

"Impressive, Miss Tremaine. You show great insight into a man's character on such short acquaintance." Lady Marion signalled a passing footman and procured two glasses of chilled champagne, one for each of them. "Fortunately for all of us, Hampton is also blessed with a streak of unequivocal integrity. It does help temper that arrogant pride of his. Most will freely acknowledge that he is not only strong and capable, but honest and forthright as well. Though I tease him mercilessly for his devotion to protecting the family name and honor, his support and loyalty have kept me alive socially on more than one occasion."

"You are fond of him?" Rebecca asked with surprise.

"Exceedingly." She took a long sip of her champagne. "Though I will be the first to confess his arrogant attitude can be maddening at times."

"He seems to possess that in abundance."

Lady Marion laughed. "Oh, I do like you, Miss Tremaine."

The object of their conversation stood on the opposite side of the room, surrounded by a group of simpering women. Rebecca hazarded a look in his direction, one he returned for half a heartbeat before deliberately looking away. Her cheeks heated slightly.

"If I may be so bold as to offer a touch of experienced advice, do not waste your time and effort setting your cap for Hampton," Lady Marion said. "He was devoted beyond measure to his late wife, Christina. Those of us who know him well doubt he will ever remarry, even for the sake of his title."

Rebecca felt her face flush even more. "I assure you, Lady Marion, I have no romantic interest in the earl whatsoever."

"Oh, dear, now I have offended you." Lady Marion frowned. "I spent far too many years searching for the right man to marry that I easily forget all women do not have a burning desire to land a wealthy, well-connected husband. Forgive me."

"Of course." Rebecca took a small sip of her

champagne, deciding she was secretly flattered that
the viscountess thought she would be able to bring
any of these men up to scratch. For so long, Rebecca
had thought of herself as a spinster, firmly set on
the shelf.

"'Tis a burden of womanhood, I fear, to devote so
much of our time and energy to securing our futures
through marriage," Lady Marion continued. "Why I
know of at least four women who are currently
wrestling between the choice of family duty and personal happiness. And one, poor dear, who is in the
worst predicament of all—the need to marry a fortune." She leaned close and whispered merrily, "Amazingly, I was the most clever of all. I fell in love with
Viscount Cranborne, who was richer than Croesus, and
was thus able to marry for love *and* money."

Lady Marion seemed so genuinely pleased with herself that Rebecca found herself smiling back at her.
The two women chatted a few minutes longer before
Lady Marion excused herself to greet some of her
husband's relatives.

When she left, Rebecca realized under different
circumstances she might have enjoyed this opportunity to meet new people, to have a glimpse into this
fascinating world of wealth and privilege.

But the lively conversation she had just shared
barely distracted her thoughts. Lily was here, beneath
this very roof. Safely tucked away in her bed? Or perhaps she was hearing a story or saying her prayers. Rebecca closed her eyes and said a quick prayer of her
own, knowing she needed all the help she could
muster to survive this evening.

When she opened them, she felt a shiver rush
through her, the overwhelming sense that she was
under observation. A quick glance confirmed her

suspicions. The earl's dark head was tilted and his eyes fixed intently on her, making her feel decidedly uncomfortable.

He started toward her and the urge to flee grew strong. But Rebecca remained in place, trying to stem the nervous quivering of her stomach.

"Afraid I am going to pinch the silver, my lord?" she asked as he drew near, firing off the first shot.

"You can have the silver, Miss Tremaine. And the crystal, if you so desire. There are other, far more valuable items in my care to protect."

His brows rose over his intriguing hazel eyes. They were really more green, she decided; green flecked with gold and brown. Beautiful eyes to be sure and decidedly unfriendly and challenging.

He slanted her a hard look, which she met directly. Damn, there it was again—a ridiculous flash of heat that sparkled between them. No man, not even Philip, had ever made her body stir with more awareness.

The dowager countess and a few other ladies joined them, breaking some of the tension. Ignoring her attraction to the earl was difficult, yet not impossible. Ignoring her feelings about Lily, however, was quickly becoming an impossibility.

Her daughter was here, somewhere inside this very house. So close, and yet so far away. The need to search for her was almost a physical compulsion. Rebecca slowly exhaled, worrying that her heart was unable to take the building stress, that her emotions would somehow unleash and burst forth and she would do something utterly disgraceful.

Rebecca cleared her throat and spoke loudly enough to be heard over the chattering conversation of the other women. "I understand you have a grand-daughter, my lady."

"Oh, my, yes. Lily is the light of our lives." The dowager countess smiled fondly. "She is upstairs in the nursery of course, though I don't believe she has yet been put to bed."

"I bet she is a lovely child."

"Delightful, but what else would a doting grand-mother say?" A glint of love and joy lit the older woman's eyes. "In fact, I might be able to persuade my son to allow her to come down and say hello to the guests. She does so enjoy seeing the ladies and gentle-men in their evening finery."

Rebecca's thoughts froze in place at this unex-pected opportunity. It was almost too perfect to imag-ine and confirmed that the dowager countess was unaware of Lily's true parentage. "Is she not shy of strangers?"

"Heavens no." The dowager countess laughed. "Even when she was very young we noticed when other children slipped behind their mother or nurses' skirts, Lily always boldly put herself forward."

"How charming. I for one would very much enjoy meeting her."

"Not this evening." The earl covered his mother's hand with his own, his smile pleasant, even as eyes bore darkly into Rebecca's. *Drat!* She did not realize he had been listening so intently to their conversation.

"Are you certain, Cameron?" the dowager count-ess asked.

"Yes. Her nurse said Lily had a touch of the sniffles this afternoon. I think it best for everyone if she stays in her room."

"Another time perhaps," Rebecca said, her heart clouding with disappointment.

The earl's displeasure was almost a physical entity. She could sense the level of mistrust he felt for her rise higher. But she had not been able to stop herself; the chance to finally see her daughter had been too tempting to resist.

"Tread carefully, Miss Tremaine," he whispered in her ear.

Startled, she nearly dropped her empty glass. Mustering her courage, she lifted her chin and stared at him. He gave her a disarming smile, that she quickly realized was for the benefit of any who might be watching. Then he inclined his head and left to play the amiable host to the rest of his guests.

Rebecca sagged a little as he strode away, slowly letting out a long breath. That was a close call, far too close for comfort. Yet in her heart she knew she would do it again.

She drew her hand across her brow, then realized she had been twisting the tiny pearl button on her glove so hard it had come loose. Seized with a sudden idea, Rebecca yanked the thread until it broke, then eagerly went in search of Lady Marion.

"I seem to have met with a slight mishap." Rebecca held out her hand, showing the viscountess where the small pearl button was missing from the top of her glove. "Miraculously, I have located the button. Is there somewhere I can repair the damage before dinner is served?"

"Yes. There is a smaller parlor three doors to your left. I will instruct one of the footmen to have a maid sent in with a sewing kit."

"Thank you."

Heart thudding with excitement, along with a touch of guilt, Rebecca quietly left the room.

Chapter 3

Rebecca Tremaine was not at all what he had expected. Cameron took a sip of champagne, that he barely tasted, and watched her openly from across the room. She was lush, her figure rounded in a sensual, almost suggestive manner. She was taller than most women of his acquaintance, statuesque really, and he was annoyed to realize the perfect match for a man of his height.

Her honey-colored hair was brushed sleekly back and twisted at her nape, showcasing the elegant line of creamy ivory skin on her neck and throat. Her face was lovely, with high cheekbones that gave her a slightly exotic look and a wide, full mouth that added a mature sensuality to her appearance. A pair of perfectly arched brows over bright-blue eyes hinted at both intelligence and humor.

The dark green silk gown she wore had short, tight, off-the-shoulder sleeves, a cinched waist and full skirt that was fashionable, tasteful and flattering. Each time he gazed at her, Cameron unexpectedly felt a stirring in his loins. A decidedly unwelcome event.

Caught somewhere between annoyance and fascination, he continued to watch her as she circulated among the guests. There were small, subtle signs of her nerves. The way she clenched and unclenched the material of her gown in her left hand, the deep sighs she took when she thought no one was looking, the ever-so-slight trembling of the crystal goblet she held.

Yet through it all she somehow managed to keep her head high, her shoulders back, her expression open and pleasant. That earned her a grudging bit of his respect.

He was surprised to admit that under different circumstances she would have intrigued him, with her lovely face, sensual body, and proper attitude. But these were hardly normal circumstances.

A part of him wished she had been a featherbrained ninny, or a brassy, immoral creature, clearly lacking refinement and breeding. Both would have been easy to dismiss, easy to ignore.

He wondered about Lily's father. Was he the first of her many lovers? Yet, much as he would like to dismiss her as a woman of loose morals, Cameron had no proof to verify that opinion. His secretary had made inquiries. Miss Rebecca Tremaine was the daughter of a respected vicar, well liked and highly regarded in her community.

Seven years ago she had become engaged to a young lawyer. It was a proper match that most agreed was advantageous for both parties. Then her fiancé had died unexpectedly, tragically in a freak accident. Calculating the dates, Cameron realized Lily had been born six months later. It seemed probable that he had been Lily's father.

By all accounts Miss Tremaine and her fiancé had been very devoted to each other and many declared it a true love match. As much as Cameron wanted to fault the couple's behavior, he could not find it within himself to be so harsh. They would hardly be the first couple in history who had anticipated their wedding vows.

It was a pity that he had been unable to persuade his sister, Charlotte, to attend this evening's dinner party. She always kept herself quietly in the background, keenly observing those around her. Cameron valued her opinion and would have wanted to know her impressions of Miss Tremaine. Best of all, Charlotte would not have pressed him for details as to why he wanted the information.

But at their parents' encouragement, Charlotte had refrained from formally entering society. They feared her physical deformity, coupled with her plain looks and intellectual mind, would practically assure her social failure.

There were times Cameron wondered if they had all done Charlotte a great disservice by keeping her so cloistered. At five and twenty it seemed almost certain she would remain a spinster for the rest of her life.

Like Miss Tremaine? Obviously, she was unmarried, but with her beauty and refinement that state could easily change. Though society held that all women desired marriage above all else, he could see that might not always be true. Perhaps it was Miss Tremaine's choice to remain single.

Cameron handed his empty champagne glass to a passing footman and accepted a full one. Miss Tremaine's marital state was none of his concern. Her interest in Lily, however, was very much his business.

Her ploy to get the child down to the drawing room before dinner had annoyed him, yet he could not entirely fault her for the attempt. Still, he would have to be on guard to make certain nothing else like that occurred. He, and he alone, would decide when, and if, she was to meet the little girl.

The thought that he needed to keep an eye on her had no sooner entered his mind when he saw Miss Tremaine slip from the room. *What now?* Nearly choking on the last sip of bubbling nectar in his glass, Cameron abruptly excused himself and raced after her. He saw her climbing the grand staircase to the third floor and promptly increased his stride.

"Looking for something, Miss Tremaine?" he asked.

Her back stiffened at the sound of his voice, and he knew she recognized it as his. Slowly, she turned around. "I have ripped my glove, my lord. Lady Marion was kind enough to request that a maid be summoned to help me repair it."

"My cousin told you to wait on the staircase for the servant? Most peculiar."

She looked him directly in the eyes, something that women rarely did. The gesture earned her another scrap of grudging admiration.

"Lady Marion instructed me to wait in the small parlor, but I neglected to listen closely to her directions and was confused as to where it was located."

A bald-faced lie, and they both knew it. He debated calling her on it, but decided it was futile to be so boorish. Besides, what exactly could he accuse her of doing? Leaving the drawing room to fix her glove and being an inattentive listener when told where to wait for assistance?

There was an awkward silence. Cameron searched for something to say, but was finding it difficult. A meaningless social exchange about the weather was an insult to both of them, given the bizarre reality of their situation. Yet this was hardly the time or place for a lengthy personal conversation. His temper was on edge, his emotions escalated, and the house was filled with guests.

"Shall we join the others?" Cameron held out his hand, opting to retreat for now.

"My glove?"

"My housekeeper will take care of the problem. It will be repaired and returned to you before dinner."

After a deliberate hesitation, Miss Tremaine reached out and placed her bare fingers into his palm. A shiver of awareness bolted through him at the touch of her hand in the center of his warm palm. He ignored it. So, apparently did she, though he saw her lower lip trembling.

"Despite what you might think, I have no wish to cause you unnecessary anguish," he said quietly.

Her brow wrinkled. "Actions speak far louder than words, my lord. We both know the real reason I am here tonight. All I ask is for an opportunity to see the child. To meet her, to speak with her."

"I assure you, there is no need to remind me of that fact, Miss Tremaine." Cameron met her steady gaze. "However, since that meeting will most definitely not take place this evening, I strongly urge you to cease trying to orchestrate a chance encounter with Lily. 'Tis already becoming tiresome and though I consider myself a fair man, my patience has very defined limits."

Her face momentarily paled and a heated flash sparked in her eyes, yet her composure never faltered. "Point taken, my lord."

An early morning drizzle had given way to a late morning of brilliant sunshine. There was a cold, though not unpleasant, breeze blowing, yet Rebecca knew it would not have mattered if there was a bone-chilling freeze in the air or a full blown blizzard blanketed the street with snow. In any sort of weather she would be standing outdoors in precisely the same spot.

The activity on the quiet, well-appointed avenue where the Earl of Hampton lived had increased noticeably over the last half hour. There were more pedestrians, more carriages, and several carts making deliveries to the back entrances of the fashionable homes. Rebecca was glad of the additional commotion, since it made it much easier for her to remain in her current position without attracting too much undue attention.

Though pressed last night by both herself and Daniel, the earl had given them no indication of how quickly arrangements would be made for her to meet Lily. For Rebecca, his attitude had been more than a disappointment; it had left her feeling numb with dread.

Daniel too had been distressed, but he had told her repeatedly that they could not fault the earl for being protective of the child. Her brother had cautioned her to remain patient and had given his word that he would pressure Lord Hampton to arrange for her to see Lily as soon as possible.

But Rebecca had run short of patience. Hungry for any information about Lily, she had pumped the dowager countess last night for details about the little girl's daily routine. Obviously proud of her granddaughter, the dowager countess had spoken of her music and dance lessons and had also mentioned that Lily and her governess made a point of visiting the park every morning around eleven, weather permitting.

And so this morning, after a restless, nearly sleepless, night, Rebecca had left her brother's town home soon after breakfast, commandeered his carriage and made her way to the earl's home. Not wanting the servants to have an inkling of her plans, she had dismissed the coach, intending to hire a hackney when she was ready to return.

Situating herself on the corner opposite the stately mansion, eyes pinned anxiously to the closed wrought iron gates, Rebecca now waited for Lily and her governess. She was staring so hard, her thoughts and emotions so intense, that it took her a moment to notice the gates had indeed opened. A woman in a dark brown cloak emerged, followed quickly by a little girl dressed in a red woolen coat, with a matching red hat.

Lily!

Rebecca's heart accelerated to an alarming rate. Trying to calm her nerves, she took a deep breath and let it out slowly. From this distance she could see none of the little girl's features. Almost without realizing it, she stepped forward.

The shout of a coachman startled her and Rebecca pulled back just in time to avoid being struck. The ground thundered with vibrations. Visibly shaking, she turned her eyes anxiously across the street, fearful that in the commotion she might have lost sight of Lily and her governess.

Thankfully they had not gone far. Eagerly Rebecca watched as the pair walked to the corner on the far end of the street. Lily skipped gaily ahead, pausing every few steps to turn and make certain her governess was near. They stopped at the intersection, waiting for a fashionable black carriage to pass. When it was clear, they crossed the road together, hand in hand, carefully skirting a large puddle in the middle of the rutted lane.

Trying to keep a respectable, undetectable distance, Rebecca hurried across the road and followed them. After several blocks, the pair stopped a few paces in front of a park entrance and waited. Five minutes later Lily began hopping excitedly from one foot to the other as she raised her hand and waved to someone Rebecca could not see.

Her breath caught in her throat. *Dear Lord, please do not let it be the earl.*

Worried, Rebecca bit her lip in vexation, but moments later a woman and young girl came into view. The girls ran to meet each other, hugging exuberantly. Then they joined hands, skipping into the park. The women followed close behind.

Rebecca slowly exhaled and moved closer.

The park was deceptively large. There was a pond in the center, banks of trees and benches along the perimeter, sections of open space and a gravel pathway large enough to accommodate a horse and carriage. On this brisk December morning there was a surprising number of people coming and going along the footpaths and across the lawns. Rebecca noticed Lily and her young friend waving to several individuals and being greeted in return.

Finally they stopped at an empty bench. The women sat, the girls stood, lingering near, hanging onto the back of the seat. Her heart pounding with the enormity of what she was about to do, Rebecca purposefully made her way toward the group.

The two women were engaged in conversation. The two girls were no longer beside them but instead were playing a spirited game of tag on the brown grass directly in front of the bench. Rebecca tried not to stare at Lily, but her eyes were continually, compulsively drawn to the child.

"Forgive the interruption, ladies," Rebecca said softly. "I was at this very spot yesterday afternoon and I believe I lost my favorite brooch somewhere in the vicinity. Perchance, I was wondering if either of you have seen it? It is gold, with three tiny pearls and single ruby chip in the center. 'Tis of little monetary worth, but holds great sentimental value for me and I would dearly like to recover it."

"Oh, my goodness, how distressing," Lily's governess said. She immediately rose from the bench and began looking around in the grass. Her companion did the same. Naturally, they found nothing.

"'Tis so kind of you to help. Would you mind if I asked the girls if they have seen it?" Rebecca inquired.

She forced herself to smile in what she hoped was a friendly, nonintrusive manner. It was more difficult than she imagined to present herself so falsely to these two trusting women.

"Go right ahead. I'm sure they would think it a great adventure to search for such treasure," the other governess replied. "Miss Jane, Lady Lily, come here please."

The girls raced over. A thousand emotions flooded Rebecca as Lily came close enough for her to finally see her face and form clearly.

Oh, my she is beautiful! She was a sturdy little girl, with blond curls and large blue eyes. Looking at her felt like a dream to Rebecca. Anxiously she searched her face, amazed to see small parts of herself and Philip in Lily's features. And then Lily smiled—a grin so reminiscent of her own that Rebecca's knees grew weak.

"This nice lady has lost her brooch," one of the women said. "Would you girls like to help her look for it?"

"Does it have diamonds in it?" Lily asked, her eyes wide with excitement.

Rebecca smiled, swallowed hard and found her voice. "No," she managed to croak.

"It's gold and shiny, so we should be able to find it if we look closely in the grass," Lily's governess announced.

"I shall find it," Jane declared confidently.

"No, it will be me," Lily chimed in with equal bravado.

They all fanned out on the small slope of lawn. Attempting to avoid being too obvious, Rebecca stayed as near to Lily as she dared. She tried not to stare too hard, but was helpless to prevent her gaze from constantly sliding toward the little girl.

It was a heady, dizzy feeling to finally see a face she had imagined countless times. Ever since she had discovered that Lily was alive, Rebecca had tried to envision what this moment would feel like, yet nothing could have prepared her for the riot of emotions that coursed through her.

This beautiful, lively creature was a product of Philip's love and passion. She had grown inside Rebecca's body, had been born and then whisked away before Rebecca had ever held her. She had grieved and mourned the loss of the child she was told had died and yet miraculously here she was; hale, hearty and happy. They were virtual strangers and yet somehow connected in the most primal, intimate way imaginable.

Hot tears burned her eyes. Rebecca forced them back, fearing her tears might confuse or distress Lily. She was concentrating so hard on reining in her emotions that she did not hear the carriage rumbling down the broad, gravel-covered pathway, nor notice when it halted near the park bench.

"Papa!"

A horrifying dread clutched Rebecca's stomach as she turned and watched Lily rush toward the coach.

A tall gentleman in a capped greatcoat stepped down, scooped the child in his arms and hugged her tightly.

Oh, please, no. Panic enveloped her. Rebecca cast her eyes frantically about, searching for a route of escape but soon realized there was none.

The moment seemed to stretch into eternity. Fortunately, Lily's excitement and chattering filled the hollow silence. The two governesses and the other little girl had noticed the earl's arrival and were making their way up the slope. Rebecca prayed their presence would force the earl to remain in control of a temper she felt certain was ready to explode. After all, he had warned her last night to keep her distance from Lily.

She could feel his gaze resting on her face, yet could only imagine the shock and anger of his expression, for she refused to look back at him. There was a pinch in her heart, a hollow ache in her chest. Not because she had been discovered. The pain radiated through her because she knew her very brief time with her daughter was over.

Rebecca pressed her lips together, uncaring that her dismay must have been keenly apparent. There was no shame in wanting to see her child. He might have warned her to stay away, yet she felt the fault was his, for refusing to allow her contact.

"There she is, Papa. We are trying to help her find her brooch. She lost it here. Will you help too?"

Lord Hampton jerked his head away from Lily's and glanced in Rebecca's direction. A small tic began to work in the earl's left cheek. "A brooch?"

"Yes." Lily nodded her head earnestly. "It's gold and shiny, but doesn't have any diamonds."

Rebecca raised her chin. The earl glared at her, his eyes narrowing, his nostrils flaring. She noticed his left hand curl protectively on Lily's back. Her smile felt brittle, but Rebecca managed to keep it on her face. She refused to shrink away from him. Or cringe or cower.

"Mrs. James, kindly escort Lady Lily home immediately."

The earl bent low, releasing the little girl, and nudging her gently toward her governess. Lily refused to be moved, and instead was standing at his side, tugging on his coat.

"But I want to look for the brooch," she whined. "If I leave now, then Jane will find it."

"I doubt that, Puss. There will be no more looking today. 'Tis time for you and Mrs. James to go home."

Lily's face darkened. "If we have to go, then I wish to ride in the carriage."

"Not today, Puss."

"But, Papa—"

"Mrs. James," Lord Hampton interrupted, his voice rising fractionally.

"At once, my lord."

The governess gave a hurried curtsy and pulled her young charge down the path. Rebecca could hear the little girl whining with complaint, but Mrs. James's steps never faltered. Miss Jane and her governess quickly followed.

And then, as Rebecca feared, the earl turned his attention to her. His expression was black as night, his mouth a grim, set line on his handsome face.

"What in blazes do you think you are doing?"

Rebecca raised a trembling hand to her forehead. She closed her eyes for a heartbeat, trying to regain some control over her thoughts and emotions. "I was merely taking a stroll in the park, my lord," she replied, her voice sharp with mounting emotion. "'Tis a public place, free to all who wish to enjoy its natural beauty."

"How did you find her?" he demanded to know.

Rebecca drew a deep breath, steadying herself inside and out. "'Tis a public park," she repeated stubbornly.

His face muscles had tightened so much that the skin seemed stretched taut over his bones. "Get in the carriage, Miss Tremaine."

"I prefer to walk. The sun is shining, the cool fresh air invigorating."

The earl reached out to take her arm, but she jerked free of his grasp.

"Anger is such a mild term for what I am feeling right now, Miss Tremaine. I suggest you tread most carefully or else you shall push me beyond it into a boiling rage."

Rebecca blinked, moving behind the park bench, as if it could somehow physically protect her from him. "I am not a child, nor a servant that you can order about," she protested.

The earl's eyes narrowed into small slits. "If you ever hope to see my daughter again, you will step into that coach. Immediately."

Helplessly, she stared at him. As threats went, it was a most effective one. Having had but a brief glimpse of Lily made Rebecca's need to see her daughter even more intense. There was no other choice. Heart and head pounding, Rebecca did as she was bid.

"Explain yourself."

The coach jerked forward and he saw Miss Tremaine frantically clutch at the seat to keep her balance. Cameron tapped on the roof twice to indicate to his driver that he wished a more sedate pace and the carriage immediately slowed.

The question remained between them, unanswered.

Cameron opened his mouth to repeat it, but Miss Tremaine began to speak.

"The waiting has been intolerable. I tried, truly, but could delay no longer. I had to meet her, to see her, to speak with her."

"To tell her who you are?" he accused.

"No! Never!"

"I don't believe you."

"'Tis the truth." Miss Tremaine stifled a sigh. "I cannot be held responsible if you refuse to believe me."

"But you can be held accountable for your actions."

Cameron jammed his gloved fingers through his hair. He was losing control and he knew it. He needed to get his temper in check. Fast. A shouting match with Miss Tremaine would hardly solve anything.

"I did nothing wrong," she insisted. "I stand behind my behavior, my lord."

His gaze rested on her hands, clutched tightly about her reticule. "I believe I made myself perfectly clear to you last night. Your actions this morning are proof that you are a false and untrustworthy woman, someone I want my child to avoid. I would be well within my rights to deny you access to Lily. Forever."

Her breath hitched in alarm and she seemed to be struggling with her emotions. "I refuse to believe that anyone could be so cruel."

"You have no earthly idea what I am capable of, Miss Tremaine."

Her back stiffened. Good. Cameron was glad to have made an impact, pleased to have made his point. But he wondered what she was thinking. Did she believe he would make good on his threat? More important, did he believe it himself? Could he indeed be so harsh as to deny this woman, Lily's mother, any contact with her child?

A weighty pause followed. "My brother and I are not without resources," she finally countered. "If necessary, we will fight to have some rights in this matter."

It was not an idle threat. Tremaine did have money, and some influence. If he were not careful, Cameron knew things could get very ugly.

"You would never win custody from me in a court of law, nor will I allow you to drag my name into every paper in England."

Her chin lowered. "Though I care little about my own reputation, I would never subject Lily to such scrutiny, such scandal."

Well, at least that was something. "Kindly look at me, Miss Tremaine."

She finally raised her eyes and he saw why she had kept them lowered. Everything she felt was bared for him to see—the pain, the frustration, the longing for what she had lost. The sight of such raw, intense emotion jolted him. When they entered the coach, Cameron had no intention of showing her any mercy, yet his resolve faltered.

His neat, orderly, predictable, comfortable world was coming apart. From the moment Daniel Tremaine walked into White's nothing was as it should be. Life was careening out of control and Cameron realized he was powerless to prevent it.

"It has been difficult for you, has it not?" he said, the question spoken more as a statement.

"It's been pure hell."

Her bluntness only emphasized the scope of her pain. As he glanced at her forlorn expression Cameron could almost feel the misery rising in her heart.

"I'm sorry for your suffering."

She shook her head. "I know the fault initially was not yours, or your wife's. Unaware of the true facts, you did what you thought was right and decent and a part of me is very grateful that my infant daughter was placed in such a loving home.

"But since learning of my child's true fate, I have been consumed with the need to see her. You cannot begin to know how I have wished and hoped and yearned for the impossible. To spend some time with my little girl."

Her voice wavered, but she heroically managed to hold her emotions in check. Still, it dismayed him to see her flushed with distress.

"Often, circumstances that cannot be changed are best left alone," he said kindly.

Her sigh was a weary resignation. "I do not dispute that, my lord. You are Lily's father and that will never change."

Cameron settled himself against the squabs, feeling overcome with a sudden sense of exhaustion. The condition no doubt due to the lethal combination of little sleep and great worry he had experienced over the past few days, ever since learning of Miss Tremaine and her predicament.

"What part do you expect to play in my daughter's life?" he asked.

"I have no idea. There are no examples for me to draw upon, no experience quite like this one." She sounded firm, but he caught the sound of a slight tremor in her tone. "Still, I refuse to believe that we cannot reach some sort of mutually acceptable agreement, my lord."

A twinge of admiration cut through him. Though the odds were hardly in her favor, she would not retreat. Instead, she faced him with simple honesty and dignity, her grace and determination unshakable.

Bloody hell. He looked levelly at Miss Tremaine.

Perhaps he had been overreacting, reading too much into her actions this morning. By her own admission, it was an act of desperation. Battling his conscience, Cameron admitted that placed in the same position, he might have done something similar. Or even more daring.

He scrubbed his face with his hands. He was not one who relished making mistakes, but was also not foolish enough to compound them by refusing to acknowledge and rectify them. In his zealous need to protect Lily perhaps he had misjudged Miss Tremaine and inadvertently caused her additional suffering.

"Have you made any special plans for the upcoming Christmas holiday?"

Her expressive eyes blinked in confusion. "Christmas?"

"Your father is recently deceased. I was unsure if you planned to observe the holiday this year."

"It has been three months since his death. My brother and I are no longer in deep mourning. However, to be perfectly frank, with all that has been going on, Christmas is the very furthest thing from my mind."

Cameron inhaled a deep breath. "Each year we host a large gathering at Windmere, my estate in Kent. 'Tis mostly family and close friends in attendance, though when the locals join in it can be quite a crush. I was wondering if you and your brother would be free to join us."

"On Christmas Day?"

"You would be there on Christmas Day, of course, but the invitation is extended for the entire celebration. The festivities continue for several weeks, both before and after the holiday. You would be welcome for as long as you wish to stay."

Her puzzled expression vanished and she stared. "What about Lily?"

"Naturally my daughter is at the center of all the activities. If you came to the manor, it would give you an opportunity to spend time with her without arising anyone's suspicions."

She schooled her features into calm but he could see she was excited. "If I may be so bold as to inquire, does anyone else know the truth about Lily?"

"Not to my knowledge. Only you, your brother and myself are aware of Lily's true parentage. And I would like very much for it to remain that way."

Her lovely face filled with uncertainty. Cameron braced himself for an argument.

"Though I prefer it to be different, I agree with your decision," she said. "It would be too upsetting and confusing for Lily if she learned the truth." She cleared her throat. "Thank you for your kind and exceedingly generous offer. My brother and I shall be delighted to attend the Christmas festivities at your home."

"Very good. I shall have my secretary send you all the pertinent details, along with directions to the estate."

Cameron tapped again on the carriage roof and instructed the coach to take them to her brother's house. He saw Miss Tremaine's expressive blue eyes widen, for she had not given him the address. He liked that; he wanted her to be a bit wary of him, wanted her to know that he was a strong, knowledgeable, formidable opponent.

They did not speak for the remainder of the short ride. Amazingly, there was no extreme tension in the air and Cameron was glad they had managed to get past the awkwardness of the situation. For the moment.

Philosophically, he realized the tension would very likely return in full force when Miss Tremaine and her brother arrived at Windmere. Unfortunately, that was the reality of this bizarre situation and the sooner he learned to cope with it, the better.

Besides, Christmas was known to be a time of hope and rebirth. Perhaps this year, when it was needed most, they would be able to resolve this matter in a way that would bring all of them some measure of peace and happiness.

Chapter 4

Rebecca and Daniel set out on their journey to the earl's estate five days later, just after breakfast, in a brand-new, recently purchased carriage. It was well sprung and plushly appointed, but could have been filled with hay, for all that Rebecca cared. It was the prize at the end of her trip that she valued; the means to bring her there was unimportant.

"You should not have accepted this invitation without first consulting with me, Rebecca."

"I know, Daniel. I am sorry."

"This is a most inconvenient time for me to be away from London. Since I've decided to stay in England for at least a year, 'tis imperative that I establish a stronger business presence. Currently, I am in the middle of some very delicate negotiations for mining rights in Cornwall. This venture needs my complete attention in order to succeed."

"Perhaps you can arrange to return to London for part of the time?"

"And leave you on your own with Hampton? Not on your life."

"There will be a house full of guests, including the

earl's mother. I hardly think my reputation, or virtue, will be in jeopardy." Rebecca rolled her eyes, but her brother was gazing out the window and did not see. "I appreciate your concern and support, but I am well beyond a time in my life when I need someone to protect me, to shield and shelter me from the world."

Daniel huffed. "Maybe if someone had done a better job of that years ago, we would not be in this particular mess."

Every muscle in Rebecca's body stiffened, surprised to feel the hurt. He did not mean it the way it sounded, she told herself. He is merely annoyed and frustrated because of the inconvenience and interruption to his schedule. "I apologize again for not conferring with you before accepting the earl's invitation, but I simply could not allow the opportunity to spend time with Lily to slip out of my grasp."

Daniel turned to her. Rebecca saw a moment of embarrassed anger cross his expression. "Curse my wicked tongue. I do not mean to vent my foul temper on you. Forgive me."

"Oh, Daniel." Rebecca appreciated his apology, yet found herself compelled to explain further. "Please try to understand. I have no real desire to spend the holiday with Lord Hampton at his grand country estate. Truth be told, the very notion intimidates me. But this might be the only chance I will ever have to be with Lily and I know in my heart if I do not do this I shall waste far too many of the days ahead dwelling in bitterness."

"Hush, now. Of course you must go. We must go." Daniel darted her an embarrassed look, then awkwardly patted her hand. "I know it is necessary for you to seize this opportunity. Though no one who knew the truth of the matter would fault you for wallowing in pity and resentment. 'Tis monstrously unfair what our parents did.

"As for Great-Aunt Mildred, let me just say it is a blessing she is already deceased or else I would not be held accountable for my actions toward her."

Rebecca heaved a small sigh and smiled at her brother. It did her bruised spirits good to have him play the champion for her. "I know this visit will not be easy for either of us, but at least it is a happy time of year. Celebrating Christmas often brings out the best in people."

Daniel grimaced. "I find the holiday can oftentimes be a foolish combination of sentimentality and over-blown piety."

"But you always loved Christmas when you were a boy."

"That was a very long time ago, Becca."

Knowing she would never win an argument on that subject, Rebecca felt it prudent to change the course of their conversation. "How long before we are there?" she asked.

"The coachman told me another hour."

Rebecca straightened and looked out the carriage window. There had been a subtle transformation in the landscape that had previously escaped her notice. The more densely populated area outside the city proper had given way to a gently rolling countryside, the fields now bare, the meadows still boasting a few sparse patches of green.

The woodlands and copses were without leaves and the bareness was a fitting accompaniment to her mood. Though she had professed her great desire and determination for the necessity of this upcoming visit to her brother, Rebecca worried if she was doing the right thing.

Would it be easier or harder to leave her daughter once she had become acquainted with the little girl? Was she possibly making a most difficult situation even more intolerable? Would it be better to try to forget about Lily and simply move forward with her life?

And what of the earl? Was her attraction to him merely the natural female instinct of admiring a handsome, powerful man? Or was there a deeper, more complex connection that she could not begin to define or understand?

These thoughts plagued her for the next hour, but when they passed a sign announcing they had entered Kent, Rebecca threw off her worrisome mood. It was a lovely, charming, rural area, one that reminded her a bit of her home in Taunton. They rode through a prosperous village, with a fine selection of goods displayed in the shop windows and numerous, well-dressed people frequenting those establishments and her mood lightened further.

Beyond the shops were clusters of houses. Some of the dwellings had thatched roofs; others were constructed of stone and slate. All had bare gardens neatly tidied and dormant in the winter cold and there were hedgerows or painted white fences marking their boundaries. As the carriage reached the outskirts of the village proper, it clattered past an old Norman church, then turned onto a curving road that crept up a hill.

In the distance, Rebecca could see the manor house and its extensive grounds. The sun was high in the sky, its wintry rays brilliantly reflected in the many small-paned windows of the four-story house. There was smoke curling from the ten chimneys she counted, an inviting, welcoming sight.

Her excitement and delight held until they pulled into the long gravel drive, but then as she thought of the days ahead, the emotions in her gut began to churn. *However was she going to manage?*

A trio of liveried servants encircled the carriage even before it came to a complete stop in the courtyard. The men bustled efficiently around the coach, assisting Rebecca and Daniel from the interior, then organizing the luggage, horses, coachman and grooms with a skilled efficiency that bespoke of extensive experience with visitors.

The front door was opened by a stiff, unsmiling butler, but his severe greeting was softened by the immediate appearance of the housekeeper, an older woman dressed in black with a white lace cap perched on her head.

"Welcome, welcome, to Windmere manor," she said with a happy smile. "'Tis always a delight to have guests among us, but never more so than during Christmastime. I am Mrs. Evans, the housekeeper. If you find yourself in need of anything, anything at all, during your stay, please be sure to ask me."

There was no chance to reply, for the dowager countess next appeared. She too smiled with delight and welcomed them graciously, apologizing for her son's absence by explaining he was away from the manor attending to estate business.

"We are so pleased that you were able to join us this year," the dowager countess said. "We look forward to your joining in our outings and soirees. There is always something lively and delightful to do at Windmere during the holidays."

"Splendid," Daniel said with a congenial smile.

"I know you must be tired after your journey," the dowager countess continued. "The servants will show you to your chambers. We are having an informal luncheon served at one o'clock. I look forward to seeing you both then."

Rebecca smiled her thanks, pleased their arrival turned out to be slightly less of an ordeal than she had feared. A footman assisted Daniel while she followed the housekeeper up the grand staircase, through the hall, then down a long corridor.

After assuring the housekeeper she needed nothing further, Rebecca took a moment to enjoy the solitude in her bedchamber. As she walked by the four-poster bed, she could smell the lavender-scented sheets. The room was pleasantly appointed in shades of blue and cream, dominated by a subtle pattern of forget-me-nots in the wallpaper and repeated on the silk bed coverlet.

A small settee featuring the same floral pattern in brocade was at the foot of the bed, facing the hearth. There were two thick rugs, one blue, one cream, covering the floor.

In addition to a dressing table, with a matching mirror, and a large cherry armoire, there was a writing desk on the far wall and a plush blue chaise cozily positioned in front of the fireplace. Though Rebecca assumed all the bedchambers in this stately home were equally impressive, the accommodations chosen for her made her feel like an honored guest.

No sooner had Rebecca removed her bonnet than a housemaid arrived, setting a pitcher of hot water beside the porcelain basin, along with a pile of clean, fluffy towels.

"Whenever you are ready for luncheon, Miss Tremaine, just pull on the bell rope and someone will come and show you the way. Or you can have a tray prepared and brought to your room, if you prefer."

"I think I shall join the rest of the guests after I have changed out of my traveling clothes," Rebecca decided. "By any chance, do you know where my brother's room is located?"

"The single male guests are housed in the west wing of the manor. Shall I have a footman bring him a message?"

"Yes, please. Ask my brother to fetch me before he goes downstairs."

The housemaid curtsied, then left. As she departed, the personal maid that Daniel insisted Rebecca bring along arrived. Her presence momentarily flustered Rebecca, who was not used to such attention. For most of her life she had managed to dress and undress herself on her own. On the occasion that help was needed, the family's housemaid, Anne, was pressed into service.

But Daniel was adamant that she arrive with a proper maid, and he with a proper valet, and Rebecca decided it was easier to agree than argue the point. Her maid, Maureen, was a pleasant middle-aged woman who seemed to have a considerable amount of experience in the position and knew a great deal about women's fashions.

She tactfully suggested which gowns would be most appropriate to wear for the afternoon, and Rebecca selected a simple ivory lace-over-silk day gown. Maureen then deftly produced the accompanying accessories.

After fixing Rebecca's hair, the maid set about unpacking the rest of Rebecca's clothes, sorting out which gowns would need immediate attention and hanging the remainder in the armoire. Even though he had repeatedly assured her he could easily afford it, Rebecca felt a pang of guilt as she viewed the expensive new wardrobe that Daniel had insisted be ordered for the house party.

Once it was over, where in the world would she ever wear such lovely, fashionable garments? Perhaps she could repay her brother's kindness and generosity by acting as his hostess, though she assumed the majority of his social interactions would involve his business ventures and might not even require the presence of a woman.

Deciding that was something she would broach when they were alone, Rebecca answered the knock at her door. It was Daniel, with a footman in tow, coming to escort her downstairs. The casual luncheon the dowager countess had mentioned was being served in the long portrait gallery and Daniel had wisely brought the servant along to guide the way.

When Rebecca and Daniel arrived, they were greeted by a crowd of nearly thirty people, though the gallery was so large and spacious it could have easily accommodated a hundred more.

Long, white linen–covered tables were laid out with covered silver trays and large platters of every type of food imaginable were placed upon them. Arrangements of red and white hothouse roses lent color and fragrance to the room, adding a festive touch. Guests were busy helping themselves to the artful buffet and then finding seats among the smaller round tables that were set near the windows so everyone could enjoy the view of the rolling countryside.

"Do you think the informal arrangement was planned for our benefit?" Daniel asked. "No doubt in this exalted company we would have been seated far below the salt at a formal setting."

"Goodness, I had not even thought about it," Rebecca

replied, wishing her brother had not found yet another thing for her to feel nervous about.

Her eyes anxiously scanned the room and she was further disappointed to discover there were no children in attendance. It was not unexpected, yet she had hoped for a chance to see Lily again as soon as possible.

They joined the group clustered around the buffet, made their selections and started toward one of the round tables when they were waylaid by a middle-aged man carrying two goblets of wine.

"Tremaine! What a delightful surprise. I had no idea you would be here."

"Lord Bailey, hello. This is a lucky occurrence. May I present my sister, Miss Rebecca Tremaine."

"Charmed." Lord Bailey bowed elegantly from the waist, simultaneously lifting the goblets filled with wine higher in the air. Rebecca was impressed that he did not spill a drop.

"Won't you join us? Selby and Reynolds are here too. If you have a mind, we'd like to discuss that mining operation in Cornwall. We all have questions we are hoping you can answer. You are invited too, Miss Tremaine, though I cannot vouch for how interesting you will find our conversation."

Rebecca noticed Daniel glance longingly at the table filled with men. He would not willingly abandon her and yet she thought it might be the best thing for his mood if he spent some time talking business.

"You go ahead, Daniel. I have spied Lady Marion on the other side of the room and will happily join her."

"Are you certain?"

"Yes, go." She smiled with encouragement, then excused herself and deliberately headed toward the table where Lady Marion and another woman were seated before she could lose her courage.

"Miss Tremaine, you are here!" Lady Marion exclaimed. "How delightful. Please, take a seat."

The words were courteously spoken, but the grin on Lady Marion's face was genuine and welcoming, making the invitation sincere. She introduced the woman seated next to her as Lady Charlotte, the earl's sister. She was a plain-featured woman, with an oval face and brown hair that was topped by a lace-edged spinster's cap.

After a breathless greeting, Lady Charlotte shyly cast her hazel eyes down to her plate. But her smile had been sweet and kind. Rebecca gratefully joined them.

All the food that had been piled on her dish looked appetizing, but Rebecca found her nerves compelled her to push the food about on her plate while making a pretense of eating. Fortunately, the other two women did not appear to notice.

"I do hope that Cameron has invited some eligible gentlemen this year," Lady Marion said, her eyes twinkling with mischief. "Christmas is one of the best times of year to indulge in some serious matchmaking."

"Not with me!" Lady Charlotte looked horrified at the notion.

"Of course with you. And with Miss Tremaine."

Rebecca was glad she had not just put a fork filled with beef in her mouth, for she surely would have choked.

"But it is December," Lady Charlotte sputtered. "The marriage mart has ended."

"Don't be so silly. Husband hunting is a year-round pastime," Lady Marion insisted. "Thankfully, there are not too many young misses in attendance, which makes it much better."

"Not for me." Lady Charlotte met Rebecca's eyes with a panic-stricken gaze. "If there were a few pretty young girls here you would concentrate your efforts on them and shift your attention away from me."

"And me," Rebecca chimed in, hoping Lady Marion was teasing. The very idea of being matched with any of these exalted gentlemen set her teeth on edge.

"Oh, posh, young misses can be so boring and grating on the nerves," Lady Marion said. "Most have a tendency to giggle and titter like hens around a rooster when in the company of an eligible man. 'Tis maddening and most unbecoming."

"Ah, I believe we have found our escape from this matchmaking nightmare, Lady Charlotte. We need to learn to giggle and titter." Rebecca smiled, more confident now that Lady Marion was being lighthearted and amusing.

"Titter?" Lady Charlotte repeated, lowering her gaze. "Oh, dear."

"Yes, and we must learn to cackle also, for a loud cackle will surely drive everyone in the vicinity mad," Rebecca added, warming to the spirit of fun.

She turned to Lady Charlotte and noticed a slight grin appear. Rebecca flashed her an encouraging, reassuring smile. Lady Charlotte sat up a fraction in her chair.

"There now, you have been given fair warning, Marion," Lady Charlotte said. "If you persist on your matchmaking quest, Miss Tremaine and I will be forced to take drastic action."

Lady Marion's gaze narrowed. "I see that you are both planning to be difficult, but that will not deter me," she replied. "You forget, but I was arguably the most impossible debutante for more Seasons than I can recall. My mother used to repeatedly tell me it was her greatest fear that I would never have a home of my own."

"That is because she knew how bossy you can be," Lady Charlotte said with a shy grin. "She *needed* you to be in charge of your household in order to gain peace within her own home."

"Oh, how true." Lady Marion laughed. "But Mother also wanted me to have my own happiness."

Rebecca looked at Lady Marion. "Not every woman's happiness is found with a man."

"Another excellent point, Miss Tremaine, which proves that in addition to your beauty and charm, your intelligence is but one more of your outstanding qualities."

"Must I again remind you that it is December?" Lady Charlotte interrupted.

"Oh, fiddle. Courtship is a sport that is conducive to any time of year."

"And a husband is the prize?" Lady Charlotte squeaked.

"In a manner of speaking." Lady Marion took a bite of her fish and chewed thoughtfully. "Yet I prefer to think of a husband as the trophy."

"That would look best when displayed on a mantel?" Rebecca asked.

"Since you are unmarried ladies, I shall not say precisely where, and in what condition, a husband looks best, though I will give you a strong hint and remark that a prime location is above stairs. Behind a closed bedchamber door."

Rebecca was so surprised she let her fork go limp. The sizable serving of creamed potatoes that was resting there slid off, missed her plate and dropped on to the linen tablecloth. Lady Charlotte, she noted, had blushed to the roots of her hair.

"Marion, you are wicked!" Lady Charlotte exclaimed.

"I am indeed and it is one of my finest qualities. Richard tells me so all the time."

After a heartbeat of stunned silence, all three women burst into laughter.

"You truly must have set the *ton* on its ear," Rebecca said. "I do believe I would have enjoyed seeing you in action."

"I was willfully incorrigible, truly a sight to behold," Lady Marion admitted modestly. "But then I met Richard and everything changed."

"How?" Rebecca wanted to know.

"I fell in love. I fought it at first, rather spiritedly. But in the end I discovered a fundamental truth. No matter how hard you try, you cannot control love. It controls you. The heart wants what it wants. And my heart wanted Richard."

"It was terribly romantic," Lady Charlotte said with an envious sigh. "And a great relief to the family to have you safely wed at long last."

"Ha! They are mainly relieved that I am Richard's problem now and not theirs," Lady Marion exclaimed.

"Well, yes there is that too," Lady Charlotte concurred and all three women burst into another round of laughter.

They finished their meal in companionable conversation. Lady Marion was droll and witty, while Lady Charlotte proved to be a gentle foil to her cousin's rapier tongue. Rebecca was surprised to find herself enjoying the company very much. It had been years since she had indulged in fun, female dialog, and she realized she missed the unique perspective and companionship that could be found among women similar in age.

Yet as much as she was enjoying their company, Rebecca declined Lady Marion's invitation to join her and the larger group of women who were anxious to engage in holiday activity planning. Lady Charlotte also declined to join the group in the green salon and took her leave. Rebecca commented that she was feeling slightly fatigued from the trip and would probably indulge in a nap.

It was, of course, a lie. Knowing that Lily was so close would make it impossible to sleep, no matter how exhausted Rebecca felt. But she could hardly barge into the nursery at this time of day. During lunch Lady Charlotte had mentioned it was filled to near bursting with children, since all the guests were bringing their entire families. What possible, legitimate reason could Rebecca give for wanting to be among all that chaos?

She was nearing the staircase when she heard her name called. Rebecca turned to see the earl hailing her. As he drew near, she was briefly distracted by his handsome, chiseled features, his wide shoulders and firmly muscled physique. She was confused too, because her reaction to him was almost physical. Her heart thumped in an uneven rhythm, the breath rushed from her lungs, the foyer suddenly seemed too stuffy and warm.

Nerves? Fear? Or something else that was too dangerous, too distressing to acknowledge?

The sophisticated elegance she so naturally associated with him was once again in evidence this afternoon, which was odd given his casual, country attire. With no small measure of regret, she concluded he was one of those rare individuals blessed with the confidence, good looks and poise that put women at a disadvantage.

"I apologize for not greeting you earlier, Miss Tremaine. Estate business called me away."

"Your mother kindly explained."

"Have you eaten?"

"Yes, with Lady Marion, and your sister Charlotte. Everything was lovely."

"Good." He glanced at the staircase, then back at her. "And now?"

Rebecca felt a pang of guilt. He was trying to give her the benefit of the doubt and thus refused to accuse her outright of trying to find Lily, but he must be wondering where she was heading at this time of the day. "I thought I might rest in my chamber. The journey from London was tiring."

"Pity. I was hoping to persuade you to join me in the nursery."

Her hopes soared. Rebecca gazed up at the earl, testing his sincerity. His expression was unreadable, yet in truth his motives did not matter. As she had previously told him, it was his actions that interested her.

"Of course I would like to visit the nursery. I assume Lily will be there?"

"She should be. If she hasn't run off from Mrs. James."

Rebecca's eyes widened in concern. "Does she do that often? Run away from her governess? It can be dangerous, you know."

The earl smiled. "She enjoys more freedom here in the country than when we are in town, but whenever she "hides" she does so within the house. She is always safe."

Rebecca nodded in relief. The thought of Lily in any sort of peril frightened her more than she could say.

Silently, they climbed to the top floor of the manor, the earl leading the way. As they neared their destination, Rebecca could hear the shrieks of laughter on the other side of the closed nursery door. The instant the earl opened it, silence fell. A multitude of small heads jerked up, anxious to see if it was another young friend coming to join in their playtime.

Discovering it was only two adults, most of the youngsters returned to their activities. Several were congregated in the center of the room around an impressive castle they were constructing out of painted wooden bricks. Others were sitting together at tables, a few of the younger children were contentedly nestled on the laps of their nurses.

Rebecca counted nine children before the ear-splitting cry of "Papa!" cut through the air.

Lily hurled herself at the earl, literally jumping into his arms. He caught her easily and swung her high.

"She enjoys being dramatic," he explained as he carefully set the little girl back on her feet.

Well, she certainly does not get that from me, Rebecca thought.

"You are the lady with the brooch," Lily said. "Did you find it at the park?"

"Alas, no, but I do believe I left it somewhere else," Rebecca answered, feeling so pleased that Lily had remembered her. "Thank you for taking the time to help me search."

Lily squared her shoulders. "I wanted so badly to find it before my friend, Jane. She looked again the next day, you know, but Mrs. James wouldn't take me to the park because we had to come to Windmere."

Hmm, dramatic and competitive, Rebecca thought, unsure about the origins of those qualities. She wondered what other things she would discover about the child, but then her attention was momentarily diverted from Lily by a loud commotion in the center of the nursery.

The earl was playing with a boy she judged to be seven or eight years old. The child was yelling and laughing with delight as Lord Hampton dangled him upside down. Beside them, two others were jumping with excitement, anxiously waiting their turn. Seeing all the fuss, several of the other boys abandoned the castle building and crept closer.

The sizeable group crowded in and the earl set himself on his knees. Making a menacing growl deep in the back of his throat, he spread his arms wide and swept up four of them. There were squeals of delight and excitement as they wrestled on the thick rug with great merriment, while the various nurses and governesses regarded the earl with an amused expression.

Rebecca was fairly amazed at the sight, highly doubting she would have been so calm if someone had riled her charges to this extent. Still, she was grateful for the distraction of noise and chaos, for it gave her time to gather herself.

She glanced over at Lily and a rush of longing filled her. Her heart was racing as she stared into a face that seemed so new and yet so familiar. This was her daughter. Her baby. There was joy, but there was sorrow.

Rebecca's anticipation of this moment mingled strongly with a deep feeling of apprehension. Though more than anything she longed to see Lily, to spend time with her, the simple act of starting a conversation felt daunting. Fortunately the little girl did not have the same problem.

"Papa likes to play rough," Lily explained. "'Tis something that boys do." She shook her head as if puzzled by the entire concept.

"I remember my brother Daniel being much the same way," Rebecca offered.

"You have a brother?" Lily asked. "Is he a little boy?"

"No. He is older."

"Oh." Lily shrugged with disappointment. "No matter. There are far too many boys here already."

Rebecca glanced over at the earl, who by now had every male in the nursery under his spell. They were climbing on, over and under him, clinging to his back with arms clasped around his neck, tugging on his hair, laughing. It struck her how comfortable he appeared, how much he was obviously enjoying himself. Clearly, he was a man who should father many children, for he seemed to like them a great deal.

"Will you play with me?" Lily asked. "I have lots of paper dolls with pretty clothes. Nothing new, because Christmas hasn't come. Papa will buy me all the latest fashions to dress my paper dolls, and my real dolls too, but we can play with the old clothes today."

Rebecca swallowed hard, touched by Lily's invitation. "That sounds like fun."

Lily led her to a child-size table with two matching chairs. Gingerly, Rebecca sat in one, hoping it would hold her weight, while Lily retrieved her toys. She watched closely as the little girl opened the different boxes and carefully removed the contents.

Rebecca felt a tightness suddenly rise inside her. A powerful sense of regret for all that she had missed in Lily's life, a bitter resentment at what had been so cruelly stolen from her. Pushing the feelings aside, she attempted a smile. Now was not the time to dwell on the unfairness of the past. She must seize this opportunity and make the most of it.

"This is Little Fanny," Lily explained as she held out one of the paper figures. "She has five different hats."

"She is pretty," Rebecca remarked.

Lily shrugged. "Queen Victoria has much prettier clothes and lots of extra things, because she is very special. I like her best. Here is my ballerina, Marie. I will be Queen Victoria. Who do you want to be?"

"You decide."

The child's answering smile let Rebecca know she had said the right thing. They began an imaginary game with the queen and the ballerina and Rebecca had to agree that Queen Victoria did have an extraordinary wardrobe, one that could easily rival the silken fashions worn by real ladies. She had many outfits with a stunning array of accessories, a few of which Rebecca could not identify. And her clothes were not just made of paper, there were bits of cloth, real lace and tissue paper attached to several of the ball gowns.

Alas, poor Marie's clothes were far simpler, though her dancing outfits were very frilly. Time flew by as Lily directed their play, deciding what was happening, where the dolls were going, what they were going to wear. Rebecca was delighted to play along, taking it all in, reveling in the chance to be with her daughter.

Secretly, Rebecca had been terrified that Lily would not like her. The uncertainty was not completely gone, but she was less worried, more confident. In gratitude, she turned to properly thank the earl for his generosity in allowing her this opportunity. But he had already left the nursery.

Chapter 5

Daniel lingered over luncheon, pleased at the surprising turn of events that afforded him a chance to accomplish some business. It had been a stroke of good luck indeed to find Lord Bailey and a few other potential investors among the guests, and even better that they had an opportunity to discuss business.

When the meal concluded, Daniel left the long gallery alone, with no particular destination in mind. Though she had said nothing specifically, he assumed Rebecca was hoping for a chance to see her daughter again. As for himself, Daniel knew he was not yet ready to meet the child, nor was he in the mood to converse with any of the earl's other guests. If the conversation went much beyond business he felt out of his element.

This niggling doubt of insecurity was in part due to his birth. Though he knew they respected his business talents and accomplishments, Daniel never forgot the majority of men he dealt with were of noble birth. And he was not.

He was the great-grandson of a baron, the grandson of a solicitor, the son of a vicar, in turn a man of little social significance. He currently moved in these aristocratic circles because of his recently acquired wealth and was astute enough to realize if his circumstances ever changed, these doors would be forever closed to him.

Hell, if not for the most bizarre connection between Rebecca's child and the earl, he would not be at Windmere at all. A fact he had every intention of keeping to himself.

Deciding a walk in the brisk air was always a good way to chase away these strange moods, Daniel retrieved his coat, hat and walking stick from the butler and set out to explore the gardens.

The many flowering plants were dormant on this winter day, but the evergreens were thick and lush, the hedges full and green. He followed a brick path through a winding curve, momentarily wondering if he had entered a maze. Realizing it was just an intricate pattern of hedges, he rounded the corner and saw a woman seated on a marble bench.

He had no idea who she was, which was hardly surprising since he knew almost none of the guests. Daniel's first inclination was to turn and hurry away or else smile, nod and walk swiftly passed her.

But then she suddenly looked up, noticing his approach. *Damn!* He had hesitated too long. Courtesy demanded he speak to her.

"Good afternoon," he said cordially, tipping his hat. "I'm afraid we have not yet been formally introduced. I am Daniel Tremaine, a guest of the earl's."

"Charlotte Sinclair, the aforementioned earl's sister."

"A pleasure to meet you, Lady Charlotte." Out of habit, he extended his hand. Lady Charlotte blinked in puzzlement, then mimicked his gesture. Her fingers quivered in his, the bones slender and fragile. She shook his hand hesitantly, briefly, as Daniel realized his mistake.

He had been too long in the company of business-men; too long living in the informality of the Ameri-can Colonies. A proper English gentleman did not offer to shake hands with a noble lady. 'Twas damn decent of Lady Charlotte not to say anything about it.

Grateful for her tolerance, Daniel decided to join her for a few minutes. Without asking he took a seat on the opposite end of the bench. She seemed shocked at the move, sitting straight-back on the edge of the bench, folding her hands in her lap. He wondered if she preferred her solitude and felt sorry that he again had not considered his actions carefully. He was probably intruding.

The silence between them was long and uncomfort-able. Daniel's mind turned blank as he search for a safe topic of polite conversation. He was about to excuse himself when he saw a gray tabby emerge from the cover of the thick hedgerow and stroll past them. It moved at an odd gait and Daniel realized the cat was missing one of its hind legs. Lady Charlotte reached down and scooped the animal up in her arms. She placed it in her lap where it settled comfortably.

"Misty's leg was crushed by a carriage wheel when she was a kitten," Lady Charlotte explained in a soft voice. "The break could not be repaired, so the leg was removed. She has thrived well."

"Animals are most resilient, are they not?"

"Sometimes far more than people."

The cat was large and furry, with big green eyes and pronounced white whiskers. Normally, Daniel ignored cats, but he reached out to pat the animal on the head.

Both Lady Charlotte and the animal stiffened.

"She is afraid of strangers," Lady Charlotte said.

"I mean her no harm." The cat sniffed his hand suspiciously, then raised her chin slightly. Daniel obligingly scratched the top of her head, running his fingers behind her ears. She stretched her neck toward him and began to purr loudly.

"How strange," Lady Charlotte exclaimed. "She likes you."

"Females do, on occasion." Daniel smiled.

Lady Charlotte blushed and lowered her gaze. "There are some who might be offended to see Misty walk so oddly, but I begged for her to be saved when she was injured and my brother indulged me. I suppose you could say he has a soft spot for cripples."

"As any decent man should," Daniel responded. "It's proper to show pity for those less fortunate."

She shot him a startled look, and then a charming blush raced upward from her throat creating two rosy spots on her cheeks. Daniel remembered when making inquiries about the earl for Rebecca there had been mention of a sister who was a cripple. But surely that information had been exaggerated, for he saw no cane or crutch in sight to aid the lady when she walked. Perhaps there was another sister?

"Do you have other siblings besides your brother?" Daniel asked.

Her fingers went still. Misty squirmed on her lap and she allowed the cat to jump down. It scampered off into the bushes. "No, 'tis just the two of us. And Mother. What about you, Mr. Tremaine? I have met your sister, Rebecca. Do you have additional family?"

"No other siblings and our parents are deceased. There is a stray cousin here and there, but no family with which we share a close relationship."

"I imagine you and your sister are very close."

Daniel felt a stab of regret. They had been close

when they were children. But he had been gone for such a long time and so much had happened. To both him and Rebecca. He wondered if now that he was back in England they would be able to recapture the family bonds they had once shared so effortlessly.

"Do you ride, Lady Charlotte?" he asked, deciding a change of subject was sorely needed. "I know the hour is late, but I would appreciate the chance to enjoy some fresh air after being cooped inside my carriage for most of the morning. Will you join me?"

"I . . . uhm . . ." She stopped to clear her throat. She kept her eyes downcast and hidden, but he saw her fingers twined together in her lap, revealing her agitation.

"There are easily two to three hours of daylight remaining," he prompted, for some reason not wanting her to refuse.

She lifted her head, and he saw a flicker of yearning dance across her face. "I suppose it would not take me long to change into my riding habit."

"Excellent. If you will excuse me, I shall speak with the head groom to make the arrangements and then also change. Shall we meet back here in half an hour?"

"Yes." She smiled suddenly, and the radiant expression completely transformed her face. For an instant she almost seemed pretty.

He hastily bowed, then left. Returning twenty-five minutes later, Daniel was delighted to see Lady Charlotte already mounted on her horse. She had seemed so shy and hesitant when she accepted his offer, he half-expected her to send her regrets and avoid him.

"Ah, you are a serious rider," Daniel commented when he was close enough to view her horse. It was a magnificent animal, white with gray hindquarters and a thick silvery mane that flowed to its shoulder.

"I confess I do love to ride," she said. "There is

nothing more exhilarating than the sound of hooves hitting the ground, harness jingling, rider and horse moving as one. It makes one feel so joyful and alive. I imagine it is as close to flying through the air as a person can achieve."

Daniel was surprised at the passion in her voice, the rapture on her face. As he swung himself up to the saddle of the chestnut gelding the stableman had chosen for him, Daniel could easily think of something else that was even more exhilarating and pleasurable when two were joined as one, man to woman.

Fortunately, he had the brains to hold his tongue. It would hardly be prudent to shock the earl's sister on his first afternoon. Despite her somewhat advanced age, it was clear she was an innocent miss. But even more obvious, she was a lady.

"Shall we?" she asked, with a lighthearted smile.

Daniel let his mount prance for another moment, then deftly brought the spirited horse alongside Lady Charlotte and her mount. He followed her lead down the gravel drive, but they turned off almost immediately onto a grassy incline.

"Ready for a bit of a run?" he asked as the open valley stretched out before them.

"Splendid idea." She touched her heels to the horse's flanks and raced ahead. He followed immediately.

They thundered over the turf and Daniel exalted in the feel of the brisk wind whipping against his face and tugging at his hair. Side by side they galloped across the open field, startling birds from their roosts, forcing the occasional squirrel to hurry out of their path.

Suddenly, Lady Charlotte's hat came free and flew off onto the grass. Daniel reined in his mount, turned around and trotted over to retrieve the errant bonnet.

"I believe this is yours," he said, extending his hand with a gallant flourish.

She brushed a smudge of dirt off the top of the bonnet and hastily pinned it back on her head. It listed awkwardly to one side. "Gracious, I must look a sight," she said in a breathless pant.

"Actually, I prefer the bonnet set on your head at that angle. It makes you look daring and dangerous."

Daniel grinned and Lady Charlotte predictably blushed. He was enjoying himself. The fresh air was invigorating, the riding excellent, the company congenial.

By unspoken agreement, they kept to a more sedate pace, urging the horses into a walk, angling down a hill, then starting up the next rise. They stopped when they crested the hill, the panoramic view a magnificent sight.

"Will you tell me something about yourself, Mr. Tremaine?" Lady Charlotte asked. Her horse bent his head and nibbled contentedly at a few remaining shoots of green grass he managed to find. "I believe I heard someone mention that you are involved in various business ventures."

"I will gladly tell you if you are truly interested, though some would say it is vulgar to speak of finance to a lady."

Her eyebrows wrinkled. "Why? In my experience, most ladies seemed to like money a great deal."

Daniel stared at her in amused surprise. She was not being coy or flirty, she was merely stating her opinion. One he agreed with, to a large extent.

"The majority of my business holdings are in the American Colonies, but since returning to England I have started several new projects."

She pressed him for details. Believing her interest

to be genuine, he told her of the coal mining project in Cornwall, then mentioned his most recently completed real estate project in the Cotswolds.

Even as Daniel spoke, a part of him was concerned that she would find his ambitions crude and unworthy. In her world men were wealthy by birth and expected to live as cultured gentlemen of leisure. Most indulged in a life filled with privilege and pleasure. Or, like her brother, in service to queen and country as influential men of politics.

She would no doubt find him a most peculiar fellow and for some reason that rankled at him. She asked a few more intelligent questions and Daniel relaxed. He was pleased at her grasp of matters, flattered at her genuine admiration for his accomplishments.

"You have led a most adventurous life, Mr. Tremaine." She tugged at the base of her riding glove, pulling it tighter on her hand. "Is it true that in the Colonies there is little regard for class?"

"Not precisely. Those with wealth lead a far easier life than those who are poor. Yet in America, a person is mostly judged on his merits and accomplishments rather than family lineage and connections. Most appealing for me, however, are the endless opportunities. The possibility for great wealth and success exists for every man."

"And every woman?"

Daniel laughed. "Not really. Americans are progressive, not crazy."

She shifted slightly in her saddle, her features serious. "I have read and heard all sorts of stories. Are the women truly bold?"

"I met a few who were more outspoken, but I do not believe they are in the majority. By and large, the women I encountered dress and act and speak like ladies. 'Tis actually the men who display a marked difference. They are endowed with more spirit than most and display a sense of daring and adventure."

"Are you saying Englishmen are stuffy?"

"To do so would be to proclaim myself a stuffy, formal man."

"Oh, horrors." She chuckled softly and Daniel decided he liked the sound. Perhaps it would not be so dreary and difficult to spend the next few weeks at Windmere.

He turned his head and met her eyes. In them he saw so much sweetness, so much innocence. In the faint afternoon light she suddenly looked young, almost whimsical.

She was not a pretty woman. Her features were too plain, her coloring too ordinary. There was a smattering of freckles across the bridge of her nose and wisps of her hair had come loose when she had repinned her hat. Yet her eyes were sparkling with intelligence and charm and there was something he found indefinably appealing about her.

Daniel's eyes dropped to her lips. A strange exhilaration arose in him, along with the sudden urge to kiss her. To bury his hands in her hair, inhale her sweet female scent, to frame her face and hold it in place so his mouth could cover hers.

His desire rose and he cursed himself for being a fool. It was beneath him to have such base thoughts about a true lady.

Still, he found himself wanting to draw closer. Daniel's masculine instinct told him she might welcome his attentions. But she was so sweet, so delicate, he could not bring himself to touch her.

Her horse neighed, prancing an anxious step backward. The mood was effectively broken.

"The sun is setting quickly." Lady Charlotte remarked, her voice breathless. "We need to return. It will soon be time to change for dinner."

Daniel shifted his gaze down to the valley where the golden red orb was starting to dip below the horizon. "Are all the meals at Windmere formal?"

"Usually. But especially when there are guests."

Daniel shrugged, reminded anew at yet another difference in their worlds. While he always washed and freshened up before his evening meal, he did not change into formal evening clothes every night. Nor did he see the need for such a pretentious practice.

Together they turned their horses and side by side rode back to the manor. A groom stood at the ready to take their horses to be cooled, watered and fed. Daniel dismounted and turned to assist Lady Charlotte, but she shook her head slightly to discourage him, remaining on her horse while a stable lad held the reins.

Oddly disappointed that he would be unable to slip his hands around her waist and lift her down, Daniel bowed in farewell. "Thank you for a delightful afternoon, Lady Charlotte. I will see you at dinner."

"I look forward to it, Mr. Tremaine."

Charlotte kicked her heels lightly into her horse's flanks and the animal obediently moved forward. Once inside the dimness of the stable, she allowed a groom to help her down. It took several moments for the strength to return to her limbs. Her leg tingled and ached and she held steadily to the servant's arm before taking a few awkward steps. As she moved she could feel the blood gradually flow through her leg.

"Thank you, Hodges," she said, smiling her appreciation at the groom. "I believe I can manage now."

She limped forward, holding tightly to the wooden

stall. Her leg cramped as her hip suddenly seized. A flash of anger and pain tore through Charlotte. But it was not the physical pain that caused her greatest suffering, it was the anguish of her deformity.

She waited for the discomfort to pass, all the while despising her body for its ugliness. And she despised herself too, for being a coward, for trying to deliberately hide her infirmity from Daniel Tremaine.

But then she recalled the kindness in his eyes, the softness of his voice, the delight of his company. It had been a thoroughly wonderful afternoon. One that would have been ruined utterly if it had ended by revealing the truth, for she felt certain she would have seen pity in Mr. Tremaine's eyes, or even worse, disgust, when he discovered her affliction.

Slowly, Charlotte walked back to the manor, entering through a little used side door.

"Goodness, Charlotte, have you been out riding?"

Charlotte turned and smiled at her mother, assuming her riding habit and windblown hair had given her away. Her cheeks still held the blush put there by Daniel Tremaine's invigorating company, but her mother would merely assume it was the result of the crisp air.

"At his request, I took Mr. Tremaine on a short tour of the estate," Charlotte answered.

"Really? Well, that was most accommodating of you."

Charlotte smiled at her mother's decidedly shocked expression and continued up the stairs to her bedchamber. Dinner was to be served in a few hours and she wanted a warm bath before the meal, along with sufficient time to fuss with her appearance.

As she waited for the maids to fill the copper slipper tub with hot water, Charlotte firmly told herself she needed to be sensible. Daniel Tremaine was merely being polite, or else he just needed a riding partner today. He had not intentionally sought her company. Yet he did seem to enjoy it.

Charlotte was not a woman given to flights of fancy, to starry-eyed romantic dreams. She had no illusions about herself. She knew all too well that she was a vulnerable female, starved for male attention and affection. It was therefore logical that she would be drawn to Mr. Tremaine's powerful charm.

It meant nothing. Nothing at all.

"No cap tonight," Charlotte recklessly decided as she began to dress for dinner.

"Yes, my lady." With a surprised lift of her brow, her maid, Lucy, carefully set the lacy spinster's cap to the side.

Charlotte took a deep breath. "I was wondering, do you think there might be a way to fix my hair so it is not so severely pulled away from my face?"

"Oh, yes, my lady." The maid's eyes brightened with delight. "There are any number of styles that would look lovely on you. You do have such pretty hair."

"Not really," Charlotte mumbled as the maid brushed it out.

Yet when she glanced in the mirror she had to admit that she looked different with her hair styled out of its usual prim knot, the scrap of lace she constantly wore no longer on her head. Her long, brown shimmering tresses were draped around her shoulders, shiny, thick and slightly wavy, softening her features, making her look younger.

"'Tis a shame we can't leave it just like this," Lucy commented.

"Mother would be scandalized," Charlotte said with a nervous laugh.

The maid smiled in agreement. Charlotte sat

patiently, allowing Lucy to coil and twist and braid and work her magic on the long brown strands. She did not wince or flinch, even when the servant had to tug hard or use the very hot curling tongs.

"All finished," Lucy finally announced, stepping back to admire her handiwork. "Do you like it?"

The maid held up a large mirror so Charlotte could admire the back as well as the front. The artful decoration was truly a masterpiece. The maid had woven a few small white flowers among the curls that set off the darker color of Charlotte's hair and brightened her entire face.

A warmth curled inside Charlotte, along with a frisson of excitement. In years past she had always dreaded the holiday season, the house filled with people, the days and nights a continuous round of social events.

To survive, Charlotte remained in the background, withdrawn into her own tight little cocoon so that nothing and no one could upset her. Often, she would avoid as many of the larger events as possible, to save herself the misery of being ignored, or worse, pitied.

Yet this year her nerves seemed to have dissolved, replaced by a faint edge of hope. She found herself humming with each ungainly step she took toward the drawing room, her heart filled with anticipation and restless excitement, her mind replaying her cousin Marion's teasing words about matchmaking.

Perhaps husband hunting truly was a year-round pastime.

Rebecca sat in a chair in a corner of the drawing room amid the crush of guests gathering to await the call to supper. A steady hum of conversation drifted around her. The group of ladies and gentlemen closest to her sought to include her as they discussed the latest London gossip. Rebecca pretended to listen, nodding and smiling, yet she had no real interest and nothing to add since she knew none of the people involved.

Though never a master at casual conversation, she usually was not so tongue-tied when in company. But the day had been filled with wonderful moments and what she really wanted was the chance to be alone, to reflect on her thoughts and emotions toward Lily.

She had stayed in the nursery, playing with the paper dolls and later reading a story Lily requested, until an afternoon snack had arrived for the children. Reluctantly, she had taken her leave, promising to return tomorrow.

Rebecca could hardly wait.

Her gaze traveled across the room to where the earl and his mother stood. They made a striking pair, mother and son. Their physical resemblance was limited to the same shade of eye color and a similar smile, but no one could have mistaken the relationship. They both held themselves with an aristocratic confidence, assured of their worth and place in this world.

Rebecca realized sadly it was not a trait that the third member of their family, Lady Charlotte, had been able to emulate. She seemed to keep herself deliberately on the fringes, almost hiding from life. Pity, for she seemed a kind and deserving woman.

Rebecca wondered how Lily would grow up. Would she feel the same confidence as the earl? Would she exude this same aura of privilege and power? Or would she be like Lady Charlotte, shy and withdrawn? Given what little she had seen of her daughter thus far, Rebecca suspected the child would grow to be a proud, formidable, secure woman.

"Hungry?" inquired a masculine voice.

Her gaze flashed upward to meet Lord Hampton's. She had been so engrossed in her thoughts she had not heard his approach.

"Famished," she said, flustered as her pulse started racing at the sound of his voice.

It was not fear, she admitted to herself, for he no longer purposely intimidated her. True, there was an attraction, but she found other men attractive, too. What was so unique about him? So irresistible?

She tried to dispassionately, logically examine the conundrum, hoping that by solving the mystery she could eliminate the feelings. Was it the forbidden allure, knowing this would never amount to anything, for she was the very last woman on earth the earl would consider for a relationship? Perhaps it was an underlying resentment that caused her emotions to react so strongly, since no matter what she said or did, Lily would always remain his child?

Shaking off her unfathomable emotions, Rebecca told herself firmly that dwelling on this attraction was a course fraught with peril and temptation. Lily was living proof that her will to resist forbidden temptations could, at times, be lacking.

"Did you enjoy your afternoon in the nursery with Lily?" the earl asked.

Rebecca felt a rush of emotion fill her eyes, but she blinked back the tears. "'Twas a joy that surpassed even my expectations, my lord. I thank you again for your kindness. You have no idea how much it meant to me."

For a moment he hesitated as if he were about to say something more, but the butler arrived to announce the meal was served. The earl excused himself to escort his mother into the dining room.

Rebecca found her brother and they followed the crowd. Though it seemed to be a large crush, there was a smaller number of people for the evening meal. Only those guests sleeping at the manor were in attendance; lunch had included additional guests from the neighboring estate.

"Oh, hell," Daniel muttered under his breath.

Rebecca swallowed hard in perfect understanding of her brother's remark. The dining room fairly glowed from the twinkling candles in the chandelier, which reflected the shimmering light off all the crystal, silver and gilt-edged china formally arranged on the table. There were five large flower arrangements set on high crystal pillars in the center of the table, along with numerous smaller vases of the same flowers and a single bloom at each place setting in a silver vessel.

As she glided down the table to find her seat, Rebecca counted no fewer than six goblets in assorted sizes and twelve forks at each place setting. Twelve! Gracious, how much precisely was one expected to eat?

They began with a choice of pheasant soup, mushroom soup, nettle soup or clear soup, followed by turbot with tartare sauce, sweetbreads in wine sauce, lobster cream, pigeon pie, vegetable souffle and wild duck. Rebecca stopped counting courses when the saddle of mutton was served and at that stage gave up all pretense of eating. Thankfully, she noticed several of the other ladies had done the same.

Though nervous about the elaborate meal, Rebecca felt she did an acceptable job with her dinner companions, saying all the correct, polite things about the weather and the evening and the plans for the upcoming holiday.

After the trifle, creams and puddings were served, the dowager countess rose from her seat. All the ladies did the same and they withdrew from the dining room, leaving the men to their brandy, port and cigars.

For the next half hour the ladies conversed in the drawing room, sipping tea and cordials. Rebecca marveled how anyone could manage to fit anything else in their stomachs, since everyone was wearing tightly laced corsets and evening gowns cinched in at the waist.

"We need some entertainment to finish out the evening," the dowager countess said as the gentlemen rejoined them. "Who will play the piano for us? And sing? Miss Tremaine?"

Rebecca felt her skin flush. She had a passable voice, but was intimidated at the idea of singing in front of so many strangers. Still, it would be rude to refuse. She was a guest who had been afforded an honor by being asked. With effort she restrained the grimace that rose to her face and nodded in agreement. The dowager countess beamed with approval.

Pulse skittering, Rebecca walked to the opposite side of the room and sat at the padded piano bench. "I shall play, my lady. Perhaps Lady Marion will sing?"

"No!" Several individuals shouted in unison, while others started shaking their heads emphatically to and fro.

Rebecca was startled by the chorus of negative responses. Her surprise must have shown on her face, for the earl, who stood near the piano, leaned close and whispered, "My cousin's voice has been compared to the sounds made by a screeching wet cat left too long in the rain. To be honest, that would be far more pleasant to hear than listening to Marion. I fear if we allow her to sing, everyone's stomach will sour."

"It cannot be that bad," Rebecca whispered.

"'Tis worse," Lord Hampton insisted with a shudder. "To say it is caterwauling is a kindness."

Lady Marion look exasperated. "I grant you that my voice is unusual, but it has a classic quality," she declared, tapping her finger against her knee.

"Classic, Marion?" the earl asked with a raised brow.

"Indeed. And I give you all fair warning. I am in charge of leading the Christmas carolers this year and I expect to be a full participant."

Several of the men groaned. "With you leading us, and lending your voice, we shall all get dosed with buckets of water," one of them said.

"Or pelted with rotten fruits and vegetables," another chimed in and several others laughed at the quip.

"Christmas is a time of joy and brotherhood, when we all celebrate the birth of our savior," the dowager countess insisted. "I hardly think the neighbors would toss refuse at a hapless band of carolers, coming to spread holiday cheer."

"They will if they hear Marion sing, Mother."

"*Et tu*, Hampton," Lady Marion uttered with an exaggerated sigh, but then she burst into laughter and everyone joined her.

Rebecca noticed Viscount Cranborne move near his wife and lay a hand on Lady Marion's arm. It was a simple gesture that conveyed love as well as comfort and Lady Marion preened under the attention. 'Twas obvious they had a strong union, with a deep sense of commitment and passion for each other, though in many ways they seemed an unlikely pair.

Lady Marion was a diamond of the first water, a

woman of great beauty and style. The viscount was beyond thirty, of medium height, stocky, pleasant-looking, yet unremarkable. His brown hair was starting to thin at the crown. Seeing them together made Rebecca think of the ironic truth in one of her mother's favorite sayings; as God made them, he matched them.

A wave of sadness washed over her as she acknowledged the man she had always believed was her match was gone. With the passing of time she had been able to accept the finality of Philip's death, but the memory of that loss was something that would remain a part of her.

She glanced over at the earl and wondered if he felt the same about losing his wife.

"Charlotte will sing. She has a charming voice," Lady Marion suggested.

Lady Charlotte, sitting at the chair nearest the piano, blushed so red Rebecca thought for certain she would refuse.

"I need someone to accompany me," Lady Charlotte finally said. "Cameron?"

The earl shook his head slowly. "A duet is far too ambitious for me. I will not be able to do it justice."

Rebecca turned to her brother. "Daniel? You sing well. Won't you accompany Lady Charlotte?"

Daniel obediently came to the piano. Rebecca carefully read through the sheet music, consulting with the pair until they agreed on a final selection.

Rebecca steadied her hands on the keys and began to play, soon realizing she need not be so nervous. No one would notice any slight mistakes she made, for they were all enraptured by the sound of Lady Charlotte and Daniel's voices.

Their talents were well matched. A light, lilting

soprano and a vibrant, emotional tenor. Each had a musical ear, as well as a strong singing voice and though they had not rehearsed, they sang as if they had practiced for weeks.

Rebecca felt a chill at how beautifully their voices melded together, noting how everyone appeared moved by the emotion of the pretty ballad. As the piece concluded, Rebecca saw Lady Marion dab at her eyes and several other women lift a handkerchief to their faces.

"Though I know it was not your intent, you have convinced me," Lady Marion said. "I shall gladly lead the carolers, choosing the songs and the places where we will serenade. But I promise, I shall only mouth the words."

There was but a moment of silence, and everyone began to clap. Lady Marion loudest of all.

Chapter 6

"Which gown will you be wearing for this afternoon's visit, Miss Rebecca?"

Rebecca set down her writing quill and looked over at Maureen. The maid had opened the cherry armoire and was standing in front of it, hands on hips in consideration.

"I'm not sure," Rebecca confessed, slightly panicked that this was yet another test of fashion sense that she might fail. Life was far more complicated for society women, with pitfalls too ridiculous to consider. It made her glad to realize this was but a short venture for her into the world of the highest privilege and nobility.

"Do you know specifically where you are going?" the maid asked.

Rebecca frowned, wondering what possible difference it could make. "The dowager countess mentioned we would be stopping at the rectory to visit with the vicar and his wife to discuss Christmas activities and gifts for the parish families. Is there something you think is appropriate for that sort of call?"

The maid nodded enthusiastically and pulled out a

lovely day dress in a deep shade of blue. She paired it with a multicolored paisley shawl and a small hat done in shades of blue that could be comfortably worn while taking tea.

Properly clothed, with her hair neatly styled, Rebecca decided to wait in the front courtyard, eager for a chance to enjoy some fresh air. The first thing she noticed as she stepped outside was the sharp drop in temperature and the visibility of her breath.

Pulling the collar of her wool cloak higher to ward off the icy chill, Rebecca was glad to note the coach had been pulled around to the front, the driver and grooms waiting patiently for all the passengers to arrive. Standing too long out in the cold would not be pleasant.

"The weather has turned biting. It feels like it might snow very soon."

The masculine voice was deep and measured. Rebecca turned to find the earl by her side. He looked dashingly handsome garbed in traditional riding clothes and knee-high black boots. Predictably, her heart quickened. He offered his arm, and she laid her hand on the top of his sleeve, ignoring the little shiver of awareness that traveled through her limbs.

"I did not think snow fell much in this area," she said, glancing up at the collection of clouds drifting across the sky.

"'Tis a rare, but not impossible, occurrence," he replied. "Actually, under the proper conditions, anything is possible, don't you agree, Miss Tremaine?"

She smiled vaguely. He is merely making polite conversation, she told herself sternly. There is no hidden innuendo in his words, though once again Rebecca acknowledged she was at a loss to comprehend why the earl captivated her so thoroughly. She was not a completely naive woman; she had been exposed to handsome men before. Yet even after several days in his company, being around him still unnerved her.

Their conversation was interrupted by the arrival of the dowager countess and Rebecca was glad for the distraction. Then to her complete surprise, Lily and her governess, Mrs. James, also appeared.

"Are we all here?" the dowager countess asked, nodding her head in answer to her own question. "You are such a dear to accompany us, Miss Tremaine. I sent the other ladies into the village to do a bit of shopping, explaining that I did not think it fair to overwhelm our young vicar with too many visitors this afternoon."

Rebecca licked her lips. "Perhaps it would be better if I too stayed behind?"

"Oh, no, I very much want you along. Cameron told us your late father was a man of the cloth. Your presence will ease the vicar's nerves, I am certain."

Giving her no opportunity to protest further, the dowager countess practically shooed Rebecca into the coach. Lily began to climb in next, but suddenly stopped.

"Papa, I want to sit next to you in the carriage."

"That's impossible, Puss. I'm not riding in the coach."

Indeed. The earl had vaulted onto a large black stallion and the pair were eagerly prancing about the courtyard. It was almost sinful how strong and virile the earl looked.

"I will ride with you on your horse," Lily declared. Jumping down from the small carriage step, the little girl ducked under her grandmother's raised arm and ran over to Lord Hampton.

Her sudden movement startled the earl's horse. It

reared, front hooves pawing wildly in the air. Rebecca felt a scream build in her throat as the little girl came perilously close to the stallion's large, deadly hooves. But Lord Hampton managed to expertly control his mount, alleviating any danger to the child.

"Be careful, Lily!" the earl shouted.

Rebecca waited for the scolding. It was reckless, dangerous, behavior and Lily deserved a harsh reprimand. But no one said another word to the child.

In shock, Rebecca watched a groom hustle over and boost the little girl into Lord Hampton's waiting arms. She squirmed and shifted, finally sitting sidesaddle. The earl held her firmly in the circle of his arms.

"Is her coat warm enough?" Rebecca asked, wanting to bite her tongue the moment the question fell from her lips.

Mrs. James gave her an odd look, no doubt wondering how it was any of Rebecca's business.

"Cameron will keep her from catching a chill," the dowager countess replied. "At least with Lily on the horse he will be forced to ride at a sedate pace, keeping the wind at bay. And that shall make it a far safer ride for both of them."

The earl and Lily took off ahead of the coach. Rebecca could hear the little girl's laugh of delight as they raced off and hoped the dowager duchess' comment about the earl riding slowly was true.

It was not too long a drive to the rambling stone cottage that housed the vicarage. The three women stepped out of the coach just as the earl and Lily arrived. Lord Hampton carefully handed his daughter down to a waiting groom before dismounting. Then offering his arm to his mother, he led the way to the front door and banged briskly on the lion's head knocker.

An elderly housekeeper opened the door, asking to

take their coats and gloves and the earl's hat the moment they were inside. After removing her cloak and straightening her shawl, Rebecca's attention was drawn to the vicar and his wife, who crowded together into the foyer to greet them.

Clad in the somber clothes of his profession, Vicar Hargrave was a kind-looking man with alert brown eyes and close-trimmed dark hair whom Rebecca judged to be but a few years older than herself. His expression was eager and a bit anxious as he bowed to greet them. His wife looked younger, no more than nineteen or twenty, a small, slender woman with strawberry blond hair, innocent features and a shy smile.

They were ushered into a cozy parlor that smelled faintly of lavender and beeswax. The furniture was well used, but in good condition. Nothing exactly matched in terms of style or even wood grain, yet nothing seemed out of place. It was a comfortable and inviting room.

A pretty landscape depicting the village square, done in oil, hung over the fireplace, instantly drawing Rebecca's attention. She moved closer for a better look, peered at the signature, then smiled in surprise.

"I must commend your talent, Reverend Hargrave. 'Tis a beautiful picture."

The vicar bowed his head modestly. "Painting is merely a hobby of mine. Mrs. Hargrave insisted we hang it in here, though I believe it would be better suited for a back room."

"Nonsense," the earl replied. "This is first rate."

The housekeeper wheeled in a tray and they sat for tea. Rebecca noticed Mrs. Hargrave's hand trembling slightly as she poured from the pretty china pot. Tendrils of steam spiraled into the air as she passed the nearly full cup of tea to the dowager countess.

Rebecca had to restrain herself from leaping forward to rescue the shaking china, fearing a disaster, but the dowager countess was a woman experienced with flustered young females. She clasped the cup firmly in her hand, then set it gently on the low table in front of her.

After serving the ladies, Mrs. Hargrave poured for the gentlemen. The earl accepted his cup with a nod and a grin of thanks. Mrs. Hargrave blushed and nearly dropped the teapot in his lap. Rebecca felt a flash of sympathy, knowing all too well the effects of that devastating smile.

Cakes and small sandwiches were served next. Compliments were extended to Mrs. Hargrave when her husband revealed she had baked two of the delicacies herself. Rebecca thought fondly of the many hours she had spent in the kitchen, learning the same skill, then realized it had been weeks since she had last done any baking.

"We'd like your advice about the Christmas baskets we are putting together for the village families, vicar," the earl said. "My steward has given me a list regarding my tenant farmers, but I should like to know if there are others you feel are in special need this holiday season."

"'Tis so good of you to inquire, my lord." With a smile of relief directed at his wife, the young man stood. "Forgive my presumption, but I have been working on a list. If you will wait, it will take but a moment to retrieve it from my study."

Mr. Hargrave was good as his word. He returned in short order with a piece of parchment he handed to Lord Hampton. The earl smiled in thanks and pocketed the paper. "I shall make certain this is taken care of promptly. After all, we want to make sure that everyone has a happy Christmas."

With business concluded, they were able to chat more easily. Lily had moved to sit beside her father on the opposite settee and Rebecca contented herself by stealing glances across the way, gratified to catch occasional glimpses of Lily watching her back.

She winked at Lily and the girl giggled. Rebecca watched anxiously as Lily lifted the delicate china cup and took a small sip. She feared she might slosh some over the edge and burn herself, but the child had no difficulties. Placing it back on the saucer, Lily grabbed the earl's arm and snuggled against him.

Lord Hampton glanced down and smiled at the little girl. She grinned back, her expression pure mischief. Lily ate a cream cake, then Rebecca noticed Mrs. James put a gentle restraining hand on Lily's arm as she reached for the silver sugar tongs and attempted to plunk a third cube of sugar into her teacup.

"You'll get worms if you eat too much sugar," Mrs. James muttered under her breath.

Rebecca's eyes widened at the lie, but it seemed to do the trick. Lily obediently let go of the tongs. She sank back in her chair and sullenly took a bite of a crumpet topped with raspberry jam.

The child's fidgeting grew with her boredom and Rebecca wondered again at why Lily had been brought along. It was unheard of to bring a child of her age on a social visit, even if that visit was to a country reverend. It seemed to Rebecca to be yet another troubling example of the vast indulgence afforded Lily by Lord Hampton and frankly she did not like it.

Fortunately, they finished their refreshments without incident. As they prepared to leave, Mr. Hargrave suggested a tour of the newly completed village school, which was located across the road from the vicarage. Rebecca was impressed when she learned the building had been constructed using funds donated by the earl. In her experience, most aristocrats were not in favor of educating the children of the families who worked their land.

"Now that we have such a wonderful new meeting space, we are organizing a nativity play with the older school children. It shall be performed before church services on Christmas Eve," Mrs. Hargrave announced.

"What a perfectly splendid idea," the dowager countess replied. "I hope there will be room for us to attend?"

"We would be honored to have you, my lady," Mr. Hargrave said with an anxious, delighted smile.

"You will need to reserve two, no make that three, rows of seats for us," the earl said. "I promise to fill them with a most enthusiastic audience."

Rebecca did not have to pretend interest. "Please do not think me too forward, but I would like to offer my services, Mrs. Hargrave. I often helped my father stage similar events. I understand that many hands are needed when working with such a large group of children."

"Oh, thank you, Miss Tremaine." The young woman looked enormously relieved. She leaned closer and whispered confidentially. "Mr. Hargrave wants so much to make a favorable impression upon the earl and his family and in turn I fear is taking on too many responsibilities. I am trying to lighten his burden as best I can, but my experience in these matters is limited."

Rebecca nodded in understanding, knowing all too well the kind of pressure the vicar was under. "I am certain it will be a splendid success, but if there are any glitches, you must blame me."

"Why are you whispering?" Lily asked, tugging on Rebecca's sleeve to gain her attention.

Rebecca glanced down in surprise. She thought the little girl had moved to the next room with the other adults.

Mrs. Hargrave smiled. "Miss Tremaine and I were discussing the nativity play."

"My papa goes to the theatre in London to see the plays. And sometimes Grandma goes with him. She always wears a pretty dress." Lily turned to Rebecca. "What's a play?"

"A play is a story that people act out by pretending to be the characters of the tale as they tell the story. They wear costumes and stand on a stage in front of everyone so they can be seen and heard," Rebecca explained.

"Who will be telling the story in the play? The people from London?" Lily asked.

"No, the children from the village who attend our schools will play all the parts," Mrs. Hargrave said. She pointed to the front of the room. "We are going to build a small stage over there and sew costumes for them to wear and when the performance is over, we shall have a party to celebrate. It will take place in the evening, but not too late. I hope you will come with your father and grandmother to watch it."

"No." Lily shook her head. "I don't want to watch the play. I want to tell the story and be on the stage and wear a pretty costume."

Mrs. Hargrave hid her shock well, though her eyes betrayed her inner concern as they widened. "I'm not sure if your father would approve."

"My papa tells me all the time he loves me and wants me to be happy. I will be happy if I am in the play." Lily folded her arms across her chest.

"But all the other children are all much older than you," Mrs. Hargrave added.

"So?" Lily huffed in annoyance.

"I suppose we can ask Lord Hampton," Mrs. Hargrave said, wringing her hands nervously. "Though all the parts have already been assigned."

"If you ask him, my papa will say yes," Lily responded confidently. "And then I will play the part of the baby."

"Oh, goodness. We were going to use a doll." Mrs. Hargrave took in a rather shaky breath. "How about an angel? Would you like to be an angel, Lady Lily?"

Lily's brows knit together in a suspicious frown. "Everyone knows that you can't see an angel."

"Angels can be seen in our play," Mrs. Hargrave answered. "They wear very pretty white dresses and have golden haloes on their heads."

Lily's lower lips thrust out. "I do not want to be an angel. I want to be the baby Jesus."

Mrs. Hargrave blanched. Rebecca crouched down and took the little girl's hands in her own. "You are a growing girl, not a baby. I think you will make a lovely angel."

"Will there be other angels?"

They turned to Mrs. Hargrave. She attempted a smile. "Oh, yes. At least four or five."

Lily pulled her hands away. "I won't be special if there are other angels," she said, sounding most aggrieved.

"I am sure you will be the prettiest angel of all," Mrs. Hargrave said with false heartiness.

"I don't want to be an angel." Lily hitched her shoulders in a gesture of defiance. "My father is the earl and I am a lady and I will have the best part! I will be the baby, the one that everyone comes to see and brings special gifts."

The last sentence came out in a shrieking scream.

Mrs. James, who had come back into the room, rushed forward to take charge of Lily.

Mrs. Hargrave looked horrified. Rebecca's embarrassment over Lily's disgraceful behavior quickly turned to sympathy. Poor Mrs. Hargrave had been nothing but kind and considerate to the child. She certainly did not deserve to be treated so rudely by an ill-mannered little girl.

Mrs. James managed to stop Lily's screaming, but the child looked furious. Her arms were crossed in defiance, her face scowling and red, her sobbing loud and dramatic.

It was embarrassing to see Lily so peevish and perverse. Rebecca had been around children enough to know they often misbehaved and on occasion acted badly. But she had never witnessed such a spoiled, violent reaction. It was disgraceful and she would have said so, if her remarks could have been heard above the din.

The earl poked his head into the room. "Is there a problem?" he asked.

"I have things well in hand, my lord," Mrs. James replied as she hastily pulled the sniffling Lily out of the room.

"Excuse me." Eyes downcast, Mrs. Hargrave also hurried away.

Poor thing. Rebecca sighed. Mrs. Hargrave had wanted so badly to impress the earl.

Lord Hampton's face darkened. "Was Lily crying?"

"Yes." Rebecca hesitated. Instinctively she wanted to protect her daughter, yet she was too upset by the incident to conceal it. "Lily was excited to learn about the Christmas play. Mrs. Hargrave kindly agreed to allow her a part, but Lily became difficult and kept insisting that she be given the role of the newborn savior in the production."

Unruffled, the earl turned to Rebecca. "She does like to get her own way."

Rebecca darted a cautious glance at the earl. After hearing and now seeing this behavior he did not question or denounce it?

"She was rather rude," Rebecca said pointedly.

"She must be tired. My mother was most skeptical when I suggested Lily be brought along on today's visit. But I overcame her apprehension and insisted that one was never too young to begin learning about social duties." He blew out a sigh. "Of course the real reason I pushed to have her along was because I knew you would be accompanying us and assumed you would enjoy being in Lily's company."

Rebecca stiffened. That was a low blow. So now it was her fault that Lily was brought along? Was he trying to say she was also responsible for the child's inappropriate behavior?

"She needs to apologize to Mrs. Hargrave," Rebecca said.

"Mrs. James will see to it."

His casual dismissal of the incident angered her. "You are her father. You should see to it."

"I beg your pardon?"

"Her disgraceful behavior is a direct result of your overindulgence," Rebecca said. "Lily is a smart, observant little girl. She knows that ultimately she does not have to behave because you will excuse her from anything that she does, no matter how naughty."

"That is preposterous!" Faint color tinged his cheeks.

"Is it? Earlier today she jumped from the carriage and ran in front of your horse. If not for your expert skill with the reins she might have been seriously injured. Yet you barely scolded her."

"Are you inferring that I cannot take proper care of the child?"

"I am not inferring it at all. I am stating it as fact."

His nostrils flared. "You overstep your bounds, Miss Tremaine."

Rebecca bristled at the comment, shrugging off the warning. "I have a vested interest in this also, my lord."

"You most certainly do not!" Lord Hampton's voice rose with his anger, but he brought it under control and lowered his tone before speaking again. "Though you gave birth to her, you are not, nor will you ever be, Lily's mother."

His words seemed to hang in the air. Potent, angry, truthful. "I still have the right to care about her," Rebecca replied, her voice quivering with emotion.

"That may very well be," he said in an irritated voice. "Yet I give you fair warning. Do not ever again presume to tell me how to handle my daughter, Miss Tremaine. I promise you will be most distressed at the consequences."

Their gazes locked in a silent battle of wills until Rebecca realized she was in no position to win this argument. He was right. The earl held all the power. He was Lily's father. And she . . . she was nothing.

Rebecca bowed her head. Inside she was quaking. The unfairness of it all made her temper blaze as hotly as his. But she held back the angry words that sprang to her lips, knowing it would only make matters worse to speak them.

The knot of tension inside Rebecca's chest tightened, yet somehow she managed to keep her expression calm, serene. Using every ounce of willpower she possessed, Rebecca looked him straight in the eye.

"As you wish, my lord."

The ride home seemed twice as long to Cameron as it had on the way to the vicarage. Lily rode in the carriage with the rest of the women, and he missed her distracting chatter. Without it, Rebecca Tremaine's biting words about the child's behavior echoed too loud and too long in his head.

Despite all his many other duties and responsibilities the earl had always considered Lily his most important responsibility, one he took on with the greatest enthusiasm and love. He knew the level of his involvement with his child was unusual for a man of his class. Whenever he visited other friends and acquaintances children were hardly ever in evidence. Occasionally there would be a brief appearance where a youngster would bow or curtsy and perhaps say hello. For their efforts they received a pat on the head and an indulgent smile and were promptly ignored.

Cameron knew several lords who went weeks without setting eyes on their children; ladies who spent no more than twenty minutes a day in the company of their offspring before the youngsters were whisked away by a nurse or a governess.

Yet from the moment she arrived, both he and Christina had taken an overt interest in everything about Lily, had spent an extraordinary amount of time fussing and cooing over the baby girl. As young parents they would often sneak into the nursery to have a look at her while she slept, marveling at the good fortune that had brought this tiny blessing into their lives.

When Christina died, it was the distraction of Lily that kept Cameron's grief from overtaking him. She quickly became the center of his life. Concentrating on her needs had saved him from thinking too hard about his own life; about the emptiness that was there, the loneliness that invaded his heart.

The child had been his salvation and he adored her completely. It was unthinkable to accept any sort of criticism about her from Rebecca Tremaine.

Cameron reached the front courtyard of Windmere manor ahead of the carriage. He dismounted and tossed the horse's reins to a young groom who had rushed forward. Tapping his hand impatiently against his thigh, Lord Hampton waited for the women to arrive.

The coach had barely come to a complete stop before Lily jumped out of the door and ran toward him, ignoring Mrs. James's admonishments to slow down. She lunged at him, arms open wide, body quivering. Cameron stooped down, pulling her close, hugging her tightly.

"I am sorry that I was a naughty girl, Papa," she said, her voice muffled against his greatcoat. "Please don't be mad at me."

"You upset Mrs. Hargrave a great deal with your display of temper," Cameron said as he set her down on her feet.

"I said I was sorry," Lily wailed, a stream of tears coursing down her cheeks.

"I know." He removed his linen handkerchief from his coat pocket and wiped her face. Her sobs instantly quieted to periodic sniffles.

"Am I a disgrace?" Lily whispered, a frown of worry on her brow.

"What? No! Who said that you were?"

"Mrs. James."

Cameron's head shot up, his ire roused. He spotted the governess standing at a respectful distance and turned a piercing gaze upon her. "Is that what you told her?" he accused.

Mrs. James gave him a dazed look. "Oh no, my lord. I told Lady Lily her *behavior* was a disgrace and now that she has had time to think about her actions, she agreed."

Hmm. The earl quelled his anger. There was no way he could reprimand the woman for saying that, though he vowed to keep a closer watch on the governess. Cameron nodded, then looked at Lily.

"I know you did not mean to upset Mrs. Hargrave, Puss. You must remember, however, that a great lady strives to be gracious to everyone at all times."

"Truly?"

Her innocent expression of trust was nearly his undoing. "Truly."

"Was my mama a great lady?"

Mama? Miss Tremaine? Cameron nearly fell to his knees, he was so shocked by his thoughts. Upon hearing Lily say "Mama" his first thought was not of his beloved wife Christina, but rather Rebecca Tremaine.

Even though not more than twenty minutes ago he had been bellowing at the woman proclaiming that she would never be Lily's mother, somehow she had been melded into the role of "Mama" in his mind.

A most troubling development.

"Yes, your mama was a grand lady," the dowager countess interjected. "We all loved and admired her tremendously. Just as we love you. Come along, Lily, let's go inside. All this excitement has rattled my nerves."

The little girl turned on her heel and skipped

over to her grandmother. "I can't wait to tell Aunt Charlotte about the play and my angel costume. Won't she be surprised? Oh, how I wish Jane Grolier were here so she could see me wearing my gold halo. I think I shall take it back to London with me so I can show her. Can I, Grandma?"

He could not hear his mother's reply, for they had entered the house, with Mrs. James trailing behind. He turned to follow them and found himself face-to-face with Rebecca Tremaine, who was staring up at him with unblinking eyes.

"I wish to apologize for my earlier comments," she said stoically. "I did not mean to interfere."

"Well, you did," he replied peevishly. "Lily is my responsibility. You must never forget it."

She looked at him in chagrin. "Believe me, I know that very well."

Her expression remained calm, but the bitterness in her voice was evident. He cleared his throat a little guiltily, knowing he was the cause. "If you will excuse me, I need to confer with my secretary about the list Vicar Hargrave gave me."

"Of course. Good afternoon."

She took an awkward step, stumbling on the uneven gravel. Instinctively, Cameron reached for her, grabbing her arm at the elbow and holding her upright. At the same moment Miss Tremaine reached for him with her other flailing hand, seeking something solid to grasp and steady herself.

She was closer than he realized. He glanced down and found himself staring into her enchanting blue eyes, becoming lost in their bottomless depths. Beneath her woolen cloak he could feel the enticing curves of her body, could smell the delicate scent of her floral perfume.

She looked achingly beautiful and he was momentarily dazzled by her. But this sudden awareness was not a welcome occurrence.

"Are you all right?" he inquired, his tone clipped to hide his reaction.

"Yes. Please, pardon my clumsiness."

She sounded breathless. He released her and she straightened, brushing her hands nervously down the front of her skirt. Then she bobbed a quick curtsy, turned and walked swiftly away. Cameron fought to keep his feet planted in place, squashing the most ridiculous compulsion to follow her.

Lord, what rubbish! He had no wish to think such idiotic, dare he admit, romantic thoughts about Rebecca Tremaine. He had more than enough problems trying to negotiate this bizarre situation as it stood. Adding a romantic element would make things quite impossible.

'Twas nothing more than a physical reaction, he told himself. A healthy male too long without a sexual release responding to the nearness and scent of a beautiful female.

Yet he knew the body and the spirit were not so easily separated. There was something undefinable beneath the physical allure that drew him to Rebecca Tremaine and that worried him.

He slapped his riding crop sharply against the top of his boot trying to snap himself out of this fanciful mood. It didn't work. Striding toward the house, Cameron mentally counted off the days until Christmas. Like a child of Lily's age, he fervently hoped it would come quickly.

For when the holiday was over, Rebecca Tremaine would be gone.

Chapter 7

Charlotte sank back against her chair, sighing as the majority of the crowd partnered for the next dance. This evening the music room was serving as a makeshift ballroom, since several of the guests declared an interest in dancing after supper. Charlotte was very disappointed with the choice, for it would exclude her from the festivities. But worst of all, it would also deny her a chance to be with Mr. Tremaine.

It was a stroke of bad luck that their paths had not crossed once in the past three days. Tonight she had not actually seen him until supper was being served— had not had any opportunity to speak with him since they had sung their duet three nights ago. Charlotte had been terribly nervous when Marion suggested she sing, and near panic when Mr. Tremaine had agreed to accompany her. But the result had far exceeded anything she could have imagined.

For the first time in her life she had lost her shyness and inhibition. Since she was already seated near the piano, she did not have to take any steps with all eyes upon her, watching her uneven, ungainly gait. With the distress of revealing her limp removed, she had been able to relax, to indulge in the beauty of the music.

The moment Miss Tremaine's fingers began to play, Charlotte could feel herself being transported by her emotions. And when she and Mr. Tremaine had started to sing . . . Charlotte sighed at the memory. Their voices had sounded so beautiful together, so perfectly matched.

It was by far the most intimate experience she had ever shared with a man, which was ironic since it occurred in front of a crowd and she had never once looked at Mr. Tremaine as they sang. And still it had been magical.

The experience had deepened her connection to him, had stirred a primal need inside her for companionship and understanding, for stimulation of the senses she had been conditioned to repress. Miraculously, in those few amazing moments, Daniel Tremaine had become a beacon to Charlotte, a comforting refuge, a place of safety and promise in a world of darkness.

Yet the victory and delight of the other evening were now ended and tonight reality once again reigned. As she watched her cousin Marion gracefully pirouette in front of her dance partner, Charlotte felt herself slipping back into her usual quiet, self-contained self. Back into the world where she dwelled, where all was dull and gray and lonely.

She brushed a hand over the burgundy silk skirt of her evening gown, feeling foolish for giving into the temptation to wear it. Her maid had enthusiastically encouraged her to don the brightly hued gown—one of the very few in her wardrobe. She had smiled when Charlotte asked about her lace spinster's cap, claiming she was unable to fetch it because it now resided in the dustbin. And she had once again created an elaborate, fashionable hairstyle that made Charlotte feel attractive and vibrant.

But it had all been for naught. Mr. Tremaine did not even notice her. He and his sister had been the last guests to arrive for supper, barely glancing at anyone as they had hurried to take their places. They had been seated at the opposite end of the table from Charlotte, precluding any chance of conversation.

Despondent, Charlotte had actually stared at Mr. Tremaine for a good portion of the meal yet he never once glanced in her direction.

She spied him now on the far side of the room, surrounded by several gentlemen. He cut an undeniably attractive figure in his black formal evening clothes. She could not help but admire his handsome face with his dark hair and twinkling eyes, his charming smile.

There was a smattering of applause as the dance ended. Lady Bailey, who had graciously consented to play for the dancers, asked for a cup of tea and with a bit of prompting Mrs. Halloway took her place at the piano.

Charlotte craned her neck to see where Mr. Tremaine had gotten himself off to, momentarily panicking when she could not find him. She shifted restlessly in her chair, then caught a glimpse of him moving across the room.

Tall and well built, he moved with power and purpose. She monitored his progress as he kept coming closer, finally realizing he was walking directly toward her. Their eyes met. Gooseflesh prickled Charlotte's arm.

"Will you do me the honor of partnering me for this dance, Lady Charlotte?"

He bowed and extended his hand. Her mouth

went dry. She stared into his gentle brown eyes, unable to breathe, to stammer out a single syllable.

"Oh . . . I . . ." Charlotte stuttered, totally at a loss.

"Please?"

Charlotte struggled to swallow. Gracious, where was her fan? It suddenly felt unbearably warm as a blast of heat flushed up from her chest and settled on her cheeks.

"I believe you to be too kindhearted a woman to so cruelly reject me," he continued, his eyes entreating her with a whimsical twinkle. "Please, dance with me."

A sense of light-headedness swept over her. Charlotte put a hand to her head to still the throbbing pulse at her temple. *Now what was she to do?* For the past few days she had taken such great pains to hide her infirmity from him and clearly her ruse had been successful. He had no inkling she was a cripple.

She gazed up at him in alarm. What could she say? More than anything she wanted to say yes, but it was impossible. She rarely danced and never in public.

And then he smiled.

Mesmerized, Charlotte felt her arm lift toward him. It was madness, certain to end in disaster, but in that instant she did not care. All she could think about was how he would haunt her heart for the rest of her life. Seizing this one chance to be in his arms seemed to be worth any humiliation.

She placed her trembling gloved finger in the palm of his hand and stood; then took two steps revealing her uneven, unsteady gait. Flushed with mortification, Charlotte waited for him to stammer with puzzlement or embarrassment or worst of all with pity, and withdraw the offer. Instead he took a step closer, offering his entire arm, rather than merely his hand, to support her.

"'Tis a waltz," he said with an easy grin. "My favorite."

Before Charlotte had an opportunity to reply, Mr. Tremaine's arm slid around her waist and they went whirling onto the dance floor.

Tension radiated through her. She feared that she would stumble or fall and make a complete fool of herself. But Mr. Tremaine seemed oblivious to her distress, acting as if nothing was amiss. With another captivating smile he tightened his arm around her waist. Pulling her close, he expertly led her in a patterned circle.

He was very strong. He was also an excellent dancer. Assured, confident in his abilities, smooth and graceful. Gradually, Charlotte began to relax and let him take control, enjoying the movement and energy of the dance. Her injured leg lagged behind slightly to the beat of the music, but Mr. Tremaine twirled her so expertly it did not seem to matter.

It reminded Charlotte of the time she had seen Cameron dancing with Lily. The little girl had placed her feet atop her father's and the earl had danced about the room, taking the child with him.

Lost in thought, she did not catch Mr. Tremaine's remarks. "Pardon?"

"You look so solemn, Lady Charlotte. Are you not enjoying yourself?"

"Oh, no, 'tis marvelous," Charlotte replied, for indeed it was heavenly. It was like floating, like flying as they whirled around the ballroom at a dizzying speed. But most delightful of all was the joy she felt at being held in his arms.

She had seen others waltz before and was surprised at how private it felt, how personal. Being held this close afforded her the opportunity to gaze at his handsome face without seeming intrusive. She admired his white, straight teeth, the small dimple that appeared in the depths of his cheek when he smiled,

even the tiny lines that formed at the corners of his
eyes when he laughed.

He pulled her closer to avoid a collision with another couple and Charlotte was suddenly aware of her
breasts crushed against his chest. She faltered a step.
He caught her, steadied her, saved her from making
an embarrassing fall.

A rush of feelings and emotions swamped her. Her
face was burning. She hoped Mr. Tremaine would not
be able to see the color creeping into her cheeks. He
twirled again and she could feel his muscular thighs
pressing against her own through the gown.

Charlotte began to tremble. She told herself it was
due to the tight stays in her corset that restricted her
breathing, but she knew it was a lie. It was being near
Mr. Tremaine. Daniel. She glanced up at him, fearing
he had guessed she was attracted to him.

He smiled back at her, his features relaxed with
amusement. If he did know, it apparently did not trou-
ble him. Charlotte nearly asked, but bit her tongue
before she spoke and made a complete ninny of herself. Deciding it must be the intensity of being so near
him that stole her wits, she wisely did not attempt any
conversation.

Instead, she allowed herself the luxury of concentrating on the moment, telling herself it was essential
that she remember each and every small detail, so this
dance could be savored again and again in the coming
days and weeks.

Mrs. Halloway ended the waltz with an impressive
crescendo on the piano, her arms shimmying. Everyone began to applaud, except Charlotte, who sighed
with genuine regret. Reluctantly she allowed herself
to be led from the floor, back to her solitary seat on
the outer edge of the room.

After a slight pause, she forced herself to relinquish her hold on Mr. Tremaine's arm and sank into her chair. She was attempting to summon the courage to invite him to sit with her, but felt shy at the presumption and guilty at ruining his chance to enjoy himself. Just because she was a cripple did not give her the right to inflict her limitations on him. He should partner another lady and enjoy more dances.

"I noticed you were limping when we came off the dance floor. Did you injure yourself today?" he inquired.

Her heart sank and a vise of cold tightened her chest. She blinked quickly to avoid the sudden rush of tears. "The injury is of long-standing, one I have had since birth."

"You dance beautifully. Better than I, certainly." He gave her a questioning look, then glanced down as if trying to ascertain precisely what was wrong.

Somehow she conjured a smile, to let him know she was not offended, though in truth she was mortified at having to explain. "I was born with the defect. My hip socket is not correctly formed and thus affects my left leg. It is crooked and slightly shorter than the right."

"Oh, is that all? I thought it something far more serious." He cocked his head to one side. "Are you feeling tired?"

"No," she squeaked.

"Splendid. Shall we try the quadrille next?"

Charlotte found herself nodding, for speech was a total impossibility. *Is that all? Is that all?* Had he truly said it just that way? Casually, simply. As if it were nothing. As if her cripple leg was but a mere inconvenience, something insignificant, of little, nay, of almost no consequence. Something that did not matter.

Her chest constricted and her heart began a too-rapid beat. The euphoria she felt was all inclusive. Though she tried to contain it, 'twas impossible not to let her heart soar.

Long ago, when she had turned eighteen, her mother had gently warned her that she needed to be careful of men, careful of love. The dowager countess explained how she feared her only daughter would be vulnerable, suspecting if Charlotte ever fell in love, she would fall hard and fast and with all the impulsive passion of a lonely, neglected woman.

Charlotte had heeded her mother's advice. From that day forward, she had closed her mind to the idea of finding a gentleman to love, one who would care for her in return. Worried she would turn bitter, Charlotte had strived hard not to be the sort of woman who railed and lamented her fate, who brooded endlessly about what she could not change. Countless times she had endeavored to find the strength within herself to accept the future that fate had forced upon her.

But tonight—well, tonight she was ready to risk her heart and allow her dreams to fly free. Tonight she was going to savor ever minute of this magical feeling, she was going to embrace it utterly.

"I would very much like to dance the quadrille with you, Mr. Tremaine," Charlotte said. "Though I might be a bit clumsy at some parts."

"I'm sure you will be graceful as a gazelle, Lady Charlotte." He lowered his head toward her and she could feel his warm breath against her cheek, their mouths only inches apart. "But even if you are not, I shall not mind in the least."

Charlotte grinned broadly, a smile bright enough to put the sun to shame. Then with her head held high, she allowed herself to be led back on the dance floor.

* * *

Cameron tossed back the last of his drink and placed it on a nearby table, wondering how many times he could circle the music room and still not approach Miss Tremaine. Upon reflection, he had come to regret his outburst with her earlier today. It was creating an awkward, underlying tension between them that did no one any good. Least of all him.

The sadness and vulnerability on her face as he railed at her had made him feel like the worst sort of bully. It brought home hard the wounding power of his words, never more potent than when spewed in anger.

And yet there was a part, albeit a small part, of him that felt justified in his intense reaction to her criticism. It was not Miss Tremaine's place to dictate how Lily was being reared. That was his responsibility and he was pleased with the results.

He was a man used to being in control, of having things he directed go in a correct, proper manner. Few, if any, ever questioned his authority or the rightness of his behavior and actions. He was not, as unfortunately were many others of his class, a pompous ass who would book no criticism. He had on more than one occasion freely admitted a mistake and done whatever was necessary to correct it.

Perhaps that was the crux of his dilemma. He honestly did not believe he said anything wrong and yet somehow she made him feel that he was in the wrong. How the devil had that happened? Was she a witch or a sorceress or just a bloody clever woman?

Cameron wanted to curse himself for having a weak moment and bringing her here in the first place, but in the end he knew he could not regret inviting Miss

Tremaine to Windmere manor. Given the circumstances it was the right thing to do. She had been dealt a harsh, unfair blow and genuinely suffered from the loss of her child. It was within his power to ease some of that pain and his conscience would not let him turn his back on his duty.

Still, he could not help wishing that she was merely another guest at his home, someone who would briefly touch his life and then be gone. He knew now that would be very unlikely. It was staggering, really, when he considered the ramifications of this relationship.

Complicating it further, as the afternoon had clearly demonstrated, if he were not constantly on his guard he could far too quickly lose control of his temper and emotions. Determined to purge the incident, and her, from his mind, Cameron had spent the remainder of the afternoon locked in his study reviewing year-end financial statements. Those dull tomes, combined with several glasses of fine wine, had caused his mind to fog, his eyelids to grow heavy.

He had briefly fallen asleep. And while asleep had dreamt about Rebecca Tremaine.

In the dream it had been Christmas morning. As was their family custom, he, Lily, Mother and Charlotte had been gathered together in the private parlor exchanging gifts. Lily was especially excited, dashing from one person to the next, her eyes bright and happy, her face flushed with childish, innocent delight as she waited for the signal that they could begin tearing into the pretty, wrapped packages.

There was another woman in the room. Christina. Seated in her customary place on the settee, wearing her favorite royal blue dressing gown, her long blond hair loose and flowing down her back. A warm, comforting feeling had invaded his soul at the sight of her.

Grinning, he had laid one hand on her shoulder while extending a Christmas present toward her with the other.

Slowly, she turned. And smiled.

Startled, he felt the package fall from his hand. It was not his beloved Christina staring back at him with a joyful smile, a glow of happiness on her lovely face. It was Rebecca Tremaine.

Lily had begun to cry, and Cameron had awoken with a jolt, the sound of his daughter's misery echoing in his heart.

"Pretty woman, that Rebecca Tremaine. I'm surprised she isn't married," Viscount Cranborne remarked as he came to stand beside Cameron.

The earl blinked. "Her father was a vicar," he replied, glad of the distraction from his disturbing thoughts. "I imagine her dowry is exceedingly small."

"With a face and form like that, a dowry should be the last thing on a gentleman's mind," Cranborne remarked. The viscount took a sip of wine. "It looks as if her circumstances might improve. Her brother is a very successful man, by all accounts quite wealthy. 'Tis possible he will gift her with a substantial settlement, though her age might be a deterrent for some men."

"She isn't that old," Cameron answered, quick to defend.

"Of course not, but there are those who prefer a very young, impressionable, malleable bride." Viscount Cranborne directed his wine goblet in a small salute toward his wife, who merrily danced by them. Marion lifted her eyebrow suggestively in answer and the viscount laughed. "Never could understand why a man would want a milquetoast as his lifelong companion. Damn boring, if you ask me."

Cameron had to agree. Yet for some unexpected

reason the idea of Rebecca marrying did not sit well in his mind.

And why was that exactly? The earl sighed, deciding it had to be a question of attraction. If he were able to view Rebecca Tremaine as simply an available woman—without the tangles and complications of Lily—he might at this moment be acting upon the attraction he felt for her.

A most disturbing revelation, indeed. Cameron rubbed his brow in exasperation and gazed again at Miss Tremaine, who was now dancing with Lord Bailey. She was stylishly attired in a gown of violet silk, a few artfully arranged curls bouncing around her face, drawing attention to her lovely eyes. She had danced with two different gentlemen, smiling often with each one, though showing no particular favoritism toward any.

She had not once smiled at him. Not through supper, not when evening tea was served, not when they had begun the dancing.

He knew this because he had been watching her. Like a curious lad caught in the throes of his first crush his eyes had compulsively traveled in her direction time and again. Ridiculous behavior. One that surely would be cured with a stiff drink. Or two.

Cameron started toward the table where the crystal decanters of spirits were prominently displayed, then in midstride suddenly switched directions. The music had ended, the couples were milling about waiting for the next piece to begin. Purposefully he strode over to Miss Tremaine. A hint of wary curiosity entered her expression.

"Care to dance?"

A spark of surprise showed in her eyes. She glanced away as if looking for a polite, reasonable way to refuse and he felt a surge of embarrassment. Damn!

Did she truly hold so low an opinion of him that she would decline a simple dance?

Without waiting for her reply, Cameron took her hand. She resisted slightly, leaning back on her heels. He tugged and she obediently moved forward. With a grimace, he led her to the makeshift dance floor.

Initially, conversation was unnecessary, since the patterns of the dance required them to part often. But since this was a more casual affair, and not a formal ball, couples were lingering longer together and sets of dancers were merrily talking and laughing.

He sought his mind for some safe subject on which to converse, but came up empty. In frustration, he gripped her elbow too tightly, causing her to pull away. His hand slipped and accidentally grazed her left breast, softly caressing its roundness, tenderly brushing over the nipple.

Cameron heard the quickening of her breath, could feel her start to tremble at the unexpected contact. He opened his mouth to apologize, for it truly had been an accident. But his lips shut when he caught the expression of flushed desire on her face. She did not find the incident offensive or repulsive. Quite the contrary, in fact.

An odd sense of satisfaction filled him at the knowledge that this unwanted attraction enthralling him was not one-sided. Clearly, it also affected her. He angled his head and caught her eye. Her answering gaze nearly burned through him. Cameron laughed. Affected her and annoyed her as much as him. Perfect.

They came together for the next figure and she held herself rigidly as if fearing contact. He was tempted to move his hand over her shoulder and caress the exposed flesh of her delicate, creamy neck, but restrained himself. Instead, he offered a branch of peace.

"I sincerely hope you did not get the wrong impression this afternoon from our conversation, Miss Tremaine. Granted, I was peeved at your criticism of Lily, however, upon reflection, I realize my tone and attitude might be misconstrued as dictatorial."

He had to wait until she rejoined him in the dance before hearing her reply.

"You were quite clear when stating your position on this matter, my lord. I am not ignorant. I understood precisely what you meant."

He frowned. He anticipated that she would most likely not make it easy for him to extend a peace offering, but he had not expected such a frosty reaction.

Determined, the earl tried again. "Any distress I might have caused you was unintentional," he said.

She glanced at him askance. "Frankly, I am shocked that you have given the conversation any additional consideration. I did not for one moment imagine that you spent the remainder of the afternoon cursing and gnashing your teeth over my remarks. Especially since you made it adamantly clear that my opinion is neither sought nor welcome."

Cameron craned his neck forward as his collar suddenly felt a bit too tight. "That is not precisely true."

She scrunched her brow. "Really?"

"Yes."

"Hmm. Forgive me if I am skeptical of that idea, but I fear that my opinion is only sought if it concurs with yours, my lord. Is that right?" She daintily raised herself up on her toes and skillfully executed the next steps of the dance.

He snuffed his rising temper. "What I mean to say is that it was not my intention to intimidate you."

"I assure you, my lord, you did not."

Her tart response put an unexpected smile on his face. The woman had gumption, that was certain. "What is it you want, Miss Tremaine?" he asked. "Truthfully."

She looked startled at the question and then uncomfortable. "I highly doubt you want to hear it."

"Oh, but I do."

She made a graceful turn, her back to his, then whispered over her shoulder. "I want what I cannot have and realize in order to survive, I need to discipline myself to amend my desires. I want peace in my soul when I wake in the morning and a feeling of contentment during the day. I want the heaviness in my heart to lessen, to be replaced with laughter and the occasional joy of real happiness. In short, my lord, I want the impossible."

"Those seem like reasonable, attainable things," he countered.

"I want to mother my daughter."

His footstep faltered, his heel skidding on the hard wood floor. She was correct. He did not want to hear that bitter truth. He opened his mouth, speaking without thought. "You are a young woman. You could marry, have other children."

She gasped, stiffened and he was certain would have ceased dancing if he had not been holding her hand in his own.

"A child is not an interchangeable item, with one being just as good as another," she hissed.

Something inside his chest wrenched. *God help him, his tongue could be lethal at times.* "Forgive me. That was an appalling, insensitive remark." He lifted her arm aloft and she twirled beneath it in perfect time to the music. "I made the assumption that because you were critical of Lily you held her in little regard."

She swallowed visibly, drawing his gaze to her throat, which was bare of jewels. "One has nothing in the least to do with the other. I care for Lily far more than I ought. More, you tell me, than I have a right."

"You have misconstrued my words, Miss Tremaine. I do not object to your having an affection for Lily."

"An affection?" She shook her head. "I am supposed to be content with something as tepid as affection when my heart longs to be someone important, someone special to her?"

The earl felt a wash of unwelcome guilt. "Unfortunately, we do not always get what we want in this life."

"An interesting observation from a man who has everything." Cameron was looking directly into her beautiful blue eyes when she spoke. He saw a flare of emotion, quickly shuttered. "I know I must learn to be content with what I can get or else I shall constantly be miserable. But pray, do not expect me to be pleased about it."

He wanted to dismiss her reaction as melodramatic, but the honesty of her words and the heartfelt emotion in them haunted him. "Miss Tremaine—"

The music ended and the room became suddenly quiet, forcing him to hold back any further comments.

"Thank you for the dance," she said, tugging her hand out of his grasp. "And the enlightening conversation."

She dipped a shallow curtsy, low enough only to avoid insult. Cameron grimaced in understanding. He could not blame her.

He wondered how she would react if he grabbed her hand and tucked it in the crook of his elbow, forcing her to stay at his side. He did not take her for a woman who would make a scene, but his judgment had been so poor in so many things concerning Rebecca Tremaine, Cameron knew the risk was too great.

She glided away from him and he felt an unexpected wave of longing. It had been a mistake to ask her to dance, a mistake to probe too deeply into her feelings. If he had any sense he would cease tormenting them both and keep himself as far removed from her company as possible.

He made his way toward the opposite side of the room. As he lifted the crystal decanter of port, the earl heard the rustling of a silk gown. He turned, glowering when he caught Marion's interfering gaze upon him. Sometimes his cousin saw too much.

"I sense an undercurrent of romance in the air tonight, Cameron," she declared, holding out her empty wine goblet for a refill. "The Christmas season does carry a very special kind of magic for these sorts of things, you know. I think it is absolutely marvelous."

"And I think you have drunk too many glasses of wine," the earl responded, adding but a splash of liquid to the goblet.

"Nonsense." She drained the small sip he had given her and extended the glass, demanding more. "'Tis about time you thought about your future. You aren't getting any younger, you know."

"Marion," he warned in his sternest voice, regretting that he had not bolted from the room the moment his dance with Miss Tremaine had ended.

"Oh, do stop trying to be so fierce," she countered. "I have known you far too long to take that sort of behavior seriously."

And he knew Marion too well to argue. The effort would hardly be worth the result. Thankfully, Marion's husband was within earshot.

"Take charge of your wife, Cranborne," the earl

called out. "Or else I will not be held responsible for my actions."

The viscount obligingly came forward. Marion's face pulled into a sour expression as she turned to her husband. "That's it! First thing tomorrow after breakfast we are going to organize an outing to the woods."

"The woods?" the viscount questioned.

"Yes," Lady Marion answered. "We need to gather mistletoe. This manor needs a lot of mistletoe."

"Why mistletoe, my love?"

"Because my cousin is a pig-headed brute!"

The viscount blanched. "I fail to see the connection."

"I have my heart set on at least one Christmas romance this season and it will never move forward unless there is some kissing. No, a lot of kissing." She lifted her goblet and took a long sip. "I fear if I leave it to my cousin, there will be no magic this season. And I am determined to have some. Mistletoe is but the first step in my plan."

Chapter 8

The moment she was able, Rebecca quietly slipped away. The music room had become stuffy and she told herself she needed fresh air. She was feeling light-headed, a belated reaction, she was sure, from her encounter with Lord Hampton.

She should not have danced with him, even though he had given her little choice. Ostensibly he appeared to be trying to make amends for his dictatorial behavior earlier in the day, trying to clarify his position on the matter of Lily. Yet despite any initial good intentions, the result had fallen far short of the mark.

His attempt at an apology had merely succeeded in distressing her further. And the things she had said to him! Rebecca shut her eyes in mortification, aghast that she had revealed to him her inner pain about Lily. A pain she had yet to fully comprehend, one she certainly had not mastered. A pain that she knew now would never completely heal.

But it wasn't only thoughts of Lily that rattled Rebecca tonight. Being so near the earl emphasized and illuminated this baffling attraction she felt for him.

An attraction that frankly embarrassed her because it was so ludicrous.

She thought she was being fanciful when she suspected he glanced at her bosom before leading her onto the dance floor. And then his fingers had brushed across her breast. Accidentally? Who could say for certain? Yet more disturbing than the act was her shivering, physical reaction to his touch.

It was a basic, primal feeling. She tried to ignore it, to pretend it did not exist. Tried and failed because something inside her wanted to acknowledge it, and even more scandalous, answer it. No matter how many times she sternly told herself she could not tolerate another minute of these discomforting feelings, they refused to retreat.

Rebecca went down the hall, thinking to make use of the stone balcony off the second floor sitting room as a place for private reflection. As she walked down the candlelit corridor, the clock chimed the quarter hour.

The door to the sitting room stood open and she paused for a moment to see if there was anyone about. Thankfully, the room was deserted. Rebecca entered, telling herself she would stay only a few minutes, no more than a quarter of an hour.

Unlocking the French door to the wide balcony, she stepped outside and filled her lungs with slow, deep breaths of air. The air was chilled, the night sky clear and twinkling with stars. She shivered, and a feeling like ice traveled down her spine and settled in the pit of her stomach. Knowing it was more than the weather that put this chill in her heart, Rebecca nevertheless decided she could not stay outside too much longer dressed in only her evening gown.

She returned indoors, thinking briefly about retiring for the night, but that smacked too much of cowardice.

She would not hide from the earl. She moved to the hearth, seeking the warmth of the modest fire glowing in the fireplace. From the corner of her eye she noticed something moving into her line of vision.

A man!

She jerked her head, her heart beating like the fluttering wings of a bird, fearing it was Lord Hampton. Fortunately, it was her brother, Daniel, who stood in the doorway. Releasing a small sigh, Rebecca collected herself.

"Is everything all right?" he asked, coming into the room. "Lady Charlotte and I noticed you left the music room in a hurry."

"I thought I had been discreet when I exited."

"I doubt anyone else was aware." His brow wrinkled in concern. "Are you feeling ill?"

Rebecca considered her words. Daniel had stood by her these past weeks, supplying comfort and advice as best he could, a solid reminder that she was not totally alone. Yet what could she say? The earl is being territorial about Lily, but even more distressing there is an unwelcome attraction between him and me.

What lunacy. Rebecca sighed, deciding there was no need to muddy the waters trying to explain something she did not even pretend to understand herself.

"It has been a trying day," she finally admitted. "We went to see the vicar and his wife this afternoon. Lily came too."

"That's unusual." Daniel settled himself in the chair closest to the fireplace. "I thought children were relegated to the nursery for most of their day."

"Apparently Lily is not like other little girls. It seems that there are many unusual, far from ordinary things occurring when it comes to raising her."

"You don't approve?"

Rebecca could not contain her most unladylike snort. "My opinion is neither sought nor appreciated."

"Are you certain?"

"Oh, yes." Rebecca began to pace. "Lily threw a tantrum in front of the vicar's wife when she did not get her way. It was disgraceful behavior for a child of her age and completely unwarranted. When I commented upon it to the earl, the lethal warning in his voice to keep my opinions to myself was hard to mistake."

She paused, took a deep breath, then resumed her pacing. "He cannot seem to understand that my motives were pure. I only want what is best for her. I thought that by being honest and direct with him he would appreciate my concern, would consider my admonition in the spirit upon which it was offered."

"I take it that is not what happened?"

"Alas, no. I was merely fooling myself when I believed he would listen to me. Even worse, he seized the opportunity to make it more than clear that my future contact with Lily rests on his whims. 'Tis maddening."

Daniel scowled. "We are here at the earl's good will, Rebecca. Which could evaporate at any time. I assume you wish to stay and spend more time with the little girl?"

Rebecca stopped her pacing abruptly. His impersonal tone struck at her emotions. "For pity's sake, Daniel, she isn't just any little girl." *She's my daughter!* The thought reverberated in her mind, the pain of being denied her rightful place in Lily's life burned at her soul.

"In the eyes of the world, and the law, that is precisely what she is to you."

"Oh, God." Rebecca covered her face with her hands. Hearing the words, the truthful words, felt like a knife-point stabbing her heart. How could she bear it?

"If you'd like, I shall consult another lawyer," Daniel offered, his voice contrite.

Rebecca lifted her head. "Do you think that would help?"

He shrugged. "This situation is so unique, so odd, 'tis impossible to find someone with experience in a similar matter. Yet there still might be some legal recourse for you."

She hesitated. Having to conceal the truth about her identity was the most bitter experience of her life. More than anything she wanted a chance to be a true mother to her child, to love and nurture her. But at what cost?

Sadly, Rebecca shook her head. Though she initially believed she was desperate enough to do whatever was necessary to have Lily in her life, she realized it was far more complicated.

"I fear my chances in court are slim, the risk of failure too high. Besides, any small legal victory would be clouded by the potential harm this would cause Lily. I cannot, in good conscience, subject her to this sort of turmoil. It would be far too selfish."

"I should like to believe there is something we can do to give you some leverage in this situation," Daniel insisted. "Something that would not involve a public airing of our dirty laundry."

"Perhaps there is, although we must both agree to weigh carefully any considered course of action against the possible harm it would cause."

"Agreed."

Rebecca felt the weight on her chest ease slightly. It was so good to know she was not completely alone. "For now, I know I need to try and manage this as it stands. I always thought of myself as a pragmatic person. A survivor. But there are times that I suddenly feel like a very foolish woman, deluding herself about the future."

"It's not all that bleak." Daniel smiled encouragingly at her.

"You're right. By some divine miracle we now find ourselves in the earl's home, readying ourselves to share in a traditional Christmas celebration." She tried to smile, but ended up letting out a short, sharp giggle as the irony of it all was not lost on her.

Daniel cleared his throat. "As usual, life has a way of dealing one the hand that is least expected."

"Least expected? Even an individual with the most fertile imagination would never dream of my situation." Rebecca tried once more to laugh, yet this time it came out as more of a groan. "I keep telling myself I need to try to change what I can and accept the rest."

"Sound advice. Yet far more difficult to enact, I assure you."

"As well, I know. But I must try." Finally she succeeded in releasing a small laugh. "Goodness, listen to me prattle on! It seems as if some days I simply cannot stop myself from babbling. 'Tis so very unlike me."

"If you talk a great deal, you have less time to think."

"Or else you merely speak without thinking." Rebecca rubbed her forearms briskly, her emotions deflating. "Are you certain you don't mind staying at Windmere? You were hardly eager to celebrate Christmas and you certainly had no wish to stay here in the country, away from London and your business interests."

Daniel lifted his shoulders in a shrug. "As luck would have it I've been able to conduct business here, since two of my principal investors in the Cornish mines are guests. And Viscount Cranborne has expressed interest in a land development deal that could prove to be even more successful."

Rebecca glanced closely at her brother. Was that a faint hint of a blush on his cheek? "It does not appear that this visit has been all business for you, Daniel. I noticed you dancing with Lady Charlotte earlier this evening."

Daniel shifted forward in his chair, picked up the fireplace iron and poked nervously at the burning logs. "I was merely being polite to my hostess."

"Stop blushing. I like her and I think it is wonderful that you have taken an interest in such a refined, kind woman."

Daniel prodded the logs once more. "Nothing can ever come of it," he said quietly. "She is too far above me in station."

"Not so very far, Daniel," Rebecca responded, offering her brother a smile she hoped was encouraging. "True, our ancestors were not of the highest nobility, well, actually they barely had any aristocratic blood, but we are hardly descended from peasant stock."

"Compared to the earl and his family we are mongrels." Daniel slowly lowered his hand, returning the poker iron to its stand. "I have not lived so long out of the country that I have forgotten how things are done in certain circles. It would be humiliating for me to be thought of as a man who married for social position. Besides, Lady Charlotte's family would never view me as a proper suitor."

"If it is what you really want, then you must change their minds."

"Rebecca!"

"Determination, brother. 'Tis a quality I know you possess and it will serve you well if you find yourself seriously interested in Lady Charlotte."

"'Tis hardly that simple," he protested.

"I am not suggesting that it is; I am merely pointing out what is needed to succeed." Her expression lightened, as her resolve hardened. "I never was much of a fighter. I solved conflicts with reason and compromise or simply retreated, abandoning my desire and accepting the will of others. Perhaps if I had been more forceful with Mother and Father, I would not be in this position today. But I am trying to change, Daniel, because now I have something of great importance for which to fight."

Bolstered by her own words, Rebecca walked to the door and opened it. She turned expectantly toward her brother. With a skeptical expression, Daniel rose from his chair and followed. They walked arm in arm down the hall, pausing briefly at the base of the staircase.

"Do you wish to retire or return to the music room?" he asked.

"The music room," she answered honestly. She would stay for at least another hour. *Determination.* No matter that one look from the earl could make her thoughts scatter. If he deemed to cast any attention in her direction, she would simply ignore him.

It was overcast the following morning, with a raw chill in the air that bespoke of the possibility of snow. Rebecca tarried in her room until breakfast was over, needing the time to gather her thoughts. When she left, she headed directly toward the nursery, hoping for a chance to spend some time with Lily.

She met Lady Charlotte in the hall and discovered that many of the guests, and children, were meeting at the stables. An impromptu party to gather greenery to decorate the house for the upcoming holiday had been decided upon at breakfast.

"I do not usually attend these outings," Lady Charlotte said with a reserved smile. "My hip is not that strong and I find it difficult to walk for great distances. But it seems as if nearly everyone is going." She blushed and lowered her gaze and Rebecca assumed Daniel was among those hearty souls who were venturing outdoors.

"It sounds like a merry time."

"Yes, it does." Lady Charlotte's eyes lit up with excitement. "Cameron has arranged for carriages to bring us to the west woods, though in truth it is more for my benefit. And the children. I hope you will join us."

Knowing she would never forsake an opportunity to be with Lily, Rebecca nodded in agreement. She returned to her room to dress in warmer clothing, then made her way to the stables to join the rest of the group.

There was an air of happy excitement when she arrived. There were four children, including Lily, darting about, laughing, shouting, playing tag and generally getting in everyone's way. Instead of elegant coaches, simple pony carts were being made ready and servants were scuttling between the main house and the stable yard bringing lap blankets and braziers of hot coals to warm the passengers.

Rebecca greeted several people, then walked beyond the crowd to gaze at the expansive grounds, admiring the beauty of the landscape. Though dormant in winter, the elegance and design of the estate's many gardens could be seen. She found an odd sense of contentment as she gazed at myriad curved paths lined with well-tended borders that meandered through acres of lawn and manicured hedges.

It must be spectacular in spring and summer, when

all was in bloom. Idly she wondered if she would ever be afforded the opportunity to view it at that time of year.

Beyond the acres of gardens were sloping hills that led to the woods. Suddenly, the ground seemed to shake with thunder. Looking over to the small clearing in front of the woods Rebecca saw a large dog crest the rise of the hill and charge toward them.

A few of the ladies shrieked in concern. Rebecca considered moving back into the crowd, but when she saw the beast's tail wagging, she remained where she stood. He was an enormous animal, quite possibly the largest canine she had ever seen and he seemed to grow in size with each long stride that brought him closer.

His was of indeterminable breed, though she was hardly an expert on the subject. For all she knew he could be some sort of rare, highly prized dog yet his shaggy brown fur and a lolling tongue suggested otherwise.

He skidded to a stop when he reached her. Lowering his head, he sniffed eagerly at her boots. She slowly extended an ungloved hand. The dog's head instantly lifted. He stretched out his neck and nudged at her palm with his cold, wet, black nose.

Apparently satisfied with what he found, he sat directly in front of her, and raised a massive wet paw in greeting.

Rebecca laughed. She had always liked dogs, especially large, friendly ones. She bent over to shake his paw, then patted him on the head.

"Apollo, come." The command was followed by a sharp whistle.

The dog stood and ran obediently to his master's side. Rebecca straightened and watched the earl enter the stable yard.

"Papa!"

Lily too ran toward Lord Hampton, arriving nearly at the same time as the dog. The earl greeted the enthusiastic pair, then turned his gaze to Rebecca.

"I hope Apollo did not frighten you, Miss Tremaine."

"Hardly, my lord." The animal had returned to her and she bent down to scratch his ears, unconcerned about the brown hairs shedding onto her black woolen cloak. He was a delightful beast with liquid brown eyes and a sweet, friendly disposition. "He is quite lovable. Though very heavy."

The earl bristled at her comment. "He is a trim hunting dog, bred for strength and muscle."

"Well, he must weigh ten stone."

"How do you know how much Apollo weighs?" Lily asked in curious fascination.

Rebecca smiled. "He is sitting on my foot."

Three pairs of eyes looked down. Sure enough, Apollo's rump was parked squarely in the middle of Rebecca's left boot.

"Apollo!" The earl gestured with his hand and the dog stood. "Heavens, Miss Tremaine, even my dog lacks the proper manners to appease you."

Rebecca's spine stiffened at what she perceived was a veiled reference to her comments about Lily's behavior. She turned sharply toward the earl, ready with a rebuke, but then noticed the twinkle of amusement in his eyes and her ire quickly deflated.

"I do not fault Apollo's manners." She reached out and rubbed his silky brown ears. Apollo's tail thumped rhythmically against the ground and his tongue darted out to lick her hand in appreciation. "I believe he suffers mostly from the belief that he is a lapdog and therefore wishes to be cosseted and spoiled with attention and affection."

"Isn't that something all living creatures crave?"

"Hmm. Perhaps I should scratch your ears, my lord? It might improve our relationship."

"Indeed."

He smiled. Rebecca nearly sighed out loud as her awareness of him kicked into high gear. Lord Almighty, the man was almost too handsome for his own good. But it did not matter. She simply refused to explore her thoughts or feelings, refused to even fully acknowledge the attraction. Today she was simply going to enjoy the moment, every moment and not think beyond it.

It was time to set out for the woods and begin the task of collecting Christmas greenery. They broke into groups and loaded themselves into the pony carts. Rebecca found herself in the same conveyance as her brother, Lady Charlotte and Lord and Lady Bailey.

In high spirits, they chatted amicably. Servants drove them to the edge of the forest where they disembarked. The earl led the way into the woods, with the rest of the party straggling behind. They walked slowly, talking as they went and soon the ladies were clustered together and likewise the gentlemen were a separate group.

The three boys and Lily ran between them. The six gentlemen, of disparate ages, interests and temperaments, soon found common ground for conversation—what they quickly labeled the ridiculous demands of the women in the party.

"Whose idea was it to allow the women along anyway, Hampton?" Viscount Cranborne grumbled in a teasing voice. "This is man's work. The females will be in the way."

"Hampton invited the women because he knows you can't bear to have your wife out of your sight for more than ten minutes," Mr. Halloway replied.

"Actually, 'tis twenty," the viscount replied with a good-natured smile. "But I could stretch it to an hour—or more—if she doesn't stop telling everyone where to go and what to do."

"My cousin is a woman inclined toward strong opinions, lovable teasing and occasional blasts of temper, but it has gotten much worse since she married," the earl said. "You indulge her every whim."

Cranborne made a rude noise and the men laughed. "This criticism from a man who spoils his daughter beyond reason? Mark my words, Hampton, you are creating a miniature Marion."

The conversation ended as a thicket of lush holly bushes was discovered, with their dark green leaves and bright red berries. Several of the men, including the earl, began to cut sections of branches with the small saws they had brought along.

Lady Marion, ever the organizer, energetically arranged the pile of holly into bundles, then instructed the men to each carry one.

"It's prickly," the viscount declared, shaking his finger.

"It's holly, dear. It's supposed to pinch." Lady Marion broke off a small sprig from the bundle in her husband's arms and carefully tucked it in the ribbon band on the brim of her bonnet. A few of the other women imitated her actions. Rebecca selected a sprig also, but placed it in Lily's bonnet. The little girl smiled with delight and preened for anyone who glanced her way.

"The Druids believed that good spirits lived in the branches of holly," Lady Charlotte told everyone.

"Then I will help you find a few more branches to bring back to the manor," Daniel said. "One can never have too many good spirits sprinkled around the house."

Lady Charlotte smiled a shy reply. Rebecca noticed a flush of additional color beneath the rosiness that the wind and cold had whipped into Lady Charlotte's cheeks. The other woman's reaction called to mind the conversation she had with Daniel last night.

She hoped he would pursue his interest in the earl's sister, for clearly the lady held him in regard. How foolish of Daniel to forsake a chance at love, at happiness, on the ridiculous belief that the conventions of society were of greater importance.

Next on Lady Marion's list were evergreen boughs. After much discussion, it was decided to leave the holly bundles behind while the evergreens were gathered.

"You need to talk with Tremaine about some of his business ventures, Hampton," Sir Reynolds said as they continued tromping through the woods. "I'm certain he could find some project that needs investors."

The earl's brow lifted. "Why do I need additional investments?"

"Clearly you are hard up for cash. Or else you would have your servants taking care of harvesting the greenery."

"It is a tradition for the lord to participate," Lord Hampton said. "If you are feeling tired you are welcome to return to the manor to rest in front of the fire, Reynolds."

"Don't tempt me."

"A roaring fire sounds glorious, but my wife would have my head if I didn't participate," Viscount Cranborne admitted.

The men laughed.

"I give you fair warning, gentlemen, we also participate in decorating the manor," the earl said.

"'Tis a matter that my mother claims cannot be left for the servants and she takes great pride in her lavish decorations."

Several of the men groaned in mock horror. "Lord save us!" Mr. Halloway cried. "Days spent climbing up and down ladders and in and out of various niches and alcoves trying to hang greenery in a way that meets with the approval of an exacting female. If not for your well-stocked wine cellars, Hampton, I would leave tomorrow."

"I will take you all shooting in a few days," the earl promised. "That should lift your spirits."

"Cranborne can pretend the bird is holly and exact some revenge," Sir Reynolds quipped as he added another large bough to the ever-growing pile of greenery.

"Mistletoe, gentlemen," Lady Marion cried. "We have enough evergreens, so now we search for mistletoe. And as we all know, the very best of it grows in the tallest oak trees."

"My mother gave me specific instructions to make sure there was an abundance of it," Lady Charlotte informed them all.

"For the kissing boughs," Lily pipped up.

They turned to look at her and she covered her mouth with her hand and started giggling. Rebecca realized then that the little girl knew exactly what happened when a person was caught standing beneath one.

Once again the earl took the lead, bringing them through the woods to a section of tall oaks. For all their complaining about the indignity of climbing trees and ruining their perfectly polished boots, Rebecca thought the men scrambled rather nimbly up and down. And seemed to be enjoying themselves greatly in the process.

The women and children clustered around the base of the trees, shouting encouragement and spotting those particularly fine specimens that simply must be retrieved. Good-naturedly the men complied as they joked with each other at how ridiculous they must appear.

"We will all need naps when we return to the manor," Lady Marion declared. "All this fresh air and exercise is exhausting."

"I am too old to take a nap, cousin Marion," Lily declared.

"You will be a very grumpy little girl if you do not rest," Lady Charlotte warned.

Lily shook her head vehemently. "Papa promised to play backgammon with me today."

"That is a very grown-up game," Rebecca commented.

"I like it better than piquet," Lily said. "But Papa will play both if I ask him."

Startled, Rebecca turned to Lady Marion, certain she must have misheard. "Cards? But she's only six!"

"Smart as a whip, that one." Lady Marion clucked her tongue. "She plays better than many adults I've seen. Wagers like a professional, too."

"She gambles?" Rebecca squeaked in astonishment. "Her father allows it?"

Lady Charlotte blushed and lowered her gaze. "My brother is the one who taught her."

Rebecca's eyes widened in astonishment. As the daughter of a clergyman, she was raised to believe gambling was something to be avoided, especially for a lady.

"Why would he do such a thing?" Rebecca asked.

Lady Charlotte cleared her throat, then hastily glanced at Lady Marion. Neither woman said anything.

"It's because of my mother," Lady Marion finally

said. "A wonderful woman, to be sure, but bless her dear soul she lost a fortune at the card tables. We did not realize the extent of her problem until her death, when my father discovered the majority of her jewelry was paste."

"I don't understand," Rebecca admitted.

"Mother had sold the real gems to pay her gambling debts. To keep this disgraceful secret from my father, she had copies of her jewelry made in paste."

"Goodness."

"Precisely, and yet another reason I felt it imperative to marry a wealthy man." Lady Marion tilted her head upward, calling out to her husband. "Be sure to grab that lovely bunch on your left, dearest. It's so full and lush we can simply tie a ribbon around the stem and hang it over a doorway."

"If I can reach it without breaking my neck, it's going in our bedchamber, my love," the viscount replied.

Rebecca's glance swung back to Lady Marion. "Do you gamble, also?" she whispered.

"Gracious, no. I have never wagered on anything, not even a horse at the market day races. I know all too well this sort of thing can run in the blood," Lady Marion said ruefully. "I believe that is why Cameron taught Lily how to play. 'Tis far better to know how to wager properly—and win. It will save her grief in the end."

"Wouldn't it be better to encourage Lily never to gamble in the first place?" Rebecca inquired, astonished at this reasoning, when the earl obviously knew very well this gambling sickness could not be in a drop of Lily's blood.

"I expect he will do so when she is older," Lady Charlotte said.

"I, for one applaud his efforts to educate Lily," Lady Marion said in a firm tone. "And taking the time to do so himself is nothing short of extraordinary. Parents are rarely so avid and considerate. Christina and Cameron were quite unusual in that regard; always making time for their daughter. I intend to do the same whenever Richard and I are blessed with wee ones."

Viscount Cranborne, who was descending from the tree, nearly lost his footing as he caught the tail end of his wife's conversation. "Wee ones, Marion? As in babies?"

Lady Marion's face reddened. "Alas, I have no announcement to make at this time, but I hope soon to have . . ." She cleared her throat. "To have news."

Viscount's Cranborne's face turned pale and he leaned against the tree trunk for support. "Amazing."

"Don't look so triumphant," Lady Marion said with an affectionate grin. "We Sinclairs are a brazen lot. High strung and terribly spoiled, always getting into one scrape or another. Our children will no doubt be a singularly ill-behaved brood."

"Nothing would please me more," Viscount Cranborne replied in a dazed voice.

Lady Marion patted his arm. "Hush now. Such matters are not to be spoken of in genteel and mixed company."

Seeming not to care that anyone noticed, the viscount put his arms around his wife and kissed her soundly on the lips. Rebecca watched their obvious affection with a pang of envy. How wonderful, wonderful beyond imagining, it must be to share the excitement and anticipation of the birth of your child with the man you loved by your side.

"Enough of that, Cranborne," Sir Reynolds shouted. "You'll wear out the kissing power of the mistletoe if you keep it up much longer."

The couple parted, but Rebecca noted the viscount kept his arm around his wife's waist.

"Have we gotten everything on your list, Lady Marion?" Daniel asked.

"All that remains is the Yule log," she answered.

"To save time, we shall split into groups and each search a different section of the woods," the earl decreed. "The team that discovers the finest specimen will be granted a special prize on Christmas Eve."

"Come, Papa. You must help me and Miss Tremaine find the best Yule log!"

Then to Rebecca's utter astonishment Lily grabbed her hand and pulled her toward the earl. Rebecca could not tell if Lord Hampton was pleased or annoyed with the arrangement of having her as the third member of their group, but if he was, she knew he would not make a scene in front of Lily.

Everyone scattered, most in groups of two and three. Lily scampered eagerly ahead, bounding over fallen branches, skipping over roots, frolicking along like an eager young puppy.

"There's one," Lily shouted, pointing to a fallen branch. She ran over and the adults dutifully followed.

"Too small, Puss. It needs to fill the hall hearth and be thick enough to burn for many hours."

Undaunted, Lily tromped over the mossy earth, stopping at nearly every piece of wood she found.

"Too thin," the earl proclaimed.

"Too rotted," Rebecca judged.

"Too funny-looking," Lily decided, getting into the spirit.

"I have found it!" Rebecca declared with a happy yell. She stepped forward and patted the felled trunk of a majestic oak, heavy, thick and solid. It lay a few feet off the woodland path, resting atop a tangle of crushed underbrush.

"That's perfect," Lily squealed. "Isn't it perfect? Wait, I want to sit on it. Help me, Papa."

Lord Hampton lifted the little girl and settled her in the middle of the log.

"Up you go, Miss Tremaine," the earl said. With no warning, he reached around her waist and lifted her to sit beside Lily.

Rebecca's pulse skittered at the contact of his hands on her waist. Even through the layers of clothing she could feel the heat of his body. Though trembling, she forced herself to hold his gaze and sternly admonished herself to remain detached.

His face was smoothed into a blank, firm mask, but his hazel eyes had darkened to a shade that was nearly green. Scrambling to retain her balance and keep her dignity, Rebecca held her back ramrod straight. Then Lily snuggled closer and Rebecca felt herself relax, felt the tension and reserve melt away.

It was a moment of pure and simply joy. She looked down at their dangling feet and a lump of emotion swamped her throat, knowing this would be a memory to cherish. A bit of liquid dripped from the end of her nose. She fumbled in the pocket of her cloak, startled when the earl pressed a clean, white square of cloth into her hand.

She daintily blew her nose into the linen handkerchief, telling herself it was the cold, brisk air making her eyes water and her nose run.

"You too, Papa." Lily swung her feet rapidly and the log shifted slightly. Rebecca yelped in surprise, her hands clutching the wood. How utterly ridiculous would she feel if she fell off?

"Easy," Lord Hampton admonished Lily.

"I want you to sit up here too," Lily said.

Lord Hampton shook his head. "I shall break the log in two and then we will need to start our search all over again."

"But I liked the looking," Lily said.

"'Tis getting late. And cold. We need to signal the others and share our find," the earl countered.

"And then we will win the prize!" Lily shouted, her excitement restored. "I hope it shall be a very spectacular prize, Papa."

"I will endeavor to make it as special as possible, Puss." He reached out, placing his hand on Lily's knee to still her swinging legs. "You really should thank Miss Tremaine for our victory. After all, she was the one who found this magnificent log."

"Oh, yes, thank you ever so much," Lily cried with excitement.

Then she unexpectedly turned and threw her arms around Rebecca, pressing herself close. Startled, Rebecca gathered the child within her embrace, for a few precious seconds holding her tightly to her breast, inhaling her sweet, little girl scent.

Fresh tears gathered in Rebecca's eyes as a rush of pure love washed over her. It was, without question, the most emotional, joyful experience of her life and she greedily wished she could freeze this moment in time and hold it in her heart forever.

Chapter 9

Daniel smiled kindly at Lady Charlotte and offered her his arm, which she took after a moment of hesitation. With the Yule log found and their tasks completed, the cheerful group began the long walk back to the waiting pony carts. The earl promised a variety of refreshments, including hot cider and mulled wine, and to a person they all eagerly agreed they were famished. Viscount Cranborne admitted to be hungry enough to eat a horse, which struck Lady Lily as particularly funny and she giggled uncontrollably for several minutes.

Daniel and Lady Marion had tactfully slowed their steps, staying with Lady Charlotte, who by this point in the outing was no longer able to keep pace with the rest of the party. He noticed her limp had become more pronounced as the morning wore on and realized she must be very tired from walking nonstop for so long. Yet she never complained or asked that consideration be given to her infirmity and he admired her determination and inner strength.

It was difficult, though, to see her struggle, to imagine that she might be in pain. The temptation was strong to lift her into his arms and carry her the rest of the way, but he feared she would be dreadfully embarrassed by the attention. Besides, he did not have the right. And a part of him worried that she might object to being held in his arms.

"Please, do not feel you need to stay back here with me, Mr. Tremaine," Lady Charlotte said, her voice slightly winded. "I would not want you to miss any of the fun on my account."

She tried to quicken her pace, which caused a slight stumble. Daniel reached out to catch her, but she righted herself on her own. However, the sprig of holly she had jauntily placed in her bonnet ribbon dislodged and tumbled to the ground.

"Please, allow me." Daniel swooped down and retrieved the bit of greenery that had escaped the ribbon. Yet instead of replacing it, he pocketed the holly and placed a sprig of mistletoe in the original spot.

"I really am far too old to be doing something so frivolous as putting holly in my bonnet. Does it look silly?" she whispered.

"It looks lovely," he replied. "Just as you do."

He suspected her question was a direct reflection on the opinion she held of herself. Clearly, she thought she was staid and prim and matronly, and perhaps that is what others saw when they looked at her. If they even gave her a passing notice.

But that was not how he viewed her. Though her features were plain, he would not classify them as ordinary. She had a lopsided grin he found intriguing and a mouth blessed with plump, sensual lips. He had spent far too many hours these past days gazing at those lips, imagining what it would feel like to kiss them.

Today there was color in her cheeks from the chilly air and a light in her eyes from her enjoyment of the activities. She had a low, sweet voice he found especially appealing and he liked hearing her speak. There was an intelligence in her conversation that he appreciated and a dash of humor that often escaped when she allowed herself to relax.

He enjoyed being in her company. The opportunity to have a sustained discussion with a woman that went beyond the superficial, social niceties was unique to Daniel and in its own way oddly seductive. While others might easily dismiss her from consideration, Daniel thought her interesting and charming and utterly delightful.

"Oh, Charlotte, you are a bold one," Lady Marion said. She tapped her finger to her own bonnet and giggled. "I am so proud of you."

"Whatever do you mean, Marion?"

"I am caught, Lady Marion," Daniel interjected, belatedly realizing his little joke might embarrass Lady Charlotte. "The mistletoe is my doing."

"Mistletoe?" Lady Charlotte repeated in a faint voice.

He had done it on impulse, the fun and delight of the morning putting him in an uncustomarily frivolous mood. He had done it too because he had wanted to kiss her, had wanted to give in to the temptation of tasting those enchanting, sensual lips.

"You are a sly one, Mr. Tremaine," Lady Marion declared. "I approve."

With a parting smile, she hurried ahead to catch up with the others, leaving them alone.

"Whatever did Marion mean, Mr. Tremaine?"

"Daniel," he said softly. "My name is Daniel. Won't you please address me as such when we are alone?"

It was a bold, improper suggestion. As he expected, she blushed, yet he thought it a good sign that a hint of a mischievous smile curved at her lips. "If you will call me Charlotte."

"May we sit for just a moment?" He guided her to a fallen tree trunk belatedly realizing it would have served as an excellent Yule log.

"Now will you tell me what Marion meant about the mistletoe?" she asked as he sat beside her.

"I assume she was referring to the Christmas custom, invented no doubt by a gentleman, giving him the right to kiss any lady he catches beneath the mistletoe without the worry of having his face slapped."

"I know about the custom, Mr. Trem . . . Daniel."

"Yes, but what you did not know is that I replaced your sprig of holly. Instead, I have put a fat bunch of mistletoe in your bonnet, making it ridiculously easy for me to catch you standing beneath it and thus claim the right to kiss you."

He raised his hand and touched the rim of her bonnet, showing her where the mistletoe rested. Her mouth dropped open in an exclamation of surprise as her hand lifted to touch the spot on her hat. He saw her fingers curl over the greenery, which was soft and delicate and very different from the prickly holly she had put there earlier in the morning.

She turned away and dipped her head so far down that he could see the tender flesh at the arch of her neck and the wisps of hair that had escaped from the tight coil of her chignon. *Damn it!* She appeared mortified and he cursed himself silently for having embarrassed her.

There was a tense, short silence. He was just about to apologize when she lifted her head to look at him.

"And now that I am caught beneath the mistletoe, Daniel, what will you do?"

It was far more than he could have hoped. "I will

follow the custom, dear Charlotte. It would be rude not to, don't you agree?"

Heart pounding with anticipation, Daniel lifted his hand and cradled the back of Charlotte's head in his palm. Then he leaned forward and pressed his lips against hers. He did not give her a token, swift kiss, as was the custom between newly acquainted couples. He kissed her fully, deeply, with all the pent-up emotions swirling in his heart.

Her lips trembled noticeably and he felt her breath release just as his lips touched hers. Her mouth was exquisitely soft and he kissed her gently, tasting the fullness of her lips, those incredibly, sensual lips, that had driven him crazy for days.

He slanted his mouth this way and then the other, teasing at her mouth, first running his tongue lightly across her bottom lip, then drawing it between his teeth and gently sucking on it.

Her body relaxed and she melted toward him. Her unique, particular scent of lavender and lemon permeated his senses. Daniel tightened his hold on her neck, then eased his other hand down from her shoulder to the small of her back and urged her closer. Her lips parted on a small sigh and he took advantage of the opportunity to deepen the kiss.

Warm and sweet, she tasted so good. So incredibly delicious. Pleasure shuddered from her into him and he lost all sense of time and place.

Yet reality slowly intruded. They were in the woods, with others, including her brother, nearby. It had to stop. Reluctantly Daniel pulled away, though it felt as if every cell in his body was screaming for him to continue.

Charlotte's lashes fluttered and she slowly opened them. Her eyes were huge and deep and he fleetingly thought that if he gazed into them long enough he would catch a glimpse of her soul.

"I think, perhaps, that you were wrong about the mistletoe, Daniel," she said, her voice a breathless whisper. "In my humble opinion, the custom of kissing beneath it was surely started by a woman."

She smiled. He answered the grin with one of his own. More than anything Daniel wanted to sweep her into his arms and kiss her again. And again. If only circumstances were different! How much easier things would be if she were but a poor relation, or even a governess to the family? Then his interest would be accepted by her relations. It would not matter that he was not a member of society's elite or that he had made his money in *trade*.

A shout was heard up ahead.

Charlotte's head lifted and she gazed down the path. "We had better join the others or else we shall be left behind," she said.

Daniel felt a muscle in his jaw twitch. He wanted to protest, to suggest that they deliberately stay behind. However, he felt uncharacteristically hesitant with her, unsure of his position. A sharp contrast to how he usually handled all other aspects of his life.

He stood, extended his hand and helped her rise to her feet. She lifted her head and smiled her thanks and he noticed her face was flushed with a rosy glow of pleasure. He grinned, knowing his face would also reflect the same pleasure, for she had made him feel better than he had in a very long time.

Still, his mind was in turmoil as they started walking. He was a man who trusted his instincts, who had been successful because he made smart, calculated choices. And now that sensible, practical part of his brain was telling him rather forcefully how foolish indeed it would be to allow himself to fall in love with her.

Cameron stood at the window of his private study and stared out at the gathering clouds. It might actually snow soon and the very thought soured his mood. A blanketing of white would surely increase the excitement of the guests, not that it was needed. It seemed that nearly everyone was aglow with the anticipation of Christmas.

Except him. All this Christmas frivolity and good cheer was giving him a headache. He would be glad to return to London in a few weeks, back to the normal, predictable routine of his life. Yet now that Rebecca Tremaine had made her presence known, would his life ever be the same?

Cameron blew out a frustrated sigh and pondered what else he could do to diffuse the underlying tension permeating the air whenever they were together. He had managed to do an admirable job of being pleasant this morning, and she had responded in kind, but he suspected that was because Lily was near. One thing he had learned about Miss Tremaine these past few days; she would not make a scene in front of her daughter.

Her daughter. Good Lord, precisely when had he come to think of Lily as being *her* daughter?

Cameron made an impatient sound, annoyed with himself for dwelling too long on the matter. He wondered again if he had made a mistake by inviting Miss Tremaine and her brother to Windmere for the holidays, then felt irritated that he was second-guessing his decisions, something he rarely did under any circumstances.

Still, his choices had been limited. Ignoring the

problem because it was difficult and unpleasant was not going to make it go away. What he needed were distractions. Yes, that was it. He needed to fill his days with some of the distractions easily available at the estate, something that preferably had nothing to do with Christmas.

Several of the gentlemen had mentioned they would be gathering in the billiards room and Cameron decided he would join them shortly, even though he seldom played. But first, he needed to venture upstairs to the nursery and play one quick game of backgammon with Lily, as he had promised her.

It was unusually quiet when he reached the nursery doors and he suspected most of the children were napping at this time of day. It was part of the normal routine for the younger children, but after all the fresh air and exercise searching for greenery this morning, he would not be surprised to find the older boys asleep. Maybe even Lily was resting.

One benefit of this holiday was the number of children visiting. A few of the other parents had commented that it was too chaotic, but the earl was glad to see the nursery filled with boisterous youngsters, making the room alive with their laughter and joy and innocence.

As a boy he had loved his sister dearly, yet had longed for a larger family of brothers and sisters with which to play. He wondered fleeting if Lily too felt the lack of siblings in her life.

The nursery door was ajar. Cameron peered inside and saw Lily was the only child in the room. She was seated at her favorite wooden table, which was covered with a collection of her paper dolls and their ensembles. One of the younger maids, Molly, sat beside her. They were both engrossed in some sort of game.

"The tabs on this riding habit have come off," Lily complained. "I can't get it to stay on my doll. How will the queen go riding if she isn't wearing her habit?"

"Why, that's no problem at all," Molly said cheerfully. "I'll show you a trick. All we need to do is use a wee bit of wax and the dress will stay in place."

"Are you sure it will work?"

Molly nodded. Heads pressed together, they worked on getting the outfit affixed to the doll.

"There!" Smiling, the maid held up the paper doll for Lily's inspection and the little girl clapped enthusiastically.

"Let me try." Lily reached out and pulled the doll to her side of the table.

"Be sure to use just a small amount of the wax, Lady Lily," the maid warned. "Here now, be careful. And gentle, be very gentle. You don't want to rip the dress."

Her expression rapt with concentration, Lily fumbled with the wax and paper. Cameron saw Molly reach out to help, but Lily deliberately pushed the maid's hand away. Typically, she wanted to do it herself.

"Look what you did!" Lily cried out. "The hem is torn and the feather is ripped. Queen Victoria's gown is ruined. It's ruined!"

"No, it's not," the maid answered calmly. "We can fix it. Just wait a minute."

"No! Stop it! Don't touch it, you'll make it worse!" Lily's hand shot out and she tugged on the paper dress the maid held. The sound of it tearing filled the room.

"Oh, goodness," Molly exclaimed.

"It's ripped all the way! You are a stupid, stupid girl!" Lily threw the two halves of the paper dress onto the floor. Screeching with anger, she then swept her arms across the table, sending all the paper dolls and their various clothes flying about the room. Her usual sunny disposition disappeared completely as a full temper tantrum began.

"Now, what did you go and do that for?" Molly asked. "All the pretty dolls and their nice clothes are thrown on the floor."

"It's your fault," Lily cried. "You ruined everything, Molly."

The maid slowly shook her head, as if puzzled by that conclusion. "Well, then, who is going to clean up this mess?"

"You will!" Lily crossed her arms and stomped her feet. "You are the maid and I am the lady, so you need to clean it up. Do it now! This minute. Or else I am going to tattle on you and Mrs. Evans will be mad."

Cameron blinked, not certain if he was more stunned or angry at Lily's behavior. What he did know was that he had heard more than enough. He pushed the door completely open and stormed into the nursery.

"Oh, Papa." Lily's eyes filled with tears and she ran to him. "Molly is being ever so mean to me and she has ruined my very favorite outfit for Queen Victoria."

The maid jumped to her feet and turned toward him. She stood nervously next to the table, wringing the material of her white apron in her hands, the paper dolls and dresses scattered around her feet. He felt a bolt of sympathy for her.

"Where is Mrs. James?" Cameron asked.

The maid's eyes widened. "She went down to the servants' quarters to have her tea. She asked permission from Mrs. Evans and she said it would all right if I stayed with Lady Lily until Mrs. James returns."

"What happened here?" he asked.

Lily's eyes looked innocently back into his, her expression sweet and calm. "Molly made a mess, Papa. She ruined everything."

Cameron looked into the visibly frightened eyes of the maid and frowned. "Is that what happened, Molly. You made this mess?"

"No, my lord." Molly dropped to her knees and hastily began to scoop up the various paper dolls and their paper dresses.

"She did so make that mess!" Lily said in a high-pitched voice. "You need to send her away from here and tell her never to come back. She is disgraceful."

Disgraceful? Hmm, that sounded familiar. Was that not precisely how Mrs. James had described Lily's actions at the vicarage the other day?

Molly's features turned to stone. She slowly rose from her knees and carefully placed the items she had gathered from the floor onto the table. She bent down to continue with her task, but Cameron reached out a hand to stop her. The maid's eyes clouded with confusion.

Cameron tensed slightly as he considered the best way to handle the situation. In the face of so much childish emotion, he knew calm was called for, knew it was important to keep his own feelings of annoyance at bay.

He went down on his knees before Lily, meeting her face-to-face. Her crying had stopped, but her continued distress was evident in the way she bit her bottom lip.

"Will you look me in the eye and tell me precisely what happened?" Cameron asked.

She nodded.

"And will you promise this time to tell me the truth?"

Another nod.

"Molly ripped Queen Victoria's riding habit and

then threw the dolls and their clothes on the floor," Lily declared in a breathless rush.

He glanced at the maid. She looked back at him in mute appeal, obviously unsure if she could contradict Lily.

"Molly already told me she did not make this mess. Clearly, one of you is lying."

"It's wrong to lie," Lily whispered. She bit her lip and shut her eyes very tightly for a few moments.

"Yes it is wrong," he agreed. "I was outside the nursery door, Lily. I heard and saw all that happened."

Lily's eyes popped open. "Mrs. James says it's rude to eavesdrop on other people and listen to what they are saying."

"That might very well be, but in this case it was a good thing that I heard and saw what I did or else I would never have learned the truth. It was you who behaved badly and made this mess, not Molly."

He could practically see the denial spring to Lily's lips, but then she hesitated, thinking before she spoke. "I'm sorry."

Relieved she would not be so bold as to continue with the lie, Cameron decided to be lenient. "I am not sure what is worse, Lily, behaving so badly or lying about it. Now pick up your dolls and the clothes."

Her contrite attitude quickly vanished. "I don't want to," she declared, placing her hands on her hips.

Cameron slowly rose from his knees, his patience wearing thin. "If you do not clean this up, then I will put everything back in the box, take the box from this room and you will never see your dolls again."

Lily's eyes rounded with shock. "You can't do that! Those are my toys."

"They were given to you by me, a gift for my well-behaved daughter."

Her expression mulish, Lily contemplated her options. Eventually realizing she had none she stomped over to the table. Grumbling, she tossed the items Molly had placed on the table into the box, then picked up the few remaining paper items from the floor and threw them in too.

When she finished, she sat in her chair, crossed her arms and glared at him.

Cameron nearly laughed. She was a miniature version of a grand lady in a temper, her mood spoiled, her pride pricked. Heaven help him when she reached womanhood if she did not learn to control her temper.

"Now, you will apologize to Molly for your rude remarks," he ordered.

Lily jumped from the chair, her face a mask of six-year-old indignity. "Molly is a maid! I am a lady! Jane Grolier says you must always be bossy to your servants and give them orders. It keeps them in their place."

Cameron blew out his breath. When had his sweet-tempered little girl turned into such a tyrant?

"A lady treats everyone with kindness and respect. Your grandmother would never act so poorly toward anyone, be they servant or queen. Neither would Aunt Charlotte or cousin Marion. I am very ashamed of you, Lily."

Her lower lip jutted out rebelliously. Geeze, now what? Cameron worried that he might have to push the issue, but then Lily relented.

"I am sorry I yelled at you, Molly."

The maid's face relaxed in relief. "And I am sorry, that Queen Victoria's riding habit was ripped. If you'd like, I'll try to fix it for you."

Lily's eyes sparkled with eagerness. "Oh, yes. That would be grand."

"Tomorrow, Molly," Cameron said.

The maid nodded. She picked up the box of paper dolls and placed it carefully on the shelf. She straightened the area around the play table, then awaited further instructions. He dismissed her but before she left, Molly leaned forward and spoke to him in a confidential whisper.

"Lady Lily is tired this afternoon, my lord. That's why she was a bit out of sorts."

Cameron blinked in surprise. Being tired was hardly an acceptable excuse, but it bespoke well of Molly's character that she would defend the little girl after Lily had acted like such a brat.

The maid dipped a curtsy, then a second one, and whisked herself from the room.

Cameron's gaze returned to Lily. She was leaning against the table, her head bent, her finger idly moving over the surface of the wood. He knew he needed to mete out some sort of punishment for her behavior, nothing too severe, but something with enough impact that would make her think twice before acting so rudely again.

As a boy he had suffered an occasional caning for his youthful misdeeds but the idea of striking Lily made him physically ill. It would be better to punish her by taking away a privilege or refusing to allow her to participate in an activity she enjoyed. Yet it seemed especially mean-spirited to deny her during this holiday season, when many events would not take place again until next year.

Still, he had to do *something*.

"You have greatly disappointed me, Lily."

"I was very naughty," she agreed, her head still lowered.

He heard the regret in her voice. "Apologizing to

me for lying and to Molly for behaving so rudely was a proper start. But you must be punished."

She nodded solemnly.

Cameron swallowed. This was proving to be much harder than he thought. Her contrite, dejected attitude tore at his heart. He liked his feisty, spirited little girl, not this timid, sad creature.

Frantically, he racked his brain, trying to remember the type of discipline used to keep Charlotte from misbehaving. Yet he could not recall a single incident where his shy, gentle sister had disobeyed, though surely there must have been a few.

"I think it best if you not be allowed to have dessert for the remainder of the week," he finally proclaimed. "I shall inform Cook and Mrs. James."

Lily's shoulders rose as she let out a deep, shuddering sigh. He felt as though he was taking the breath with her. Relieved it was over, Cameron lifted her chin. She stared up at him, her eyes large in her small face.

His heart lurched. Cupping her face, he gently wiped away the tears coursing down her cheeks with his thumbs.

He was used to Lily's dramatic flux of emotions, the noisy, gulping sobs she seemed to be able to start and stop at the drop of a hat. Yet as much as it upset him to hear her loud wailing and noisy sobs, there was something far more disturbing about a child crying so silently.

"Please don't be mad at me anymore, Papa. Please."

"Oh, Puss."

He lifted her into his arms. She twined her arms around his neck and buried her face into his shoulder. Slowly, he rocked back and forth on his heels. This was part of the discipline, too. Forgiving her, but more importantly, reassuring her that he still loved her no matter how badly she had acted.

He continued moving to and fro and the gentle swaying motion calmed them both. Soon he felt the steady rise and fall of her breathing and realized Lily had fallen asleep. He walked out of the nursery, down the hall to her bedchamber and placed her on the bed.

She barely stirred when he removed her shoes, let out a soft, sleepy moan as he pulled the coverlet up to her chin to keep her warm.

Cameron's mind was heavy as he gazed down at the slumbering child, looking so innocent and angelic. But he knew it was an illusion. Her behavior this afternoon went beyond what could be blamed on exhaustion. Lily had been spiteful and nasty. Hearing her words and the tone she used had made his blood run cold.

It forced him to think back, to remember the times Charlotte had timidly suggested he not indulge Lily's whims so easily and so often. The occasions where his mother declared she needed a respite from Lily's high spirits. The numerous conversations where Mrs. James had tried to tactfully elicit his support in enforcing stricter behavior from her charge.

The distress and concern in Rebecca Tremaine's voice when she declared herself appalled at the temper tantrum Lily threw when they were at the vicarage. He almost laughed as he recalled his staunch defense of the child, his accusations that Miss Tremaine was overreacting to a situation she did not comprehend.

He knew now it was he who had been in the wrong and it was high time he faced the truth of the matter. Lily had many good qualities and those needed to be nurtured and encouraged. Likewise, she had several unattractive qualities, of which he had to claim partial responsibility. He had spoiled and indulged her too much, was in part a reason she was fast becoming a tyrant. And that was behavior he could not, and would not, tolerate.

With an exclamation of disgust, the earl moved from Lily's bedchamber and descended the staircase. This problem with Lily needed to be addressed head-on and he knew it was his duty to set the example and approve and as well as enforce the changes that were needed.

But even more daunting than tackling the challenge of getting his child's unruly attitude and behavior under control, was knowing that he owed Rebecca Tremaine an apology.

Chapter 10

Charlotte sat at her dressing table and stared at herself in the mirror. Her evening gown was a cream-colored creation that brought out the rosy hue in her cheeks. The flattering neckline allowed her to show-case a single strand of perfectly matched pearls with a diamond clasp, a gift from her parents on her twenty-first birthday. Her hairstyle was a cascading mound of soft, dark curls accented with a single satin ribbon woven through the design.

Was it possible? She looked almost . . . pretty. She shut her eyes at the fanciful notion, then quickly opened them. Amazingly, the same attractive woman was still reflected in the mirror. Yet Charlotte did not believe this fleeting glimpse of beauty she found came from her outward appearance. It was not the result of a gown of a flattering shade, nor a hairstyle that was softer and more youthful.

The beauty came from within. It came, she was convinced, from the kiss she had shared this afternoon with Daniel Tremaine. Her first kiss. The most perfect kiss in the world.

It was still difficult to believe it had actually happened. 'Twas a moment void of reality, a dream, a secret longing come to life. For her, Daniel's kiss was a perfect treasure, a memory that she could hold in her heart and cherish. A memory that she could revisit, a moment that she could relive, when the loneliness and emptiness in her life became too strong.

Charlotte sighed. Raising her hand she slowly skimmed her fingertips over her lips, remembering every sensation, every feeling. Never in her wildest dreams had she imagined the delicious sensations that would claim her body, the emotional fullness that would embrace her heart when he held her close. When his lips claimed hers.

Daniel's kiss had been the most wondrous event in her dull, staid life. It had been enchanting, intoxicating and far more spectacular than anything she had ever experienced. Or hoped to experience.

For one brief, enchanting moment, it felt as if anything were possible. For the first time in her life, Charlotte dared to believe that she could indeed achieve the secrets of her heart. She could somehow miraculously find the love she had always craved, but had long ago ceased dreaming she would be lucky enough to share.

Fluttering with a sudden dash of nerves, Charlotte cleared her throat. Too much thinking, too much wishing and too much hoping was dangerous. Her heart, so fragile and innocent, was vulnerable. It would take very little for it to shatter.

She shook her head sternly, telling herself that she had to be mistaken, had to be reading too much into the kiss. Leaning forward, Charlotte studied herself more closely in the mirror, then released another sigh of confusion. She saw nothing in her reflection that would inspire passion, nothing that would entice a man as handsome and accomplished as Daniel Tremaine to kiss her.

Charlotte made an impatient sound, annoyed with herself for being so fanciful and impractical. It was just a kiss! One of many for him, no doubt. Determining her only course of survival lay in being practical, she pulled her gaze from the mirror.

Joining the guests gathered in the drawing room before the evening meal, Charlotte reminded herself that she needed to be casual, to forget that the kiss was anything of importance or significance.

Yet the moment she entered the room, her eyes deliberately sought out Daniel. He was engaged in conversation with several gentlemen, no doubt talking of business. The thought made her feel proud. She sensed he was uncomfortable with his extensive involvement in business, for he believed it marked him as less of a gentleman, but she thought his accomplishments were admirable, a clear example of his good character and intelligence. In her eyes, they made him more attractive, not less.

She suspected he worried that living too long among the Americans had left him with some of their uncouth manners, but Charlotte could not have disagreed more. She thought his manners impeccable and felt his forthright manner was honest and refreshing.

He might misguidedly think that earning his own way and making his own fortune somehow made him less of a gentleman, but she believed it made him more of a man.

"You seem preoccupied lately, Charlotte. Is everything all right?"

Startled, Charlotte pulled her gaze away from Daniel and looked up at her brother. Cameron was smiling pleasantly at her, but the corners of his eyes were wrinkled with puzzled concern.

"I'm fine, Cameron. Just feeling a little tired from today's outing, that's all."

"If you are tired, then you should rest. I will call for your maid to help you to your bedchamber. It's not necessary for you to be in attendance for every event."

"You shall do nothing of the kind," she replied sharply. "I wish to stay. 'Tis only dinner, for goodness sake. I'm not so frail and fragile that I am unable to sit at the table and eat my meal without exhausting myself."

She flushed slightly as Cameron's brow rose in surprise. Her unaccustomedly strong reaction startled her brother, but she was pleased she had made her opinions known. Though it might have been wiser to express them more serenely. Fearing he might begin to suspect there was another reason she was so insistent on being at dinner, Charlotte turned to walk away.

"We seem to have a lively group this year," Cameron said, clearly not wanting her to leave.

The opening was simply too good to miss. Charlotte slowly pivoted to face her brother, who was now smiling again. "It is a nice mix of old friends and relations and new faces," she said. "Though I was curious about Mr. Tremaine and his sister. How precisely are you acquainted with them?"

The smile remained in Cameron's face, but his body went taut at the question. "Tremaine and I are exploring various business ventures."

"Over the holidays? That cannot be the only reason you invited them. I understand that the focus of Mr. Tremaine's life is his work, but that is not true in your case."

"My hands may not reek of trade, but I do have

various business interests," Cameron said vaguely. "Some of them involve Mr. Tremaine."

Charlotte's brows lowered. Somehow this did not seem quite right. At her encouragement, Daniel had spoken with her about several of his current projects. He had mentioned that Lord Bailey and Mr. Selby were significant investors, but never said anything about her brother.

"I'm surprised to hear this," she said. "On the few occasions I have been in company with the two of you, I sensed an undercurrent of animosity."

"We are exploring business ventures," he repeated. "Various business ventures."

Was that true? He spoke too forcefully and one too many times to be so easily believed, she thought. There was more to this than Cameron was going to say, of that Charlotte felt certain.

She studied her brother closely, noting his increasing discomfort. His agitation stirred her own. What was he hiding?

The sound of laughter reached her ears. She turned away from her brother and saw Marion had insinuated herself in the middle of Daniel's group of the gentlemen. In her customary style, Marion had them all joking and smiling, but Daniel had averted his attention elsewhere.

To Charlotte.

He was looking at her in open admiration. Charlotte felt a flash of joy followed immediately by a jolt of suspicion. Was Daniel's interest in her a sham? Was he using her in hopes of gaining greater access to her brother for these various business ventures?

Or even more humiliating, had Cameron arranged for Daniel to pay attention to her? As a favor, or a condition, of investing in one of his projects.

How horrifying if that were true? Yet Charlotte knew her brother would not consider Daniel a proper suitor for a woman of her rank. But he was certainly acceptable as a holiday flirtation. The very idea was almost too humiliating to consider, but it might explain his interest in her.

"How lovely to see you, Lady Charlotte." Daniel had broken away from the group and come to her side. Cameron had also disappeared. They were alone together.

He brought her trembling hand to his lips and pressed a gentle kiss against the back of her glove. All the while his gaze remained on her face and a serious, intent expression favored his features.

Charlotte's heart fairly tripped over itself. She knew it would be best to ask him directly about his relationship with her brother, to discover if there was some ulterior motive for his interest in her. She opened her mouth to ask the questions, but could not get the words to come out.

"Is something wrong, Lady Charlotte?" he asked.

"Ladies and gentlemen, dinner is served," the butler announced.

Oh, bother. More than anything, Charlotte wished she could take Daniel's arm and be escorted into the dining room, but he was not her partner for the meal. Reluctantly, she accepted Sir Reynolds's escort, vowing to have a hand in the seating arrangements for tomorrow night's supper so she would be seated near Daniel.

She noted that Marion was his dinner companion and the stab of jealousy she felt at her cousin's good fortune to be near him was staggering. Embarrassed at her uncharitable thoughts, Charlotte made a special effort to engage her dinner companions in conversation, yet time and again her gaze strayed to the opposite end of the table.

She had just lifted a fork full of creamed peas into her mouth when Daniel looked back and his gaze met hers. Instantly Charlotte felt as if all the air had been pulled from the room. The buzzing conversation and merry laughter faded away and for a moment, a splendid, glorious moment, it seemed as if they were the only two people in the room.

She struggled to keep her features composed, but she realized he would be able to see his effect on her. Daniel knew everything.

It got even worse when the meal ended. Music and dancing was abandoned for the evening in favor of cards and backgammon. Charlotte hesitated, waiting too long to join a table, then found that she and Daniel were left as the odd couple without partners. They made their way to a comfortable couch secluded in the corner of the room.

"Shall we play Beggar My Neighbor?" he asked with a smile.

"I haven't played that since I was nine."

"Excellent. I am assured of a win."

Charlotte laughed. "Hardly."

He produced a deck of cards and expertly shuffled. Her eyes stayed on his hands, which were large, yet elegant, with strong, tapered fingers. She thought them beautiful.

"So, what shall our opening wager be?" he asked.

"Though I have not played since I was a little girl, in all fairness, I must warn you. I am very good at this game."

"Ah, I appreciate your honesty. I fear my fortune is in grave peril. We must therefore find something else of value to wager. I confess, I can think of only one thing, but 'tis most improper."

Charlotte's face heated at the innuendo. Daniel gave her a rakish grin and began to deal.

She adjusted her position on the couch, reached over and began absentmindedly rubbing her left calf. It had begun to cramp and the pain was intensifying. She pressed her fingers into the knotted muscle for a few moments, until she suddenly realized where she was and what she was doing. Mortified, she pulled her hand away and sat up straight. But it was too late. Daniel had seen.

She had long ago accepted her disfigurement as something she could not ever change. Railing against the unfairness of fate, crying about it, wishing and hoping for it to be different was simply a waste of time and energy. Though he professed not to notice, she could not help but feel embarrassed by her limitations, by her imperfections. In front of Daniel she did not want to appear less of a woman.

He said nothing about her odd behavior and she was grateful. But then he set the remaining cards he had not yet dealt down and moved to sit in the padded footstool in front of her. Curious, Charlotte watched, then nearly jumped out of her seat when he put his hand on her calf.

"My goodness, Mr Tremaine . . . Daniel. Whatever are you doing?" she asked, attempting to push his hand away.

"I know this is inappropriate, but please forgive me. I cannot bear to see you suffer," he replied. Carefully keeping her foot and leg covered, he held her knee with one hand and began rubbing her calf with the other. "Is this where it hurts?"

It was precisely the spot. Charlotte could feel the muscle tighten and spasm and her embarrassment grew. No one, except a doctor or physician, had ever touched her feeble leg.

"This is highly improper," she hissed.

"Everyone else is involved with their gaming," he said. "No one is taking any notice of us."

Unsuccessful in pushing him away, she instead tried to pull her leg back, but his grip was too strong. Not wanting to create a scene, and draw attention to what they were doing, Charlotte sat very still. His fingers continued to massage and she gradually began to relax.

"The cramp is easing," she said, sitting up higher against the cushions. "Thank you."

He patted the top of her knee, then gently placed her foot on the floor. "I want you to tell me if it begins to tighten again."

"Oh, yes." She agreed only to shift his attention away from her leg, knowing she would sooner hack off the limb than say anything.

"I mean it." Daniel put his index finger beneath her chin and turned her head with the barest touch. Unmistakable warmth flickered in his eyes. Charlotte felt herself suddenly quiver with expectation. *Kiss me. Oh, please, kiss me.*

He seemed tempted, yet he did not lean any closer. He removed his hand and Charlotte nearly screamed in vexation, her disappointment keen. If she moved just slightly in his direction, perhaps then he might . . . ?

The kiss in the woods had been so glorious. She had thought of little else, except an opportunity to have another. And this seemed like the perfect chance.

Her eyes darted toward the ceiling, wishing there was a sprig of mistletoe near, but the greenery collected this afternoon had not yet been hung. Discomforted, she lowered her chin and narrowed her gaze. Daniel continued to smile pleasantly at her, seeming not to understand her wishes. Or perhaps he did not want to kiss her?

More than anything she wanted to lean forward and touch her lips to his, but her inhibition and fear of rejection held her back. Ladies did not throw themselves at handsome, virile gentlemen. Especially spinsters with ungainly limps.

A sense of emptiness suddenly filled her, along with a deep, painful ache for the things she might never have in her life. A wonderful romance, an enduring love, a grand passion. A husband and children to love and share the joys and trials of life.

With a sigh of real regret, she leaned back against the cushions. At her movement, the indecision in Daniel's eyes vanished and without further warning, he leaned forward and kissed her.

By necessity it was quick, since they could easily be seen by others in the room. Yet it was deep and passionate and full of exquisite promise.

Charlotte was quite breathless when it was over. A quick scan at the gaming tables verified that no one had seen. She flicked up the fan that dangled from her wrist, opened it and fanned away the sudden rush of warmth from her face.

He gave her a roguish smile when he noticed the gesture and she felt a blush starting anew. But along with the blush, a niggling sense of doubt bloomed at the true reason for the kiss. Dare she believe he wanted her for herself?

"Excellent play, Miss Tremaine," the earl said as she put down the final card. Their opponents groaned and she tried not to gloat at another victory. It was rather bad manners to continually trounce one's opponents at cards, but the earl seemed to be having a grand time and Rebecca was enjoying it as well.

After observing the quiet, steady determination the earl had displayed during the past few hands, she understood why he was such a formidable man. Though they played as a team, she acknowledged that she mostly followed his lead. Their constant wins were due to him.

It was not just the earl's experience at the card game that set him apart. It was the way he played. True, this was but a friendly game, with no real wagering. Nevertheless, the earl's quiet, confident demeanor rattled Lord Bailey, forcing him to make foolish errors and costly mistakes.

If not for the ladies present, the amiable atmosphere might have deteriorated to a cold tension. As it was, it seemed prudent to end the competition before it moved beyond a friendly evening of cards.

Congratulating the opposing couple on a well-played match, Rebecca excused herself and pushed her chair back. The earl did the same and somehow their knees bumped beneath the table. A heated spark rushed through her limbs.

Rebecca's head turned. Amusement mixed with a hint of challenge gleamed in the earl's eyes. She opened her mouth, preparing to give him a royal set-down. But then he shifted, increasing the contact between his leg and hers.

"Do you have a moment?" he asked. "I need to speak with you."

Rebecca offered him a smile she prayed did not appear as tight as it felt. "I am listening."

The earl shook his head. "Not here. Meet me in my private study in ten minutes. Do you know where it is located?"

She nodded. It was hardly proper, or prudent, to be alone with him, but she assumed the conversation would involve Lily. For that, privacy was needed.

It seemed that several of the other tables of card players were also shifting partners. The dowager countess was insisting Lady Marion team with her for the next set, while Viscount Cranborne joked with Mr. Halloway about wanting to face a far less clever opponent than his wife. Seizing the moment, Rebecca slipped away unobserved and made her way to the earl's study.

A fire burned in the hearth, but no candles had been lit. Rebecca quickly remedied that and the room was soon bathed in the soft glow of candlelight. She started toward the grouping of chairs near the fireplace, but did not sit down. Instead, she gazed up at the portrait of a young woman hanging above the marble mantel.

She was gorgeous. A blond angel with huge, expressive eyes of an unusual shade of violet that matched the color of her stylish gown. Her eyes twinkled, her face glowed with a vibrancy that went beyond an artist's skill. Even on the flat surface she was embodied with beauty and vigor.

She was smiling, confident and happy. And achingly young. There was no name placard, but Rebecca knew it had to be the earl's late wife. How sad and tragic to be cut down in the prime of one's life. And how true that life, as usual, was seldom fair.

"The portrait was painted the year before Christina fell ill," the earl explained, as he came into the room to stand beside her. "It was only recently taken out of storage. For a long time I could not bear the sight of it, but now I am very glad I have this memory of her at a time when she was happy and healthy. It brings some measure of comfort."

Clearly, he had loved her deeply. The remnants of pain were still evident in his voice.

"I am sorry," Rebecca said softly.

He accepted her sympathy with a nod. "Even with the passing of time, it is still difficult."

"Yes."

He drew a deep breath. "For a while, after she died, the grief unmanned me, nearly paralyzed me, really. Through necessity, I learned to live with it." He regarded her through serious eyes. "I imagine it has been the same for you."

A deep pain seared through Rebecca's heart. Though she thought of Philip nearly every day, she rarely spoke of him. "One does learn how to go on, but it's a pain that never completely heals."

"There are those who say it makes you stronger."

"Rubbish."

A ghost of a grin appeared on his face and Rebecca was glad he agreed. Dare she believe that she and the earl had more in common than either of them wished to acknowledge?

"Would you care for a drink?" he asked.

Rebecca knew she should decline. She was nervous enough in his company and needed to keep her wits about her. Yet without waiting for her reply, the earl poured wine into a glass and took it to her.

She accepted it routinely, yet this close she had to look up at him to meet his gaze. He continued to stare at her and she found the sensation disconcerting. He took a step closer and her breathing deepened. His eyes darkened with emotion and for one wild moment she thought he meant to try and seduce her.

Which was utterly ridiculous. She was most certainly

the last person on earth the earl would find appealing. Still, his nearness shattered the calm she was struggling to achieve.

"Are you afraid of me?" he asked.

She laughed softly, pride forcing her to lift her head higher and stare steadily back at him. "I do not fear you, my lord."

"Then you don't like me very much."

"Nonsense," she answered, tempted to tell him that a part of her liked him far too much indeed. Rebecca lifted the glass to her lips to prevent herself from blurting out that humiliating fact.

"Tell me what is wrong."

"If I tell you, it will anger you and I do not wish to argue." *Especially when I know I will not win!* "Let me say only that I am struggling to accept the fact that you are in control of how Lily is being raised. Especially since we cannot seem to agree on the proper way for her to behave. In fairness, I presume you will concede it is a difficult situation for me, but let us leave at that, please."

He gave her a perplexed glance. "You will no doubt be pleased to learn my opinion has recently undergone a change."

"Really?" Rebecca studied the contents of her wine goblet, surprised to see half the liquid gone.

He poured more wine in their glasses.

"Thank you, my lord," she said, even as she told herself firmly she would not drink it.

"Cameron," he said.

"Pardon?"

The earl studied her over the rim of his wineglass. "My name is Cameron. I would like you to call me that when we are alone."

Rebecca's brow rose suspiciously. It seemed far too

intimate a gesture and not at all in keeping with his character. "Why?"

"It pleases me." He took a swallow of his wine and she did the same, stopping abruptly when she realized what she was doing. "My sister asked me earlier this evening about you and your brother. How I knew the two of you? How you had come to be invited to the Christmas celebration this year?"

Rebecca went very still. "What did you say?"

"As little as possible."

"I am sure that was best," she said, her face growing warm.

"Her inquiries were innocent, to be expected, I suppose. Yet I confess to worrying that someday, somehow the truth about Lily will come out," he admitted. "'Twould be disastrous."

"Secrets of such magnitude are difficult to keep," she said slowly, trying to sound matter-of-fact. "But it is possible. It helps also that there are so few who know the truth. There are only three of us; you, me and Daniel."

"Hmm."

A dark heaviness pressed against Rebecca. More than anything she wanted Lily to know the truth, but the risk seemed too great, the consequences too high. If others in society learned she was a bastard, even Lord Hampton's position and influence would not fully protect the little girl.

"Do you want us to leave? Has the chance of exposure become too great?" she asked, her heart thumping with fear. To go now after having a brief taste of being with her child would be agony, but if it was necessary, Rebecca was prepared to make the sacrifice.

He gave her an alert glance. "Would you go?"

"Reluctantly." The moment the word was spoken, Rebecca was swamped in a feeling of bleakness, a sorrow almost beyond tears. "Today was a wonderful day. I did not realize, but I have not truly celebrated the Christmas season for many years. Six to be precise."

She saw he seemed to grasp the significance of the number.

"Lily enjoyed herself too."

"She did. I saw her briefly this evening before I came down for supper." Rebecca smiled as she recalled the conversation. "For some reason, she seemed very interested in the dessert at dinner tonight. She mentioned several times that a raspberry trifle would be served, which she informed me was her very favorite. I'm not sure why, but she did not have any with her meal, so I promised to ask Cook if she would set a portion aside for Lily to eat tomorrow."

"Oh, she did?"

"Why are you scowling? Did I do something wrong?"

He stared at her quizzically. "Did Lily happen to mention why she did not eat the dessert?"

"No."

"She is too clever by half. Regrettably I must admit you were right about Lily's behavior." He lowered his head and stared into his empty wine goblet with a brooding expression. "I heard her this afternoon with one of the housemaids. Molly was kind enough to entertain her, but when Lily did not get her own way the situation rapidly deteriorated. It was not pretty."

Rebecca could only imagine the tantrum. "She can be willful. And demanding."

"She was incorrigible. And rude. And certainly old enough to know better."

A light of understanding dawned on Rebecca. "So you punished her by denying her dessert this evening."

"That was the plan. First I had to wait until the

raging tears had degenerated into sobs and hiccups before meting out my verdict. Yet she managed to neatly outfox me."

"Well, she hasn't gotten her trifle yet. Nor will she, now that I know the situation."

"Don't be too sure," he responded. "You are not the only one she can ask."

"She is clever. But at her core, she is a good child, with a kind and generous heart," Rebecca said, feeling strange at assuming the role of champion and protector. "What Lily needs is practical guidance and a firm hand."

Cameron darted a worried glance at her. "Is Mrs. James up to the task?"

"I don't know."

"Would you speak with her? I have never before questioned her methods of dealing with Lily, but I'd like your opinion of Mrs. James's abilities and temperament."

"I am honored that you would consider my opinion on the matter and would be more than pleased to do as you ask. Though from my observations, I will say that Mrs. James seems perfectly adequate; a competent and caring woman."

Rebecca set down her wineglass to prevent herself from drinking any more, though she acknowledged the alcohol was responsible for her honest bravado in their conversation.

"Forgive my blunt manner, but from what I have observed, you are the problem, not Mrs. James. Lily knows she can get away with most things because no matter how awful she acts, you will protect her from any substantial punishment."

"I did make an attempt to change that perception by being firm with her today." Cameron's voice roughened with misery. "And all I can say is that it was bloody difficult punishing her."

She saw the despondency in the earl's eyes and it gave her pause. His confusion was complete, his frustration genuine.

Rebecca settled a gentle hand on Cameron's arm and leaned closer. "Lily worships you and loves you unconditionally. I know 'tis hard to disillusion someone when they hold you in such great esteem, but in this case it must be done."

"Am I so pathetic that I need the approval of a six-year-old girl?"

Rebecca squelched the impulse to wrap her arms around him, denying her instinct to soothe and ease his mind. But something in her expression must have alerted him to her feelings of empathy. He moved closer, no longer standing a respectable distance from her.

Rebecca's maternal instincts to comfort vanished, replaced by a sexual awareness. With each breath she drew in the scent of him, the tartness of his subtle cologne, the intoxicating aroma that was so unique to him. Her entire body suddenly ached, almost as if the intense emotions of the past few days were bubbling to the surface.

The subtle power of the earl's hard, masculine essence surrounded her, enveloped her. Rebecca felt her body leaning toward him, in anticipation of what would come next. A tension simmered between them.

"Rebecca."

She gazed up at him. His face lowered toward hers, his hand slid to the back of her neck. He brushed against her mouth with his own very gently, a soft, wisp of lips touching lips. It felt warm and firm. It felt wonderful.

She felt his hand go around her waist, gripping her

flesh with a force that should have caused her discomfort but felt secure instead. He kissed her again, angling his head and pressing strongly.

All question of right and wrong fled from Rebecca's conscience as she parted her lips and allowed his tongue to caress the softness of her mouth. She stayed quietly in his embrace, feeling a delicate warm glow start in the pit of her stomach.

Their tongues twined, playfully, erotically. It felt so achingly good. She spread her hand over his chest and let herself go, let herself enjoy the moment, savor the sensation. How long had it been since she had felt wanted? Desired? A long time. A very long time.

He was so careful, so gentle. Her body hummed with the desire for more. She heard herself moan. Rebecca was filled with the urge to press her entire body against him, but she held back. She feared this could so easily escalate into unbridled passion.

Boldly she ran her tongue over his bottom lip, lingering for a moment. Then slowly, almost regretfully, she pulled herself away.

Their final kiss ended with a soft murmur. He ran his lips across her cheekbones, down her jawline to her throat, pausing for an instant on the vulnerable spot along the curve of her neck.

And then his touch was gone.

Their arms dropped, nearly at the same time, as they each took a step back, a step away. For a long moment Rebecca just stood there, stunned by the kisses. Cameron stared down at her and made a sound that was midway between a laugh and a groan. His breath came quick and hard as his eyes bore into her.

She forced herself to hold his gaze, even as it made her tremble. He blinked and in that moment she glimpsed his puzzled vulnerability, his equal amazement at what had just happened between them.

Acting instinctively, Rebecca put her hand on his cheek. Cameron pressed his head against her palm. She raised herself on her toes, leaned in toward him and then surprised herself by pressing her lips against his other cheek.

"Good night, Cameron," she whispered.

Turning, she left the room, her heart and mind in a whirl. Lord only knew what complications would emerge from this new twist in their relationship!

She let out a slight, nervous laugh and climbed the staircase to her bedchamber. It was time to retire, time to reflect and regroup. She did not regret the kisses precisely, for it had been wonderful and something they both clearly wanted. Yet Rebecca could not deny that in hindsight, it might have been better to have stayed at odds with each other.

Chapter 11

Hell and damnation, what have I just done?

Cameron stared about the empty room and groaned. Of all the idiotic, undisciplined, insane things! He was embarrassed and angry with himself as he realized for all the momentary pleasure it had brought him, kissing Rebecca Tremaine had been an extremely bad idea.

He scratched his head, at a loss to comprehend why she had captivated him so thoroughly. Was it the forbidden aspect of the association, the knowledge that he wanted her so intensely simply because he knew it was unwise, almost dangerous to get involved? Was he honestly that shallow a man, that narrow a thinker?

True, he had not been with a woman since Christina, which would account for his sexual response. Frankly, he had not been interested in other women. Not respectable, decent women. After experiencing a loving, monogamous relationship, the idea of bed hopping among those women of society willing and eager to engage in an affair held no appeal for him. Likewise, the idea of keeping a mistress smacked of a business arrangement, devoid of emotional commitment.

He missed the physical release of a passionate sexual

encounter, but had learned to adjust. Yet Rebecca's kiss had breached his defenses; her kiss had somehow unleashed his sexual desire, yet it was more than sex. She had awakened within him all the tender, vulnerable feelings he thought had been buried with his wife.

What in the hell had ever possessed him to kiss her? Impulse? Opportunity?

He had been aroused by her nearness, but had managed to ignore it on other occasions. What was so different about tonight? She had looked fetching, of course, but then she always did. It had been fun trouncing Lord Bailey and his partner at cards. He and Rebecca had played well together, synchronized in strategy, near equals in skill. Had that created the connection?

Perhaps it had been the way she took the news about Lily, with sympathy and understanding of his dilemma? She had not tossed his mistaken attitude back at him with a superior air, claiming she knew the truth all along, berating him for not seeing it sooner. She had been kind and gracious.

And in return he had acted upon his base impulse and kissed her. Worse, he knew he should not and yet he had done it anyway. To his discredit.

Frowning, Cameron shifted to relieve the growing discomfort in his trousers. This unwanted desire for her was bloody unacceptable. Yet even more volatile was confirming that she felt the same degree of attraction for him.

The fervor of her response was something he needed to push firmly from his memory. And when the kisses had ended, instead of slapping his face, she had offered him comfort and understanding in a gesture nearly as intimate as the kiss they had shared. That almost bothered him more.

Cameron tossed back the wine remaining in his goblet, but refrained from refilling it. Alcohol was not the answer. Besides, his wits were befuddled enough.

As much as he wanted to deny it, he did admire Rebecca. She had character and principles. A quick mind and a sharp wit. She did not find it imperative to fill silences with nervous chatter or silly questions as so many other women he knew did. There was also a quiet patience and self-possession in her manner he found restful and comforting.

Cameron headed toward the fireplace, his eyes drawn to Christina's portrait. In many ways their life together seemed like a very distant memory. Had it truly been three years since her death?

The sharpest pain of loss had dulled, thankfully overtaken by a recollection of the happy times they had shared. Cameron felt grateful he could still recall Christina's musical voice, her merry laugh, her loving touch. He remembered too, her generous spirit. There was no doubt in his mind that she would want him to move forward with his life, that she would want him to be happy.

With Rebecca Tremaine? Christ, where had that thought sprung from? A life with Rebecca. Was it possible they would find happiness together given the peculiar circumstances that formed their initial connection or would it be a disaster?

Heaven help him, he simply did not know.

He should return to his guests, yet Cameron remained near the fireplace, one arm resting across the mantel, the other hand deep in his pocket. His expression was perturbed, as he was reminded of those kisses, something he should forget. Or better still, something that never should have occurred.

He heard someone enter. For a moment his heart

raced, thinking Rebecca had returned. But it was his mother who stood in the doorway.

"Oh, here you are, Cameron. I was wondering where you had gone." The dowager countess peered about the room as though she expected to see another person. "Is everything all right?"

"Yes, of course." Cameron picked up the poker and stirred the fire, angling himself so his face, and other parts of his anatomy, were concealed in the shadows.

"First Charlotte disappears and then you. I'm not sure what to make of it."

Cameron cleared his throat. "I apologize, Mother. There was an urgent matter that needed my attention. As all of our guests seemed occupied, I did not think it rude to leave for a few moments."

"It seemed that you were gone for more than a few minutes." The dowager countess crossed to the fireplace and held out her hands to capture the warmth. "I noticed Miss Tremaine in the hall on my way here. I presume she was your important business?"

Cameron's eyes darkened. The last thing he needed was his mother's involvement. She had broadly hinted for the past year that he needed to think about marrying again. It was his duty, to his family and his title. As much as they all loved and adored Lily, she would be unable to inherit the earldom or any of the entailed property. For that, a son was required.

"I had but a brief word with Miss Tremaine," Cameron said. "And I presume Charlotte has taken herself off to bed. You know how company tires her."

"I am not certain of that at all. Your sister has been acting a bit oddly. Surely you have seen it too? Did you notice her gown this evening? And her hairstyle? Something is definitely different and it is more than just the absence of her spinster's cap. It troubles me."

Cameron sighed wearily. "I am unaware of any significant changes."

His mother eyed him sharply. "Then clearly you have other matters on your mind. One would have to be blind not to notice Charlotte's transformation."

Cameron gave the fire one final jab, then replaced the poker. His mother was not by nature a meddlesome woman. She had shown a marked, though not overbearing, interest in her children when they were younger and offered counsel as they grew older. No matter what their age, she had championed them in times of crisis.

She had not, nor did she appear, interested in dictating the course of their lives as they became adults. Cameron sincerely hoped that was not about to change.

"I will make certain to compliment Charlotte on her looks the next time I see her," he said.

"I doubt 'tis you she is trying to impress. I have noted that she seems to be spending a great deal of time with Mr. Tremaine." He heard her skirts rustle as she came near. She sent him a significant glance. "What can you tell me of him?"

Cameron held back a grimace. What was going on with the women in his family? First his sister and now his mother. Why was everyone so bloody interested in Daniel Tremaine?

"He is a business acquaintance," Cameron said, deciding if this kept up he really was going to have to make an investment in one of Tremaine's projects in order to give validity to that claim.

"I see." The dowager countess paused to make sure she had her son's complete attention. "You know I never bother my head with that sort of thing, so perhaps that is why I have never heard of him until recently. However, I still do not understand exactly how he and his sister came to be part of our holiday guest list. You rarely entertain your business contacts at home and certainly never over the holiday season."

"Are you questioning who I may invite to share our holidays, Mother?" he asked, scowling.

"I assure you there is no need to take that tone with me, Cameron." His mother looked offended for a full heartbeat before continuing. "I only ask because I am concerned. About your sister. I cannot help but think if she is forming an attachment to Mr. Tremaine, as I am beginning to suspect, it will most assuredly lead to heartache for Charlotte."

Cameron shook his head. "Tremaine is a businessman. I am hoping to finalize an important deal with him over mining rights to some property I own in Cornwall. Selby and Lord Bailey are also partners in this venture and they like him very much. They have repeatedly told me he is an honorable man. A wealthy one, too."

"Then why is he so interested in Charlotte? If he has money, he can't be a fortune hunter."

Cameron looked down, suffering a sharp pain of guilty concern. How had he missed all of this drama? True, he had been wrapped up in his concerns over Rebecca Tremaine and Lily, but that was no excuse for being so oblivious to his surroundings.

Or perhaps his mother was exaggerating? Perhaps there was nothing at all between Charlotte and Daniel Tremaine except his mother's imagination? "Are you saying Tremaine is courting Charlotte?"

The words, spoken aloud, sounded ridiculous. Cameron almost smiled with relief, but then he caught the expression of genuine concern on his mother's face.

"Well, I don't know exactly what Mr. Tremaine is doing with Charlotte," the dowager countess mused.

"One would assume if his intentions are honorable then he would be planning to court her properly, within all bounds of propriety."

"He damn well better stay within the bounds of propriety!"

"Cameron please, language."

"Pardon."

"I do not mean to imply that Mr. Tremaine has a nefarious purpose." The dowager countess wrinkled her nose. "Though the improvements in her appearance are impressive, no one will ever call Charlotte beautiful or even pretty. At her best, she is passable."

"Men do not only consider a woman's looks."

"Precisely. Which is why I am even more confused. Charlotte is shy and retiring. She does not have the sparkling wit or impish charm men find so irresistible. With neither good looks nor an effervescent personality there is very little to recommend her. I do not mean to be cruel, but what would a man with Mr. Tremaine's looks and wealth want with Charlotte?"

"I hardly think it has reached that stage."

"I'm not certain. For a moment during our card game, I thought I saw . . ." the dowager countess hesitated.

"What, Mother?" Cameron prompted. "What did you see?"

"I thought I saw Mr. Tremaine and Charlotte kissing!" She cleared her throat nervously, her face flushed with astonishment.

"Surely you are mistaken?"

"I know that sounds rather ridiculous, but I do believe it happened." His mother looked aghast. "And yet 'tis such impulsive and improper behavior, two things that one would never associate with Charlotte." She shook her head, then began muttering. "Every time I think about it, I tell myself I must have been mistaken. Though a social inferior, Mr. Tremaine does have a handsome countenance and a fortune. He has no need to accept a crippled wife."

"There is much more to Charlotte than her infirmity. You do her a great disservice not to look beyond it."

"I know, dear. She is my daughter and I love her with all my heart. Naturally we, as her family, know what a treasure she is, what a sweet, caring and wonderful woman." The dowager countess's eyes narrowed. "However, as her mother it is my duty to be suspicious, given these circumstances. You must not forget that Charlotte is also innocent of society and naive of men, despite her years, which we both know is well beyond the age when she could be expected to make a favorable match."

"She is hardly an old woman," Cameron mused.

"But she is not a young woman either. I worry that she might be dallying with a man who has mischief in mind. Or worse, will attempt to trick her into accepting an unfavorable match. I will not see her hurt by a social climber."

"I am fairly certain that Mr. Tremaine has no specific interest in Charlotte. Romantic or otherwise," Cameron replied, wishing he was at liberty to tell his mother the real reason the Tremaines were here. It would alleviate her worries and give him the opportunity to unburden his own distress by revealing the truth.

Yet, what had Rebecca said to him earlier? Some secrets were harder to keep than others. "I will keep an eye on things, Mother."

"Thank you, dear. I know I can always depend on you."

Seeing the emotion in his mother's eyes made Cameron feel guilty. In addition to keeping secrets from his family, he had been neglecting his duties to them.

Six more days until Christmas. Less than two weeks beyond that, the guests would start leaving. Then gradually things would begin to return to normal.

Or would they? With an inward grimace, Cameron admitted that was highly unlikely.

The next morning Rebecca dressed carefully, anticipating her outing to the vicarage. She had promised Mrs. Hargrave she would help with this year's nativity play, never realizing what a welcome distraction it would be. The commitment would take her from the house for the entire morning, thus eliminating the possibility of having to spend any significant time in the earl's company.

She splashed the warm water her maid had brought on her face, her lips tingling with the memory of the earl's kisses. It seemed to almost burn through her, but Rebecca gulped back the storm of emotions. It had truly happened, she mused. They had kissed. And it meant . . . ?

"That nothing will change," she said firmly, her voice echoing throughout the room. "Nothing at all."

Unwilling to examine the events of last night too closely, Rebecca made up her mind. She was going to do what any well-bred woman of character was taught to do when faced with confusing, overstimulated emotions. Firmly ignore them.

Bolstered by her decision, Rebecca finished dressing. Her plan remained in place through breakfast, where she ate her toast and sipped her hot chocolate and engaged in a lively conversation with Lord Bailey and his wife. They joked and laughed and it made her feel better knowing there were no hard feelings over last evening's card game.

She had not realized how tense she was until Cameron . . . no, the earl, entered the room, Lady Charlotte at his side. He spoke a general greeting to all, then resumed his conversation with his sister. His gaze did not so much as flicker in Rebecca's direction.

Feeling his presence acutely, Rebecca's hand trembled as she lifted her cup of hot chocolate to her lips and took a small sip. Oddly, the fact that he was acting perfectly at ease, as if nothing at all had happened, as if nothing had changed between them, pricked at her pride. Or else maybe he was a more accomplished actor than she, better skilled at hiding his true feelings?

Rebecca stared straight ahead, afraid her face would give away her inner turmoil. Telling herself she was going to ignore any strong emotions brewing inside her and actually doing it were quite different, but she was determined. The kisses between them last night might have awakened a hunger deep within her, but that hunger could be contained and controlled.

Understanding what she faced was important. She knew now to be on her guard, to be careful not to place herself in a position where she would need to fight the temptation of desire she felt for the earl.

For she was honest enough to acknowledge she could all too easily surrender to it.

"Are you sure I should not have brought my angel costume with me?" Lily asked for the third time. "I bet Mrs. Hargrave would like to see it. And Reverend Hargrave, too. It is ever so pretty."

"I know Mrs. Hargrave will indeed be very pleased to see you dressed as an angel, but it is not necessary today. The players are all going to practice their lines and learn where they need to stand. You don't have to wear a costume to do that correctly," Rebecca replied.

Lily hesitated for a moment, clearly wanting to debate the point, but a stern glare from Mrs. James silenced the girl.

The morning was fair, the sun bright, the grass lightly browned from the freezing temperatures of the past few days. As they arrived at the vicarage, Mrs. Hargrave stood at the door to bid them welcome. Rebecca fixed a smile on her face and looked at the young woman with what she hoped would be interpreted as enthusiasm and not the apprehension she really felt. Despite a long lecture on proper behavior, Rebecca knew Lily could turn ugly with the slightest provocation. Real or imagined.

"Good afternoon, Miss Tremaine. Lady Lily. And Mrs. James. How nice to see you all again."

Rebecca smiled back at the vicar's pretty wife. Mrs. Hargrave looked anything but pleased, managing only a closed lipped smile as they drew near. As she had been told, Lily curtsied to Mrs. Hargrave. She seemed touched by the respectful gesture, but her eyes remained wary. Nervous and fluttery, her eyes darted toward the little girl as if waiting for another explosion to erupt at any moment. Given the tantrum displayed at their last visit, Rebecca could hardly blame the woman.

They retreated to the schoolhouse. A bevy of children, boys and girls of various sizes, awaited their arrival. All were at least five years or more older than Lily and considerably taller.

Mrs. James retreated to the back of the room. Rebecca removed Lily's cloak and bonnet. The little girl's eyes were bright with excitement as they kept glancing toward the other children.

The rehearsal began promisingly. The children had been well coached and knew their lines. Still, it was difficult to keep everyone standing in their proper place and fidgeting was inevitable. Rebecca curiously noted Lily's interaction with the other children. Though by far the youngest, and a stranger to them, Lily was the center of attention.

The older girls treated her like a prized doll, cosseting and spoiling her, vying for her favor. The boys mostly ignored her, though Rebecca could see a smile or two emerge when they caught a glimpse of Lily's antics.

It was good to see Lily laughing and giggling with the others, her face flushed and happy. The one sticky moment came when the final placement of the angels was decided. Rebecca had served as Mrs. Hargrave's assistant throughout the entire rehearsal, allowing the other woman to make the decisions. After all, this was her production and she was doing an admirable job.

"You shall stand here, Amanda, with Julie beside you and Lady Lily in front," Mrs. Hargrave instructed.

Dutifully the girls complied and Rebecca grew nervous. Lily was standing directly behind the cradle laid with straw. She continually glanced down at the spot where the newborn babe would be placed. Rebecca could almost see the wheels turning in the little girl's head.

Chewing thoughtfully on her bottom lip, Lily left her position and headed toward Mrs. Hargrave, who was organizing the three wise men. Rebecca sprang forward to intercept her.

"Is anything wrong?" Rebecca asked, fearing the renewed demand to play the part of the baby Jesus was forthcoming.

"Will everyone be able to see me if I stand behind

the cradle?" Lily asked. "I am much smaller than all the other angels."

"That is why Mrs. Hargrave has placed you there, at the center. All eyes will be drawn to that very spot," Rebecca answered.

"Good." Content with the response, Lily skipped back to her assigned position and the rehearsal concluded without incident.

During the carriage ride back to the manor, Lily chattered merrily about the play and the other children, prompting an impulsive thought to enter Rebecca's head.

"Do you have any special plans for Lady Lily this afternoon, Mrs. James?"

The governess, who had been lightly dozing, blinked rapidly as she brought herself to full alertness. "Why no, Miss Tremaine."

"Excellent." Turning to face the child, Rebecca asked, "Would you like to help me this afternoon? I am going to bake Christmas cookies to put in the holiday baskets, but I thought it might be nice to bring some cookies to the school on the evening of the performance. I'm sure all the children would enjoy a special treat."

"What kind of cookies?" Lily asked.

"Gingerbread. Do you like gingerbread?"

"Yes, very much." Lily smiled with enthusiasm, but then her lips curved down into a frown. "But I cannot eat any dessert for the rest of the week. Papa said so."

"We are not going to be eating the cookies. We shall be baking them," Rebecca clarified. "Though I suppose we will be forced to eat one or two, just to be certain they are good. After all, the majority of them will be given away and it would be dreadfully embarrassing if they were inferior-tasting."

"Can I taste them too?"

"I believe your father will allow it."

Lily's smile returned, brighter than ever. "Can we start the moment we get home?"

Rebecca replied with a nod and an enthusiastic smile of her own.

"I like the kitchen," Lily said when she arrived. "I can see the cat."

Rebecca, in the process of organizing her baking supplies, turned and noticed a large calico cat sprawled on top of a tall closed cupboard, its legs and tail drooping over the edge.

"That will be Horace," Cook informed Rebecca. "He likes to stay in here on cold days where it's warm and cozy."

Rebecca nodded. "Cats are very smart creatures. No matter where they are, they always seem to be able to find a snug spot to curl up."

"Aunt Charlotte's favorite cat is Misty, but I like Horace better," Lily said. "I can't ever catch Misty when I chase after her and she only has three legs."

Three legs? That could not possibly be true. Rebecca glanced over, intending to lecture Lily on how it was best not to exaggerate the truth, when she caught Cook's eye.

"Aye, that Misty is one fast critter on her three legs," Cook agreed. "Even the dogs can't catch her."

Rebecca muffled her surprise. She found a clean white apron and wrapped it several times around Lily's waist. Then she gathered together the rest of the ingredients needed for the cookies while Lily watched. Not wanting to deplete any of the household stores and disrupt the menu that Cook had planned

for the holidays, Rebecca had arranged for extra
flour, butter, eggs, sugar and molasses to be delivered,
along with cinnamon and ginger.

In her experience, cooks tended to be territorial. It
was odd enough to have one of the earl's guests using
the kitchen. She did not want to further disrupt Cook's
domain by pilfering her larder.

As it was, she thought the earl's cook was being
more than tolerant of her presence. The older woman
was polite, helpfully bringing out the mixing bowls,
wooden spoons, cookie cutters and other baking uten-
sils as asked, yet her gaze was openly curious.

Rebecca understood. Society women did not cook.
Most ladies consulted on menus and brought a few
prized recipes from their mother's homes, but had no
idea the proper way to prepare even the most simple
foods.

It was yet another facet that set her apart and reminded Rebecca that she was not a society woman.
She had been raised in a genteel household, where a
servant did the majority of the cooking, but Rebecca
had learned a few basics.

From an early age she had developed a particular
interest in baking. As she grew older, she found it relaxing and enjoyable and had the added bonus of
producing something one could eat.

This knowledge and skill was something she was
eager to share with Lily. Another Christmas memory to
create and cherish in the years ahead. She explained
what all the ingredients were and how they were going
to be mixed together while Lily listened patiently.

Rebecca was soon grinding lumps of sugar into a fine
powder while Lily, under Cook's watchful eye, was
counting out scoops of flour. She unceremoniously
dumped them in a large bowl, stirring up a white cloud.

Within minutes, the little girl had herself, and Rebecca, covered in a fine dusting of flour, and poor Cook was continually sneezing.

"Maybe I should put in the rest of the flour?" Cook volunteered, no doubt out of self-preservation.

"Then what will I do?" Lily asked, the question soon forgotten when her eyes saw the pile of eggs neatly stacked in another bowl. "Oh, may I break the eggs?"

Cook blanched. Rebecca hesitated, but knowing the best way to learn was by doing, she demonstrated the proper technique, cracking the egg carefully on the side of the bowl and adding it to the dry ingredients.

With great concentration, Lily copied the movements. When she eagerly reached for another egg, Rebecca slid her fingers into the batter, removing the majority of egg shell Lily had also managed to put in the bowl.

Once properly mixed, the dough was kneaded and rolled out. Rebecca cut off a section for Lily to work with and showed her how to use the cutters. As soon as a tray was filled, Rebecca placed it in the oven. The enticing smell of warm ginger and spices soon filled the air.

Unfortunately, Rebecca left the cookies too long in the oven. The delicious smell vanished, replaced with an unpleasant, burnt aroma. Lily held her nose as Rebecca lifted the cookies off the tray, their bottoms a solid black.

"You can feed those to the dogs," Cook suggested.

"Apollo eats anything," Lily concurred cheerfully.

Disheartened, Rebecca piled the cookies on the edge of the wooden table, wondering if the dogs would even bother to eat them. They looked awful and smelled worse. Reaching for the flour, she began mixing a second batch of dough, telling herself the constant glimpses from Cook were sympathy and not smirks of superiority.

Vowing to be more vigilant, Rebecca diligently checked the next batch several times, removing them when they were crisp, but not too dark. She was silently congratulating herself on her success when the earl entered the kitchen.

"Papa! Come and see what I have done."

"Are you cooking?" he asked in an astonished tone.

Rebecca looked up. He was watching her with an expression of amusement that might have been considered patronizing if not for the genuine warmth in his smile.

"Baking!" Lily corrected him.

"Really?"

"Yes, Miss Rebecca is teaching me."

"Extraordinary."

Rebecca could feel her face heat and knew it wasn't just from the hot oven.

"And how is my little angel, today?" the earl added. Lily giggled. Lord Hampton moved closer and whispered to Rebecca, "Just to clarify, I was referring to her part in the play, not her behavior."

"I am glad to hear that, my lord. I for one believe your change in attitude and actions toward Lily will serve you in good stead."

"And hopefully assure peace for the rest of the household," he added. "And the surrounding community."

"Gracious, she isn't that bad!" Rebecca removed a ball of dough from the large bowl and began to slowly knead it. "Try to think of it this way. If you cannot control her at six, you will never be able to control her at sixteen."

His face paled. "Suitors and young bucks sniffing around my little girl? You are giving me heart palpitations."

The earl leaned close. When he spoke again, she felt his breath caress her cheeks. Rebecca's wits scattered and she barely comprehended his question.

"Pardon?"

"Did Lily truly behave herself this morning?"

Rebecca blinked. "Yes. There was a small problem with where she was standing on stage, but she held her temper and behaved properly. I was very proud of her."

"A good start. After all, one cannot expect miracles in a day. We must celebrate the small victories. And brace ourselves for the defeats."

"My lord!"

"I thought we agreed you would call me Cameron."

"Only when we are alone."

He was watching her intently, with an expression that caused her breath to quicken. She deliberately turned her attention to the cookie dough, dipping the metal cutter in flour and then carefully cutting out the shapes. She put them on the metal sheet, then walked them to the oven.

Rebecca transferred the hot cookies they had previously baked onto a platter. The earl scooped one up and popped it in his mouth.

"Wait!" Rebecca warned. "They haven't cooled,"

She saw him gasp, and realized it must have scorched his tongue. But he valiantly managed to chew and swallow it.

"Do you like it, Papa?"

"It's delicious," the earl choked out.

Lily's eyes widened. "Really? Do you really like it?"

He swallowed again. "'Tis most assuredly the very best Christmas cookie I have ever eaten, Puss. My compliments to the chef, or rather, the baker."

"We are going to wrap them and put them in the Christmas baskets. For the tenants."

"I am certain everyone will enjoy them."

Lily smiled. "I want to give some cookies to Mrs. Hargrave too, as a special present."

"What a lovely idea," Rebecca said. "As a baker herself, she will doubly appreciate your efforts."

Lily nodded her head enthusiastically. "I can't wait to go back to London and tell Jane Grolier that I baked cookies myself and gave them to everyone as a present. And they were wonderful."

The earl raised an ironic eyebrow at his daughter.

"Her intentions are good," Rebecca interjected.

"Hmm, we just need to work on her modesty. And her motivation. I shudder to think what other deeds will come into her mind when the need to impress Jane Grolier is foremost in her thinking."

"Perhaps when Lily sees the genuine appreciation that others feel from her efforts, it will make a more lasting impression."

"We can only hope."

He reached for another cookie and Rebecca felt oddly pleased to see him enjoy them so much. Lily, having grown bored with the work, wandered off to the other side of the kitchen. Crouching down, she was trying to coax the calico cat who had moved under the large wooden cupboard.

Seeing Lily with Horace solidified the thought Rebecca had been tossing around in her head. "I have an idea for a Christmas gift for Lily I would like to discuss with you," Rebecca whispered to the earl.

"Really? What is it?"

"I can't speak of it here," Rebecca replied. "I wish for it to be a surprise."

Lord Hampton nodded in understanding. "Fine.

We will meet later and discuss it somewhere private."
He flashed her a conspiratorial grin.

Rebecca's heart skipped. He looked boyish and
young and happy. Shaking her head, she turned back
to the gingerbread dough, pressing too hard as she
rolled out the next batch, simply refusing to identify
the reason that thrilled her.

Chapter 12

"A kitten?"

Rebecca nodded as the earl frowned. They had but a few moments alone together until evening tea was served and she wanted to share her idea of a Christmas gift for Lily.

"She adores cats. She had fun baking cookies this afternoon, but spent half her time chasing after Cook's cat, Horace," Rebecca explained. "Plus, I thought having her own kitten would give her a sense of responsibility. And the best part is that cats require a minimum amount of care."

"Whatever will Apollo think?" the earl asked with a grin.

Rebecca's own smile faded. She had not considered the earl's large dog. "Surely Apollo is used to seeing cats about the estate?"

"Yes, and he likes nothing more than to chase them. Cook bars him from the kitchen, so Horace is safe." The earl crossed his arms over his chest. "Apollo might think of a kitten as a breakfast treat."

"Gracious!" Rebecca gulped back her alarm. "That would be most disastrous. But if you honestly believe the two animals won't get on together, then I suppose I need to come up with another idea."

"It is unnecessary for you to give Lily a gift."

Disappointment slammed into Rebecca's heart. She had thought of little else but the kitten since the idea came to her, but was willing to forgo the notion if the earl deemed it unsuitable. Yet being denied the chance to give Lily something, anything, for the holiday was deeply upsetting.

"It would mean a great deal to me to give Lily something to celebrate the season," Rebecca stated. And perhaps remember me by, she thought with longing.

"Cameron, Miss Tremaine," Lady Marion interrupted. "We are forming teams for a game of charades. Will you play?"

"We will join you in a moment," the earl answered. Turning back to Rebecca, he added. "I shall ask my steward to find out which of my tenants currently have feline litters. With so many farms in the vicinity, I am sure there are several."

His remark drew a glance of startled disbelief. "I may get Lily a kitten?"

"I am not a complete villain, Rebecca. Clearly, it would please you to give her one and I admit you are correct in your assumptions. Lily will be thrilled." He smiled slightly. "I only wish I had thought of it myself."

"I would like to choose the animal," Rebecca added quickly, delighted and a bit stunned.

"I assumed that would be the case. I will accompany you. Now, let us join the others. If Marion finds out about Lily's gift, the surprise will be in serious jeopardy. My cousin has never been able to hold a secret for more than twenty minutes."

"Ah, you fear if she knew, Lady Marion would let the cat out of the bag?" Rebecca could not resist asking.

He groaned at the obvious pun, but the spark of teasing in his eyes made her pulse jump.

As good as his word, the earl told Rebecca at breakfast the following morning that they might find what she was seeking at the Braggs's farm. They rode out together on horseback directly after luncheon. The air was cold, the sky a milky gray. Rebecca found the journey invigorating.

Their conversation was safe and innocuous and Rebecca told herself she preferred it that way. This bond of peace between them was too fragile to risk with serious discussions and highly felt emotions.

After a little more than an hour they arrived at their destination. It was a well-kept property, with a house that looked like a stone box perched on the top of a gradually inclining hilltop, surrounded by several smaller buildings of a similar design.

Mr. Bragg greeted them cordially, his manner reserved and respectful. Rebecca could not help but note that the earl went out of his way to put the man at ease, remarking several times how much he appreciated Mr. Bragg's assistance.

The litter was cozily housed in the barn. The kittens were sleeping on a thick bed of straw, jumbled atop one another in a single ball of fur. With a slight bit of urging, they awoke and began exploring the area.

Rebecca took her time observing the brood. They were all sweet and adorable, but her eyes kept coming back to one in particular. "I think this one is perfect," she decided, after Mr. Bragg had told them it was a female.

"A gray cat with black eyes," the earl observed. "Very pretty."

Rebecca reached down and scooped the kitten into her arms. The animal squirmed, then settled against the palm of Rebecca's hand, purring loudly. Rebecca tilted her head, peering into the kitten's face and laughed. "Her eyes are not black, my lord. They are green. The black you see is her pupils. She is simply wide-eyed with excitement."

"Is my household ready for such an excitable creature?"

Rebecca laughed again. "The kitten will no doubt liven things up."

"Hmm, precisely what I need. Another spirited female living with me." He scowled, but Rebecca could see he was teasing. "Is she ready to be weaned from her mother?" he asked Mr. Bragg.

"Nearly. We can start feeding her right away, so you can take her in a few days."

"Excellent. Then I will send a servant to retrieve the kitten on Christmas Eve."

"Very good, milord."

The two men shook hands on the matter.

"We'd best be on our way, Mr. Bragg. I thank you again for your help."

The farmer glanced down at the ground, rubbing the toe of his boot in the hard earthen floor of the barn. "Mrs. Bragg was hoping you might have a moment to share some refreshments before you leave."

"We would be honored." The earl turned to Rebecca. "Miss Tremaine?"

"How very kind of you to offer, Mr. Bragg," Rebecca answered, knowing it was a point of pride for the tenant and his family to extend this hospitality to the earl.

They walked up the hill to the house. No sooner had they reached the top when the door of the cottage flew open. "Lord Hampton, how wonderful to see you," a voice sang out. A plump woman stood at the front door, her face wreathed in a broad smile. "And you've brought a lady with you."

Rebecca felt herself blush at Mrs. Bragg's implied tone that she had some sort of special relationship with the earl. Heaven forbid if anyone knew the real truth!

"I am Rebecca Tremaine, Mrs. Bragg," she said, trying to hold off any further speculation. "My brother and I are visiting Windmere for the holiday season."

"Miss Tremaine? Are you the lady who has been helping Mrs. Hargrave with the nativity play?"

"She is indeed, Mrs. Bragg," the earl answered. "And doing a fine job, from what I hear."

"Oh, my yes. My Jamie came home full of tales from the last rehearsal."

"That play is a lot of foolish nonsense if you ask me," Mr. Bragg grumbled. "But his mother had her heart set on him being a part of it."

"Hush now, George. It is an honor to have our boy chosen."

"If you don't mind my saying, Mr. Bragg, young Jamie does you all proud," Rebecca offered.

Upon hearing that news, Mrs. Bragg positively beamed. "See, I told you. Miss Tremaine is a fine lady and she knows best."

Mr. Bragg mumbled a few words. Rebecca could see he was not entirely convinced, but he wisely let the matter drop.

They were ushered through the doorway into a cozy sitting room. Mrs. Bragg insisted the earl sit in the only armchair while she and Rebecca settled on the settee. Mr. Bragg stood. The house smelled of wood smoke, cinnamon and freshly baked bread. Rebecca felt very much at ease.

A young girl entered with a tray of refreshments. She was introduced as Anna, the Braggs's oldest daughter and baker of the delicious rum raisin cake they were served. It was a pleasant visit. The earl and Mr. Bragg discussed various local matters, including the fall harvest and plans for the new crops to be planted in the spring.

Rebecca found she did not have to contribute much to the conversation with Mrs. Bragg. A simple question here and there and an occasional encouraging remark kept her talking for the majority of the visit.

As they mounted their horses to leave, Rebecca noticed Lord Hampton discretely slip a few coins into Mr. Bragg's palm.

"I should like to reimburse you for the money you gave Mr. Bragg," Rebecca said the moment they had ridden out of the farm's front yard.

"It is not at all necessary, yet I have a feeling you will not let this matter drop."

"I most assuredly will not," she replied. "The kitten is to be my gift."

"Very well. You owe me ten guineas."

Far from being appalled at the sum, Rebecca was pleased to note the earl's generosity. The farm had seemed prosperous and in good repair, but she had caught the reference to Mr. Bragg's eight children. With such a large brood to feed and clothe and care for, any additional income would be welcome.

They rode across a pasture bordered by a stream, setting a comfortable pace for the horses. The sky had turned a darker gray, the air was heavy with moisture. Still, the storm swooped down so unexpectedly it at first seemed like a momentary apparition.

"It's so pretty," Rebecca exclaimed with amusement.

She lifted her face to the sky, laughing as the damp snowflakes tickled her lashes and cheeks.

"Viscount Cranborne will be pleased," the earl commented. "He bet a tidy sum with Lord Bailey that there would be snow before Christmas Day."

Rebecca abruptly turned her head. "Is nothing sacred? Wagering on the weather. How absurd."

"Did you not know, Rebecca? 'Tis a favorite pastime of bored aristocrats. Cranborne's snow wager is hardly the worst of it. The betting book at White's is filled with the most ridiculous predictions imaginable, along with some of the most scandalous."

"Such as?"

"Which do you prefer? Ridiculous or scandalous?"

"Ridiculous," she answered honestly.

"Well, there is Lord Alvanley's three-thousand-pound bet as to which of five raindrops would first reach the bottom of the pane on the bow window at White's."

Rebecca smiled. "That happened years ago. Believe it or not, I've actually heard of that one."

"Then how about the Duke of Hampshire's more recent wager on which of two flies would crawl first up the window and reach the top?"

"The members seem to have a fascination with windows," she remarked.

"I suppose you could call it that." The earl shook his head and drew his horse next to hers.

She thought she heard him mutter something that sounded like *pompous asses,* but wasn't certain. They continued their conversation in the same lighthearted tone, yet all too soon the falling snow thickened. Countless large, wet, fat flakes fell, seeming to form a curtain between them and the rest of the world. They slowed their pace considerably, yet Rebecca could still not see more than a few feet in front of her.

"Is it my imagination or has the storm gotten worse?" she asked, nearly shouting to be heard over the gusting wind and swirling snow.

"Worse," Cameron replied, grimacing at the sky. "We need to take shelter before we become hopelessly lost."

"Are we closer to the Braggs's farm or the manor house?"

"Neither. We are somewhere in the middle."

A strong gust of wind nearly drowned out his answer. Her horse tossed his head, sending a shower of wet snow all over Rebecca. She sputtered and wiped it from her eyes, then reached over and patted the animal's neck reassuringly. He calmed noticeably. If only that was all it took to reassure her.

The wind whipped her cloak and skirts and the wet precipitation seeped through her gloves. The snow fell so heavily Rebecca could barely see. They slowly climbed a hill. The frozen ground beneath the horse's hooves was slippery and the animal struggled to stay on its feet.

Barely at a walk, they plodded through the storm. At some point, the earl grabbed her leading rein and Rebecca was glad to be secured behind him. She would not want to be out here on her own, with no idea of her direction.

Ten minutes later a faint outline of a building arose through the white mist. Rebecca sighed with relief. She noted the earl sitting taller in the saddle and surmised he had also spotted the shelter. He urged their horses on and they soon trotted through the gate, which was swinging madly on its top hinge.

Rebecca was so glad to see shelter she did not at first notice there was no smoke curling from the chimney, no light shining from the windows. They dismounted and fought their way through the swirling winds to reach the front door. The earl lifted the latch, but it did not budge.

"Is it locked?" Rebecca asked, her teeth chattering.

"No. Rusted shut." He slammed his shoulder into the door.

"Gracious!" Rebecca screeched.

He ignored her outburst and shoved again. This time the rusty latch gave way and the earl went tumbling through the doorway. Rebecca hurried into the house and shut the door behind her.

She was immediately thrust into gloomy darkness. "Are there no windows?"

"The wooden shutters are secured tight. Best to leave them closed or else we will feel the bite of the wind. Can you see?"

"Barely."

"Stay where you are," he instructed. "I need to shelter the horses. When I return, I will build us fire. The warmth will be welcome and it should provide enough light so we don't trip over anything."

Rebecca nodded. The earl left. She smoothed her skirts, then thrust her hands into the pockets of her cloak, trying to appear calm and nonchalant. Inside, however, she was jittery and nervous. Being stranded alone in a cottage in the middle of a raging snowstorm with Lord Hampton had the potential for disaster written all over it.

The door opened and the earl entered. His greatcoat and hat were coated in snow, his cheeks red. He stomped off the snow that had accumulated on his boots, then gingerly moved from one foot to the other trying to warm himself. He was soon panting from the exertion, his breath puffing in the cold air.

"The horses?" Rebecca asked, managing a casual tone with great effort.

"They are fine. I found the barn nearly tumbling down, but two walls and a section of the roof are intact. I secured the horses in an area that will shelter them from the worst of the wind and snow."

"But is the structure sound enough to withstand high winds and pelting snow? It would be horrible to have the roof or walls collapse and trap the poor creatures."

"I am no architect, but I feel confident they will be safe." He looked about the room. "Is there any wood? I need to build a fire to keep us from freezing."

A task. Good. It was important to stay busy, focused. That allowed less time to dwell on the situation. She needed to find wood or something they could burn. Ignoring the lump that had sprouted in her throat, Rebecca took stock of her surroundings.

The room was completely bare. The previous occupants had not left any furniture or small items behind. The wood floor was covered in a fine layer of dust and as she moved, the motes flew about the room, tickling her nose. Waiting until her eyes adjusted more thoroughly to the gloom, Rebecca cautiously entered the only other room on the first floor. There she discovered a small pile of logs neatly stacked in the corner, covered in dust and cobwebs.

Triumphantly she returned with her arms laden. The earl quickly relieved her of her burden. She stood near while he attended to the fire. Her teeth were chattering loudly by the time a small orange flame curled around the log.

The earl crouched and gently blew on it, coaxing the flame to life. At his command, Rebecca obediently handed him several of the smaller sticks she had found. He added them slowly to the fledgling fire and the tiny flames grew larger, brighter, licking around the wood.

"How long do you think this place has been abandoned?" she asked.

"I'm not sure." The earl sat back on his heels. "A year at least. Maybe more. Let's just hope the chimney isn't clogged or else we'll soon be surrounded in smoke."

They waited anxiously, but the smoke drafted upward.

"I don't suppose anyone will come looking for us?" she asked, not sure if that would make matters better or worse. A search party would ensure a faster rescue. Yet it might be better to keep this entire incident confidential and thus avoid any questions about their being alone.

"I doubt anyone realizes we are gone," he said. "Which is probably good. It would be foolish for someone to try to find us. Even a local who knows the area well would soon become disoriented and lost. The snow squall is near blinding." He stood. "Thankfully, these storms rarely last long. No doubt the sun will appear within the hour."

An hour! Her knees wobbled. Rebecca averted her stricken eyes, not wanting him to think she was overreacting. "And if it doesn't end in an hour?"

"Then it will end in two." He turned a curious face her way. "You look frightened. Are you, Rebecca?"

She lifted her chin. "Is there reason for me to be afraid, Cameron?"

He smiled. "Answering a question with another. A clever technique of avoidance."

"More of an opportunity to gain perspective before saying the wrong thing," she said lightly. "Is it something you would like to try yourself?"

"Should I?"

Rebecca smiled. She had removed her wet leather gloves and was attempting to warm her hands in the folds of her woolen cloak, but that too was wet.

Cameron took another step closer and faced her, lifting her hands and holding them between his own. She looked down and noted his hands were large and well shaped. Surprisingly, his skin felt warm against the coldness of her flesh. It must have been warmed by the fire he just built.

She fisted her hands and tried to pull away, but he increased his grip. Giving up the effort, Rebecca told herself she was being silly. He only meant to warm her, to prevent her from catching a chill.

Their fingers entwined. Her skin prickled.

"I like holding your hand," he said softly.

"I like it too. Which is why it also disturbs me." She sighed, wondering if he could read the uncertainty and vulnerability in her eyes. "Sometimes I miss the touch of another person so much I feel near tears."

He nodded, as though he understood. "I miss the conversation, the laughter. The security of knowing I am loved for the man that I am, be that good or bad on any particular day."

His words brought her emotions to the surface. How many nights after Philip died did she lay awake at night, trembling with fear, knowing there was no longer that special, marvelous person who cared for her utterly, unselfishly?

"'Tis not always easy to push aside the temptation to give in to the despair, is it?" she whispered. "Yet we must both hope to someday find someone who would find comfort in being with us."

"If you said that to me a year ago I would have dismissed it without a thought. Yet I have recently discovered that people are not designed to live alone, to live without affection or caring."

Her heart suddenly leapt and her breath turned choppy. Was she the reason for his change of heart?

"We are lucky to have family," she said. "There is Lily, your mother, your sister. Though I had my father, I felt alone for a very long time. At least now I have my brother."

Rebecca blushed and turned her head, looking at the crackling fire with annoyance. Had the stormy weather brought about this maudlin mood?

Cameron cleared his throat. "The room is warming. We should remove our wet garments."

He peeled off his dripping coat and hung it on a peg on the wall, then turned expectantly toward her. Rebecca shrugged off her cloak and hung it on the peg next to it.

Now what? she thought as they regarded each other with uncertainty.

"There must be a second story loft," Cameron said. "I'll explore it and see if there is anything there that will make our stay a bit more comfortable."

He walked to the back of the room and for the first time Rebecca noticed the crudely made wooden ladder. He quickly climbed it and soon returned carrying two blankets. "They are none too clean, but will offer some protection from the chill in the air."

He spread one meager blanket on the floor in front of the fire, reserving the second blanket to lay across their laps. Feeling self-conscious, Rebecca obediently sat down. He gingerly sat beside her. Their thighs momentarily touched. She felt her heart thump with the speed of a galloping horse.

But he made no inappropriate advances. It was necessary to stay close to keep warm, but her awareness of him beside her gradually became a pleasant feeling. Watching the crackling fire, they began talking of inconsequential matters. Rebecca decided he either did not notice her awkwardness or chose to ignore it. Whatever the truth, she was glad of it, for it gave her time to collect herself and settle her rioting emotions.

Cameron asked her about her home and her childhood and she told him about her parents and her brother and some of the more eccentric members of their small community. She talked for a long time, prompted by his questions and his genuine interest in her answers. Then she turned the tables on him, wanting to know of his life as a young man.

He soon had her laughing at his mischievous pranks and daring escapades, both at home and during his tenure at Eton. She expressed pity for his parents at having to cope with such a high-spirited child and he told her another tale, far more outrageous than the others.

Laughing heartily, Rebecca turned to look at him. She was enjoying herself far more than she could have possibly expected. She wanted so badly to believe they could eventually become friends, that she could form a relationship with him that would allow her to see Lily, but even more important, would allow her to be comfortable and secure in his company.

Their eyes met and suddenly there was an awareness between them; an awareness that they were a man and a woman alone together. She took a deep breath, then had difficulty letting it go.

"Your hair has come loose." He reached out and very slowly brushed the stray wisp back behind her ear. The tips of his fingers feathered across the sensitive skin on her cheek.

"Thank you," she whispered, closing her eyes in yearning.

His hand lingered at her nape. She moved forward, felt the warmth of his breath caress her cheek. *One kiss. Just one, sweet kiss.*

"I'm going to check on the progress of the storm." He dropped his hand abruptly, breaking the unbearable tension. "There is a window on the second floor with a western view."

Rebecca's eyes sprung open. She watched him once again climb the ladder leading to the loft. She waited below, her emotions mixed in turmoil.

What would happen if the storm worsened and they had to stay the night? Would their relationship escalate? Or even if it did not, would she be compromised to a state that would require a marriage proposal?

The cottage remained eerily quiet and she grew nervous. Grasping the sides of the wooden ladder, Rebecca slowly climbed. The second story loft was far more spacious than she would have imagined. The ceiling was just high enough for Cameron to stand erect. The room air was chilled and she shivered.

She crossed to where he was and he smiled when he saw her, stepping aside. He had rubbed away the grime on a section of the window glass revealing a view that evoked a sense of otherworldliness.

The snow had ceased falling, though it clung to every surface. The sky was a deep gray, yet in the distance, above the far horizon a single shaft of sunlight made the ground sparkle like diamonds, glittering and fanciful.

There was a light breeze wafting through a crack in one of the windowpanes and Rebecca could smell the fresh, crisp, clean air. Her breath fogged up the glass and she stepped back from the draft, but she continued to view the snow-encrusted countryside. Icicles hung from the edge of the roof like frozen tears, glistening in the light.

As far as the eye could see there was white, with no dwelling or structures to break the landscape. The vastness of barren land made one feel small and insignificant, yet instead of emptiness, the clean purity of the snow made Rebecca feel reborn.

The pristine blanket was so pure and perfect, covering any flaws beneath it. It was like a blank canvas, full of hope and promise, rife with the opportunity to start fresh.

"It's so quiet," she said, a huge welling of emotions rumbling through her voice.

"Aye." His head bent close to hears, his breath warming her as he murmured, "It feels as if we are the only two people on earth."

If only that were true. The thought popped into her mind and Rebecca blushed with embarrassment. Under different circumstances she knew she would have allowed herself to act upon the attraction she felt so strongly for him, would have allowed herself to feel the emotions she firmly believed had died along with Philip.

If only . . . ?

Deliberately breaking the spell of intimacy, Rebecca turned away. "Now that it has cleared, we can leave."

"Wait!" Cameron slid his arm around her, his grasp so powerful she could not move. Slowly, she raised her chin and looked up.

Rebecca gazed into his eyes, becoming still, as Cameron stared down at her with a smoldering look. His face was inches from her. This time he was going to kiss her. She was certain.

Her heart fluttered wildly, hopefully.

"I'm glad we were stranded," he said roughly. "I enjoyed our time together."

It took a moment to find her voice. "Me too."

His right hand lifted and he touched her cheek. His gaze unwavering on hers, he stroked her face, traced her ear. He fingered her earlobe lightly, moving downward to caress the side of her throat. Rebecca heard herself breathing hard as she waited. Waited for him to lower his mouth and press it to hers.

She leaned closer, lifting her chin, angling her head. Finally, he moved. The light brush of his lips against hers caused a shiver to race down her spine. She ceased to think. His lips were warm, soft, comforting. The tip of her tongue darted out to meet his lips. He pulled it into his mouth, instantly turning the kiss into a deeply intimate connection.

Their mouths fussed hungrily. The feel of his tongue, the taste of him, the groan of desire he made when he deepened the kiss were emblazoned on her mind. She felt him shudder and knew he was exercising strong control.

He broke the kiss and she bowed her head, gasping for air, her heart pounding so swiftly it was almost frightening. Silence stretched between them. Not an awkward quiet, but rather a silence filled with unspoken thoughts.

"The perfect ending to a delightful afternoon," he finally said.

"Yes," she whispered. It was precisely how she felt.

Rebecca leaned against him, nestling her head into the curve of his neck and shoulder, waiting for the intense pleasure to wane, feeling safe in his embrace. Which was strange, given the strong sexual tension and the circumstances of their acquaintance. Yet he had just proven that she could trust him to be a gentleman, that he would not take unfair advantage of her.

She snuggled into him. The warmth of his body was intoxicating. He was a large man, a solid force, a man who would fight for what he believed was right, who would protect what he cherished.

A man she could respect.

A man she could admire.

A man she could love.

A cold fission of fear shivered down Rebecca's spine and she knew it had nothing at all to do with the weather.

Chapter 13

Charlotte sat in the window seat, her face pressed against the cold glass as she gazed outdoors. Thick flakes fluttered down from a gray sky, quickly coating the frozen grass, blanketing it in white. Yet with each snowflake that fell, her spirits tumbled with it.

Snow meant she would be trapped, forced to stay inside. Snow meant the others in their party, adults and children alike, would bundle up in warm coats and hats and scarves and gloves and brave the cold to go sledding or ice-skating or engage in a snowball fight. They would build a snowman, or a snowwoman. They would laugh and joke and play and toss themselves gleefully on their backs to make angel patterns in the piles of fluffy white snow.

They would enter a magical, white world, a place where worries and cares could be forgotten, at least for a brief time. But all Charlotte could do was stay indoors and watch. With envy and regret and a spark of jealousy.

Snow was slippery. Snow hid the dangerous, almost lethal ice beneath it. As her mother had so often told her, it was difficult enough for Charlotte to get around in the best of circumstances. Why would she endure the indignity of trying to wade inelegantly through a mass of snow, risking grave injury, unless it was absolutely necessary?

Sighing deeply, Charlotte turned her head away from the wintry scene and gazed across the room. Apollo, who lay sprawled in front of the roaring fire, picked up his head and stared at her. As if sensing her distress, the large dog got to his feet and padded over. He sat beside her, leaning his considerable weight against her leg. Whimpering, he rested his head on her knee and lifted his soulful brown eyes to her face.

Charlotte smiled in spite of her sour mood. She petted his head, stroking her hand rhythmically over his silky ears. The action soothed her nerves and delighted Apollo. When she finished, he stood, circled in place several times, then settled at her feet, his nose practically tucked under his tail.

Charlotte sighed again, envying the dog with his simple needs and easy pleasures. Suddenly, she wanted her old life back. In the past she would not have thought twice about being left behind. It was a foregone conclusion that she would not participate in most winter outings, especially if there was a large group. Due to her crippled leg, her indoor activities were severely limited, her outdoor activities almost nonexistent, especially in this sort of weather.

Charlotte is too weak, Charlotte is too unsteady on her feet, Charlotte is too delicate, she will surely catch a chill and become gravely ill. She had heard those words in various combinations all her life and had come to accept them as gospel. But being with Daniel Tremaine these many days had altered her view. He expected more from her, and thus she expected more from herself.

By necessity, she had been content with calm and

quiet, had been accepting of her solitary existence. It was not wonderful, nor was it so terribly awful. But now . . . now she wanted something more. Much more. She wanted excitement and thrills. She wanted intense emotions, be they happy or sad. She wanted to be more of a participant and less of a bystander to life. She wanted laughter and lightness in her heart, along with those special emotions that only a man, a man devoted to her, could provide.

Pipe dreams, every last one.

"Oh, there you are," a male voice called from the doorway. "I've been scouring the house looking for you."

Charlotte did not have to turn her head to identify the speaker. "Hello, Daniel."

"Nearly everyone is preparing to go outside to enjoy the newly fallen snow. Childish, I know, but it will be fun. I came to find you so we could go out together."

"The weather is too harsh for me to go outside," she answered flatly.

"Nonsense." He came closer, avoiding tripping over Apollo with nimble skill. "The snowfall is beginning to ease and it isn't that cold. Many of the children are going; you'll be fine."

"I would be a burden, miserable in the snow and cold, and most assuredly spoil the outing for everyone else," she said in a dismissive tone.

"Not for me," he responded earnestly. "It will not be half as enjoyable if you are not along."

Charlotte slowly turned her head back to the window. She pretended an interest in the lessening snowfall, but in actuality she was studying Daniel's reflection in the window glass.

"Do you like the snow, Charlotte?"

She shrugged, feeling peevish and childish and despising herself for it.

"I like the snow," he continued. "It can be beautiful when it first falls and clings to the tree branches and bushes. And at night, it often seems to glow, as it lights up everything around it."

She frowned, disliking his cheerful, enthusiastic mood, resenting the feeling of vulnerability that overcame her at his inquiries. How could she possibly like the snow? It was as alien to her as walking on water.

"Snow is cold," she said flatly. "And wet. And slippery. 'Tis dangerous."

He looked momentarily disconcerted by her response and she vowed from that moment on she would try her best to be a bit more direct with him. It was past time he learned the realities of living in her world.

"You sound like you are afraid of it," he joked. "Which is utterly ridiculous."

Charlotte sucked in a breath, then leapt to her feet, too restless to sit. Apollo instantly stood, alerted, agitated by her mood. She patted the dog reassuringly on the head. "You know nothing about what I fear, Mr. Tremaine. What is ridiculous is that you presume a knowledge you obviously lack."

"Then tell me."

The spark of fighting spirit so quickly ignited, was swiftly extinguished. Charlotte's shoulders slumped forward. She suddenly felt old and tired.

"I am clumsy enough in calm weather, 'twould be foolish to tempt fate in such poor conditions," she admitted, trying to keep the emotion from her voice, but there were tears threatening in her eyes.

"You are not clumsy, Charlotte." He touched her cheek, his eyes warm with affection. "True, you might have to exercise a bit more caution than others, but that hardly precludes you from participating."

"I cannot possibly ice-skate," she blurted out.

"Nor can I," he said. "Anytime I have tried, I have fallen on my arse."

"Daniel!"

He gave her a mischievous smile. "'Tis the truth. I am a complete failure at ice-skating. However, I have considerable skill with a sled and I insist that you go sledding with me."

"I've never been."

"Then it is past time you tried. I will summon your maid. You need to put on a warmer gown and forgive my indelicacy, warmer stockings."

Charlotte could not help the smile that broke from her lips. Now he was concerned about being indelicate? After he had just spoken the word *arse* within her hearing?

He turned to walk away, no doubt to summon her maid. Charlotte's mood sobered. Unable to stop herself, she whispered, "Why are you doing this, Daniel?"

His shoulders stiffened. He stopped, then pivoted to face her. "It makes me happy to be with you. And I believe you will enjoy being outside in the snow, if only you give it a chance. I suspect, Charlotte, that you shut yourself away on purpose, you deliberately keep your distance from others. But I think deep down you would prefer to end your isolation."

Gracious. He seemed able to read her mind, which certainly gave him an unfair advantage. She hesitated, caught between common sense and longing. Then he gave her a smile that melted her fears. Surrendering, she followed him out the door.

With her maid's help she changed into a simple gown of soft wool and at her suggestion donned two pairs of woolen stockings and a pair of sturdy boots. It took longer than expected and by the time Charlotte reached the front hall foyer, it was deserted.

"Everyone is on the lawn, Lady Charlotte," a passing footman helpfully informed her.

"Thank you, Jenkins."

Pulling on her warmest gloves, Charlotte gingerly walked out on the back terrace. Bracing her hands on the railing, she inhaled the cool, wintry air. And smiled.

The lawn was teeming with people. The snow was about four inches deep and still falling, though very lightly. Everyone was dressed warmly in layers of coats and hats and scarves, laughing and talking merrily. Right in the thick of it all she could see Lily, her red woolen coat blazing as she dashed about, screeching with excitement.

Pink-cheeked, eyes bright, her hair slowly freeing itself from her braid, Lily was the picture of carefree joy. She was clearly the leader of the group of seven children who were busy chasing each other and trying to slide on the snow. Nearly all landed on their rears. Or arses, as Daniel would say.

He was, unfortunately, the one person Charlotte did not find among the crowd. Growing nervous, she continued to scan the many faces and then suddenly he appeared, emerging from the center of the group. Charlotte remained on the terrace for several minutes, then cautiously made her way down to the bottom, clinging to the rail, hand over hand.

Everyone was so full of wild, uninhibited joy she was nearly overwhelmed by it. Being so close to all the merriment made Charlotte feel a real part of it. It was a good beginning. If she did nothing else today but contentedly stand near and watch everyone else make fools of themselves, it would be progress. She would be happy.

But Daniel Tremaine had another idea.

He came toward her, his eyes bright, his face flushed from the cold. Lacy flakes coated his forehead and dusted his dark lashes. He looked fit and virile and oh, so very handsome.

"Give me your hand," he said when he reached her.

She slowly set her hand in his, feeling a warm tingle through the layers of their gloves. "The snow is very slippery. I fear I might fall," she confessed.

"I'll catch you," he promised.

She went trustingly toward him, her limp more exaggerated due to her slow, careful movements. To her relief, she did not fall, but her foot suddenly slipped and she swayed badly, teetering to one side. Daniel caught her around the waist.

Her body sagged against him. "Be careful!" she screeched. "If I fall, I will most likely bring you down with me."

"Why, Lady Charlotte, nothing would please me more than to take a tumble with you."

She blushed to the roots of her hair, which were hidden beneath her bonnet. She straightened, then planted her feet firmly in place. Daniel's arm remained around her waist.

"Where is everyone going?" she asked.

"To the edge of the south garden. We have it on good authority there is a hill worthy of a sled ride."

Charlotte knew the spot. "It is an impressive hill, but when you reach the bottom, it trails into some fairly dense woods."

"Then we must take precautions to make certain nobody crashes into any of the larger trees."

"Daniel!"

"I'm teasing, Charlotte. We shall all be very responsible adults. No one will come to any harm."

He gazed at her solemnly to emphasize his sincerity,

but his assurance that there would be adult behavior was soon challenged as a snowball swished by, coming perilously close to his head.

"Sorry, Mr. Tremaine," Lady Marion yelled. "I was aiming for my cousin."

"Oh, my." Charlotte huffed out a cold breath of air.

"Quick!" Daniel grabbed her hand and pulled her forward.

"There is nowhere to take cover," she hissed as another snowball was hurled at them. This one struck Daniel on the nose. He sputtered and was trying to clean off his face, when a second snowball hit him squarely in the chest.

"For heaven sakes, woman, help me!" he shouted.

"Oh, my," Charlotte repeated. She reached up and tried to brush the cold, wet snow off his cheeks, but he anxiously pushed her hands away.

"We are being ambushed, Charlotte. We must fight back."

Demonstrating the point, he reached down and packed a large handful of snow into a ball. While still bent over he hurled it through the air. It landed neatly on Viscount Cranborne's shoulder, who let out a roar of laughter.

In rapid succession, Daniel threw several more snow-balls, each hitting a target. An equal number then zoomed through the air toward them, but all missed.

"Thankfully, my cousin Marion has dismal aim," Charlotte shouted, to be heard over the giggles and squeals.

It had now escalated into an unruly brawl, with everyone hurling snowballs in all directions. For an instant Charlotte wished she was standing on the sidelines, away from the frantic, frenzied activity. She wanted to be back inside, sitting in front of the fire, where it was warm and safe and dry. And sane.

Daniel was doing an admirable job of protecting her. He made and threw snowballs faster than any of the other gentlemen and his missives seemed to always reach their intended targets. Protected by his deadly accurate aim, Charlotte began to relax, to enjoy herself until she felt a soft snowball splatter against her thigh. Charlotte turned and found Marion grinning smugly at her from a few yards away.

"Come on, Charlotte, you need to retaliate," Marion declared. No sooner had the words left her cousin's mouth, Marion was struck in the back with a large snowball. By Daniel.

Charlotte laughed and felt suddenly, unexpectedly free. She knelt and gathered a handful of snow, formed a ball, then zeroed in on her target.

"Wait! Stand up. 'Tis very hard to make an accurate throw from your knees," Daniel advised.

Charlotte obligingly stood, reached back with her arm and hurled the snowball with all her might. It made a pleasing, splattering sound as it connected with a warm body. Problem was, it connected with the wrong body.

Daniel's face was covered in snow. It dripped down his forehead to his nose, then slid past his mouth to his chin. "You look like a deranged snowman," Charlotte whispered, before a pealing laugh broke free.

"And you dare to criticize your cousin's aim," he said. "Unless I was the true target?"

"Oh, my, no." She moved awkwardly toward him, thinking to help brush the snow away. But a closer look had her pealing with laughter again. He looked utterly ridiculous.

Fortunately the battle was winding down. A truce

was called. A few stray snowballs hurled through the air and then none. Exhausted, yet happy, the merry group gathered together and began walking toward the edge of the south lawn, with Lily and several of the other children leading the way. Someone started singing a Christmas carol and soon they all joined in, singing and marching along in rhythm to the song.

Lily dropped back from her position at the front of the line to walk beside Charlotte. Grasping her aunt's hand, the little girl gazed up, her eyes bright with excitement. "I so wish Papa was with us. Will he come home soon?"

Charlotte nearly stopped walking, startled to realize her brother was not among them. "Did he tell you he was going out?"

"Yes, on an errand with Miss Rebecca. But I want him to come back so we can play in the snow together."

"I'm sure he will be back soon," Charlotte said.

The matter was promptly forgotten by both females as they reached the top of the hill. The servants had brought the sleds and left them neatly lined in a row. There were five in total, all in good condition, most large enough for two or even three riders.

"I want to be first!" Lily demanded, possessively grasping the rope of the largest sled.

"Best let one of the adults do a trial run, just to be certain there are no unexpected difficulties," Lady Marion suggested. She turned to her husband with a saucy smile. "Shall we do the honors, my love?"

"Delighted!" Viscount Cranborne rubbed his gloved hands together before taking the rope of the sled. He sat first, then patted the space in front of him. "For you, my dear."

Marion giggled like a schoolgirl and promptly sat where he indicated. Daniel and Lord Bailey stood behind the sled, their hands on the viscount's back. On the count of three, they pushed the pair forward and the sled careened wildly down the hill, disappearing at an alarming speed.

Marion's shrieks of laughter could be clearly heard even when the pair safely reached the bottom.

"Excellent run," Lord Bailey cried. "Who's next?"

"Me! Me!" Lily pushed herself forward.

Lord Bailey frowned. "You need at least one adult to go with you, Lady Lily."

"Aunt Charlotte will go."

"Oh, dear, I'm not sure—"

"I will take charge of the sled," Daniel offered.

"Capital idea," Lord Bailey answered. "Now we just need to wait for Cranborne to get out of the way."

"I want to go as fast as lightning, Aunt Charlotte," Lily proclaimed.

"Mr. Tremaine will steer our sled," Charlotte answered. "He will determine our speed."

"Actually, the condition of the hill will determine our speed," Daniel replied. "And based on how quickly Lord Cranborne and Lady Marion reached the bottom, we shall go very fast indeed."

Charlotte swallowed back her sudden rush of panic. Gracious, was she about to make a colossal fool of herself? She turned her head toward Daniel, searching for assurance, but he was staring at the bottom of the hill.

Her gaze went to his jaw. A shadow of whiskers was forming. The dark, faint stubble was surprisingly intriguing. She had a sudden, mad urge to reach out and touch it, to discover the feel of his masculine face.

Charlotte wrenched her gaze away and wiped a few flakes of snow that had fallen on her cheek with a hand that shook slightly. It appeared that along with her courage, she was in danger of relinquishing the last shred of her common sense.

"You are not going to lose your nerve now, are you, Charlotte?" Daniel asked.

"A lady never goes back on her word," she said with conviction. "But I will ride only if you promise to hold me tightly."

"Nothing would please me more."

For all her bravado, Charlotte was terribly nervous. She could hear her heartbeat thudding in her ears. She clasped her gloved hands loosely before her and concentrated on relaxing, hoping at the very least she was not revealing the turmoil of her feelings.

Up close the sleds looked alarmingly narrow and frail. Charlotte swallowed hard, telling herself if she tumbled off it was unlikely she would be seriously injured. The layers of snow would provide an adequate, if cold, cushion.

Daniel sat first, then indicated she should seat herself in front of him. "Now move back and make room for Lady Lily," he instructed.

Obediently Charlotte wiggled until her back was pressed snugly against Daniel's front. Lord Bailey helped Lily get into place, in front of Charlotte. The moment the little girl was settled, Charlotte set her arms tightly around her niece.

"I think I shall scream," Lily announced with an excited giggle as Lord Bailey pulled them back and then with a mighty huff shoved them off the edge of the slope. "What about you, Aunt Charlotte?"

Charlotte answered Lily with a shriek of her own. The sled hurled down the slope at a speed that left Charlotte nearly breathless. Just when she was certain she would lose her balance she felt Daniel's arms tighten around her. She could feel him lean to the left and realized he was trying to steer their course. Instinctively she mirrored his movements, but in her inexperience leaned too far over.

"Charlotte, no, just stay in place," Daniel muttered, but it was too late.

As they reached the bottom, the sled tipped over, dumping them into the soft snow. They rolled in it, a tangle of arms and legs. From the top of the hill, Charlotte could hear giggling and shouting and a few male cheers.

Slowly, she began to right herself. It was then that she saw Lily lying facedown in the snow. Reaching over, she rolled the little girl until she was lying flat on her back. "Are you all right?" she asked anxiously, brushing the snow from Lily's hat.

Lily stared up at her, saucer-eyed. Charlotte worried she might be hurt, or upset by the wild ride and subsequent tumble in the snow. She ran her hands nervously down Lily's arms and legs, searching for signs of injury. Her touch seemed to bring the child back to life and the little girl struggled to sit up.

"Again! I want to go again!" Lily's excitement could not be contained. She bolted upright, nearly fell over, then straightened. Her head turned toward the top of the hill. "Wait, Lord Bailey! Wait for me! I want to go again. There is room for me on your sled."

Scrambling through the snow, Lily began to run back up the hill. One of the boys sat with Lord and Lady Bailey on the sled and Lily let out a cry of disappointment. But Viscount Cranborne waved, then pointed at his sled, indicating he was saving a spot for Lily. The little girl squealed with delight and redoubled her efforts to quickly climb the hill.

Charlotte let out a loud sigh and sank with exhaustion down into the snow.

"Good Lord, that was fun," Daniel exclaimed.

"I'm freezing," Charlotte answered.

Daniel scooted over, half-sitting, half-sprawling on the ground next to her. He drew her into his arms so that her spine was pressed into his stomach and her bottom was against his groin. He began rubbing the chilled length of her arm.

"I hope you are getting warmer. I know that I am." His voice was dryly humorous. "Are you tired? Shall we return to the house to get dry and warm?"

"No. Let's ride again. But this time, let me steer."

He laughed and she joined him. They stood. Charlotte held out her hand and allowed Daniel to tug her back up the hill. Snow had gotten in to the top of her boot, numbing her left ankle. Actually, both her feet were wet and cold, her nose near frozen. She was sore in places a lady never mentioned, much less thought about.

The line for the sleds moved quickly, since several of the adults had stopped after taking a single ride. Charlotte stomped her feet in the snow and slapped her hands against her sides, trying to get warm. She was certain her cheeks must be fiery red and her nose a similar shade, thanks to the cold. Yet as she settled herself for a second time on the sled, an errant thought past through her mind.

She had never been happier in her life.

Rebecca was feeling anxious about returning to the manor house, wondering how many people were aware they had been gone so long. Though unsure precisely what time it was, she feared they would arrive just as afternoon tea was being served, thus bringing additional unwanted attention to themselves. She dreaded the speculation that might occur, the curiosity about where they had stayed and what they had done while the storm raged.

It seemed truly ironic that she should suffer such extreme pangs of guilt when they had not done anything so terribly scandalous. An intimate conversation and one passionate kiss hardly constituted a torrid, immoral afternoon. They had sought shelter to remain safe, not to steal time alone.

Yet the guilt intensified. Possibly because deep down she had wanted something more to happen between them? Something more intimate, more physical, more compromising?

Whatever the reason, she tried to ignore the guilt, deciding she was going to leave the explanations to the earl. It was his house, his family, his guests.

They entered a thicket of woods that bordered the earl's estate. After a time they emerged on the other side, totally unprepared for the sight that greeted them. A substantial gathering of adults and children were clamoring up and down the large hill on sleds, shrieking with laughter, shouting out to each other and generally having a marvelous time.

"Shall we join in the fun?" Cameron asked.

Rebecca steered her mount next to his, then turned to find him close enough so that she could see the faint lines that fanned from the corners of his eyes. Eyes that normally held depth and maturity, that were often serious and considering. Eyes that were suddenly twinkling like a lad.

"The horses must be tired, my lord. We should bring them to the stables as soon as possible."

"Tom can do that for us."

It was then Rebecca noticed a young groom running toward them. The earl dismounted. He advanced on

Rebecca, wrapped his hands around her waist and practically pulled her from the saddle. When she reached the ground, he paused a moment and looked at her. She stared back, losing her thread of thought, forgetting that she wanted to ask him what story they would tell to explain their long absence.

Movement stirred beside them. Rebecca blushed and noticed the groom patiently waiting, his eyes carefully averted. At the earl's command, the lad obligingly took hold of their horses' reins and led the animals away.

Slowly they climbed the hill. There were shouts and waves from the sledders as they careened down the hill. When they reached the top, they separated. Rebecca noted the earl entered the middle of the pack of men, confident and commanding. They crowded around him, all seeming to speak at once.

"We noticed you arrived on horseback. 'Tis a rather odd time of day to be taking a ride, Hampton," Lord Bailey commented.

"We set out earlier to visit one of the tenant farms," the earl explained. "Fortunately, we were able to stay ahead of the worst of the storm on our journey back."

"Papa!" Lily's shout echoed through the trees, flushing a flock of birds from their nest. "You must ride on the sled with me."

"Is it our turn?" he asked.

"Oh, yes. Now hurry."

Laughing, he allowed the child to tug on his hand and pull him away. He gestured with his other hand, indicating that Rebecca should join them. She hesitated. Too long, unfortunately. One of the boys jumped on the sled and the trio went down the hill.

Lady Marion approached, tucking her arm through Rebecca's. "Come stand with me while we wait our turn on the sleds," she said, but Rebecca was not fooled by the ploy. No doubt Lady Marion wanted privacy for a different reason. Rebecca swallowed hard, fearing the other woman would quiz her about how long she and the earl had been away from the manor together. And what they had been doing.

"Have you been having fun out in the snow, Lady Marion?" Rebecca asked.

"I have indeed, Miss Tremaine and I am so pleased that you have joined us. It's been a grand afternoon, even with the antics of the men. They are acting more like boys than the young lads who came along. But no matter. There is something of extreme importance I need to discuss with you."

Oh, no. Rebecca did not like the sound of that request. She cast her eyes about, hoping for a means of escape, but found none. "Is there some sort of problem, Lady Marion?"

"I would not classify it as a problem at this stage. But unless something is done, I fear it could escalate into a deep concern. For both our families." She drew closer to Rebecca. "Charlotte is enamored with your brother. And I am convinced, he in turn has fallen in love with her."

Rebecca stared at Lady Marion in amazement. Of all the things she feared the good woman might say, this was one thought that had never entered her mind.

"What? How in the world can you be so certain? My brother is barely acquainted with Lady Charlotte."

Lady Marion dismissed her comments with a dramatic wave of her arm. "Love can happen in an instant. With one look, one touch, one whispered compliment. Isn't it marvelous?"

For an instant all Rebecca could manage was a

thunderstruck stare. "I am sure you are mistaken," she finally remarked.

Lady Marion looked offended. "I most definitely am not mistaken. Why, 'tis as obvious as the nose on your face, Miss Tremaine. All one need do is to observe them. Have you not noticed how your brother's eyes follow Charlotte around the room and the way he grins like a besotted fool when he looks at her?" Her tone was serious, but there was a smile lurking in her eyes. "On, no, he is in love. Trust me, I am an expert on these matters."

"Daniel and Lady Charlotte?" Rebecca's voice trailed off in astonishment. She and Daniel had discussed his admiration for Lady Charlotte soon after they arrived at Windmere and Rebecca had encouraged him to follow his heart. Yet she never honestly believed it would come to anything.

Could Lady Marion be right? Had Daniel developed a tendre for Lady Charlotte?

"I suppose it is possible," Rebecca began.

Lady Marion silenced her with another dramatic wave of her gloved hand. "It's more than possible. It's very real! Of course the one sticky wicket in this lovely romance is Cameron. As you know, I adore my cousin, but like all men he can be a bit of an idiot sometimes."

Amazingly, Rebecca understood what Lady Marion was trying to say. "Yes, the earl would not approve of a match between Daniel and his sister."

"Probably not," Lady Marion agreed. "At least initially. But with the right argument, he could be convinced. After all he has invited you into his home to share the Christmas holiday. That must mean he holds you both in high regard."

Rebecca shifted uncomfortably in the snow. If Lady Marion knew the real reason they had been invited, she would no doubt quickly change her tune. "The earl is generous and kind, but extending his hospitality to us and welcoming us into his family are two entirely different matters. We hardly move within the same social circles and certainly cannot lay claim to any significant noble ancestry."

"You are well educated and genteel and your brother is a highly successful businessman. In these matters, wealth does count for something."

Rebecca shook her head. "It should, yet I'm sure Lady Charlotte is an heiress in her own right. She hardly needs to marry for money."

"No, but she does need to marry for love." Lady Marion reached down, took Rebecca's hand and squeezed it briefly. "Don't look so glum. There is always hope. After all, Christmas is the season for goodwill, brotherhood and most important of all, miracles."

Chapter 14

"Ah, Daniel, I'm so glad I caught you. Do you have a moment to spare?" Rebecca asked as she hurried down the hall toward her brother. "I need to talk with you."

After a restless night thinking about everything Lady Marion had said yesterday afternoon, Rebecca decided the only way to get to the truth of the matter was to speak directly to her brother.

Daniel frowned. "Can it wait? Lord Hampton is taking us shooting. It would be rude to keep the other gentlemen waiting."

"Shooting?" Rebecca shuddered. "That hardly seems like a charitable Christmas outing."

"Don't be so softhearted, Becca. Many of the birds will starve if we don't thin out the flocks. And those we do shoot will be given to the local families. They will grace many a Christmas table and no doubt provide a good deal of cheer."

Rebecca forced a smile. "I suppose that makes it a bit better. But just a bit. Are you certain you need to dash? This won't take long. I worry if we don't speak now, we will never find the time to be alone."

"True, there does always seem to be something going on around here."

"Precisely. Who ever knew that socializing could be so very time-consuming and exhausting?"

Daniel consulted the large clock in the hallway. "I can give you a few minutes. Come, let's step in here." He opened the nearest door.

They went inside. It was a lovely chamber, boasting a cozy sitting area in front of a pair of French doors that led out to the terraced gardens. A cheerful fire was lit, giving the space a warm, welcoming feel. It seemed the perfect spot to gain some privacy, and Rebecca could not help but wonder how many rooms there were in this enormous, rambling mansion.

"I wanted to speak with you about Lady Charlotte," she said.

Daniel stiffened noticeably, his expression growing guarded. "Lady Charlotte? The earl's sister?"

"Yes." Alarm bells began to clang in Rebecca's head, but she forced herself to be calm. She paused, trying to frame her question in such a way as to not offend. "When we first arrived, you expressed an admiration for her. I was wondering if you still held such an opinion."

"About Lady Charlotte?"

"Yes, Daniel, about Lady Charlotte."

He shuffled his feet, moving closer to the fire. "She seems like a perfectly respectable lady. Kind, thoughtful. Rather shy."

"Have you been spending a great deal of your time with her?"

He inhaled sharply. "Why do you ask?"

Rebecca rubbed her brow. This was proving far more difficult than she imagined. They were simple, straightforward questions, but Daniel's reactions made her feel as if she were prying into something very personal. Something that was not any of her business.

"Your attention to Lady Charlotte has been noted by another, who remarked upon it to me," she said.

"Who? Was it the earl?" Distress flickered in Daniel's eyes. He paced toward the French windows, stopped, then turned. "Has there been a great deal of gossip about myself and Lady Charlotte? What are people saying?"

"I don't think they are saying anything. Well, not that I know of, anyway. As far as I am aware, only Lady Marion seems to believe there is something going on between you and Lady Charlotte." Rebecca took a step closer. "Is that true, Daniel?"

Her brother was now prowling restlessly about the room. "Nothing unseemly has happened between us."

The look in his eyes made her feel self-conscious. "I never thought that it had. I know you are a gentleman, a man who respects a lady."

A wary expression crossed his features, which then took on a decidedly guilty look. "I did kiss her, though. Twice."

Rebecca swallowed her surprise. "Two kisses? Goodness, you must be smitten." She tried to make light of it, but the teasing lilt in her voice fell flat.

"Two kisses hardly constitute a torrid romance, Becca. Charlotte is a lady, a tenderhearted, innocent woman."

Rebecca tried to smile, but she was still struggling with her shock. "I think she is delightful."

"She is more than delightful. She is exceptional. A rare jewel. Intelligent, kind, unspoiled." He ran his fingers through his hair, then after an interval of silence added, "Would you kindly stop looking so horrified. I know my growing obsession is not good for me. Or her."

Rebecca could not have disagreed more. "Why-ever not?"

"Nothing can ever come of it."

"You sound so sure. Has she rejected you?"

"No."

"Then I don't understand."

He stopped pacing, but drummed his fingertips nervously on the edge of the padded armchair. "Your, hmm, shall we say, *unique* situation with Lord Hampton precludes me from making any serious considerations about my relationship with Lady Charlotte," he said. "Though I'll own I have a tough hide, and sometimes have acted with far more bluster than brains in my life, 'tis damn hard to be put in a position where you have to threaten your future brother-in-law. Even I would be unable to pull that off."

"Threaten?" She stared at him wordlessly.

"You are my sister. I owe you my loyalty, Becca. Lord Hampton has been more than fair by allowing you to see Lily, but we know he could change his mind on a whim and deny you access to the child. If that happens, we must be prepared to do whatever is necessary. Including threats."

Oh, dear, this was all because of her? "I am humbled by your support, Daniel. Far more than you will ever know." Her eyes jerked up to meet his. "But my problems with the earl are my own. They should not affect your feelings or your future with Lady Charlotte."

He looked at her closely, then looked away. "Even if I wanted to consider a future with Charlotte, it would be impossible. I would never be warmly greeted as a potential suitor. We are not of the earl's social stature and in his world, breeding, rank and position are everything."

"But you are more than his equal," Rebecca cried

out in protest. "In character, in wealth, in social graces. You have nothing to be ashamed of, Daniel."

Her optimistic statement did not coax a like response from her brother. There was something else, something he wasn't telling her. She was just about to ask, when he spoke.

"There is another reason. A foolish one, really. Born of my insecurity."

"Tell me."

A flicker of something entered, then left his eyes. "Charlotte has led a pampered, yet difficult life. At her core she is lonely and has not very often been in the company of men. She seems to return my regard and yet I cannot help but wonder if her interest is merely a result of my being the only man who has paid her any significant attention."

"I doubt that very much." Rebecca would have smiled, but her brother looked so serious, so concerned. He really was unsure. "Lady Charlotte is an intelligent woman, for all her naivete. I don't believe she would be so easily taken in by a handsome face and some witty conversation. And she allowed you not one, but two kisses. Clearly she cares for you, perhaps even loves you. But you know there is only one way that you can discover the truth."

"One way?"

"You must ask her, Daniel."

"Egad, I'm acting like a lovesick fool, aren't I?" His voice rose a notch.

"I find it rather endearing."

"I find it rather nauseating."

Rebecca understood his embarrassment, sympathized with his predicament. Yet she would have considered herself a poor sister indeed if she did not encourage him to act upon his feelings. Love was a rare and wondrous emotion, not to be squandered if one was lucky enough to find it.

"Listen to me, Daniel. If you search your heart and discover that you do indeed love Lady Charlotte, then you must act. Do not allow this real chance at happiness to slip away from you because of a few difficulties."

He pressed his fingers to his temples, rubbing them furiously as though he had a searing headache. Then he lowered his hand and let out a short, gruff laugh. "I should have known you would go all starry-eyed and sappy on me. Women are such romantics."

"We are, indeed." Rebecca stretched our her arms and gave him a tight hug.

"I will consider everything you have said most carefully, Becca," he whispered.

"Good." She pulled back and gave him what she hoped was an encouraging smile. "Just remember, you do not have much time to make a decision. It will be Christmas in a few days and we shall depart Windmere soon after the holiday."

"I know." The porcelain clock on the fireplace mantel chimed the hour. "Goodness, I need to hurry," Daniel exclaimed as he rushed out the door.

Rebecca followed slowly, almost laughing at her own bravado as she recalled their conversation. She sounded so sure of herself, so confident in the rightness of her opinion. Yet she could not help but wonder, if the opportunity to express her growing feelings for the earl ever presented itself, would she have the courage to follow her own advice?

"I want to go ice-skating," Lily said. "Papa promised we would go today, but I can't find him. Will you take me, Miss Rebecca? Please?"

Startled, Rebecca looked up from the basket she was arranging. Several of the ladies were assisting the dowager countess with the final touches on the gift baskets for the local families. She had joined them directly after speaking with Daniel. Rebecca was pleased to help, for it was a familiar task, one she had done often with her parents for the families of their parish.

Lily had wandered in to watch and then surprised Rebecca with her request. With her grandmother and aunt present, why had the little girl chosen Rebecca? She would have liked to think it was because Lily craved her company, but was realistic to know there was probably another reason. Most likely Lily thought she'd have the best chance of getting her way with Rebecca, especially with this outdoor activity.

"I would very much like to take you skating, Lady Lily," Rebecca said sincerely. "But I'm afraid I too am busy right now. Would you like to help with my baskets? As you see, I am putting some of the cookies we baked the other day in each one."

Lily glanced over at the basket, then pulled a face. "I want to tie the bows on the top, but I can't tie very well."

"You can hand me the fruit," Rebecca suggested.

"Or help me count out the candy sticks to make sure everyone has an equal amount," Lady Charlotte interjected.

Lily ran her finger over the polished surface of the dining room table and slowly shook her head. "That's not much fun."

The women concentrated on their tasks and with a mulish expression Lily soon drifted away. Rebecca assumed she might visit the kitchen to beg a treat from Cook or attempt to corner Horace for a cuddle. She thought briefly of the sweet gray kitten at the

Braggs's farm and smiled. Lily was going to adore her Christmas gift.

The remainder of the morning passed quickly. While not entirely comfortable, Rebecca did enjoy her time with the other ladies. Lady Marion could always be counted upon to lighten the mood and the dowager countess was gracious, though reserved.

Everyone went her separate way when the job was finished, many promising to assist in the delivery of the baskets on Christmas Eve. Deciding it was the perfect time for some solitude, Rebecca dressed warmly, put on her sturdy walking books and set off for a walk at a brisk pace.

Apollo was her uninvited companion, joining her the moment she stepped beyond the stables. He barked a friendly greeting and ran to her side. The large dog seemed thrilled to be out in the snow. He jumped, leapt, then buried his nose in it, rolling blissfully on his back. Rebecca could not help but laugh at his silly antics.

It was a glorious afternoon. The sky was a brilliant cloudless blue, the shining sun reflecting off the frozen tree branches glistening merrily. Apollo romped happily beside her, occasionally abandoning her to chase after a squirrel or bark at a winter bird nestled in the bushes.

He uncovered a sizable stick from beneath the snow and brought it to her, dropping it expectantly at her feet. Rebecca laughed and threw it. Though her attempt was a modest effort, Apollo tore off after it, returning quickly to continue the game.

Rebecca continued to walk and throw until her arm began to ache from the exercise. Deciding it was time to head back to the manor, she turned, then paused as she heard the distinct sound of skate blades cutting against the ice. On impulse she moved toward the noise, expecting to come across a party of skaters.

Instead she discovered one lone figure on the ice twirling merrily in the center of the pond, the skirt of her red coat billowing out with each spin.

Lily.

The little imp. Obviously, she had talked someone into taking her skating. It was not totally surprising, given the child's determined nature. When she wanted something, she persisted until she got it. A lesson that perhaps Rebecca could learn from her child?

Rebecca's eyes searched the bank for signs of the earl, but she did not see him. Strange, she assumed he had been the one to finally succumb to Lily's fervent pleas and accompany the little girl to the pond. Mayhap it was Mrs. James instead?

Rebecca continued to look around and soon realized that neither the earl, nor Mrs. James, nor any other adult for that matter was in attendance. Obviously, Lily had come on her own. A willful, foolish and defiant act.

"Lily!"

Startled, the little girl turned, then waved enthusiastically. "I've been practicing ever so hard and I can finally spin. Watch me, Miss Rebecca."

The scold on Rebecca's lips was momentarily silenced as she watched Lily carefully glide forward on the ice, then tuck her arms to her side and spin in a circle. It was a rather impressive feat for a child of her years.

"Very pretty, Lady Lily. But I insist you come off the ice now. As you well know, you should not have come here on your own."

"But I wanted to go ice-skating. Papa said he would take me, but he never did. Neither did you."

"I was planning on surprising you after luncheon."

Lily clapped her hands together in delight. "Maybe Papa can come too."

"We won't be coming back to skate this afternoon," Rebecca answered. "I'm not sure how your father will feel about our outing after he discovers what you have done this morning."

"But Papa doesn't know! Can't it be our secret?"

Rebecca gave her a grimace. "No."

Lily's expression grew troubled. "Please don't tattle on me, Miss Rebecca. Papa will be ever so cross."

Her answer sealed her fate. There was no question now that the child knew she was doing something wrong. For her own sake, she would have to be punished.

"I am afraid that you have given me no choice," Rebecca said gravely. "I will however try to explain—"

Rebecca's words were cut off by a harsh, horrible cracking sound. Lily, who was weaving her way from the middle of the pond toward Rebecca halted suddenly. They glanced simultaneously down at her feet. Water began to run beneath the cracks of the ice, surrounding Lily's skates.

Rebecca did not hesitate. She ran as fast as she could, scrambling down the slight bank to the edge of the pond, heedless of the snow that fell into the top of her boots, ignoring the branches that tore at her coat and scratched her cheek.

"Don't move!" she screamed.

Lily froze. But it made no difference. Another sound, another crack and the ice splintered further.

Rebecca tested the surface gingerly with the tip of her boot. Up close, she could see that the water was not entirely frozen. Some sections were thick with several solid inches of ice, while other parts of the pond were nearly translucent, with only a thin glaze covering the surface.

It was a miracle that Lily had not broken through sooner. Rebecca shuddered to think what might have happened if the little girl had fallen into the water while out here alone.

"I'm scared," Lily wailed. "I don't want to be on the ice anymore."

The fright in her voice twisted Rebecca's stomach. She nearly sobbed at the child's fear, knowing all too soon Lily might get her wish. She would not be on the ice, but rather in the freezing water beneath it.

"You must make your way over to me," Rebecca said, her voice hitching with emotion. "But you must go very slowly and very carefully. Can you do that for me, sweetheart?"

Lily's brow wrinkled in concentration as she started forward. Head bowed, she stared at her skates. She moved but a few inches and there was another loud snap as the ice beneath her cracked further. Her head flew up, her eyes widened even more. "I can't do it! The ice keeps breaking! Please, oh, please, Miss Rebecca, come and get me."

Rebecca glanced down at the thinner ice in front of her and nearly screamed in frustration. Her first instinct was to scramble across the pond as fast as she was able and snatch the child away from harm. But she was fearful of putting too much pressure on the thin sheet of ice, knowing in its present state it could easily fracture, tumbling them both into the water.

"I'm too heavy to go out on the ice, Lily. If I walk toward you, it will certainly crack."

"I want my papa."

"So do I," Rebecca muttered as she tried to remain calm. The last thing they needed was for Lily to panic further.

Rebecca circled around the side of the pond,

searching desperately for a section where the ice appeared firmer, more solid. Some area where she could get herself onto the pond, or failing that, a safer way for Lily to get off the ice. But she found nothing.

Apollo ran over, happily wagging his tail, eager to be a part of what he thought was another game. He barked a greeting to Lily and set his large paw tentatively on the ice, but quickly pulled it away. Smart dog. With an expression Rebecca could only define as worry, the animal began to pace along the banks of the water's edge, as if searching for a way to reach the child.

Knowing she had little time, Rebecca quickly formulated a plan. "You must slowly get down on your knees and then lie on your tummy, Lily. See, like this!"

Rebecca knelt in the snow, then laid down, gingerly placing her stomach, upper torso and shoulders on the frozen pond, praying the distribution of her weight would prevent the ice from breaking.

It held. Encouraged, she cautiously pushed herself away from the edge toward Lily, as far as she dared. Ahead, she could see the cracks in the ice had lengthened and knew it would not hold together much longer. "That's right, Lily. On your tummy. Very good."

Clearly frightened, the little girl valiantly tried to follow Rebecca's instructions. "It's cold," she moaned. "I'm getting wet."

"I know, but you are also getting closer to me." Rebecca stretched out her arm. "Now wiggle like a worm Lily and reach for my hand."

"Wiggle like a worm," the child repeated in a trembling voice, her eyes glossy wet, her lashes spiked with tears.

Lily took a deep breath and thrust her arms forward, trying to do as she was told. The ice cracked and shifted beneath her and Lily screamed.

"Ignore it!" Rebecca shouted. "Just keep moving forward." The child lay completely still for several long moments, her shoulders heaving as she sobbed.

"I can't."

"You must trust me, Lily. Move! Now!"

Whimpering, Lily moved another foot. Just a few more pushes and she would be close enough to grab. Rebecca stretched her body forward, her muscles screaming in protest. She could see the largest crack begin to widen, like a deadly snake poised to strike.

Hurry, please, oh please, hurry. Wild with fear, Rebecca carefully slid across the frozen pond, desperate to get closer. Encouraged, Lily reached for her with both hands, but they were still too far away. Clearly frustrated, Lily tried to pull herself forward by planting her hands on the ice and the horrible snapping began as the ice broke beneath her palms.

"Help!" Lily yelled.

The panic inside Rebecca was so complete she tried to scream, yet lost her voice. Heedless of her own safety, she propelled herself forward and grabbed Lily's wrist. "I've got you."

Her relief lasted a fraction of a second. Lily's wrist was wet, Rebecca's hold tenuous at best. Within moments Rebecca could feel her grip slipping, could feel the child start to slide from her fingers. This time she did scream, powerless in her fear to prevent it.

Suddenly, there was an immense crack as the ice gave way beneath the child. Her legs and upper body fell into the frozen water; the rupture widening as Lily thrashed, shrieking in shock and fear.

Rebecca put both her hands on Lily's wrist and yanked with all her might, but it was useless. The water had soaked the child's clothes and was pulling her under.

Letting out a grunting yell, Rebecca wrenched her shoulder back, throwing all her weight and strength into the motion. But all she succeeded in doing was to slide herself forward.

Then suddenly her wet grip faltered and Lily was cruelly wrenched from her grasp.

In utter horror, Rebecca saw the child move away, saw water close over the little girl's head. Lily's face was pale, her mouth open in a soundless scream. A cry escaped Rebecca's lips as she lunged forward, ignoring the freezing wet water engulfing the front of her body. She frantically plunged her hand beneath the broken ice into the freezing water, but found nothing.

Terrified, Rebecca put both arms, up to the elbows into the water, doubling her efforts. Twice more she reached down, each time coming up empty. Her hands were soon numb, her strength quickly ebbing, yet she would not quit. Frantic, she continued until finally she touched the soggy material of Lily's cloak.

Nearly sobbing with relief, Rebecca curled her fingers tightly around it and pulled. With a strength she never knew she possessed, she continued tugging, even as she heard the ice beneath her legs begin to crack. All that mattered was freeing Lily from the deadly water.

"Miss Rebecca!"

Lily's sputtering, coughing, gasping cry was the sweetest sound she had ever heard. Rolling onto her back, Rebecca lifted the child from the water, hugging her close. Lily wrapped her arms around Rebecca's neck, squeezing tightly.

It was a good sign. Though cold, wet and scared, at least Lily was alert, breathing heavily, but breathing. A large section of ice floated by and Rebecca realized they were laying on a chuck of ice that had broken free and were bobbing toward the center of the pond.

Throwing her right arm into the freezing water, Rebecca paddled toward the shore. She soon reached a solid section of frozen water. Hoisting them both off their ice raft, Rebecca dragged herself and Lily several feet over the fragile ice. Thankfully, there were no additional cracks, or breaks.

With one final heave, Rebecca threw their bodies forward and they tumbled into the snowy bank. Ground! Solid, firm earth. They were both gasping and shivering. Lily's teeth were chattering, her lips blue. But they were alive. Safe.

Removing her cloak, which miraculously had one dry section, Rebecca wrapped it around Lily and drew the child tightly into her arms. Apollo was immediately at their side, licking their faces, nuzzling them with his nose, whimpering in sympathy.

He pushed his nose between them, anxiously pressing it against Lily's cheek, then Rebecca's. It was nearly as cold and wet as they were. Lily ceased her sobbing and started giggling and Rebecca joined her. Soon they were crying and laughing, as the dog continued his ministrations.

Apollo looked up suddenly. His ears pricked forward, as though he heard someone call him.

"Have you no sense, woman! How could you have allowed her to skate on this ice when clearly it is unsafe?"

Wearily, Rebecca turned and saw the earl sprinting toward them. He was alone and on foot, the thunderous expression on his face a mere hint of his temper.

Rebecca waited until he drew closer before shouting back, "Damn it, my lord, help us!"

His step faltered for an instant, but then he continued

to run toward the pair at breakneck speed. Kneeling, he ripped the greatcoat off his shoulders and wrapped it around both of them.

"I swear I lost ten years off my life when I saw you pull her from the water," he declared.

Lily snuggled against her father, her body trembling. The earl scooped Lily up in his arms and held her against his chest. Then he reached out with his other arm and tugged at Rebecca, pulling her close.

"Well, 'tis not how I usually like to go skating," Rebecca replied sourly.

Then telling herself it was merely her overwrought nerves, Rebecca turned her face into the earl's shoulder and tightly hugged him back.

A heavy feeling constricted Cameron's chest. He was angry and scared but the predominate feeling of protectiveness for these two females surged strongest within him. He tightened his grip, squeezing them both harder as he clasped them to his chest.

He kissed Lily's brow, worried to feel the chill on it.

"We need to get you both back to the house. Quickly."

"Take her," Rebecca answered, her teeth chattering. "My legs feel too weak to hold me. I'll only slow you down."

For a second he was tempted to rush Lily back to the house and leave Rebecca behind, shivering. She certainly deserved the treatment, a fitting punishment for her lack of sense. For putting Lily's life so callously in danger.

"I can manage you both," he grumbled.

He removed his jacket and handed it to Rebecca. Wordlessly she relinquished her section of his greatcoat and donned the jacket. He peeled off Lily's wet overgarments, then carefully wrapped her in the woolen coat, leaving only a small portion of her face exposed to the elements.

Standing, he shifted the child to his stronger right arm, then reached down for Rebecca with his left. Grunting with the effort, he helped her to her feet. With his arm solidly around her waist, they started walking.

It took two tries to make it up the sloping pond embankment, but once on flat ground they moved at a steady pace. Rebecca made a move to pull away from him, but the earl would not allow it. They went a few more feet before Cameron realized he was grinding his teeth.

"You certainly have a devil of a temper," Rebecca observed.

"It is a recently acquired vice," he bristled. "Prevalent only since our acquaintance."

"Don't be mean to Miss Rebecca, Papa," Lily said as she shivered in his arms. "She saved me."

Lily turned to Rebecca, her eyes wide with hero worship. Rebecca reached over and rubbed her hand over the little girl's cheek. Cameron drew in a sharp breath.

"Miss Rebecca's rescue of you would not have been necessary if she had acted as a proper adult and forbade you to skate on the pond in the first place. Obviously, the ice was not thick enough if it could not even carry your slight weight." He exhaled and scowled at Rebecca, his temper still simmering. "I thought she had more sense."

Rebecca let out a snort and muttered something under her breath. A word that sounded suspiciously like a curse. A word that should not have been known, much less uttered, by a lady. Cameron blinked.

"Miss Rebecca was scolding me when the ice broke and I fell in the water."

He raised his brows in question. "Why?"

"Because I was a naughty girl and went ice-skating without telling anyone."

Shocked, he turned to glance down at Rebecca. She gave him a slight, nonchalant shrug.

"You see, my lord. I did not bring Lily out here. Yet I thank the good Lord that I was the one who found her *before* she had her accident and fell through the ice."

The guilt for his hasty and unfair accusation was a sharp pain inside him. "My apologies," he said, hoping he sounded as contrite as he felt. "I had not realized."

"Perhaps next time you will wait to ascertain the facts before you start yelling, my lord." Her scowl softened.

His face paled with more guilt. "Rebecca—"

"Hush, Cameron," she murmured. "We are safe. You had no way of knowing the circumstances. It was cruel of me to tease you."

The throbbing panic in his chest eased. She lifted her head. Her lips were a hair's breath away from his own. Heedless of the little girl he held in his arms, Cameron lowered his chin and brushed his lips softly, briefly against Rebecca's.

Unhesitatingly, she kissed him back. And in that instant Cameron realized he was holding in his arms the two people that were most precious to him.

Chapter 15

Rebecca was starting to feel better. She was warm and dry, wrapped in a soft blanket, nestled in a comfortable chair in her bedchamber, relishing the peace and quiet. The household had gone into an uproar when they had returned, wet, shivering and still partially in shock.

Lily had been whisked away to the nursery and put into a hot bath. The little girl later joined the adults for afternoon tea, where she was the undisputed center of attention. After getting herself into dry clothes, Rebecca had made a brief appearance, mainly to assure herself that Lily was suffering no ill effects from her ordeal.

However, the moment she entered the drawing room, Rebecca had instantly been proclaimed a hero for saving Lily and everyone applauded her bravery and daring. The dowager countess had wept and hugged her close; Lady Charlotte also had tears in her eyes as she repeatedly issued her thanks and gratitude.

Lady Marion had declared a reward should be given and had placed herself in charge of determining exactly what that should be. Even Mrs. James had become emotional when she faced Rebecca, confiding she would have been crushed if any serious injury had befallen Lady Lily.

Rebecca felt decidedly uncomfortable with the accolades and something of a fraud. She would like to believe that she would have done the same for any other child, any other person actually, who was in similar dire straits, but she was honestly uncertain.

Lily was her daughter. Flesh of her flesh. Rebecca knew she would have given her own life to save her little girl. Would she have acted so bravely, so decisively if it was someone else who had fallen through the ice?

Rebecca sighed. Perhaps she should not have stayed in her room this evening, taking dinner on a tray, in an effort to avoid the servants and houseguests who had bombarded her with attention and praise. Perhaps it would have been better to face them again, so the furor and novelty of the situation would wear off.

She plumped the cushion behind her and settled back. Closing her eyes, Rebecca tried to relax, tried to let her mind drift away from the events of the day. It worked for a time and she gradually felt the languid peace of sleep starting to overcome her weary limbs.

She was about to ring for her maid when she heard a soft knock. Then the door opened.

"Perfect timing, Maureen. I am all done in and ready for bed."

Rebecca glanced up. It was not her diminutive maid who stood in the doorway. It was the earl.

"I'm sorry to disturb you," Cameron said. "I just wanted to make sure you were feeling all right."

"I'm fine," she replied, scooting upright in her chair. Self-conscious, Rebecca folded her legs under her skirt. She had kicked off her shoes and removed her stockings earlier and for some reason it felt strangely intimate to greet Lord Hampton with bare feet.

"We missed you at dinner," he said.

"I was tired and frankly feeling overwhelmed by all the attention," she explained.

He smiled. "A far different reaction from Lily. She was basking in the spotlight, telling and retelling the tale over and over."

"'Tis good to hear she is suffering no lasting effects from the trauma."

His lips tightened fractionally. "She seems to have fared well after her tumble through the ice, but I fear she might have a stomachache from all the treats everyone was plying her with tonight."

"Ah, so you have relented on your punishment to deny her dessert?"

"I find myself too relieved at her survival to deny her anything." His handsome face flashed an almost guilty expression of misgiving. "Is that so very wrong?"

She shook her head no, opened her mouth to explain, but then a noise distracted her. Rebecca peered around the earl and saw her maid hovering in the doorway.

"Shall I come back, Miss Rebecca?"

"No, thank you, Maureen," she answered. "You may take yourself off to bed. I will not need you any further tonight."

The maid's brow lifted in confusion. She glanced at the earl, then back at Rebecca. Dipping a hasty curtsy she withdrew, shutting the door firmly behind her.

"I should not be here," Cameron said, voicing what they were both thinking.

"I know."

Rebecca glanced down at the rug. It was highly improper for him to be alone with her, in her bedchamber of all places. Yet he made no move to leave and she said nothing to prompt his departure.

"You seem melancholy tonight," he said.

"Perhaps a bit," she acknowledged. "Spending too much time in my own company afforded me a great deal of time to think, to reflect on the past."

"And that has made you sad?"

She shrugged. "Thinking about what might have been is always dangerous, is it not?"

He moved closer. "Do you ever regret it? What happened between you and Philip?"

"No! Never!" She looked him straight in the eye, needing very much for him to understand. "I am not sorry that I had a physical relationship with Philip. I loved him without reservation and it was something we both wanted."

"But the consequences . . ." the earl's voice trailed off and Rebecca dipped her chin.

"It was devastating when I first found myself in such a predicament. Alone and pregnant, my fiancé dead. My parents took the news well, all things considered. Or at least I thought so at the time." She toyed with a length of green satin ribbon on the skirt of her gown, pleating it into neat folds. "Yet even with all that happened after, all the pain and heartache, I was never sorry there was a child. I could never regret Lily. She is a wonderful little girl, a gift from God."

A brief emotion shifted across his face. "She is a precious child."

"That is what I have always believed, even when others would refute it." A sudden pain settled in Rebecca's chest, squeezing tightly. "It annoyed Great-Aunt Mildred to no end that I was not deeply sorrowful and repentant for my disgraceful, dishonorable actions. I had broken the rules, you see, challenged society itself with my careless, wanton behavior yet I showed no extreme signs of remorse.

"I think perhaps that was why Aunt Mildred did what she did with the baby. Why she took Lily from me, claiming the infant had died. She wanted to punish me."

An anguished sorrow flickered in his eyes. "If that was her intention, then I would say she was successful."

"Initially." A shiver rose beneath her skin and Rebecca pulled the cashmere blanket from her lap and wrapped it around her shoulders. "But Aunt Mildred also protected my baby. She could have done anything with the infant. No one would have known, no one would have stopped her. Yet instead she found a fine, loving couple to take the child and raise her in wealth and privilege. Lily is safe. And for that reason alone, I cannot hate my aunt."

"And your parents? What of their part in all of this mess?"

A pang of regret struck Rebecca. "I believe they were bullied mercilessly by my aunt. She was a fierce, determined woman and no match for their gentle temperaments. Having succumbed to Aunt Mildred's dictates in the beginning, I'm sure they thought no good could come from revealing the truth to me after it was over."

He laid his hand on her shoulder. "You are an extraordinary woman, Rebecca."

"No, not really." She tilted her chin, puzzled by the obvious admiration in his eyes. "If others knew about Lily, they would shun me."

He moved his head in a sympathetic gesture. "Society is harsh and unforgiving."

"Most people are quick to accuse, quick to censure. But not you, Cameron. Why?"

He paused before answering. "'Tis not my right to

judge another so harshly, especially the woman who has given birth to Lily, the woman who has given me the very best part of my life."

"What a strange pair we are, my lord." A wry laugh faltered on Rebecca's lips. "I feel a closeness to you because you know my dreadful secret. You know about my child, the true circumstances of her birth and you do not condemn me. Or else you are simply too much of a gentleman to say."

His eyes grew soft with kindness. "I know you loved Lily's father very deeply."

"I did. I do." She drew a slow breath. "But he is gone and sometimes . . . sometimes I am angry and resentful that he left me behind. Which is monstrously foolish, since Philip hardly chose his fate."

A shadow of pain passed through Cameron's eyes. "I felt very much the same when Christina died. Her illness was long and difficult and a part of me always believed if she had fought harder, she would have survived."

"But they did not and we are here." Rebecca winced. She sounded so pitiful, yet she felt unable to hold back the tide of her words. "I am so weary of being isolated, alone. Sometimes it feels like an ache, an almost crushing pain deep in my chest. An ache that expands outward, that at times feels as though it were encompassing my entire being."

She hung her head, hardly believing what she had just divulged. Rebecca had never dared to say the words out loud, had barely acknowledged the feelings existed to herself. But they were true. She *was* lonely.

Yet even more astonishing was the realization that Cameron was probably the only person to whom she could expose her pain and hear no false pity in his voice, no quip about how it would quickly pass and she would once again be happy and carefree.

"I know the feeling of loneliness too well myself," he said in a quiet tone. "Perhaps there is a way we can ease each other's pain?"

"Perhaps."

"Shall we find out?"

Her heart began to thump with an erratic rhythm. She knew what he was asking. "I believe that would be ill-advised and foolish."

He nodded in agreement. "Lacking all sense."

She stood. The blanket fell from her shoulders onto the chair. She ignored it. Took a step closer. Sense be damned. Logic be damned. She wanted to feel his arms around her, wanted the heat of his body pressed against hers, wanted the strength of his maleness buried deep inside her. She wanted the burden of loneliness she carried so strongly and fought so desperately to hold at bay to be banished from her heart.

Cameron smoothed his thumb over her cheek and Rebecca tried to swallow the lump in her throat. She drew another deep breath. He gazed steadily at her. Her heart stirred, her pulse continued its erratic beat. Rebecca shut her eyes and mustered the remains of her courage.

"I would like very much to feel the press of a man's body against mine again," she confessed, pulling the words from the depths of her heart, from the very essence of her soul.

"Would you like that body to be mine?" he asked, his voice as low as her own.

"Yes."

Rebecca opened her eyes and gazed at him. He moved closer. Her heart clamored in her breast as she waited for him to take her in his arms, to hold her and kiss her and caress her. But instead he lifted his hand and set his palm against her cheek. The warmth and strength of his flesh seared her to her very soul. She leaned into his hand and closed her eyes again.

"I would like that too," he whispered.

"I hope that I have not offended you with my wanton thoughts, my base desires," she replied softly.

He circled her waist and drew her hard against him. "Offend me? Hardly. I am humbled by your honesty, flattered that you would choose me."

"That we would choose each other," she corrected.

Cameron released the pins of her hair and the shining mass of honey-colored tresses tumbled down Rebecca's shoulders to the center of her back. He gathered it in his hands, running the silky strands through his fingers before lifting a curl to his lips.

Rebecca shuddered, a quiver of anticipation racing through her. Cameron leaned forward. His lips traveled a path to her throat. He nuzzled her ear, then caught the tender lobe between his teeth, nipping playfully. Surprise and pleasure rippled down her spine.

"I am not very experienced," Rebecca whispered, hoping he would not judge and find her lacking.

"I, too, am rather rusty." He fanned his breath along a particularly sensitive spot on the nape of her neck. "There has been no woman in my bed for many years. Not since my wife died."

Rebecca was shocked at the admission. Yet it was somehow reassuring to know he did not hop from bed to bed, from woman to woman, something he could so easily accomplish given his looks and position.

"I thought most noblemen kept mistresses."

"Not this one."

"Oh."

She turned to look at him. The pools of his eyes had darkened with passion, his smoldering, sensual stare making her tremble and ache.

"You are a very beautiful woman, Rebecca." He skimmed her bottom lip with his fingertip in a slow, sensual caress. "I would very much like to kiss you."

"Only kiss me, my lord?"

His breath hitched and he smiled wickedly. Oh, dear. He was mesmerizing. Captivating. His sensual male essence surrounded her, making coherent thought impossible. She swallowed and inched her head forward. Just a fraction. Enough to let him know it was precisely what she wanted too.

A kiss.

There was another flash of a wicked smile and he fulfilled her wish. He kissed her.

Rebecca's eyelids fluttered closed. His lips were warm and firm as he pressed them against hers. Eagerly she opened her mouth to let his tongue slip inside. It circled hers slowly, then stroked the tip before moving to caress the edge of her lips.

It was heavenly. She clutched his lapels, groaning into the kiss, deepening it. Their tongues dueled, caressed, teased. Again and again. Restlessly, she moved her hands to his shoulders, then down to his upper arms. She squeezed tightly, fascinated by the power she felt in his firm, hard muscles, excited by the difference in their bodies.

He was a large man, solid, firm, yet beneath his strength there was gentleness and caring. She was confident he would be a generous lover, would take care to give her pleasure even as he achieved his own.

They continued kissing. The sensual delight he gave her was an intense escape, a magical invitation she was eager to accept. Rebecca felt his fingers at her back and soon realized he was unhooking her gown. Her mind seized and she suddenly panicked. There were candles lit *everywhere* in the room. It was nearly bright as day.

"Shouldn't we extinguish the candles first?" she asked weakly.

"No."

Dear Lord. Her stomach fluttered. To be exposed so completely was a frightening notion. Would he be pleased by what he found? Excited? Would he find her pretty, desirable?

"I need to see you," he declared in a rough voice.

The sound intensified Rebecca's nerves, but he moved so fast she had no time to protest. Her bodice was opened, the silk ribbons of her chemise untied and then lowered. She felt a chill of cool air on her nipples and then a sensual warmth as his hands curved around them. His fingers molded her breasts, stroking the nipples until they hardened and peaked.

"They are magnificent. You are magnificent." His voice shook.

Rebecca turned her head away, then caught a glimpse of his hands so possessively on her skin. They looked dark against the paleness of her flesh. Dark and rough and undeniably male.

"Oh, my." She shivered.

He stilled, yet his hands remained cradling her breasts. "Are you certain you want me to stay?"

A rush of feminine power filled her. A sense of control. A control that was quickly fading for both of them. "Make love to me, Cameron."

To emphasize the request, Rebecca grabbed the material bunched at her waist and deliberately pushed it off her hips. Her gown and chemise fell to the floor. She stepped out of the garments. Neatly kicking them aside, Rebecca boldly moved into the glare of the candlelight, standing naked before him.

"Christ!"

A muscle in his jaw flexed. She noticed a small bead of sweat break out on his brow. Then with a growl of predatory excitement, Cameron lifted her in his arms and carried her to the bed.

After setting her in the middle of the mattress, he tore off his jacket, removed his waistcoat, yanked off his cravat. The garments sailed to the floor in rapid succession. Rebecca found herself smiling as he pulled his shirt over his head, but her amusement was quickly distracted by the sight of his bare chest.

Broad shoulders showcased a sculptured and muscular chest. There was a mat of crisp, dark hair swirling in the center that trailed across his abdomen and narrowed provocatively downward until it disappeared into the waistband of his trousers.

The sight held her in rapt fascination. She almost reached out to touch one of the flat, dark nipples that so intrigued her, but held back. Raising her eyes, she met his. A frisson of embarrassment shivered through her at being caught staring so boldly, but he seemed pleased at her interest.

Without taking his eyes from hers, Cameron began to unfasten his trousers. Rebecca gasped when she saw his rigid penis exposed. It was so swollen. So large.

He preened under her gaze, thrusting his hips forward to emphasize his size. The carnal sight filled her with heat, making the sensitive flesh between her legs grow moist with anticipation.

The mattress dipped as he put his knee onto the bed. He reached for her with both hands and Rebecca practically rolled into his arms. His fingers caressed her shoulders, then smoothed down her arms, crossed over her belly, and finally delved into the sweet curls below.

Rebecca averted her eyes, not knowing where to look. An insistent throbbing began to pulse between her legs. She felt slick and swollen and very aroused. Cameron cupped her hips and shifted her so that she was at the edge of the bed. Then he lowered his head.

At first all she felt was the gentle warmth of his breath. It made her jump with tension.

"Shh, relax," he murmured. "It will feel wonderful. Trust me."

Rebecca trembled. She shouldn't let him. It was too personal, too intimate. She tried to find the words to explain, but then he parted her tenderly, slowly and gently stroked her clitoris with the tip of his tongue.

Rebecca nearly came off the bed. He pressed deeper and she strained beneath the flicking torture, a scream building in her throat. Sensation built upon sensation as his tongue swirled and dipped. Too much, then not enough.

She began to undulate her hips forward. His hands settled over her stomach, rubbing it in smooth patterns, keeping her in place so he could taste and tease her tender flesh.

Rebecca blazed with heat; she shivered with cold. She panted breathlessly, unable to get enough air to fill her lungs. The sensations intensified and then suddenly broke. Rebecca dug her heels into the mattress, arching higher as she felt the pleasure shake and rumble through her.

Cameron held her as she shuddered, his tongue moving slower, barely touching her flesh. When the final tremor ended, she felt him shift, felt the bed creak as he moved. He gathered her in his arms and she was surrounded by his strength, his heat.

Boneless, Rebecca closed her eyes and let herself drift, let the lightness and satisfaction of her climax bathe her in warmth and comfort. But her peace was short-lived. His erection, long and stiff, was pressing insistently against her hip, poking, probing at her.

Her body reawakened. She shifted so she faced him, until only inches separated their faces. His eyes had darkened to near blackness. The smoldering look nearly brought a blush to her cheeks, which was ridiculous considering the intimacy she had just allowed him. With an impish grin, Rebecca leaned forward and bit his earlobe. Hard.

At the same time she boldly dragged her hand over his flat stomach and cupped the heavy sacks of his balls. He sucked in a sharp breath.

Lightly dancing her fingers upward, she wrapped her hand around his stiff penis, his width so thick her fingers barely met. Gliding her hand upward, she stroked him, pleased to hear a sharp moan escape his lips, delighted to feel his body shudder.

She set a pace that seemed to please him, stroking up, then down. His hips pumped forward to meet her hand and she felt a drop of moisture form at the tip of his erect shaft. Touching it with her fingertip she rubbed it sensually over the head, massaging with a circular motion.

"So bloody good," he moaned.

Rebecca pulled back so that she could see his face. His expression was tight, his eyes heavy lidded with desire. Watching him in his pleasure brought forth the wetness between her own legs. She moved them restlessly against his upper thighs as she increased the pressure of her grip on his rock-hard penis.

"Cameron."

Her voice was a whisper, a call of passion. Yet it seemed to pull him away from the moment. He groaned again, then clasping her wrist, he dragged her hand away.

"Enough," he growled, his voice filled with want and need.

He turned away from her and Rebecca cried out. The musky scent of their arousal filled the chamber and her frustration mounted. She should have kept silent, should have allowed him to gain his release.

"I'm sorry," she muttered, feeling terribly gauche and inexperienced.

"For what? Nearly killing me?" She heard the humorous irony in his voice.

"I . . . uhm—"

"Thank goodness you spoke," he said. "I was nearly too far gone to hold myself back."

"Oh. So you're not angry with me?"

"Rebecca, I can assure you that anger is most definitely not an emotion I am feeling at this moment."

Catlike, he stretched his naked body, rubbing against her in a slow, sensual caress, from her breast to her belly, to her sex. Then linking her fingers with his, Cameron slowly raised her arms above her head.

Suddenly she was spread before him like a wanton feast, a woman waiting to be conquered, possessed. The vulnerable position heated her blood, made her feel wicked and desirable. He kissed her again, his lips hot, his tongue merciless. She began to struggle for breath, her chest rising and falling rapidly.

Cameron rose to his knees above her. She watched the play of candlelight on his handsome face. There was a yearning in his eyes, so honest, so intense it nearly stole her breath.

"You are mine," he stated hoarsely.

"I am."

Slowly she spread her legs. She felt him reach between them and part her most tender flesh before easing himself inside. Their bodies slid together intimately, naturally. It felt extraordinary.

He flexed his hips forward and went deeper. Rebecca gasped at the feel of him filling her, digging her fingertips into the tight muscles of his upper arms.

"You are very tight," he whispered. "Am I hurting you?"

She shook her head, fighting to think beyond the confusion of intense pleasure and intense emotions.

"No . . . I feel . . . I . . ." her eyes filled with tears.

"I know," he whispered. "I know. You cannot help but remember the past, the memories of another."

"I'm sorry." She blinked and two tears rolled down her cheek. "I want you, Cameron. You. No one else. Truly."

"Ah, sweet Rebecca. I understand."

He held himself perfectly still inside her. Gradually, Rebecca felt the emotions begin to ease from her heart, felt herself drawn back into the sensuality and passion of the moment.

He does understand. He knows as much as I want this, as much as I want him, my heart needed a moment to say a final farewell to the only other man who ever shared this total intimacy with me.

Cameron touched the side of her face, then leaned down. She angled her head so they could kiss. Mouths joined, Rebecca parted her lips and sucked in his tongue. His scent invaded her senses. Need rushed through her like a lightning storm and she melted under the delicate, caring assault.

She shifted her buttocks and arched herself against him. It felt right, this passion between them. He was everything she could desire in a lover; passionate, giving, caring. Rebecca embraced the moment utterly, allowing the last of her defenses to fall.

She took his hand and brought it down between

their bodies to the place where they were joined. His fingers were gentle, almost delicate as they stroked her. Gasping, she bucked to take him deeper and he obligingly thrust harder.

She wrapped her legs around his hips, holding him in place. Cameron quickened the pace and moaned. They surged together, then came apart, each seeking release, oblivion, fulfillment.

Then all at once he seemed to reach a crisis. Cameron stiffened and shuddered in her arms. A guttural, masculine shout of pure satisfaction rang in her ears. She felt his heat and power seep into her and it filled her with a soaring sense of joy and completion, different totally from anything she had ever known.

Visibly exhausted, he sank down and buried his head against her cheek. His breath came in great, rasping billows. The sound flooded her heart with a strange, intense warmth.

Rebecca sighed. His body lay heavily on hers. It felt wonderful. Her hair was damp, her face covered in a fine sheen of sweat. It felt wonderful. Her limbs were stretched and sore and aching. They felt wonderful.

"Sorry. I must be crushing you." Cameron levered himself away and started to roll off her.

"No, don't leave me," she cried, holding him close for a tender kiss.

He obliged. Then he smiled wickedly, flexing himself inside her. "Eventually I shall have no choice but to go, dearest Rebecca."

"Perhaps." She smiled back, clutching his hips with her thighs. "Perhaps not."

"Here, let's try this instead," he said.

He disengaged himself, but before she could protest he shifted to his back and gathered her on top of his body, holding her in a possessive embrace.

She lifted her chin and set it squarely in the center of his chest. He reached up, brushing her damp, disheveled hair back from her temples. Their eyes met. His gaze was still intense, his face still hard with passion.

Rebecca's heart swelled with emotions she could not define. Was it love? She was unsure. She had loved Philip deeply, completely, yet those feelings were different from these emotions.

Worse? Better? She honestly did not know.

"Now what?" she whispered.

He pushed a stray tendril of damp hair behind her ear, then lifted himself forward and kissed her temple.

"We sleep."

And remarkably, they did.

The bedchamber was filled with quiet, peaceful stillness when Cameron awoke a few hours later. It was dark outside, but he knew morning must be fast approaching. Sitting upright, the earl tossed back the sheets and left the warmth of the bed, searching the floor for his discarded clothing.

He kept glancing at the bed, but Rebecca did not stir once as he dressed. Though he was loathed to disturb her slumber, Cameron knew he could not leave without speaking with her.

He had to call out to her twice before she moved. Finally, she sat up in the bed, clutching the sheet to her breast. She looked tousled and sleepy and incredibly sexy.

"Are you leaving?" she asked, her expression unfathomable.

"'Tis late. I must return to my room." He held up

the night rail he had found. "Will you be needing this tonight?"

"Oh, yes, thank you." She reached for it, but he held it back.

"Would you like to wash first?"

She blushed. He handed her the night rail, then turned his back. She scurried to the washstand, and he imagined her naked body. Sweet, lush, tempting. He hardened quickly. Needing to toss that delightful image from his mind, Cameron busied himself by picking her garments off the floor and placing them neatly on the chair.

"You make a fine lady's maid, my lord," she joked when he was finished.

"I shall remember that, if my fortunes ever change and I am forced to seek employment."

She scrambled over to the mattress and sat on the edge, apparently waiting for him to leave before getting beneath the covers. It should have felt awkward, but somehow it did not.

He hesitated at the foot of the bed, then cleared his throat. "Perhaps we should consider marriage, Rebecca. If you are so inclined."

She lowered her head for a moment, then lifted it. Her face broke into a small grin. "Gracious, Cameron. You look as though you have swallowed a lemon. Whole."

"Oh, God, I am sorry. I did not mean it to come out quite that way." The smile he was trying to force on his face withered before it reached his mouth. Damn, he was behaving like a fool. How else would she react to such a dutiful, dispassionate proposal? Of course she would say no to it.

"It's all right, Cameron. Truly. So much has changed between us and so suddenly. We need time to absorb it all before we consider taking any sort of action, before we make any decisions about our future."

"You are rejecting me?" he asked.

"Not precisely."

"I am an earl," he blurted out.

Her lips twitched. "So I have heard."

"I am very wealthy."

She glanced about the elegant chamber. "Clearly."

"I am also, apparently, an ass."

"Cameron, please." She stood and walked from the bed to him, each step graceful and elegant, not stopping until she was again in his arms.

He pulled her close against his chest. She smelled of roses. And sex. His penis began to stir with interest.

"Hmm, you are also a randy, oversexed goat," she muttered.

"Only around you," he said in an ironic tone.

"I did not say that I did not like that aspect of your personality," she teased.

"But you won't marry me," he said glumly.

"Gracious, you are worse than Lily! Stop acting like a petulant child."

He knew she was right. He was being ridiculous. Yet as he held her in his arms, he realized this went beyond a physical, sexual connection. On some level he did not fully understand, he needed her. The sum of his feelings were confused, conflicted, yet there was no doubt in his mind, or his heart, that a part of him longed for her. For Rebecca, and no one else.

Cameron dragged in a heavy breath. "We will speak of this again."

"Yes, certainly."

She looked decidedly wary. It bothered him more than he wanted to admit, but he was wise enough to know when to retreat. He could not press her now, when his thoughts were addled and hers seemed so set.

In Cameron's experience there were few opportunities in life for second chances. This was, he believed, his chance and he was determined not to make a mistake and let it escape his grasp.

Chapter 16

Rebecca pulled her woolen cloak more firmly around her shoulders. The occasional gusts of wind sent a sharp chill through her, that brought on a strong shiver.

"Are you sure you have dressed warmly enough?" Cameron asked, concern lacing his voice.

"I am fine. The exercise will warm me. Really," she insisted, before he could protest further.

To emphasize the point, Rebecca quickened her step. The earl merely took a slightly longer stride to keep pace. It was early afternoon, a crisp, cold day and they were on foot, heading toward the north woods. On a very important mission, Cameron had told her, though he had not given her any specifics.

And Rebecca had not been inclined to ask. She was in a strange mood today, her thoughts and feelings jumbled, her emotions confused, yet serene. Her body still tingled from last night, those seldom used muscles and limbs sore from the earl's ardent lovemaking. Though she did not fully understand it, she did not regret what had happened between them, yet she could not help but wonder where it would all lead.

He had not brought up the marriage proposal again and she was grateful. Her feelings were too raw, too new, too disoriented to discuss it.

The treetops moved in the slight wind, sending a fresh shower of snow to the ground. The earl tilted his head and stared at the leafless branches overhead. "We should try to stay in the center of the path or else we will soon be covered in snow."

Rebecca followed him obediently into the middle, now measuring her strides to match his. "I usually don't like the winter," she said. "Too cold and blustery. But I like the snow."

"I do too." He smiled wryly. "Just not when it is falling on my head."

Rebecca returned the smile, pleased they were able to be comfortable around each other, especially after the events of last night. How ironic that their physical closeness brought on this odd change, when logic dictated it would be precisely the opposite.

It seemed to Rebecca from the first moment she had crossed the threshold of the earl's London home, they had been at odds, so rarely at ease with each other, especially when alone. She was relieved that had finally started to change.

"Snow is a most amazing phenomenon," Rebecca commented. "Even when only a dusting of it falls, the world around you looks perfect, pristine. All the natural imperfections are so artfully hidden and everything appears so hopeful and full of promise."

"True, but then the temperature begins to rise."

"Aye." She shook her head and muttered sadly, "as it gets warmer, the snow melts and reality intrudes. The dirt beneath the snow appears, the white perfection is marred, and the chance for a fresh, clean start seems to vanish."

"Dear Rebecca, we do not need the illusion of snow to remind ourselves that there is always hope, always the chance for a new beginning, no matter what has happened."

She ceased walking. "Are you turning into a romantic, my lord?"

"Perhaps I am," he answered with an easy smile. "Or perhaps you are just hoping that I am."

The wind changed direction suddenly and blew against her side. Rebecca shivered and the earl moved so that his large body buffeted her from the chill as they continued walking.

For an instant she was shockingly aware of the strength of his solid male body. It brought forth an unbidden memory of last night, the feeling within her as his large, powerful frame loomed above her, her hips rising against the hardness of his penetration, the muscular strength of his back as she held on tightly to him.

"Ah, here it is at last. Perfect."

With a blush, Rebecca pulled herself away from her sensual recollections. Dutifully, she gazed ahead and beheld a lush evergreen. It stood at nearly her height, fuller at the bottom and tapering to a point at the top. The branches were straight and full, draping in an elegant line.

"'Tis an evergreen tree," she said vaguely.

"Oh, no, Rebecca, 'tis a Christmas tree," he corrected.

"A what?"

"A Christmas tree," he repeated.

Rebecca blinked. She had never heard of such a thing. "What precisely, does one do with a Christmas tree, my lord?"

"Decorate it."

He circled the tree slowly, carefully examining it

from all sides. His gaze traveled up and down and she could see his thoughts were centered completely on it.

"I daresay, I do not grasp the significance of decorating a tree in the middle of the forest," Rebecca said.

"It is not meant to stay in the woods. I shall have it cut down."

"And then what?"

"Bring it back to the house," he answered as if it were the most logical of explanations and she was acting foolish by asking.

"And when it is at the manor?" Rebecca prompted, still not following his train of thought.

"It will be set on a table and placed in a prominent section of the drawing room."

"The drawing room?"

"Yes, I thought that would be best." He tilted his head, studying the tree from a different angle. "Or do you think the front parlor would be better?"

"I think the forest is the best place of all to keep an evergreen, my lord."

"You are missing the entire point."

"Apparently." She stared at the tree, then stared at him, trying to puzzle it all out. "You will place this tree in the drawing room and then decorate it?"

"Yes. With small candles and ribbons and bows and some handmade ornaments. Charlotte has already started crafting a few of them, but everyone is invited to help. I imagine the children and servants will think it great fun."

Rebecca furrowed her brow. "Are you certain you wish to take a tree into the house? It will make a dreadful mess all over the carpets. And could easily catch fire when it dries, especially if you plan on putting candles on it. Frankly, the entire notion smacks of paganism, like some ancient Druid ritual."

"Precisely." He grinned impishly, delighted with her reference. The twinkle in his eye reminded her that beneath the proper, upright manner the earl had a mischievous streak. "This custom is one that is wholly embraced by our queen and I should like to try it at Windmere this year. Anyone voicing a strong objection would obviously be considered disloyal to the crown."

"Ridiculous." Rebecca shook her head. "It still seems very unnatural to me, almost foreign."

"It's festive," he insisted.

"It's odd," she retorted.

"My goodness, Rebecca, you need not look at me with a face that could curdle cream. 'Tis just a harmless tree."

"Curdle cream? What a beastly thing to say!" She flounced her head haughtily, but could not hold back her smile. There was something remarkably intimate about being teased by him. "Fortunately for you, Lord Hampton, I am a woman of little vanity and great confidence or else I should be highly insulted by your erroneous remark."

"Minx."

His gaze lowered to her mouth. A trick of the sunlight scattering through the treetops made his eyes gleam with a strange illumination. He took a step toward her. Rebecca's lips began to tingle.

"I see no oak trees in the vicinity," she said as his hand rose and his thumb slowly glided over the exposed flesh at her throat. The light stroke brought a swift, throbbing arousal to every part of Rebecca's body. "There appears to be no mistletoe hanging from any branches."

"None? Are you certain?"

"I am."

"I believe you need to look again, sweetheart."

He bent his head toward her. Rebecca lifted her chin. He touched her only with his mouth, his lips softly easing over hers. Disarmed by his gentleness, she felt herself starting to melt.

Thoroughly enjoying the tremor of her body, and his, she drank in the hot, spicy sensation. There was passion, there was comfort, there was trust. It was a perfect kiss, sending thrills along every nerve ending.

They smiled naughtily, secretly, at each other as they broke apart. Yet niggling at the back of Rebecca's brain was the notion that Cameron's kisses were something she was beginning to anticipate with far too much emotion and delight to so easily dismiss him from her thoughts or her heart.

Charlotte continued to gaze out the window of the sitting room, her mind wandering, her thoughts unfocused. Christmas was a mere two days away. Followed by the Twelfth Night celebration and soon after the guests would begin to depart. Including Daniel.

The realistic side of her nature told Charlotte she would most likely never see him again once the holiday was over. This unusual holiday invitation seemed to be some kind of impulse on her brother's part. The Tremaines were not an ordinary social acquaintance of the family; it seemed unlikely they would be included in other events. Cameron insisted it had been business that brought them to Windmere and Charlotte doubted this odd circumstance would ever again occur.

The thought saddened, almost depressed her. She knew she had to stop thinking about it, for it was beginning to make her head hurt. With a conscious effort, she turned her attention to the ribbons and trinkets scattered on the desk, telling herself she needed to concentrate on making the ornaments for Cameron's big surprise. But her heart was not in the task.

Someone knocked on the door. "Come in." She swiveled in her seat and focused her attention on the door.

Daniel opened it. He stared at her mutely, his brown eyes guarded and mysterious. "May I join you?"

It was an improper suggestion, even though they had spent time alone in each other's company on several different occasions. This section of the house was deserted except for a few servants. Being cozily sequestered in this private manner was pushing hard against the boundaries of propriety. She should refuse him entrance.

Charlotte folded her arms about herself and took a steadying breath. "We shouldn't be in here alone."

Without being invited, he paced to the window and gazed out at the frozen landscape. "I can open the door if you wish." He looked over his shoulder at her, his eyes still shuttered and mysterious. "But I would prefer to keep it closed."

Charlotte's heart, already fluttering with anxiety, skipped a beat. Propriety be damned. "Let me pour you some tea."

She reached for the teapot nestled beneath a woolen cozy that had sat untouched at the corner of the desk for the past half hour. Pouring a cup for Daniel, she set it on the desk. Taking a small plate she next selected a scone, two cream cakes, several ginger cookies and a lemon biscuit.

He dragged a chair from in front of the fireplace and put it near her own. As she handed him the brimming plate of sweets, he stroked a finger gently across her hand. Charlotte blinked, yet held his gaze, wondering if the gesture had been deliberate. His shy smile told her it might have been, though he sat back and munched on his scone as if he were unaware of the sizzling contact.

Charlotte popped a lemon biscuit in her mouth and tried not to choke.

"Have you had a pleasant morning?" she asked.

"Tolerable." He took a small sip of his tea, then placed it back on the saucer. "Is your brother about? I asked several of the servants and no one seems to know precisely where he has gone."

"Cameron is on a most secretive errand," Charlotte said primly. "'Tis a surprise Christmas treat for the guests. I assume he will be returning home by late afternoon. Was there something specific you wanted to speak with him about?"

Her question produced a most peculiar reaction. Daniel's face heated with a flush that might be construed as embarrassment. "'Tis a personal matter."

"Personal, not business?" Charlotte idly stirred her tea with a silver spoon. "Pardon my inquisitiveness, but I sense an animosity between you and my brother simmering beneath the surface of your very civil behavior toward each other."

"You are a very wise, observant woman, Charlotte."

"Does it have anything to do with me?"

He shifted in his chair. "No, it does not concern you. At least not presently." His face clouded, almost as if he regretted that remark. "'Tis a somewhat indelicate family matter that has caused this friction between us. I am afraid I cannot share the specifics with you."

Charlotte felt a odd stab of pain. "You don't trust me to keep the matter confidential?"

"You could not be more wrong. I trust you completely. The secret is not mine to reveal. It is between my sister and the earl."

Gracious! Charlotte had seen an undercurrent of emotion between her brother and Miss Tremaine, but she never suspected it was a secret that bound them together. Absently she selected a ginger cookie from the tray, although her appetite had fled.

"I have to say, this has been the most unusual Christmas season we have ever had at Windmere," she mused. "Even I confess to having felt so different these last few weeks. So very unlike myself." She twirled the cookie between her fingers. "In an odd way I am like a maiden in a fairy tale who has awakened after a long, cold sleep. I believe I have you to thank for that, Daniel."

"I cannot take all the credit for this long, overdue change, Charlotte, though perhaps I had a bit to do with your new awareness. It pleases me to think that I might. But I have not transformed you, my dear. I have merely given you the confidence to finally emerge from your cocoon.

"Years of defining yourself by but one small part of your whole have clouded the truth in your mind and in your heart. You are not your crippled leg, Charlotte. You have a depth of spirit and strength of character that any man would admire. Never forget that you are a lovely woman, a desirable woman."

She looked at his sincere expression and her chest seemed to constrict. "No gentleman has ever noticed me before. Except you."

"Fools, every last one of them."

Charlotte coughed lightly to hide her embarrassment at the remark. Her seclusion from society had ensured that there had been little chance of any man noticing her before, but even if someone had, Charlotte doubted she would have reacted this way toward them.

Daniel was unique, special. He made her feel alive in ways she never dreamed, never thought possible. It was as if she had never truly lived until they became acquainted, became friends.

But deep within her heart, Charlotte knew she wanted far more than friendship. Even more than love. Of course she wanted to love a man with all of her heart, wanted that same man to love her in return.

But she also desired a man she could confide in, a man she could reveal herself to without fear or ridicule. A man who loved her despite her weaknesses and faults and frailties. Though she had long suspected and even longer tried to deny it, Charlotte admitted to herself now that Daniel Tremaine was that man.

It was almost a relief to acknowledge the feeling, though she could have done very well indeed without the confusion and doubt that also circled her heart. Knowing she could not possibly swallow beyond the lump in her throat, Charlotte put down the ginger cookie. Yet needing to occupy her hands, she picked up a Christmas ornament she had been crafting earlier.

Daniel leaned forward. He was close enough for her to catch the scent of lemon on his breath from the biscuit he had just eaten. Bizarre what an appealing aphrodisiac lemons could be. Funny, how she had never before noticed such a thing.

He raised one hand and rested it on her shoulder as the fingertips on his other hand traced the sloping line of her jaw.

"You are making it hard for me to concentrate," she said, clumsily trying to tie a red bow on the top of the glass sphere.

"That was rather the idea." He cleared his throat. "Charlotte . . . Lady Charlotte, I have a most important matter to discuss with you."

She turned in her chair to face him. The ornament dropped from her nerveless fingers and rolled across the carpet. He ignored it, taking her hand in his, gently uncurling her fingers and placing their palms together.

Moisture pricked at the corners of Charlotte's eyes, and she struggled not to let it fall. *I love him,* she thought, looking at his handsome face and his beautiful eyes. *I love him utterly.*

Though Daniel denied it, she knew he was the reason she had been able to transform herself. If he left, she would inevitably retreat to the safety of her old self, would forever remain an observer instead of a participant. The sadness of it nearly made her cry as she wondered if it would have been easier not to have tasted this small bit of bliss, if it would have been better never to truly understand what she would be denied.

He cleared his throat. "You have a comfortable life here, with your family. All that you need."

She blinked, trying to understand what he was saying. "Well, yes, I suppose. Cameron is kind and generous. Mother loves me dearly and is a comfortable companion. Lily is the true life of the house, keeping us all on our toes with her antics."

He nodded his head. "Yet aside from your family, you have other interests."

"Yes, a few." Her brow lifted in surprise. She had never really thought much about it. "I ride, as you know. And I like to garden. I have a particularly fine hand with roses, if I may be so immodest. And there is always my embroidery, of course."

"'Tis a good life," he said quietly. "One you might not wish to change."

Not want to change! Was the man completely daft? Her head moved vigorously from side to side. "Truth be told, I despise embroidery. And while I enjoy my rides, most days I feel lonely with just a groom trailing behind me. It would be wonderful to have someone ride beside me.

"But it's more than that, Daniel. I long for a companion, someone to share the trials and joys of life, someone who shares my interests, yet would introduce me to new ones." She dipped her chin shyly. "Someone to gift one of my few perfect specimens of roses, those I am most proud of cultivating."

"You would give a rose to a man, Charlotte?"

"I would give a rose to you, Daniel. If I thought you would take it."

"Oh, my love." He put his hand around her neck, drew her close, and kissed her forehead. "'Tis a strange relationship we have developed these past few weeks. With you I have established a closeness I have never before felt, an ache I cannot conquer. You are a companion, a confidante, yet I want so much more. So much more I fear that I do not deserve, that I will never have no matter how much I wish for it. Oh, these many nights I have laid awake in my bed wondering if meeting you was a blessing or a curse."

What was he saying? He left his chair and sank down on one knee in front of her. Charlotte's chest felt so tight she had difficulty catching her breath. He was on his knee, holding her hands. Was it possible he meant to propose? Or was it just her wishful, foolish heart hoping for the impossible?

Suddenly, she had difficulty controlling the trembling of her limbs. "Pray, tell me, what have you decided? Am I a blessing or a curse?"

"A blessing. I love you, Charlotte. Though I fear I am far from worthy of the honor, I would ask you, most humbly, if you would please consider my request to marry me."

The tears Charlotte had been holding back slid

silently down her cheek. She had never before felt such joy, nor such object terror.

"We will make a most unusual couple," she said, thinking of her deformity.

He nodded his head, but she soon realized he was not referring to her crippled leg. "No doubt there will be society doors that will never be open to us, no matter how staunch the support we receive from our family and friends.

"At most I can claim a very distant relation to an impoverished baronet, several generations back. I daresay some in society will be hard-pressed to even declare me a gentleman. Clearly, you would be marrying beneath you."

"That is ridiculous!" she answered hotly, but as Charlotte thought upon it, she realized Daniel was right. There would be some people who believed he was marrying her for her social position and connections. "Well, others might think I am marrying you for your money," she countered.

He paused, his eyes alighting with interest. "Have you need of a fortune, Charlotte?"

He looked so hopeful, almost eager at the notion, she felt a twinge of regret having to tell him the truth.

"I have a substantial dowry and a generous annual allowance, that will increase when I am wed."

Wed! The word echoed through Charlotte's brain and she nearly screeched with excitement. She took a deep breath, wanting this perfect moment of joy to last forever.

Daniel's face turned glum. "I can easily support you in the style that you are accustomed to and deserve. I have no need of your money and I insist that you allow me to supply you with a monthly allowance that you may spend entirely at your discretion.

"With your permission, I shall invest your dowry funds in a variety of solid ventures and place all subsequent profits in trust for our children."

Children! She would have children. She muffled a sob of pure delight. "You are very generous, sir. Perhaps I will be accused of marrying you for your fortune?"

"Well, not to put too fine a point on it, but you have not yet said that you will be my wife."

He actually looked a tad nervous. Charlotte might have smiled if she had not been so astonished.

"Saints above, Daniel, of course I will marry you." She reached down to hug him and they nearly toppled to the floor. Laughing, they regained their seats, their hands clasped tightly.

"I will marry you, Daniel, because I love you, because I love how you make me feel about myself. You believe that I can do anything, you see me as a whole and special person, not an unfortunate woman with a bad limp. I will marry you because you make me feel special and cherished and adored. And if all I can ever do is bring but a tenth of the happiness to you that you give to me, I shall be a successful wife."

He broke into a smile so wide she was certain his jaw must ache. "With your permission, I will speak to your brother as soon as possible. But you must prepare yourself, Charlotte. The earl would be well within his rights to refuse me."

"If he dares to, he can go straight to the devil."

"Such language, my lady. Proof positive that I am already corrupting you." He laughed and pulled her out of her chair and into his lap. "We will marry, Charlotte. With or without his blessing."

"He will give it," she replied confidently. "I feel as though I am dreaming. At long last I have gotten my most secret wish, my childhood fantasy of a romantic courtship, an adoring, loving, handsome bridegroom and a ceremony in the private chapel at Windmere."

"Shall we marry in the spring?" he asked. "When the flowers are in bloom and the weather is warmer?"

Charlotte squirmed in his lap. Daniel sucked in a breath and tightened his hold on her waist. It was presumptuous and most unladylike, but she doubted she would have the patience or the fortitude to wait until next spring to become Daniel's wife.

'Twas months and months away. How could she wait? And the most indecent, tantalizing hardness she now felt pressing insistently against her bottom let her know Daniel was of the same mind.

"I have always thought January to be an excellent time for a wedding," she replied.

"January?" His breath let out in a rush. "Thank the stars. That leaves me but a few weeks to avoid your kisses."

A cold fission of fear swept through her. *Had he regretted his choice already?* Charlotte bit her lip. "Don't you like my kisses?" she whispered.

"God yes, I like your kisses. I adore your kisses. Far too much."

He shuddered. She frowned. "Then why is that a problem?" she asked.

"Because hot, sensual kisses lead to other things far too rapidly."

"We are to be married," she smiled, trying to encourage him. She really did want another kiss. Another bone-melting, blood-boiling kiss, that curled her toes and left her entire body warm and tingling. "Are the rules not more lenient for engaged couples?"

His expression softened and a shiver rose beneath her skin. He truly was a most extraordinary man. "The rules might be a bit more relaxed, but we will not be truly joined together as man and wife until our vows are exchanged. Even if it kills me."

"Then perhaps a Christmas wedding would be a better idea?"

He laughed and she joined him. "Even I know two days is not enough time to organize a wedding," he said.

"January, then. Early January."

"It takes three weeks for the banns to be read."

"Not if you have a special license." She lifted her brow saucily and he groaned.

"Charlotte, your family will be shocked at the insistence for such haste."

"I don't care." Charlotte wrapped her arms around his neck. "We want a small, intimate ceremony, so it should not be too difficult to arrange."

"What about your wedding gown?"

"How long can it take to have one silly gown made? Gracious, I shall get married in my best night rail if necessary."

She saw his throat move visibly as he swallowed hard. "Lord save us all, the sight of that will have me ravishing you on the altar."

She giggled. How amazing that he would find her so appealing, that his control was so close to the edge when he thought of her? Of course, that was very much how she felt when looking at him.

"I'm certain an appropriate gown can be made in time," she decided. "As for the rest, my wedding clothes can be made after we are married."

"Better still, I will take you to Paris and have an entire wardrobe done for you. I believe I shall enjoy dressing you in the very latest colors and fashions."

The notion totally charmed her. "I've never been to Paris."

"Neither have I. 'Tis something we shall explore and experience together."

The prospect was equal parts invigorating and intimidating. She had never traveled beyond the boundaries of the family's various estates and now she was casually talking of an extended trip to France. Her world was about to change, expand. Was she ready to face this new challenge?

"I will also have to return to America sometime within the next few years to settle some of my business affairs," he said. "'Tis a much farther journey. Will you mind?"

"Not if I can accompany you," she answered truthfully.

"I would not dream of leaving you behind."

It was precisely what she needed to hear. Slowly she raised her head. He stared at her, his brown eyes glittering with emotion. Before he could utter another word, she leaned forward and kissed him, taking his mouth with a bold determination that surprised her. Daniel stiffened for an instant, then groaned and tugged her tighter inside his arms.

Charlotte sighed with delight, darting her tongue forward to circle around his, pouring all the love of her heart into the moment. Though Daniel had insisted there was danger in too many passionate kisses, she did not worry. She knew she could depend on him, could trust him to do what was right to keep her safe.

"Sweetheart." He broke away to whisper in her ear. "Oh, Charlotte, my love. We are going to be very, very happy."

Chapter 17

Cameron leaned back in his chair, knit his brow and studied the man who sat across from him with a calculating eye. He had been uncertain what to expect when this private meeting was requested, yet even the earl's fertile imagination had not anticipated the outcome.

For the second time in less than a month, Daniel Tremaine had succeeded in shocking him. Utterly. Cameron was still struggling to digest the man's latest pronouncement. Tremaine had just asked for permission to marry Charlotte.

Well, not precisely asked. More like informed the earl that he was going to marry his sister. By special license. In a few weeks' time. His mother would most likely have heart palpitations when she heard of this nearly scandalous plan.

Though the dowager countess had warned him of her suspicions of a growing affection between the two, Cameron had given the idea little credit, for he had not observed any indication of an affection between the pair. Apparently he had been wrong. Or not?

"Tell me, why would you wish to marry Charlotte?"

Tremaine looked at him as if he were a simpleton. "Is it not obvious?"

"Frankly, no."

"I could sit here for an hour and still not enumerate all of Lady Charlotte's finer qualities." Tremaine's face was solemn, sincere. "Quite simply, she's an extraordinary woman. I am deeply honored that she has looked so favorably upon my proposal."

Cameron drummed his fingertips on the edge of his desk. They were seated in his private study, but even the serene, familiar wood-paneled walls and the book-lined shelves could not help contain the earl's suspicious mood.

"I don't know what you might have heard, or what Charlotte herself might have told you, but her finances are in my control," Cameron said. "I can, and will, withhold her dowry portion and any subsequent allowance bequeath to her by my father if I do not approve of her choice for a husband. 'Tis my right and my duty."

Tremaine did not look the least upset by that lofty proclamation. In fact, he seemed tremendously relieved. "Keep your money. Every bloody cent of it. My life will be far better without it. I want only Charlotte, not her dowry or her allowance or her aristocratic, society connections."

"Not her damn family, either, Tremaine?"

"I never said—"

"You didn't have to say it. I can read your sentiments quite clearly."

"I love her. And I will have her." Tremaine made an explosive sound deep in his throat, but kept his seat and the majority of his temper. "It would be easier on Charlotte if she had her family's blessing for the marriage and for that reason I have come to you today. Be assured, I shall always do everything within my power to shield her from hurt, to see to her comforts, to bring her happiness.

"I had hoped you would be more receptive to my offer, but was prepared for your objections. Please be advised they will not alter my plans one iota. I will marry Charlotte."

Cameron narrowed his brow and stared into Tremaine's earnest face, his serious eyes and pushed a bit further.

"Is there a particular reason you are setting the wedding date so quickly?"

Tremaine flushed, his eyes widening. "You insult your sister with such a base question."

"I will not be the only one to ask it," Cameron replied. "There will be talk."

"The petty rambling of a few society gossips do not concern me or Charlotte."

"They should."

"I disagree."

They exchanged glowers.

Cameron blinked first. *Damn.* Tremaine was obviously braced for all-out warfare. He was so certain, so determined to make this marriage happen, so convinced he would overcome any obstacles fate placed in his path.

Cameron understood. Love could do that to a man. He contemplated Tremaine for a long moment, then rose from his desk. Walking to the sideboard, he lifted the cut-glass decanter filled with brandy and poured two glasses with a generous portion of the rich amber liquid.

He returned and handed one to Tremaine. "To Charlotte," he toasted.

"Charlotte." Tremaine tossed back the drink in two long swallows. "My future wife."

This time Cameron did not blink. "We shall formally announce your engagement at dinner this evening."

"Splendid." Tremaine placed his empty glass on the edge of the desk. He looked as startled as Cameron felt. "I will tell Charlotte at once."

The other man turned to leave, but the earl stopped him. "Just one more thing." Cameron extended his hand across the wide expanse of the massive oak desk. After a moment's hesitation, Tremaine grasped it firmly. "Welcome to the family," the earl said with a smile.

At dinner that night Cameron announced his sister's engagement. Rebecca, having been told the news earlier by Daniel, joined in with the rest of the guests in wishing the couple great happiness.

After a good many hugs of congratulations and a few tears of joy, shed by the dowager countess and Lady Marion, Rebecca found herself standing with the earl. She could not tell from his stern countenance if he were truly pleased about the marriage, though he had made a pretty speech when announcing the news.

"I am happy for both of them," Rebecca said sincerely. "Though I am a bit sorry for you."

"Why? Your brother seems very devoted to Charlotte. Are you concerned about their future?"

"Not in the least." She halted at the entrance to the drawing room. "I'm afraid your holiday surprise is quite overshadowed by this news. I fear no one will make a great fuss over your Christmas tree."

They turned together and observed the rest of the guests. Rebecca could immediately see her prediction had been correct. Much of the greenery gathered the previous week had been hung during the day. Boughs of holly and evergreen draped the mirrors and pictures, swags of garland were entwined in the chandelier, a kissing ball was suspended from a high wall sconce and numerous sprigs of mistletoe were hung over the doorways and archways.

The room looked spectacular and smelled even better, the faint whiff of pine permeating the air, the bright sparkle of red and gold satin ribbons glimmering in the candlelight.

The Christmas tree was set in one corner of the room, perched on a table as the earl had instructed. It received a curious glance from Lord Bailey and a raised eyebrow from Lady Marion. Beyond that, it was ignored.

The earl frowned. "I believe everyone's opinion will change once they see the tree fully decorated and lit with candles."

"Hmm, be sure to keep a bucket of water close at hand in case there are any mishaps. Burning draperies have a most noxious odor."

His expression changed, becoming amused. "You do have a special talent for putting a damper on my fun, Rebecca."

"'Tis a gift," she said in a teasing manner.

Some raucous laughter and a smattering of applause drew their attention. Rebecca glanced over and saw that Daniel and Charlotte had discovered the kissing ball. With some pointed encouragement from the dowager countess and one far from subtle hint from Lady Marion, the newly engaged couple were sharing a kiss beneath it.

They made it seem so simple. A confused sensation of melancholy settled in Rebecca's chest. She gazed up at

Cameron. His eyelids were half-lowered, his expression almost challenging. He did not have to speak what was on his mind, for she had a very strong suspicion it was the same thought as her own.

They too could be engaged and sharing a kiss in public. Rebecca's shoulders tightened. She still had difficulty believing that such an attractive, compelling man had offered her marriage. She had been stunned, flattered and then thoroughly confused by the offer and her reaction to it.

Staying with Cameron could set to rights so many wrongs in her life. It could give her what she craved most in the world, a home of her own, a family, a chance to be a mother to Lily. Yet the reality of it all was far from being so simple. 'Twas an understatement indeed to classify their relationship as complicated.

It seemed wiser, more prudent to try to separate all her emotions and view this with calm, rational logic. But it was an illogical circumstance.

'Twas nearly impossible to imagine herself as Cameron's wife, trying to fill Christina's shoes. In many ways that seemed a proposition doomed to failure, for he had loved his wife with a passion Rebecca understood, even admired.

Still, each time Rebecca considered his proposal, a whisper of hope drifted through the anxious chaos in her mind. Initially she had thought the biggest inducement to saying yes was having the opportunity to stay with Lily, but she also admitted having Cameron as the man in her life was a tempting thought.

Given their past, was it realistic to have an expectation of success for such a union? Or could she be content with far less in her life? Could he? Was it an impossibility to hope for more than a respectful companionship, a shared goal of properly raising their children, a pleasant, easygoing friendship?

The thoughts and emotions swirled in her head and her heart and Rebecca finally concluded the certainty of one thing. If she was seriously going to consider marrying him, she needed to believe there was a real chance they could live happily ever after.

A game of charades was organized. Needing an escape from her troubled thoughts, Rebecca joined in the fun, though her mind was not entirely on the game and she played poorly. The earl contented himself with cards and kept away from her. Rebecca told herself that was best.

As soon as she could, Rebecca retired. As she left the drawing room, she unintentionally caught Cameron's eye. There was a strange, almost vulnerable expression hidden in the depths of his gaze. It remained for only a moment, but it pulled at her heart.

With her usual skill and cheery attitude, her maid helped her prepare for bed. Rebecca fully expected to lay awake for hours, but surprisingly exhaustion soon claimed her and she fell into a deep, dreamless sleep.

Startled, Rebecca sat up in bed. Her neck prickled with awareness and her eyes searched the darkness for something that seemed out of place. She knew it was beyond midnight, yet dawn must be far away, for a quick glance at her window confirmed that there was no light in the sky.

"'Tis me," a husky male voice informed her.

Cameron? Rebecca shook her head, thinking she must be dreaming. Suddenly, there was movement near the armoire and the shadowy figure stepped from the darkness and drew closer to the bed.

"It really is you?" she whispered. "I thought I was dreaming."

He lit a candle. The flickering light illuminated his handsome features. "I'm flattered to be considered a dream. Deep down I feared you would think me a nightmare."

She blushed, lowering her chin and averting her eyes. "No, never."

He seemed tense, but his tone was calm, level. "Does this complicate things? My being here?"

Rebecca bit her lip. "Probably."

"Should I leave?"

"No! Please, do not go." Rebecca felt the warmth in her cheeks. She had not meant to sound so desperate, so needy.

She lifted her chin. His vivid gaze locked with hers. *He looks as confused as I feel.* That revelation eased her nerves. She smiled shyly.

"You look very beautiful sitting there all alone in your large bed," he said hoarsely.

Her pulse quickened. He looked equally beautiful. He must have gone to his chamber first and changed, for he was wearing a dark blue silk robe with wide satin lapels. She suspected he wore nothing beneath it. A heavy sensation tightened in her chest.

"Will you join me in my very large bed?" she asked.

He closed his eyes. "I shouldn't."

"I know. Will you join me anyway?"

He was silent, his eyes now open, alert and flickering over her. He moved closer. The top of his robe parted slightly. She caught a glimpse of his powerful, broad chest and the dusting of hair that covered it. The sight gave her a delicious, shivery chill.

Rebecca shifted herself on the bed, moving from beneath the covers to sit on the edge. He joined her.

She could feel the heat from his solid body radiate toward hers. She had never been so aware of his power and strength.

They sat together for several long moments. Then he lifted his hand and slipped it under the thick cascade of her unbound hair, cradling the back of her head with his palm. She waited, the sound of her breathing filling the air.

He bent his head, kissed her temple, trailed his lips down the side of her face to the rapidly beating pulse of her throat. "I've thought of little else all day."

"What is happening between us?" she asked in a trembling whisper.

"I cannot define it," he answered, pulling back. "I only know it feels incredible. Irresistible."

His eyes kindled with affection. Cameron leaned forward and pressed his lips against hers.

It was magic.

Rebecca's response was honest, giving. Cameron deepened the kiss, lured by her sensual response, captivated by the whimpering, yearning sound she made as she opened her lips to him. It was a kiss that stunned the senses, that had the power to numb the mind.

She linked her arms around his neck. There was only a single layer of silky fabric covering her body. It took extreme discipline for him not to rip the flimsy garment from her, not to push her back on the bed and feast on the delectable flesh beneath.

It was not just the sexual desire that brought him here tonight. It was not even his selfish need to kiss her, to touch her, to join with her. It was the closeness, the comfort, the affection they gave so openly to each other when in bed that he craved most of all.

There was a contentment and a peace in possessing Rebecca that Cameron never expected to find. Until she came into his life, he had not realized how badly he needed to battle the loneliness that had filled his days for so many years. A loneliness Rebecca suffered from as acutely as he.

"I adore kissing you," he confessed when their lips had finally separated. Breathing hard, Cameron rested his forehead against hers.

She took his hand. "When I am with you, I feel the excitement of the moment, but there is more. I dare to think of possibilities. But then reality intrudes and I am not sure of anything."

"I suffer a similar fate. Is this wrong? Are we merely using each other to forget the pain of our pasts, to ease the loneliness of our future?" he asked.

"I wish I knew." She looked away, wrapping her arms around his waist. "However, I do fear we are being rash."

"Yes."

"Have we so little willpower, my lord?"

"Apparently."

She laughed, as he had hoped. Curving an arm around her body, he pulled her close, kissing the sensitive skin on her nape. He could feel the rapid beating of her pulse beneath the tender flesh. Her scent was sweet and intoxicating and uniquely her own.

Slowly, he reclined against the headboard, taking her with him. She wore a pretty white lace night rail, conservative and modest and the sight of it set fire to his blood.

"We need to get rid of this," he decided, tugging on the hem of the garment.

She cleared her throat. He took that as an agreement. One swift pull and the gown sailed over her head, leaving her naked. Cameron almost growled with excitement. She had beautiful skin. Creamy, white and smooth. He could have feasted on it for days.

Instead, Cameron placed his mouth over hers. Feather light he traced the edges of her moist lips until they parted willingly, allowing him inside. She arched forward in response. He could feel her nipples tightening, her breath hitching with excitement.

"Dearest Rebecca," he muttered, as he bent his head. "You smell so good. Like a sinful woman. My woman."

He nuzzled her naked breasts. Drawing a stiff bud into his mouth, he suckled her gently, then more strongly as she began to writhe against him. She threaded her fingers through his hair and held him close. His muscles tightened with anticipation at her wanton invitation, his cock grew harder.

The wants and needs so wonderfully satisfied last night came back to Cameron with a vengeance; stronger, more intense since he now knew what heaven he could find within the softness of her body.

"I want you to stay with me tonight," she whispered.

"I want that too," he admitted.

He removed his robe. She reached up and placed a curious hand on his chest. Her fingers sifted through the swirl of hair, then moved down to his flat belly. Cameron's heart thundered as her questing fingers moved lower, his erect penis straining toward her hand.

She closed her fist around his. *Ohhh, clever girl.* That was just what he needed. Rebecca stroked him firmly and an excited groan fell from his lips. She brushed the pad of her thumb slowly over the slit in the head and he shuddered. Dazed, he allowed her to pleasure him a few moments longer, bucking into her grip. But then suddenly he pulled away, afraid he would disgrace himself and spurt all over her hand.

Turning the tables, Cameron stroked his palm down across her belly, then cupped the center of her womanhood. She hissed, her eyes turning frantic with need as she arched herself into his hands. He felt her wetness start. It excited him terribly.

Running his forefinger up and down the tender folds, he searched for the delicate hidden pearl. She undulated her hips and cried out the instant he found it. Grinning, he increased the pressure, sliding his middle finger inside the wet, hot sheath. That brought another cry.

Whimpering, Rebecca pressed her length against him. The feel of her soft, full breasts and taut, hard nipples rubbing so provocatively along his heated flesh made Cameron a bit crazed.

Trying to regain some measure of control, Cameron gazed at her face. Her features were almost severe in the glow of candlelight, her passion extreme, intense. He could see how much she hungered for this intimacy and pleasure they shared, but there was more.

Deep in her eyes was a yearning, a plea, so open and raw it humbled him. Cameron knew the pain of her past had left her withdrawn and guarded, which made the uninhibited giving she was bestowing upon him now all the more poignant.

Slipping his fingers from her warmth, he turned her on her back and settled himself between her splayed thighs. Propping himself on the weight of his forearms, Cameron positioned the head of his erect penis against her opening and with one powerful thrust, seated himself to the hilt.

She gasped loudly. The pleasure surrounded him, sweet and thick, but Cameron held himself perfectly still, gritting his teeth as her body tightened around him.

He took a deep, shuddering breath, and slowly

pulled himself back before surging forward. The earlier urgency he had felt so strongly now flowed into tenderness as each delectable sensation engulfed him. He tamped down the raw edges of his desire and watched her closely, alert to her senses, needing to assure himself she was feeling every inch of him.

Lost in the passion, Rebecca's eyes were glazed with arousal, her breathing unsteady, her face a mask of concentration.

"Do you like that?" he asked, his voice hoarse, his muscles shaking with the effort to keep his passion under control.

"Cameron," she whispered, shifting her body forward, taking him another inch deeper inside her body.

He pulled his hips back and started pumping harder, more urgently, dragging a low, keening moan of pleasure from her throat. Her body yielded completely as he slid himself in and out of her tight, wet sheath. As the intensity increased, he still tried to go as slowly as possible, to allow the pleasure to build.

But Rebecca was not of the same mind. She bucked beneath him and he sank heavily between her thighs. Every thought and emotion was swamped in a rush of desire.

"Tell me when you are going to come," he demanded, moving a hand down to where they were joined.

"Soon," she moaned. "Now."

He pressed his mouth to hers, catching her scream, filling it into his lungs. He could feel her inner muscles squeezing his penis tightly, then a rush of wet warmth engulfed him as her body shuddered in climax.

With supreme effort he managed to hold back his own release. It made him feel powerful, though he knew control was a mere illusion. He was so near to the edge, so close himself. Still he held back, allowing her to set the rhythm.

There were a few lingering shudders wracking her body before Rebecca sagged against the mattress. Cameron waited but a moment, giving her a few seconds to catch her breath. Then wrapping his arms tightly around her, he rolled onto his back, bringing her with him.

Contact between them was broken for a second as she moved to the side and his penis slipped out of her. Grunting with distress, Cameron repositioned Rebecca atop him, spread her legs over his hips, then thrust himself back inside. Back where he belonged.

"Cameron?"

Her voice was confused, unsure.

"It's fine." To prove his point, Cameron lifted his hips. He heard her indrawn gasp and smiled. Damn, she was amazing. He stroked her deeply with his penis again, lifting himself higher this time.

"Lord, that's wicked." Rebecca inhaled sharply, trying to catch her breath.

"Now you do it," he urged in a seductive voice.

Her expression curious, Rebecca pushed herself experimentally forward. He slid deeper. Cameron clenched his eyes shut. Maybe this wasn't the best position to prolong their pleasure. A few more thrusts like that and he'd erupt.

Gripping the headboard behind him with both hands, Cameron shifted his legs, relinquishing some control. Rebecca leaned forward and the heavy mass of her glorious honey-colored hair moved like silken fire over his bare chest.

"I've never been a particularly skilled equestrian, my lord," she purred in his ear. "Then again, I have not had the privilege of mounting so fine a stallion."

Her sultry banter made him nuts. He shoved himself against her and she grunted, driving herself down hard. He nearly exploded, yet he held back, his mind and body yearning to savor each exquisite sensation.

She increased the pace. Cameron could feel her tremble, could feel his own skin heat even more as the pleasure built higher. His hands reached up to thumb her nipples. She shrieked and threw back her head. He was losing control. He could feel the excitement overtaking him, driving him harder and faster.

He thrust twice more and then he started to come, so furiously, so intently he had no time to think, no time to consider. All he could do was savor the magnificent pleasure that encompassed his entire being as his body convulsed.

Long minutes passed as he slowly, gradually drifted back to himself. He knew he should have withdrawn before allowing himself to spill his seed. It was unwise to risk the chance of getting her pregnant. But he was too damn relaxed, too completely satisfied to let that rattle him.

"That was incredible," Cameron declared when he was once again able to speak.

"It does seem as if we are improving with practice, my lord," she retorted smugly.

"Cameron," he whispered as he buried his lips in the warm hollow of her throat. "You called me by my name before. Please, do so again."

She moved her hands to rest against his damp chest. "Cameron," she whispered with a seductive smile.

He enfolded her in his arms and held her against his heart. They stayed that way for a long time. Every now and then Cameron would lean down and brush a kiss on her face or shoulder, almost to assure himself that she was real, that this was not a dream or a fantasy.

Exhausted and sated, they both gradually drifted to the edge of sleep. He awoke a few hours later, his body hard and primed and ready to take her again. But he knew he could not—'twas far too risky to stay so long in Rebecca's bed, however much he craved it.

"Don't leave," she whispered drowsily, placing her hand over his, clinging to it tightly as he slid out of the bed.

"I must," he muttered against her hair. "Time for you to go back to sleep."

He nuzzled her neck until her head fell back against the soft pillow, then waited until her breathing once again grew steady and he knew sleep had claimed her. Then he quit the room.

The light of dawn had begun to break as he left the chamber. Cameron wondered idly what he would possibly say if he met anyone in the hall. Fortunately there was no one.

The fire in the grate of his bedchamber had burned low, the room had an uncomfortable chill. Grimacing, Cameron slipped between the sheets of his cold bed. No longer feeling tired, he gazed around the room.

Spacious and comfortable, the chamber had a distinctly masculine feel to it. He had commissioned a redecoration of the master suites in all of his homes after Christina died, unable to bear the familiarity and memories they evoked.

The resulting bedchamber at Windmere was his favorite. Done in dark brown tones and accented with burgundy drapes and coverlets, it had always provided a warm refuge, a place to unwind and relax. Yet tonight it felt different. Tonight it was cold and empty and lonely.

Cameron could not help but contrast it with the peace and tranquility of Rebecca's bedchamber, the prevailing atmosphere of seclusion and delight. Achieved no doubt because she was inside.

He stared broodingly at the dwindling fire, allowing his mind to open. He was in love with Rebecca Tremaine. *There, he had admitted it.*

The realization had struck him earlier as he watched her sleep. While staring at her peaceful beauty he had felt his heart swell with emotion, had been engulfed with a yearning, twisting feeling deep in his gut that started with extreme happiness and plummeted to abject misery in a matter of seconds.

Extreme happiness because he had not believed that he would ever be so fortunate as to find a woman he could care about so completely and misery because he knew there was nothing more devastating than unrequited love. Was there anything more humiliating than to lay your feelings bare and not see those same feelings reflected back at you?

He had spoken of marriage and Rebecca had rejected the notion. Not a promising start. But he had done it badly, without revealing his feelings, without pledging his love and devotion.

Did he have the courage to try again? Rebecca cared for him, of that he was certain, or else she would never have made love with him, never have given herself to him so completely. But sex was not love, liking someone was not love, enjoying someone's company was not love. And he knew that Rebecca would not settle for anything less than solid, lasting, all-consuming love in her life, just as he demanded the same.

The last of the fire sputtered and died, but Cameron made no move to put any fuel on the few remaining sparks. He let the room grow colder, let his thoughts consider all that had happened. And for the first time in many years, the earl questioned what he wanted for himself, how he truly wanted to live out the remainder of his days.

The answer was not long in coming. He wanted Rebecca. And damn, he was going to have her!

Chapter 18

"Are you enjoying our little celebration, my lord?" Vicar Hargrave asked. "I think the ladies have outdone themselves concocting so many luscious treats for everyone."

Cameron pulled his gaze away from Rebecca, who stood with several of the other women on the far side of the room, and smiled at the young clergyman and his wife.

"It is a fine party," the earl answered. "And an excellent way to celebrate the success of this evening's play. I must commend you on all your hard work, Mrs. Hargrave, and congratulate you on doing such a wonderful job. It was a most . . . uhm . . . interesting interpretation of the nativity."

"You are far too kind." Mrs. Hargrave blushed prettily. "I confess to being greatly relieved it is over. Things did not turn out precisely as I had planned."

"Come now, my dear, you heard the earl," the vicar said kindly as he patted the top of his wife's hand. "It was a splendid play."

"Hardly." Mrs. Hargrave took a sip of her drink, wrinkling her nose after she swallowed. "I thought

I might faint when young Jamie Bragg forgot his lines and stood staring out at the audience, his jaw hanging."

"I barely noticed," Cameron lied.

"Really?" She tilted her head and speared him with a quelling look, surprising him utterly. Mrs. Hargrave was usually such a deferential female. "And were you equally unaware when Penelope Morton started sneezing uncontrollably and was unable to sing her solo?"

"Unfortunately, an overabundance of straw can have that effect on some individuals," Cameron replied. "But it made the manger look most authentic."

Mrs. Hargrave's brow rose. She took another sip of her drink and Cameron realized her glass was filled with wassail. He concluded she was a woman unused to drinking spirits, which explained her uncharacteristically bold attitude.

"You are trying to spare my feelings. That is most gallant of you, Lord Hampton," Mrs. Hargrave said, one hand pressed dramatically to her heart. She closed her eyes, then opened one and peered at him. "I suppose you also took no notice of how I wrongly cued the wise men to enter before the angels?"

Cameron struggled to hide a smile. She was a pretty woman, open, honest and very forthcoming in her slightly inebriated state. The earl was enjoying the conversation far more than he should, especially given the anxious glances the vicar was sending to his wife. Cameron supposed being around Rebecca for the past few weeks had given him a greater appreciation of opinionated women.

"The sudden appearance of the wise men before the shepherds and the angels caused but a moment of confusion," he said. "But it was quickly set to rights.

Surely you heard all the applause at the end of the performance?"

Mrs. Hargrave sighed. "I did, indeed. Thankfully the audience was filled with the families and friends of our budding thespians. I shudder to think what might have happened if that were not the case."

"Oh, my dearest, you are exaggerating." Vicar Hargrave's eyes clouded with puzzlement. Clearly he did not know what to make of his wife's odd behavior.

Cameron was about to quietly suggest Mrs. Hargrave refrain from partaking of any additional wassail, but changed his mind. It was Christmas Eve. After all her hard work she deserved a celebration.

"I am very proud of you, Mrs. Hargrave," Cameron stated formally. "I just hope your husband appreciates what a great asset you are to his career."

The vicar smiled, his attention caught by the statement, precisely as the earl intended. "I do indeed know what a treasure I have in my wife," Reverend Hargrave said sincerely.

"Good. After the delight of tonight's performance, be assured I shall look forward to next year's Christmas pageant with even greater enthusiasm," Cameron added.

The vicar's smile broadened. Mrs. Hargrave's eyes popped open. She stared at him in wordless shock.

Time for me to circulate among the other guests, Cameron decided.

The earl spotted Rebecca engaged in an earnest discussion with Marion but a few feet away. Their conversation ended the moment he joined them, leading him to suspect he was most likely the topic.

"Ah, there is Richard," Marion said. "He's standing beneath some greenery that looks suspiciously like mistletoe."

"'Tis holly," Cameron insisted, without turning his head, for he had previously searched the room for mistletoe or a kissing ball and to his disappointment had found none.

Marion shrugged. "No matter. I shall tell my husband it is mistletoe and insist he kiss me."

She scampered off.

"I was just congratulating Mrs. Hargrave on this evening's performance," Cameron told Rebecca.

"Poor dear, she was in quite a state earlier, but she seems to have forgotten some of the more glaring mistakes," Rebecca said.

"Actually, I don't think she has," Cameron remarked, remembering their conversation. "But I believe the wassail is helping her forget the few mishaps."

"One can hardly expect perfection when working with children." Rebecca took a small sip of her drink.

Cameron noted it was different from Mrs. Hargrave's. Too bad. Apparently Rebecca had opted for a nonalcoholic beverage this evening.

"I tried to reassure Mrs. Hargrave that everyone thought it was a splendid effort," he said. "Honestly, if not for the amusing mistakes, what would we have to talk about?"

"Cameron!" Rebecca drew her brows together. "I certainly hope you did not say that to Mrs. Hargrave."

"Of course not." The earl smiled, too pleased over the fact that Rebecca had just called him Cameron while out in public, in a very crowded room, to take offense at the scolding. "I did however fail to mention to Mrs. Hargrave what I thought was by far the best part of the play."

"Lily's presence on the stage?" The two lines creasing Rebecca's forehead disappeared as she smiled.

"She did appoint herself well tonight. I'm sure you were very proud."

"Naturally the highlight for me was seeing Lily so poised and confident on stage," Cameron said. "But the very best thing about this evening's play was that it was short."

She laughed, as he predicted, and his confidence soared. He did know her, understand her . . . well as much as any man could claim to know the mysterious workings of a woman's mind. Pray he would be able to convince her that she could be happy, that they both could be happy, if she agreed to marry him.

An hour later the earl and his guests were the first group to leave the party, needing five carriages to convey everyone back to Windmere. Lily's excited chatter gradually trickled to a few comments and then ceased altogether as she slumped, exhausted, in the corner of the coach. Within minutes she curled up on her seat and was soon asleep, despite the jolting of the carriage and the chill inside.

When they reached home, Cameron lifted the little girl into his arms and carried her inside. She woke up when they entered the manor and insisted on walking.

"Do not forget to make your Christmas Eve wish before you go to sleep," Cameron said as hand in hand they started climbing the long staircase.

"I did make my wish," Lily complained. "Many times and it did not happen."

"Christmas has yet to come, Lily," he reminded her gently. "You may still get what you desire."

"I wanted to sleep in the stables tonight," she declared. "But Mrs. James said I could not and Grandmother said I could not and Aunt Charlotte said I could not and you said I could not. They said because

I fell through the ice I am not strong enough to stay outside and I would catch cold if I slept in the stable all night. But I am strong, Papa. Truly."

Cameron sighed as he looked down into Lily's pleading eyes and almost relented. What could it really hurt? Yet Cameron knew he had to bow to the superior judgment of the females of his household. He could not risk Lily's health on a whim.

"I think the last thing you would want is to be sick for Christmas," he said.

Lily looked crestfallen at his proclamation, but accepted the decree with far more grace than usual. Cameron released a small sigh of relief at the change in her, knowing what a sullen little girl she could be when she did not get her way. This attitude was a vast improvement and he acknowledged that Rebecca was largely responsible for the difference.

Still, he could not help but feel sympathy for his child. It was his role, and great pleasure, to spoil and indulge her whenever he had the chance. When they reached the landing, he made a sudden decision, veered from the staircase and turned toward the manor's formal rooms.

"Where are we going, Papa?"

"'Tis a surprise."

He signaled for one of the footmen, whispered an order, then proceeded to slowly walk toward the drawing room. Coming more fully awake, Lily tugged on his hand, trying to go faster. When they reached their destination, a nod from the footman assured the earl his orders had been carried out.

At his signal, the servant swung open the drawing room doors. Lily's gasp of surprise and delight shot straight to Cameron's heart. She ran ahead, turned, then ran back to him.

"Oh, Papa, it is a fairyland!"

At his instructions, the candles on the evergreen tree had been lit. The tree literally sparkled, the glow from the many flickering candles reflected in the satin bows and shiny ornaments placed on the branches. Lily squeezed his hand, her eyes bright with excitement and delight as she beheld all the wonder of Christmas.

It was a special, tender moment. But then Cameron felt a restlessness, an emptiness, a sense that something was not completely right, that something very important, essential, was missing to complete the experience, to fulfill the moment.

Rebecca.

Cameron's heart swelled with emotion. In the beginning he hadn't even realized what he felt so strongly toward her was indeed love because it was so different from what he had known with his first wife. He hadn't seen it for what it was because he was guarding his heart, because he was shutting her out of his mind.

Thank God, she had wormed her way inside. With Rebecca it was not a sweet, uncomplicated love. Theirs was not an easy, simple relationship. It was messy and unconventional and Cameron admitted he would not have it any other way.

The nagging ache in his chest was gone, banished by the love he felt for her. This love, this passion, this devotion he felt so deeply for her was something of a miracle, really. All he needed to make his happiness complete was to convince Rebecca to be his wife. With planning, and a bit of luck, it would be done before Christmas morning.

A loud yawn from Lily brought Cameron's thoughts back to the present. Though she insisted she was not in the least tired, Cameron guided the little girl from the drawing room. She ceased her protests only after he assured Lily they would light the candles on the tree again tomorrow, promising she could stay and gaze at them for as long as she wanted.

He waited while one of the maids got Lily ready for bed. Then he tucked her in, kissed her cheek and wished her happy dreams.

Resolved to have greater success in securing the fulfillment of his Christmas Eve wish than Lily, the earl left the nursery. With a determined expression on his face and an equally determined attitude, Cameron went in search of Rebecca.

At the insistence of her brother and Lady Charlotte, Rebecca had ridden in their carriage on the way back from the vicarage. It did her heart good to see the young couple so happy and clearly in love. Though it brought to mind the tangled mess of her own romantic situation, Rebecca had managed to put a stop to those runaway thoughts. It was Christmas Eve. Only pleasant thoughts were to be allowed.

Once returned to the manor, Rebecca went directly to the kitchen. Carefully, she approached the basket set before the fire, trying not to make any loud noises. Leaning over, she peered in, surprised to see a large ball of fur curled in the center of the white blanket she had placed inside earlier this evening.

With a start, Rebecca realized the large ball of fur was Horace, Cook's cat. But where was the kitten? Worried the older animal had chased the youngster away and taken the cozy bed for himself, Rebecca leaned in for a closer inspection.

"Is anything wrong?"

Startled, Rebecca turned and saw the earl. "I was checking on the kitten."

"Is everything all right?"

Rebecca squinted into the basket, then breathed a sigh of relief when she saw a small ball of gray fur contentedly cuddled against the large cat. "Yes, the kitten appears none the worse for wear."

"Ah, so you are hiding it in the kitchen tonight. Very clever. Is it in the basket?"

"Yes, apparently Horace has taken a liking to it."

"Better Horace than Apollo," the earl quipped.

He came near the fire and they both gazed down at the basket. Horace had a decidedly maternal look in his eyes, as he watched them both warily, seeming ready to pounce if they acted in a manner he thought inappropriate or threatening.

Rebecca was pleased to see the older cat's protective instinct toward the kitten who slumbered so peacefully. She was glad too, to discover the little creature was not frightened or lonely or missing her mother or brothers and sisters.

"Has Lily gone to bed?" Rebecca asked.

"Yes, just now. She was fighting sleep, but too exhausted to give it much of a battle." Cameron made a move to pet the kitten. Horace swatted a paw as the masculine fingers drew near. The earl wisely retreated, returning his hand to his pocket. "It wasn't easy getting Lily to the nursery. She kept insisting that she wanted to sleep in the stable tonight."

"Wherever did she get such a foolish notion?"

"Apparently your brother told her on the night of Christ's birth a miracle may occur in which all the animals housed in a stable can speak. Naturally, Lily wanted to be there to witness such a magical event."

Rebecca started laughing. "I remember Daniel

would say that every year when we were children. He badgered my parents mercilessly for years, claiming he had to see it for himself, even though they repeatedly told him it was untrue. Finally they relented one year and allowed him to camp out with Papa's horse and our milk cow. Daniel caught a dreadful cold in that drafty barn and had to remain in bed all of Christmas Day."

Cameron's pensive expression vanished. "Thank you for telling me that story. It eases my guilt for denying Lily what she repeatedly told me was her very fondest wish."

Rebecca was torn between exasperation and amusement. She could just imagine the wheedling and pleading Lily had put Cameron through. Though he tried, 'twas obvious the earl still had difficulty saying no to Lily. Yet in the end, he had held fast to his position. That was progress, of a sort.

"She will forget all about it by morning," Rebecca predicted.

"I doubt that very much," Cameron retorted. "On my way down here I saw the carolers gathering in the front parlor. Will you be joining them?"

"I have not decided."

"Excellent. Now I have a chance to persuade you to stay with me instead." Cameron smiled.

Rebecca felt the blood rush to her face. His smoldering eyes put all sorts of erotic images into her head. It was most embarrassing.

"It seems rather rude not to go with the carolers," she said faintly, trying to block the sensual scenes from her mind. "And I do like to sing."

"Cranborne has convinced Marion to go to the vicarage first. Vicar and Mrs. Hargrave are good, tolerant, Christian people. They shall be far more forgiving than some of our other neighbors if Marion reneges on her promise and decides to sing. There are, unfortunately, no guarantees as to what will happen once they continue on to the next house."

A sense of mischief sliced through Rebecca. "Careful, my lord, you are unwittingly tempting me with the promise of danger and excitement. It sounds as if this will be a most adventuresome evening."

"I have something I believe you will find far more delightful." He lifted her hand, then kissed it. She nearly jumped at the feel of his soft lips caressing her skin. "Join me on a sleigh ride, Rebecca," he whispered in a silky, seductive voice. "In the moonlight."

Not trusting her voice, Rebecca nodded. In a daze, she allowed herself to be led from the kitchen. They stopped in the foyer to put on their coats, then proceeded to the stables.

Rebecca could not contain her gasp of delight as she climbed into the sleigh. There were warm bricks for their feet and heavy lap blankets to keep away the chill. Cameron settled himself beside her in the driver's seat, then with an expert flick of the reins, the vehicle lurched forward.

They were off!

Moonlight guided them across the open pasture. All around them was silence except for the sound of the jingling bells the groom had placed on the horse's harness and the whoosh of the sleigh's blades as it glided over the snow.

Rebecca let out a contented sigh and slipped her gloved hands beneath the blanket. They crested a small hill. Cameron guided the sleigh to the edge of the woods and stopped. She rolled her shoulders and sat straighter, breathing in the cool, crisp air. It was a tranquil moment, filled with peace and contentment.

"Seeing the kitten earlier reminded me of something rather important," Cameron said. "I have not selected my Christmas gift for Lily."

Rebecca smiled, certain he must be jesting. "You had best hurry. There is not much time left until Christmas morning."

An intense expression flickered in the depths of his eyes. "Actually, my choice depends very much on you."

"Me? I'm uncertain how I can assist you at this late hour," Rebecca exclaimed. "Surely all the shops are closed."

"What I desire does not come from a shop, Rebecca."

"Oh?" Her heart began to thump as she met his penetrating gaze.

"I would like to give Lily what she truly wants, what she truly needs." He paused, lowering the tone and volume of his voice. "A mother."

Rebecca's heart clenched at the word. Such a basic, important role. A mother.

"Yet I find that I am a selfish man," Cameron continued. "In order for Lily to have a mother, I must have a wife. And I am very particular when it comes to that decision."

He reached beneath the blanket, squeezed her gloved hand briefly, then released it. He looked down and she noticed his brow furrow. Then he muttered something under his breath. Straining forward, Rebecca thought she heard him say, *damn it all to hell.*

"Is something wrong?" she asked.

The earl lifted his head and grinned sheepishly. "I fear my lack of planning is quite glaring at this moment."

"Regarding Lily's gift? I should say so, Cameron. Christmas will arrive in a few short hours."

He laughed, the deep timber of his voice echoing

through the quiet stillness of the night. Amazingly, the sound brought the final clarity to Rebecca's heart, reaffirming her emotions, the depth of her feelings.

She felt a single tear escape from her eye and trickle down her cheek. She had suspected it for some time, had tried to understand what she thought was impossible, had tried to explain it, confirm it, but not until this moment did she know it was real.

She was in love with Cameron.

It had come on gradually, as she had begun to know him, begun to understand what made him so special, unique. From the first she had told herself she must not open her heart to him, but in the end her emotions and not her common sense had ruled.

She sat quietly, digesting the truth of her discovery, testing it in her mind, seeing it for what it was and knew it to be true. She loved him.

Rebecca turned her head to look at him and felt a blaze of emotion sear her chest. The words trembled on her lips, aching to burst forth, but he seemed so intent, so distracted by his own thoughts she waited to speak.

He lifted her hand and pressed it against his chest. Even through the layers of clothing she could feel the steady beat of his heart. He placed his other hand beneath her chin and tilted her face toward his.

"I will always cherish my time with Christina, but that part of my life is very firmly placed in the past. It has taken me far too long to realize what I want, but I know I am ready, eager to move forward. And I want you to be with me."

"I want that too." Rebecca sniffed. "I also have been confused. What I feel for you is so different from what I experienced with Philip. But I have come to understand these emotions are even more real, more intense, more wonderful."

"I love you, Rebecca."

"Cameron, I love you."

She felt her nose start to run. Good Lord! Horrified that she must look like a wreck at the exact moment she wanted to appear pretty and desirable, Rebecca lowered her chin. But the earl would have none of it.

He pulled a fluffy white handkerchief from his pocket and wiped her nose as if it was the most natural thing in the world. Then he leaned forward and quickly brushed his lips across hers.

"Now we come to the awkward part," he said. "I bungled it so badly before, that this time I wanted everything to be perfect."

"What needs to be perfect?"

"My proposal. I wanted to get down on one knee when I asked you, but the sleigh is too narrow."

Rebecca's heart began to thump. "And the ground is too far away. Plus it is cold and wet and covered in snow."

"I know. Dreadful planning on my part. I do apologize, my dear."

Oh, for pity sake! Rebecca nearly screamed out loud, but instead took a deep breath. Her darling, proper, intelligent earl really could be a bit of an ass at times.

"I shall close my eyes and imagine you on one knee." She shut her eyes. In the silence, in the darkness, the world around her narrowed down to this precise moment in time. A moment that took on a dreamy, romantic, almost otherworldly quality. "There. Now, please ask me."

She heard a rustle of fabric and was tempted to open her eyes, yet secretly feared what she might find. So instead she waited, breath held, emotions on edge.

"I love and admire and cherish you. I want only your happiness, for I know in my heart it will bring me mine. My dear, sweet, darling Rebecca, would you do me the great honor, nay the privilege, of becoming my wife?"

Her eyes flew open. Her lips trembled. She tried to answer him, but found her voice stolen from her. How odd that she had lost the ability to speak! Cameron was staring at her. He was unsmiling, looking more serious and intense than she had ever seen him.

Her voice might be gone, but her mind was swiftly moving. With a most unladylike, improper gesture, Rebecca threw herself into his arms, clinging to him in an unseemly manner. He enfolded her in his strong arms for a moment, then pushed her away.

"Can I take that to mean you are saying yes?"

"Of course it means yes."

"Given your answer the last time I asked, you cannot blame me for wanting to be absolutely certain."

"Oh, Cameron."

Before she could say anything else, he scooped her off her seat and placed her in his lap. She stretched her arms around his neck, then kissed him for all she was worth. The pressure of his warm lips stole her breath and within moments the first kiss led to a second and then a third.

He loved her! Truly. Just as she loved him.

Was it real? Was it happening? She couldn't recall a moment when she had been happier, more excited about the possibilities. Finally they drew apart and their eyes met. Rebecca trembled at the warm, possessive look in his eyes, still struggling to take it all in.

"I can't wait to tell Lily," he said.

Rebecca felt her expression soften. "Do you think she will be happy?"

"I know she will be thrilled," he said confidently.

"What about the rest, Cameron? Shall we ever tell her the whole truth?"

He frowned a little. "Perhaps in time. When she is older and can properly understand it."

For the first time the oppressive burden of her past, the secret of Lily's parentage, that had been lying so heavily on Rebecca's heart, eased. With Cameron's love and support it was not quite so heavy a burden. It was tolerable, manageable.

Rebecca swallowed hard, feeling close to tears as all her emotions bubbled to the surface. But then she thought about her future and she smiled. She was going to be a wife and a mother. She was going to go to bed each night with this magnificent man and awake each morning with him lying beside her.

She was going to have a partner to share all of life's joys and sorrows, a lover to bestow her passions and emotions, a companion with whom she could grow old and live with in peace and harmony.

Well, maybe not perfect harmony.

Rebecca's laugh rang out loud and clear as she realized she truly would not want it to be any other way.

Epilogue

One year later

Rebecca entered the drawing room. The glorious smell of fresh evergreen assaulted her and she eagerly inhaled the aroma. "Oh, Cameron. You've lit the candles. It looks wonderful."

The earl turned, smiled, then stepped away from the Christmas tree so his wife could gain the full effect of his efforts. "I wanted to make sure I put enough candles on before lighting it. Do you like the way it looks?"

"'Tis beautiful. Even more spectacular than last year, I think." The glow emanating from the lit candles on the branches shimmered throughout the room, reflecting off the glass ornaments and satin bows that were tucked onto the limbs. "Lily will be very excited when she sees it tomorrow."

"I do hope the sight of such a pretty tree will soften her mood," Cameron said.

Rebecca smiled. "Tomorrow is Christmas Day. Lily will be beside herself with delight. The house will be filled with even more guests and there will be singing and dancing and presents and more trifle than she could consume in a week. Plus, there is this marvelous tree."

Cameron leaned forward and kissed his wife's forehead. "I'm afraid our daughter was rather petulant tonight when she went to bed. I'm not sure her disagreeable mood will be entirely gone by morning."

"But why? We had a lovely evening."

"Lily did not get her Christmas Eve wish. Again, as she reminded me several times when I tucked her into bed."

Rebecca frowned. "What wish?"

"To sleep in the stables."

"Oh, no," Rebecca groaned. "So she could hear the animals talk? I could strangle my brother for telling her that tale."

"Don't blame Daniel," the earl said. "He said it all in harmless fun, last year. One would have hoped she had forgotten it by now."

Rebecca laughed. "Lily is not someone that easily forgets something so important. I imagine one of these years we will have to give in and allow her to sleep in the stables."

"Yes, and we shall force your brother to join her."

Rebecca leaned forward, pressing herself against her husband's strength. She was so pleased that Cameron and her brother had grown to be friends, as well as business partners, over the past year. It made every family gathering more enjoyable and helped ease the sting of social exclusion Daniel and Charlotte experienced on occasion.

"At least Lily had an important role in this year's nativity play," Rebecca said. "Recalling that might brighten her spirits tomorrow."

"Being promoted from an angel to the mother of the newborn savior was quite a coup," Cameron agreed.

"Not throwing a tantrum helped also," Rebecca reminded him.

She was proud of the progress and maturity Lily had achieved, yet knew there would be stormy times ahead. A volatile, emotional spirit was too much a part of Lily's nature to ever be totally tamed and Rebecca secretly loved her daughter even more because of it.

Rebecca was even more delighted to have the child call her *Mama*, proof that Lily had accepted her as her mother. Perhaps one day they would reveal the truth about her parentage, but it was no longer a burning need tearing Rebecca apart, for she had the joy and privilege of fulfilling that role.

Cameron positioned himself behind his wife, then put his arms around her, nestling his hand over the slight swell of her belly. "What do you think? Shall we tell Lily about the baby tomorrow?"

Rebecca's breath caught. *The baby.* Though she was entering her fourth month of pregnancy, she still had difficulty believing she was going to have another child. Cameron's child. The very idea filled her with an amazing sense of love and excitement.

"I'm unsure if we should announce our news to Lily on Christmas Day," Rebecca confessed. "I worry she will not think it much of a gift."

"It is by far one of the most incredible gifts I have ever received," Cameron promptly replied. "Second only to winning your love."

Rebecca looped her arms around his neck and hugged him close, breathing in his familiar scent. "This is delicate news. I'm not sure how she will react. I was thinking we need to wait until just the right moment to tell her she will be a big sister by next spring."

Cameron's warm hand gently caressed Rebecca's bump. "We cannot wait all that much longer. You, my dear, are starting to show."

Rebecca rapped her knuckles on his arm and prepared to give her husband a royal set-down for saying she was getting fat, but then she caught his eye. He was gazing at her with such adoration, with such love and tenderness, she blushed instead. "Lily will not realize what my bulging stomach means, except that I am eating far too many of Cook's delicious cream cakes."

"You forget that Charlotte gave birth less than two months ago and my cousin Marion had her little boy in late summer. Lily now knows an ever rounding stomach on a lady means a baby will soon be here."

"My stomach is not bulging!" Rebecca retorted. "Well, not all that much."

"You are more beautiful to me than ever, Rebecca," he declared softly.

The tenderness in his eyes melted her heart and she felt a wave of emotion that seemed to so easily claim her these days rise in her chest.

"I worry how Lily will react," Rebecca admitted, wiping at her damp eyes.

"True, our daughter has not precisely mastered the art of sharing, but I know she will come to love the baby. She delights in Charlotte's daughter and Marion's son."

"That is because they only come to us for a brief visit. This baby will be staying."

Cameron stroked his chin thoughtfully. "Maybe it would be best if we tell her a baby brother or sister is something Jane Grolier will never have, no matter how hard she wishes for one."

Rebecca smiled. "Ah, my love, you do know how

to phrase things in such a manner as to make us all content."

The earl visibly preened. "My survival depends on expertly managing the spirited women in my life and keeping them both very happy."

She cupped his handsome face in her hands. "My lord, I am very pleased to tell you that you have accomplished your task most admirably."

Rebecca stood on tiptoe to reach his mouth. She paused just before their lips met, glorying in the love that filled his eyes, knowing her own were reflecting the same commitment and adoration.

At that moment the drawing room clock chimed the midnight hour. Cameron's eyes brightened with merriment. "Happy Christmas, my love."

Rebecca kissed him, her lips lingering on his, her body nestled against his strength.

"Happy Christmas, Cameron."

"Have I ever told you that Christmas is my very favorite time of year?" he asked.

Rebecca smiled. "You might have mentioned it once or twice."

"Well, it bears repeating." Still holding her in his arms, he softly kissed her forehead. "I enjoy the Yule log and wassail and the carolers and the good company of the many friends and family who gather with us to celebrate the joys of the season."

"And your Christmas tree," she prompted.

He laughed and her heart skipped a beat. He truly was a remarkably handsome, incredibly loving man.

"Yes, I do adore all those things. However this time of year holds a special place in my heart, because Christmas brought you to me," Cameron declared, before taking her lips in yet another tender kiss.

Discover the Romances of
Hannah Howell

__Highland Barbarian   0-8217-7998-2 **$6.99**US/**$7.99**CAN

__Highland Champion   0-8217-7758-0 **$6.50**US/**$8.99**CAN

__Highland Destiny   0-8217-5921-3 **$5.99**US/**$7.50**CAN

__Highland Lover   0-8217-7759-9 **$6.99**US/**$9.99**CAN

__Highland Savage   0-8217-7999-0 **$6.99**US/**$9.99**CAN

__Highland Honor   0-8217-6095-5 **$5.99**US/**$7.50**CAN

__Highland Promise   0-8217-6254-0 **$5.99**US/**$7.50**CAN

__Highland Vow   0-8217-6614-7 **$5.99**US/**$7.99**CAN

__Highland Knight   0-8217-6817-4 **$5.99**US/**$7.99**CAN

__Highland Hearts   0-8217-6925-1 **$5.99**US/**$7.99**CAN

__Highland Bride   0-8217-7397-6 **$6.50**US/**$8.99**CAN

__Highland Angel   0-8217-7426-3 **$6.50**US/**$8.99**CAN

__Highland Groom   0-8217-7427-1 **$6.50**US/**$8.99**CAN

__Highland Warrior   0-8217-7428-X **$6.50**US/**$8.99**CAN

__Highland Conqueror   0-8217-8148-0 **$6.99**US/**$9.99**CAN

Available Wherever Books Are Sold!

Visit our website at **www.kensingtonbooks.com**

Put a Little Romance in Your Life With
Georgina Gentry

Cheyenne Song
0-8217-5844-6 $5.99US/$7.99CAN

Apache Tears
0-8217-6435-7 $5.99US/$7.99CAN

Warrior's Heart
0-8217-7076-4 $5.99US/$7.99CAN

To Tame a Savage
0-8217-7077-2 $5.99US/$7.99CAN

To Tame a Texan
0-8217-7402-6 $5.99US/$7.99CAN

To Tame a Rebel
0-8217-7403-4 $5.99US/$7.99CAN

To Tempt a Texan
0-8217-7705-X $5.99US/$7.99CAN

Available Wherever Books Are Sold!

Visit our website at **www.kensingtonbooks.com**.